THE TREASURE OF ZANZIBAR

Don't store up treasures here on earth, where they can be eaten by moths and get rusty, and where thieves break in and steal. Store your treasures in heaven.... Wherever your treasure is, there your heart and thoughts will also be.

JESUS CHRIST

(Matthew 6:19-21)

The TREASURE of ZANZIBAR

Catherine Palmer

Tyndale House Publishers, Inc.
Wheaton, Illinois

Visit Tyndale's exciting Web site at www.tyndale.com

The Scripture quotation on page 242 is taken from the *Holy Bible,* King James Version.

Library of Congress Cataloging-in-Publication Data

Palmer, Catherine, date
The treasure of Zanzibar / Catherine Palmer.
p. cm. —(HeartQuest ; 2)
ISBN 0-8423-5776-9 (softcover)
I. Title. II. Series.
PS3566.A495T76 1997
813'.54—dc21 96-37222

Printed in the United States of America

02 01 00 99 98 97
7 6 5 4 3 2 1

This book is dedicated to Geoffrey Palmer,
age eleven.
My beloved son.

"I asked the Lord to give me this child, and he has given me my request. Now I am giving him to the Lord, and he will belong to the Lord his whole life."

1 Samuel 1:27-28

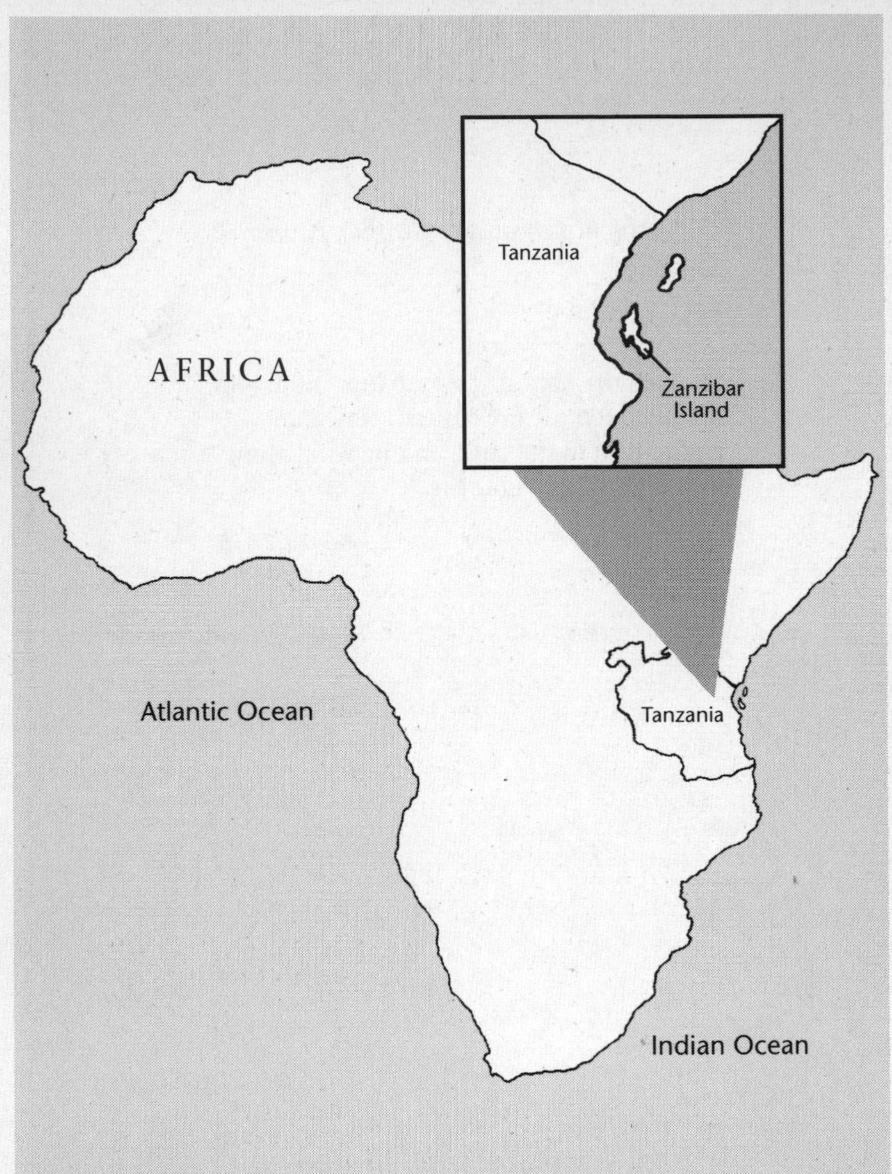
Tanzania
Zanzibar
Island
AFRICA
Atlantic Ocean
Tanzania
Indian Ocean

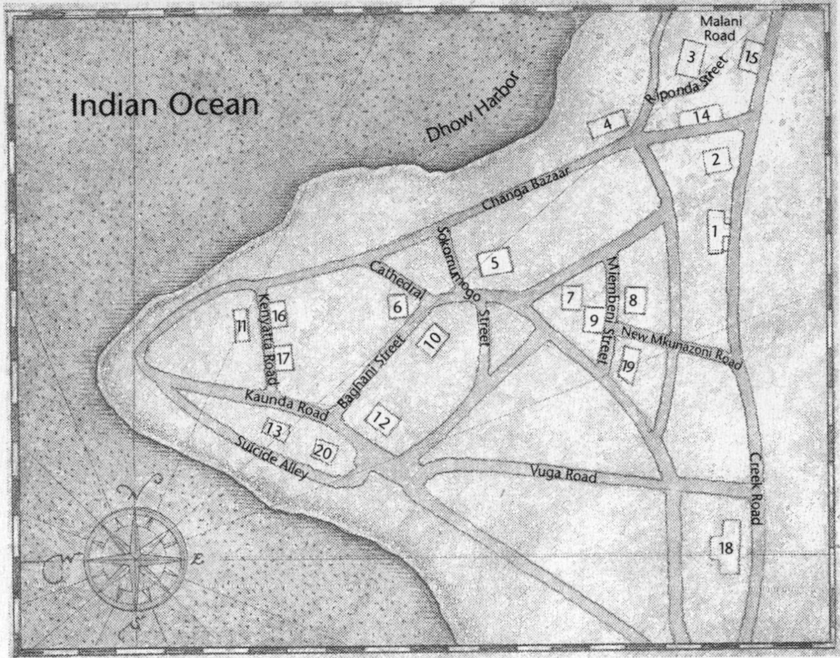

Zanzibar Town

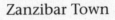

1. Emerson's House (1830s palace) House of Wonders
2. House of Spices (open timbered)
3. Bodamo
4. Witch Doctor
5. Local artist's shop
6. Arbeid
7. Tamin
8. Noorani
9. Kajole's
10. Kilau Coffee House
11. Babla's Expert Optical Service
12. Nella's Chatu
13. Africa House Hotel (former site of English Club)
14. Khod Bazaar
15. Tourist Office (Livingstone's house)
16. Post Office (former site of royal stables)
17. Dhow Palace Hotel (newly renovated) 10-room hotel
18. Mnazi Mmoja National Museum
19. Island Hospital (formerly V. I. Lenin Hospital)
20. House of Tippu Tib

Other Locations

- People's Park
- Old Arab Fort
- Square where slaves were sold
- Anglican cathedral
- Mtoni Palace
- Harem of Sultan Barghash
- Mao Stadium
- 48 mosques
- 2 churches
- 4 Hindu temples
- Roman Catholic cathedral
- El Jabir Restaurant
- Kidichi baths

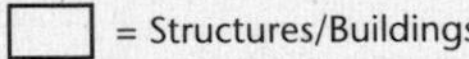
= Structures/Buildings

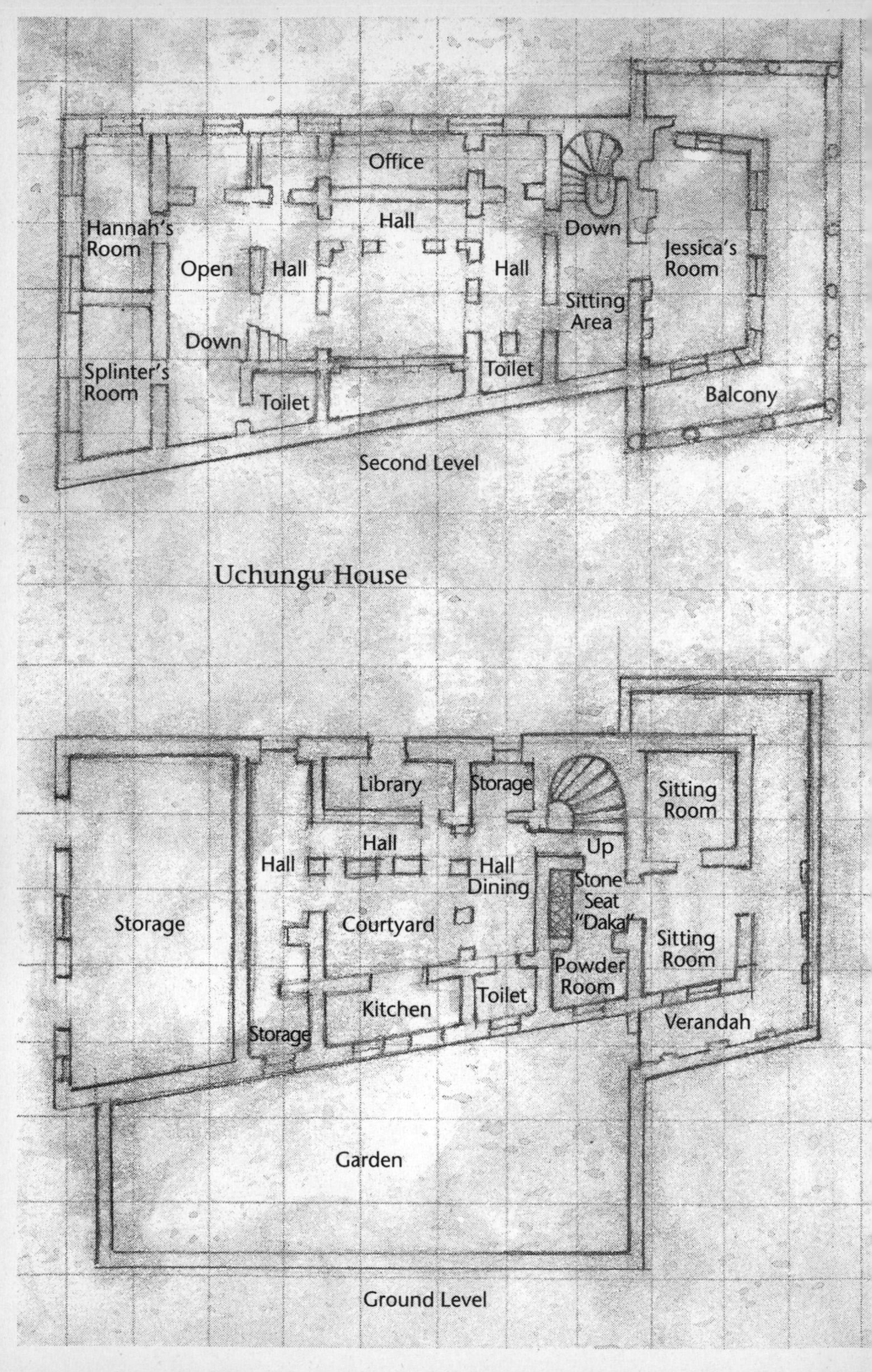
Office
Hall
Hannah's Room
Open
Hall
Hall
Down
Jessica's Room
Sitting Area
Down
Splinter's Room
Toilet
Toilet
Balcony
Second Level
Uchungu House
Library
Storage
Sitting Room
Hall
Up
Hall
Hall
Dining
Stone Seat "Daka"
Storage
Courtyard
Sitting Room
Powder Room
Kitchen
Toilet
Storage
Verandah
Garden
Ground Level

The thought of my suffering and homelessness is bitter beyond words. I will never forget this awful time, as I grieve over my loss.
—Lamentations 3:19-20

And do not bring sorrow to God's Holy Spirit by the way you live. Remember, he is the one who has identified you as his own, guaranteeing that you will be saved on the day of redemption. Get rid of all bitterness, rage, anger, harsh words, and slander, as well as all types of malicious behavior. Instead, be kind to each other, tender-hearted, forgiving one another, just as God through Christ has forgiven you.
—Ephesians 4:30-32

Prologue

"Help, help! I'm drowning!" The reed-thin voice faltered. "Somebody save me!"

Jessica Thornton planted her fists on her hips and cocked one eye at the attic door. "Spencer, are you up there?"

"A shark bit through my air hose! I can't . . . can't . . . breathe. Aaagh!"

Sounds of gurgling and choking mingled with the dull thuds of Spencer Thornton's agonized death throes. Jess shook her head. *Drowning. What an awful fate.*

"If I can just . . . swim . . . up. . . ." Spencer groaned. "Up to my boat."

Trailing a hand on the banister, Jess climbed the steep staircase. "Hey, Captain Splinter, this is your mother speaking. Grab a life buoy, and get yourself down here. I want to talk to you."

She reached the attic door and leaned against it, listening. From the other side came a loud gasp, a weak moan, and the crash of a heavy object falling onto the attic floor.

"Spencer?" Jess threw open the door. Heart racing, she searched the dimly lit room, gloomy with spiderwebs and the massive, undefined shapes of shrouded furniture. "Splint? Are you all right?"

"The treasure chest!" The voice came from somewhere near the ceiling. "I dropped it back into the sea. That gold is probably spread across leagues of ocean floor by now." The voice paused, deepened. "Well, you'll just have to go back for it, Captain Thornton. I'm not leaving the Bay of Bengal without my treasure."

Jess stepped over a box of broken Christmas balls and squinted. In the faint light coming through a round window in the gable she could just make out the thin body of a boy dangling by his skinny arms from a horizontal collar beam. Legs flailing, he was attempting to haul himself onto the wooden rafter. One end of a vacuum-cleaner hose flopped around his head; the other end was attached with silver duct tape to a football tied to his back.

"I don't think you realize what you're asking, Blackbeard," he growled at his imaginary companion. "It's a nightmare down there. Sharks everywhere. One of them bit right through the air hose on my Aqua-Lung!" He grabbed the loose end of the vacuum-cleaner hose and shook it. "See this? Cut clean in two. If I weren't as brave and powerful as I am, I would have died of the bends trying to get back to this boat."

He threw one skinny leg over the collar beam and pulled himself up to a sitting position. "I don't care if sharks tear you to pieces, Thornton," he shouted, his voice now deep and gravelly, the quintessential pirate voice. "I want my treasure!"

"And I want you to get down from there before you fall, Splinter," Jess cut in. Her son had given himself the nickname when he was too young to pronounce his real name. "I've been combing this house for you. How many times have I told you to let me know where you're playing?"

"Avast!" the boy cried, spotting his mother walking toward him. "A pirate vessel bearing down hard at starboard, Cap'n! She's coming fast, mates. A good fifteen knots, I'd say. Man the cannons!"

"I need to talk to you about something, Splint."

"Ahoy, there! Do you come in peace?"

"Aye, Captain."

"Then we'll give you permission to board. Throw the gangplank from your ship to ours and climb across."

Jess glanced at the wobbly chair her son had indicated. Then she looked up at the dusty, web-coated collar beam. *Ah, the joys of motherhood.* After kicking off her sandals, she climbed onto the chair and hiked up her jeans. She grabbed the beam, swung one leg over it, banged her knee, and nearly toppled over before righting herself.

"Welcome aboard the *Golden Crescent,"* Spencer said as his mother scooted toward him, her long legs dangling. "Speak your piece, matey. We've work to do here, and there's no time for lollygagging."

"I'm going to gag your lolly in a minute, Splint."

Jess studied her son. His violet eyes were the mirror image of her own, but where her hair glistened with red fire, the gold of sunshine danced in his. All arms and legs, he had lost the soft curves that once had made him cuddly. Now he was ropy and thin, with broad shoulders, the hint of a man's square jaw, and smooth skin stretching across high cheekbones.

Splinter had been gifted with near-genius intelligence, and creativity seemed to ooze from his every pore. Yet he was all boy. Anything dirty, hidden, explosive, or smelly held him in rapt fascination. He spent hours sketching treasure islands and building models of spaceships from paper clips and empty toilet-tissue rolls. If something could be swum in, Splinter swam in it. If something could be climbed on, Splinter viewed it as a personal Everest. He wore holes through his socks, regularly stained the knees of his jeans green, and never had two matching gloves.

"My chest of rubies and emeralds is smashed on the sea floor," he informed her. "And in case you hadn't noticed, there are gold coins spread from here to Indonesia. If I don't repair this Aqua-Lung and get back to work, Blackbeard may feed me to the sharks."

Jess regarded the broken Christmas ornaments scattered across the attic floor. Rubies and emeralds? She quelled the urge to shout, "That is broken glass! And your feet are bare! And who knows what kind of spiders are up here, and if I have to take you to the emergency room one more time, young man . . ." Instead, she reached out and laid a hand on her son's leg. "Splinter, we need to talk."

"What, Mom?" His eyes grew serious. "Is something wrong?"

"I've had a letter from someone." She searched the boy's face, praying that she could carry out the careful plan she had made to tell her son gently the incredible things that had happened in the past two weeks. "Remember the stories I told you about growing up in Africa?" she began. "About how my father was a professor and my mother died when I was just a little girl? Remember the old African lady who took care of Uncle Grant, Aunt Tillie, Aunt Fiona, and me? Hannah Wambua?"

"Yeah, so?"

"You know I've always loved Africa, Splinter, even though we live in London now so I can be near my work." She took a deep breath. "Two weeks ago I got a letter about someone I used to know in Africa."

"You found my father!"

Jessica's mouth dropped open. "Oh, Splinter. Where did you get that idea?"

"You told me you met my father in Africa. He was the son of missionaries. You got married to him. You said he didn't even know you were going to have a baby when he went away. Did my father write a letter to you? Have you told him about me yet?"

Jess stared into her son's eyes, dismayed at the light of hope burning there. For ten years she had blocked her son's father out of her mind. As Spencer had grown, she had painted for the child a vague picture of a faceless, ephemeral man who was neither good nor bad, a man who had vanished like the mist on a sunny morning.

It was clear that the boy had mentally connected Africa with his father. Jess would have to blot out that notion. She would do it carefully but firmly. Just as firmly as she always shut the door on her own bitter memories.

"Splinter, honey, the letter was from an attorney. It was about a man I knew after you were born. My old art teacher."

"Did your art teacher know my dad?"

"This has nothing to do with your father!" Tentacles of anger reached up inside her at the memory of that man. "This is about Ahmed Abdullah bin Yusuf, the professor who taught me how to sketch and paint a long time ago when I lived in Tanzania."

"Oh." Crestfallen, the boy started swinging the loose end of the vacuum-cleaner hose.

"So, anyway." Jess tried to resume her gentle revelation of the news. "You were a baby when I started taking lessons from Dr. bin Yusuf in Dar es Salaam. Hannah moved in with us, and she took care of you during the day while I was getting my education. When you were four, we left Africa and moved here to London. After I worked for a couple of years painting greeting cards and calendars, I met James Perrott."

"Why are you telling me all this stuff? I know James writes Kima the Monkey books, and you illustrate them, and you're getting ready to start *Kima the Monkey and the Irritable Impala,* and you don't know where you're going to find an impala to sketch, and you hope they have one at Regent's Park Zoo, and—"

"Splinter!" Jess gripped the beam. "I got a letter from a lawyer telling me that my old art teacher got very sick and died and left me his house on Zanzibar Island. I've decided to move there."

The violet eyes blinked. "With me?"

"Of course with you. I wouldn't leave you here alone. It's a big, old house. There's lots of room."

"Why would your art teacher will you his house? Didn't he have a wife? Didn't he have kids?"

"Dr. bin Yusuf didn't have a family. To tell you the truth, I'm not sure why he left his house to me, Splint. I know I'm his most commercially successful student, and I use a lot of his methods in my paintings. I always admired his work. He thought my technique was strong, too, and he was proud of what I've accomplished. But I think his decision to give me the house had something to do with the fact that we became very close when I was his student. In a way, he was like a father to me. Maybe he felt I was the daughter he never had."

"So what makes you think I want to live in some dead guy's house in Africa?"

Jess forced down the urge to admonish her son for disrespecting the man she had revered. This wasn't the time for a lecture. "We'll have fun in Zanzibar," she said. "Mama Hannah's going to move in with us. She'll keep an eye on you while I paint."

"Mom, I'm ten years old. I don't need a baby-sitter!"

"Mama Hannah's not a baby-sitter. She's like a grandma. You loved her when you were little."

"A grandma! I don't need some old lady looking out for me."

"Hannah's coming, and that's settled. You'll like her, I promise. I'm going to start illustrating the impala book as soon as we get there. James thinks we can work out the details by phone and fax. My editor's not thrilled with the idea of my moving so far away, but I told her I can paint with more authenticity if I'm living in Africa. An old car comes with the house. I'll be able to drive you into town to school."

"School? You mean we're going to live there forever? Like for the rest of our lives? What about Nick? What about my bed and all my stuff? I don't want to move to Africa. I like it here."

"We'll live right beside the ocean." She gave her voice the beckoning quality that sometimes worked on him. "White sand. Snorkeling. You'll be able to swim every day. You can look for shells. You can climb coconut palms."

"But I don't want to leave Nick. He's my best friend."

"You and Nick can be pen pals." She leaned over and whispered in his ear. "You can send him letters about your sunken ship."

"Sunken ship!"

"Dr. bin Yusuf told me about it years ago. There's supposed to be a wrecked ship near the reef. Sometimes gold coins wash ashore."

"You mean I might find treasure on the beach?"

"You never know. The main thing is you'll be breathing fresh air, and you won't have to go away to boarding school next term like we'd thought. We'll eat mangoes and bananas every day. We'll even see real monkeys."

"Whoa! I gotta tell Nick." He jumped to the floor, leapt neatly over the ornament shards, and spun around in midair. "When are we going?"

"About a week."

"Wahoo!" He pumped his fists toward the ceiling and threw back his head. "Zanzibar!"

Tearing off his Aqua-Lung, Splinter raced for the attic door. The football fell to the floor and bounced away with the vacuum-cleaner hose still attached. As she lowered herself to the chair, Jess heard her son's bare feet pound down the stairs.

She stepped onto the floor and picked her way through the broken ornaments to the attic door. Taking a deep breath, she stepped out onto the landing and shut the door firmly. The past was far behind. The future beckoned.

Zanzibar.

SPLINTER chewed on the cap of his ballpoint pen, working the blue plastic around inside his mouth and flicking the clip in and out like a lizard's tongue. He had been in Zanzibar only five hours, and already amazing things were happening. He couldn't wait any longer to write to his buddy Nick back in London.

After smoothing a sheet of lined notebook paper on the café table, he began to write:

> Dear Nick,
>
> Africa is awesome. First, you ride for nine hours on an airplane. Every time you push the overhead button, the stewardess comes and brings you a blanket or a pillow or a magazine. You can push the button all you want until your mom makes you stop.
>
> Then your plane lands in a city called Dar es Salaam. It's nothing like London. You could get lost there, believe me. After your mom calls the police and they find you, you get on a—

"Mom?" Splinter lifted his head. "How do you spell *hydrofoil?"*

"H-y-d . . . oh, honey, just guess."

Splinter frowned. His mom's hand was shaking as she stirred her tea. He'd never seen her face so white. The rest of her looked OK, though. She had on a blue blouse, a denim skirt, and a pair of sandals. After the hydrofoil ride, she had brushed her hair. It was bouncing around her chin as usual.

She had told him she had something called jet lag. She said as soon as Hannah came in on the afternoon hydrofoil from Dar es Salaam, they could all go out to the new house, and everything would be better. Splinter shrugged and went back to his letter.

> —hydrafol. It's like a boat with huge metal fins under it that lift the hull when it goes fast. It travels on top of the water from Dar es Salaam to Zanzibar—twenty-two miles. Mom told me not to dangle over the side anymore unless I wanted to become dinner for a shark.
>
> Zanzibar is a very old town with hundreds of winding streets. Africans, Arabs, Indians, and Europeans live here. Mom said the Arabs used to ship slaves, ivory, and gold out of Zanzibar. Now the island people grow cloves. In Zanzibar, you can get even more lost than in Dar es Salaam. Your mom can get lost, too.
>
> After she figures out how to read the map, you might talk her into buying you a lamp just like Aladdin's, but without the genie. I also got a cool model of a boat called a *dhow*. You can see the sultan's palace and the house where David Livingstone used to stay before he went exploring. Mom said to stay close to her, and I know why. We passed a witch doctor's shop, and we walked down a lane called Suicide Alley. Then we ran into a group of people, and my mom used to know some of them. Right in front of them, she—

"Mom, how do you spell *barf?"* Splinter tapped his pen on the notebook. "You know—upchuck, ralph, spew—"

"Splinter, what are you writing?"

"I'm telling Nick what happened when you got jet lag a few minutes ago."

His mom blotted her forehead with her napkin. "Maybe it was the hydrofoil. Maybe I was seasick."

"Lucky thing that guy helped you up off the street." Splinter chewed on the pen cap for a moment. The man had been awfully nice, he thought, considering the circumstances. Not everybody would mop you up with his own handkerchief and then carry you to a table at an outdoor café where you could rest. Especially not after you tossed your cookies all over his shoes.

Splinter studied his mother as she took a sip of her tea. It wasn't like her to whack somebody over the head with a camera bag. It seemed a particularly mean thing to do to a guy trying to help you. But that's what she had done—hauled off and smacked him and then yelled at him to get his hands off her and leave her alone.

She told Splinter it was jet lag. He hoped it wasn't contagious.

Splinter bent over his letter.

> —barfed. Now we are having tea at an outdoor café. I can see a cockroach right by my mom's foot. This is the most fun I've had in a long time. I'm going to like Zanzibar. Write soon.

He signed the letter with the practiced flourish of an artist. At the bottom of the letter he sketched a picture of the model *dhow* he had bought. It had triangular sails and a wooden hull. He couldn't wait to put it into the ocean and see if it would float.

While his mother sorted through the piles of official papers documenting ownership of the old house, Splint penciled a cartoon of her losing her breakfast. Nick would get a kick out of that.

It turned out to be quite a good drawing. His mom was clutching her stomach and crying out, "Oh! Oh!" in a little balloon beside her head. The man who helped her was bent over, one arm supporting her shoulders. His balloon said, "It's OK, Jessie. It's OK."

Splint frowned. How had the man known his mom's name? He turned the memory of that moment over in his mind. Very strange. There was some kind of magic here in Zanzibar. He could feel it.

He tore off a clean page and began making a copy of the cartoon to hang in his new bedroom.

@@@

Jessica Thornton had never seen a more welcome sight than the small figure of Hannah Wambua waving from the bridge of the hydrofoil late that afternoon. The morning had been an earthly image of hell. She and Splinter had gotten hopelessly lost in the winding alleys of old Zanzibar town. Despite the fact that they were late to the lawyer's office, Mr. Patel had kept them waiting an hour for the scheduled meeting. The house deed, though official, looked like it came from a Monopoly game. Mr. Patel had hinted at problems that might crop up. Something about the autopsy report and possible litigation from someone who was rumored to be considering contesting Dr. bin Yusuf's will.

"Autopsy report?" Jess had queried. "I thought he died of cancer."

"Not to worry, not to worry!" Mr. Patel had assured her. "Everything will be fine."

But how could she not worry? As the morning slipped by, things had only gotten worse. Dr. bin Yusuf's car had not been parked at the café as promised. The telephone-company supervisor had informed Jess that phone lines did not extend to the part of the island where her house was located. It was too isolated. At the post office, she had learned that her mail would have to go to a box in Zanzibar town. The house was too remote.

Even shopping for supplies had turned into a major endeavor. Groceries, she had discovered, could not be purchased at a single store. Meat came from one tiny shop; vegetables and fruit were stocked in a collection of market stalls. Sundries such as toilet paper, household cleaners, and brooms had to be purchased from a variety of little booths tucked here and there along the winding alleys. Comparison shopping was unheard of, and there was no such thing as a fixed price.

"Is that Mama Hannah?" Splinter asked as the hydrofoil drifted into port. "She's not very big."

Jess smiled. "She has a big heart."

Bright yellow scarf tied around her hair and pale green dress fluttering on her thin frame, Hannah looked exactly like an angel to

Jess. True, she was tiny and withered, and her raised hand looked like a small, dark bird's claw. But Jess knew that those bent fingers could soothe troubles with a motherly touch. The frail body disguised the fortitude and determination of a lion. And that head, as round and brown as a coffee bean, contained the wisdom of Solomon. Joy swelled inside Jess at seeing the woman who had been a mother to her through so many difficult years.

When their birth mother suffered a violent death, the four Thornton children had been devastated. Jess wasn't sure her oldest sister, Fiona, had ever recovered from the trauma. These days Fiona lived out in the isolated African bush where she studied elephants and talked to as few human beings as possible. Grant, the family rebel, would not have survived his teenage years without Hannah's guiding hand. Now he was a successful anthropologist. And Tillie, the youngest of the four Thorntons, hardly remembered having a mother other than Hannah.

In fact, the old woman had recently arrived back in East Africa from Tillie's home in Mali. Jess could hardly wait to hear all the news of her sister. Evidently, Tillie had impulsively married some mysterious writer following a whirlwind romance. It sounded like a delicious adventure.

"Mama Hannah!" Jess shouted, jumping up and down on her toes as the hydrofoil engines shut down. "Hi, Mama Hannah!"

"Mom, you're acting like a little kid," Splint said. "It's embarrassing."

Jess rumpled her son's coarse, brown-gold hair and gave him a quick hug. "She looks the same, doesn't she? She's beautiful."

"She's wrinkled."

"What did you expect? She's old."

"How old?"

"I don't know. She's always been old."

"She has great big holes in her earlobes."

"That's because she's a Kikuyu. The men and women of that tribe stretch their earlobes so they can hang lots of earrings in them."

"Barfola."

"Aren't you the fellow who was leading a cockroach down the street on a string a few minutes ago? *That's* barfola."

"She's got a dent in the top of her forehead."

"When she was young she used to carry huge loads of firewood on her back. The leather strap cut into her head and made it that way. Don't you remember?"

"I don't remember her at all. But I do know one thing: She won't be able to keep up with me. Mom, I don't want her tagging along when I'm trying to hunt treasure and explore the bay. I won't have any fun with some weird, old, wrinkled lady—"

"That's enough, young man." Jess jerked her son's arm and marched him down the dock to where the people were debarking the hydrofoil. Splinter had a knack for finding his mother's Achilles' heel in any situation and then homing in for the kill. He sensed how much Jess loved Hannah, so he had made up his mind to dislike her. Fortunately, Jess knew that in this situation Splinter had met his match. Hannah could be every bit as stubborn, willful, coercive, and cunning as any ten-year-old boy.

"Jessica!" The old woman stepped into the younger woman's arms and gave her a hug. "How are you, my *toto?*"

"Fine. Great." Jess blinked back tears as she held Hannah. Her *ayah* smelled as she always had—of thick black coffee and rich stew cooked over a charcoal fire. Her skin felt like an old flannel blanket—soft, warm, and comforting. "I've missed you, Mama Hannah."

"'A cheerful heart is good medicine,'" Hannah whispered, repeating one of her favorite proverbs. "To see you this day fills my soul with happiness."

Hannah turned from Jess and studied the lanky young boy standing beside his mother. "And who can this be?" When he didn't answer, her sparkling brown eyes narrowed. She cocked her head. "I am Hannah Wambua. You may call me Mama Hannah, if you wish."

Jess gave her son a nudge. "I'm Spencer Thornton," he said. "I'm ten."

"So you are. When I saw you last, you were four years old. You were small. You talked a lot. You also climbed on everything. At that time, I believed you would grow up to be clever and pretty to look at." She shrugged. "But even I sometimes make mistakes."

"What's that supposed to mean?" Splinter stuck out his jaw.

Hannah placed one crooked finger under the boy's chin and

tipped his face toward the afternoon sunlight. "Now I see that God has made you more than clever. He has given you the gift of a great mind. You will astonish us with your thinking." She shook her head and gave a Kikuyu expression of dismay. "Ehh, *tsk tsk*. But you are not pretty. Not at all. Instead, your face is handsome. A handsome man's face."

Splinter beamed. "I've already got peach fuzz on my lip."

Hannah appraised the silky brownish blond hair with a critical eye. Though there was nothing resembling a whisker in sight, she nodded sagely. "Mmm. So I see. In a few years, your mother will have to buy you a razor. And what about these fingers?" She held up the boy's ink-stained hands and turned them this way and that. "I see you are an artist like your mother. A writer, too, perhaps. I think you like to build and climb and swim. But I don't think you know how to make a bird from a palm leaf."

Splint's eyes widened. "Huh? How can you do that?"

"Or open a coconut to drink the milk?"

"Well—"

"Or find living clams buried in the sand?"

"I could dig."

"Do you know the secret hiding places of the sand clams?" Hannah gave the boy a wink. "Can you turn a mango into a rocket?"

"A rocket!"

"Do you know how to roast an ear of white maize so its kernels will taste like nuts? Can you tell an elephant shrew from a lemur? Can you build a house from sand?"

"I can do that. I can make sand castles."

"Can you? Hmm. We shall see." She lifted her focus to his mother. "Come, Jessica, shall we go to your new home now? I see your car is waiting."

Jess turned to find a small white Renault parked in the lot near the harbor. A brawny African man stood beside it. Arms folded, ebony face set like stone, he stared at the approaching trio with unflickering black eyes.

"Jambo, Bwana." Jess greeted the man in Swahili, pleased at how easily the language had come back to her in the few hours she'd been in Tanzania. *"Habari gani?"*

"Njema, Memsahib Thornton. This is your car." His mouth rigid, he opened the back door. "I shall drive."

"But I thought . . . it's my car. I'll drive."

"I shall drive."

She stared into the hard eyes. "What's your name?"

"Solomon Mazrui."

"Were you the driver for Dr. bin Yusuf?"

"I drive. I cut grass and grow flowers."

"You're the gardener?"

"Ndiyo." He nodded. "I fix the house also. I am a very good worker."

"You were the man helping Dr. bin Yusuf restore the house. He was proud of what had been accomplished. But there's a problem now, Solomon. I can't afford to pay a driver and a gardener. And I can't spend any money on the house. I have a son and—"

"Miriamu will be your cook."

"No, I can't afford a cook. Absolutely not. I'm very sorry. Look, I know you worked for Dr. bin Yusuf, but I'm not as well-off as he was."

"Miriamu cleans the house."

"I'll have to clean it myself. I'm used to that. In London we lived in a flat. We had no house help."

Solomon's eyes hardened. *"Ahadi ni deni."*

Jess looked at Hannah for help. "'A promise is a debt,'" the older woman translated.

"But I didn't make you a promise, Solomon," Jess said. "You worked for Dr. bin Yusuf, but you don't work for me. I have not hired you. You and I have no contract. No agreement."

"Baas. Twende." He beckoned them to climb in, as though he had comprehended nothing Jess was saying. "I shall drive."

"Let him drive, Mom." Splinter clambered into the front seat beside Solomon. "When he gets his first paycheck and it's blank, he'll figure it out."

"And I'll be accused of slavery and thrown in the Zanzibar jail." She slipped into the back beside Hannah. The Renault chugged to life, sounding like it had lost its muffler, a few pistons, and maybe a belt or two. A puff of dark gray smoke belched from the tailpipe as Solomon eased the car out of the parking lot.

"I will show you Zanzibar town," he announced.

"We already saw it," Splinter said. "We walked all over the place this morning. Mom got lost. She barfed in Suicide Alley."

"Barf?"

"Spit up. You know, *blaaagh."* Splinter pantomimed.

Solomon's stony face didn't crack a smile. *"Ndiyo.* In Kiswahili, we say *kutapika.* To vomit."

"Kutapika," Splint repeated carefully. *"Kutapika."*

In the backseat, Jess groaned. "Great. My son has just learned his first Swahili word."

"You are ill, *toto?"* Hannah asked.

"No, it was just . . . something upset me. Maybe I was seasick or had jet lag. It's been a hard day."

"Africa has brought you painful memories?"

Jess let out a breath and rubbed her eyes. Hannah had the annoying knack of seeing straight to the heart of things. And she never held in check what she was thinking. If she had a question, she asked it. If she had an opinion, she stated it. The characteristic could be endearing. It could also irritate beyond words.

"Painful memories?" Jess said. "Worse than that, Mama Hannah. I'm beginning to wonder why I ever came back."

"This is the land which the Lord your God has given you."

"The Promised Land?" She shook her head, thinking of a house with no phone, no mail, no supermarket, and a staff of cooks and gardeners she couldn't afford to pay. "It's not going to be flowing with milk and honey anytime soon."

"What has made you ill with anger and worry? Bitterness fills your stomach, and you have no release from it but *kutapika."*

"I didn't think so until today. I thought I'd gotten over it."

"Over *him?"*

Jess looked up, concerned that Splinter might hear. Her son was deep in conversation with Solomon about the possible presence of an octopus colony in the ocean near their new house. She could barely understand them over the roar of the Renault engine.

"I saw Rick today," she told Hannah in a low voice. "Here. In Zanzibar."

Hannah's eyes widened. "How can this be?"

"I don't know. I thought he was in Kenya. If I'd had any idea he might be here, I never would have come."

"Are you sure it was him, *toto?* It has been many years. I am sure he has changed, as you have. Perhaps you saw someone else."

"Maybe. The alley was dark. A group of men walked around the corner. Europeans and Africans mixed. Maybe an Asian or two. I glanced into their faces. Then I saw those eyes . . . his eyes . . . and everything just swept over me. I felt like I was going to faint."

"You did not see him again after you became ill?"

"He picked me up off the sidewalk!" Jess heard her voice rise in near hysteria at the memory. "He cleaned my shoes, and then he picked me up, Mama Hannah. He carried me to a chair at a café."

"A kind thing to do."

"Are you kidding? I didn't want that man touching me! When I realized what he was doing, I hit him with my camera bag."

"Perhaps you were beating a Good Samaritan. A stranger."

"I don't know." Jess covered her face with her hands, recalling the moment when she had been so sure she was staring into the blue eyes of Rick McTaggart. The man who had been her husband. Spencer's father.

"Oh, God."

Hannah nodded. "It is good to call upon the Lord in difficult times. God is wise. '"For I know the plans I have for you," says the Lord. "They are plans for good and not for disaster, to give you a future and a hope.'"

"Mama Hannah, please don't quote Scripture to me, OK? You know I'm a Christian. I go to church when I have time; I've taught Splinter to sing 'Jesus Loves Me' and all that. But if you and I are going to live in the same house, I'm going to have to ask you not to turn every little thing that happens into a message from God."

"What about the big things?" Hannah was staring straight ahead, her hands folded on her lap. "Perhaps God had his hand in your meeting this afternoon in Zanzibar town."

"Oh, please! If anything, that was demon inspired. I can't think what could make my life worse than having to face that man again. And if he saw Splint . . . If he found out . . ." Her voice grew tight as a lump of fear formed in her throat. "I won't let him near my son. I swear it!"

"This is Kenyatta Road," Solomon shouted over his shoulder. "Post office."

"We already went there," Jess enunciated the words slowly and clearly, lest he miss her point. "Take us to the house, Solomon."

"Long ago, the post office was the sultan's royal stables." He gave her a dark look, as if to warn her not to interfere with his plan. "Across the street is Babla's Expert Optical Service. Very old watches at that shop. Also sunglasses, cigarette lighters, cameras."

Jess dropped her hands in exasperation. Did the man never listen to anyone but himself?

"Dhow Palace Hotel," he announced next. "Ten rooms for tourists."

Jess stared out at the maze of murky streets. Women wearing the long, black, veiled *bui-buis* that bespoke their Muslim faith glided down alleys too narrow for cars. Most of the two-story houses had been built of mottled gray coral or soft limestone. Some were freshly whitewashed; others hadn't seen paint in two hundred years. Some boasted elaborately carved doors with brass studs; some had cheap wood doors; others had no doors. Jess could look into the open courtyards of multifamily dwellings where laundry hung on long lines and children chased puppies across open drains.

With the window rolled down, the smell was overpowering. Repellent odors of human refuse and rotting garbage formed a subtle undercurrent to the rich, alluring scents of curry, cinnamon, incense, charcoal smoke, fresh bread, and the island's famous cloves. The fishy saltiness of the damp sea breeze seasoned the potpourri of aromas.

Jess dragged the humid air into her lungs as though it were a heady drug. It brought back her childhood. Her youth. Wonder, beauty, mystery. For so many years, she had ached to recapture that exotic past. Now she wondered if she'd made a mistake. What had led her back to Africa? Had it been the same foolish romantic notion that once had driven her into the arms of Rick McTaggart? He had seemed perfect to her in the early days of their young love. He was handsome, full of fun, wild, and rugged. Their marriage was to have been the ideal picture of happiness. A treasure beyond her grandest imaginings.

"Nella's Chatu," Solomon barked as he drove past a small shop. "Nella will sew clothes for you, *memsahib."*

Jess nodded absently at the shelves of *batik,* tie-dye, and *kanga* fabrics. Rick McTaggart had left her holding nothing more than the fragments of broken dreams. Ten years after he had walked out of her life, she could look back and see the truth. Her husband had been little more than a twenty-year-old child. Rebelling against his strict upbringing, he had embraced adventure. He loved to scuba dive, hang glide, and ride his motorcycle through the bush country. He had climbed Mount Kilimanjaro and boated in Lake Victoria. He could dance every night until the sun came up. And he could drink. A lot.

"Creek Road," Solomon announced. Like many native Swahili speakers, he made the pronunciation error of reversing *l* and *r* in English words. To his captive audience in the Renault, he labeled the street *Cleek Load.*

"Mnazi Mmoja National Museum," he went on. "Many things inside. You will take this boy, your son, to see the things of old Zanzibar. Here is Emerson House. Long ago, it was a sultan's palace. Now it is a hotel. Nine rooms."

Solomon seemed to know the details of every shop and hotel on the island, Jess realized. Splinter was eating it up. Always fascinated with anything old or mysterious, he was falling in love with Zanzibar.

"How come every house has iron bars on the windows?" he asked Solomon.

"Pirates." When Solomon said the word, it sounded like *pilots.* But Splinter seemed to have no trouble understanding. "Red Sea Men. Very bad. They came from America. Attacked ships and robbed houses in Zanzibar. In Kiswahili we say *maharamia wa bahari,* the bandits of the beach."

While Splinter practiced this wonderful new expression, Jess fought memories she had once so carefully locked away. Rick

McTaggart. She understood now that the man she had married had been an alcoholic. Though young when they met, he had already been drinking for several years. She hadn't recognized the warning signs. To an eighteen-year-old looking for her own freedom, he had been her dream come true.

Only after they had married against the will of their parents had she begun to understand. Her new husband was not interested in going to college, finding a job, buying a house, or building a future. The more she pushed him toward her goals, the more he drank.

One night the tension had erupted into a vicious fight. Rick had left and never come back. A week later, Jess had learned she was expecting his baby. She had taken back her maiden name and given it to her son. Spencer Thornton.

At least something good had come of her terrible mistake.

"Look at that bazaar, Mom!" Spencer hollered over his shoulder. "I bet you could find anything in there. Wow, this town is so cool! Can I come down here sometime? By myself? Solomon could bring me. He knows everything. Huh, Mom? Could I?"

"Not right away, Splint," Jess said. If Rick McTaggart was living in Zanzibar, she would never let her son out of her sight. For years she had prayed that she would never have to lay eyes on that man again. She hated him. Hated the thought of how he had looked and talked and acted. Hated the memory of the things they had done together. Hated herself for having been such a fool.

"We go now to Uchungu House," Solomon announced as he steered the Renault onto a bumpy road that followed the seacoast. "The house of Ahmed Abdullah bin Yusuf is very old. Maybe one hundred years. That house does not know children. It does not know white people. It does not like new things. But I think Uchungu House will permit this boy to live in it."

"The house does not have any say about who lives in it," Jess snapped. She didn't like Solomon scaring her son with the image of a resentful, temperamental old house. Anger at the thought of anyone harming her son—including a chauffeur who told frightening stories or a ne'er-do-well who might want to stake his claim as a father—hardened her voice. "I'm in charge here. I'll do what's right for my son and for myself, and neither you nor anyone else had better interfere with that. Do you understand me, Solomon?"

"Ndiyo, memsahib."

Jess leaned against the seat back and let out a hot breath. She felt tight and achy inside, as though a thick vine had wound around her heart with tentacles determined to twist, squeeze, and choke her. Images of pirates, witch doctors, winding alleys, octopus colonies, dark bazaars, and a hundred-year-old house on a sea cliff curled inside her, latching on with suckers of fear. But they were not the vine . . . not the source of what threatened her. That was Rick McTaggart.

She rested her head against the window frame and let the tropical air fan her face. Beside her in the car, Hannah was humming. Jess recognized the song, but she couldn't put her finger on it. Something out of the past. A hymn.

The humming stopped.

"Uchungu House," Hannah murmured, repeating the name Solomon had given the old seaside home. "Uchungu House. House of Bitterness."

NIGHT descended over the island of Zanzibar like the black veil of a Muslim woman's *bui-bui*. At the town of Mdogo, Solomon turned the car onto a gravel road, leaving behind the security of overhead street lamps and the occasional passing police car. In the utter darkness, the Renault's single working headlight picked out a series of deep potholes into which the car plunged with bone-jarring frequency. Palm trees, lush undergrowth, and a tangle of leafy brush obscured all but an occasional light from a house along the road.

"Mom?" Splinter's wide eyes located his mother in the backseat. "This isn't like the streets in London, is it?"

"This is Africa, honey. You'll get used to it, I promise." Jess knew her son's vivid imagination could play terrifying tricks with his mind. Despite his bravado and his propensity for wandering off by himself to explore, Splint could dissolve into a ten-year-old's puddle of tears if he felt out of control and alone.

"Why did they name it Uchungu House?" he asked Solomon. "It sounds spooky."

"Uchungu House is not a place of happiness," the African said. "Perhaps you will bring a change."

The travelers in the car fell silent until Hannah's voice warmed

them. "'God blesses those who work for peace, for they will be called the children of God,'" she said. "'The Lord is my strength, my shield from every danger. I trust in him with all my heart. He helps me, and my heart is filled with joy. I burst out in songs of thanksgiving.'"

"What songs are you talking about?" Splinter asked, not realizing she had been quoting from Matthew and the Psalms.

Hannah hummed for a moment. Once she had the tune in mind, she repeated the favorite African preamble to a song, "Are you ready? Let us go to heaven." Then she began to sing in Swahili. *"Mungu ni pendo; apenda watu. Mungu ni pendo; anipenda."*

"Sikilizeni, furaha yangu," Jess sang, joining in with the familiar words her *ayah* had taught her so many years ago. *"Mungu ni pendo; anipenda."*

"Wow, Mom," Splinter said. "I didn't know you could do that. What's it mean?"

"God is love; he loves all people. God is love; he loves me." She paused. "Umm . . . I forget the rest."

"Listen, everyone," Hannah continued translating. "Happiness is mine. God is love; he loves me."

"Cool. I want to learn it."

"Perhaps the Swahili will be too much for you," Hannah said doubtfully. "Swahili is a difficult language."

"No way," Splinter blustered. "I can do it. Tell me how the song starts."

"Are you ready? Let us go to heaven."

By the time the Renault's headlight illuminated the narrow driveway to Uchungu House, Hannah and Splinter were singing the chorus together in perfect harmony. Solomon, who Jess suspected was a Muslim as were so many coastal Tanzanians, did not join in.

"Uchungu House," he announced, stopping the song as he stomped on the brake in the middle of what looked like thick jungle.

"Where?" Jess asked.

"There."

Seeing nothing and hearing only the rush and crash of ocean waves on the cliffs beyond the driveway, she opened the car door and stepped out. Through a tangle of vines, the high walls of a huge house emerged like a white ghost. Both stories were surrounded by a deep verandah. Six arched doorways outlined the lower level. The upper level formed a balcony guarded by an iron railing.

"Aren't there any lights?" she asked.

"In the day we have much sunshine." Solomon flicked off the Renault's headlamp, plunging them into blackness. "Inside the house, some electric lightbulbs hang from the ceiling, but Ahmed Abdullah bin Yusuf did not pay the electric company in Zanzibar town for many years. We use kerosene lamps."

"Not anymore," Jess said. "If the place has electricity, I'm putting it back in service." Unwilling to allow the pale specter of the house to overwhelm her, she slipped her arm around Splinter and gave him a hug. "Come on, buckaroo. Let's go explore our new home."

Starlight guided the four up a walk graveled with tiny seashells. Solomon snapped on a flashlight and led them up two wide stairs onto the stone-floored verandah. The beam focused on a fifteen-foot-tall set of double doors, each built of heavy, dark wood and embedded with four rows of cone-shaped brass studs the size of a man's fist. The wide lintel and frame surrounding the door had been carved in rich Arabic patterns of twining rosettes and geometric shapes. Instead of a doorknob or handle, a thick iron bolt had been mounted at the bottom of the door. The end of the bolt was buried in the stone step and made secure by a heavy chain and padlock.

"The door of Uchungu House is good," Solomon informed Jess. "Zanzibar has nearly six hundred doors—counted and recorded. *Memsahib* will not sell this door to tourists. This house wants to keep the door."

Jess had no intention of putting the magnificent door up for sale—a practice she knew had depleted the island of some of its most beautiful architecture—but she didn't like anyone ordering her around. She watched as Solomon pulled a key from his pocket, fitted it into the padlock, and lifted the bolt.

"I'll take that," she said and held out her hand for the key. "And if you have any others, I'd like them, too."

"Ndiyo, memsahib."

He dropped the key into her palm as if he didn't want to touch her. Jess wrote it off as his Muslim reluctance to have close contact with women, but she was well aware that he would not like this female stranger usurping his authority. He pushed open one of the doors and swung the flashlight beam around the interior of the first room. Jess followed him inside, Splinter gripping her hand and Hannah close behind them.

"Sitting room," Solomon said.

He swept the beam of light across a collection of square chairs built of soft wood and woven palm leaves. The room would have been plain, almost shabby, but for the large rectangular painting that hung beside an arched opening opposite the front door. Jess crossed to it and stood enraptured.

The seascape writhed with roiling pearl gray clouds and tossing ocean waves in shades of indigo, violet, and turquoise. On a high cliff at the edge of the frame, wind bowed a palm tree toward the ground, blasting green fronds like an umbrella blown inside out. Alone in the tumultuous sky, a single bird struggled to stay aloft, its black feathers ruffled and its neck stretched forward in determination.

Immediately she recognized the signature characteristics of her mentor's work. Thick layers of oil paint formed a rough, sculpturelike texture on the canvas. Brilliant jewel tones and the mottled effect of dappled paint had led critics to call Ahmed Abdullah bin Yusuf the African van Gogh. The painting was spectacular, surely one of his best. Jess knew it would be worth a small fortune.

"What is this doing *here?"* she exclaimed. "This painting needs to be in a gallery. It could be stolen, or damaged."

"This painting has lived in the sitting room of Uchungu House many years," Solomon said. "This painting likes to live here."

"Splinter, don't you dare touch it. Not even a finger. And no ball playing in the house."

"Calm down, Mom. No need to go ballistic over some picture."

"This is not just any painting. This is a masterpiece. I can't believe it's here."

Solomon led his guests into the adjoining side room—another sitting room with more inexpensive furniture, a cotton throw rug, and two small but striking portraits that had been painted by Dr. bin Yusuf.

The first canvas depicted a light-skinned Arab boy with strange green eyes. He wore a white caftan and carried a round white shell. Half of a woman's face filled the other painting. Dr. bin Yusuf had chosen to reveal only one dark brown eye, one arching eyebrow, the side of the woman's nose, and a small part of her down-turned lip. Her skin, the color of rich coffee laced with cream, was flawless and glowing. She was beautiful, but Jess could not mistake the spark of anger in her eye.

"What are these paintings doing here?" she whispered. "I just don't believe it."

"Then you will not believe many things about this house." Solomon said. "In every room, this house wears the paintings of Ahmed Abdullah bin Yusuf. Uchungu House also holds his many carvings and sculptures."

Solomon had not exaggerated. He led the little group through countless archways into room after room of eighteen-foot walls hung with magnificent landscapes and portraits. Beyond the two sitting rooms was a small area with a traditional stone seat Solomon called a *daka.* To its left stood a bar area stocked with rows of old wines. To the right rose a winding stone staircase that led to the upper floor.

Deep in the middle of the house, a large airy courtyard opened to the sky and let in fresh breezes and rainwater to nourish the collection of exotic plants growing in clay pots set around the perimeter. A covered hall surrounding the courtyard sheltered a dining table and a set of carved chairs. A bathroom with its own elaborate arched doorway lay at one end of the hall, a storage room at the other. On the left side of the courtyard stood a long narrow kitchen with an ancient stove and a deep stone sink. It appeared to have a working faucet and running water.

"Library," Solomon stated, gesturing at a door across the courtyard from the kitchen. "Locked."

"May I have the key, please?" Jess held out her hand.

His face hardened. "Tomorrow you will see the library."

"I asked you for the key tonight."

He dropped it into her palm and turned on his heel. Jess felt her son's hand tighten on her own.

"Mom, what's that?" he whispered.

On the narrow staircase in the hallway at the far end of the courtyard, a faint moving light shone on the white wall. It began to slide down the stairwell, step by step, followed by a dark sinuous shape.

"Mom!" Splint squeaked.

"Ni, Miriamu, *tu."* Solomon strode toward the figure. His flashlight beam found dark bare feet, the hem of a colorful black-and-purple gown, two slender arms, a long neck, and finally a beautiful African face.

"Solomon, *sitaki tochi,"* the woman said, pushing the harsh light aside and lifting the kerosene lantern she carried. *"Ni wageni?"*

"We're not guests." Jess stepped forward and held out her hand. "I'm Jessica Thornton, the new owner of Uchungu House. This is my son, Spencer, and our friend, Hannah Wambua. And you are Miriamu?"

"Ndiyo, memsahib." Heavy black lashes dropped over her liquid eyes, and she gave the hint of a curtsy. "I am your cook. I clean Uchungu House for you."

Jess let out a breath of frustration at yet another situation she didn't know how to resolve. "We'll talk about you and Solomon in the morning. Right now, I want to get Splinter to bed. We both have jet lag."

"Memsahib alifanya barf *ndani ya Zanzibar,"* Solomon informed the exotic woman.

"Barf?"

"Kutapika!" Splinter burst out. Miriamu's face broke into a smile, and she covered a giggle with her hand.

"Pole sana, memsahib," she apologized. "You are ill?"

Jessica fought her growing frustration. "I'm tired. Solomon, please show us the upstairs rooms. I hope there are beds."

"Ndiyo, memsahib. Very good beds."

The upper story of Uchungu House was a warren of small, narrow rooms with high ceilings and lots of large windows. Ascending by the back staircase, Solomon led the newcomers to the balcony rail that overlooked the courtyard. At the very back of the house were two identical rooms, one of which Splinter claimed. Jess wanted the other, but Miriamu told her such an arrangement was impossible. As the *memsahib* of the house, she must sleep in the big room at the front. When Jess began to protest, Hannah elected to take the room beside Splint.

"Udongo upatize uli maji," she murmured.

Take advantage of the clay while it is wet, Jess mentally translated the Swahili saying. True, she and her son had always lived in cramped quarters. Jess had to admit that she would enjoy privacy for a change. And Splinter deserved room to grow and mature without a mother always breathing down his neck.

"This boy is very brave," Hannah said, surveying Splinter as he poked around in the corners of his chosen room. "And as you know yourself, I am a light sleeper."

In reluctant agreement, Jess moved on while Solomon pointed out a long office, two bathrooms, and a storage room. Dr. bin Yusuf's paintings hung on almost every wall, and his sinuous carvings of wood or stone guarded doorways and nestled in corners. Contemplating the responsibility of guardianship for the valuable art, Jess followed the African guide toward the front of the house. They passed through a large open hall that led to the curving staircase and then slipped through a curtained arch.

"Your bedroom," Miriamu said. *"Ni maridadi kabisa."*

It certainly was *maridadi.* One of those Swahili words that had no direct translation, *maridadi* was a perfect description of this room. The word meant beautiful, fancy, decorative, and exquisite all rolled into one. No higher compliment could be paid.

Jess walked across the thick Persian rugs that carpeted the floor and stared in wonder at the room's treasures—a huge Zanzibar chest carved in wood and studded with brass; a large fern filling a bright copper urn; chairs of ebony, mahogany, and teak; a table inlaid with silver and glass; an enormous canopied bed hung with mosquito netting; and paintings everywhere. Everywhere.

"Why?" she whispered. "Why did he leave all this to *me?"*

She had asked the question of herself in London and had found no good answer. She had asked Mr. Patel in Zanzibar. The attorney had shrugged. He didn't know. She looked at the two Africans standing before her. Miriamu's dark eyelashes fluttered down. Solomon squared his shoulders.

"Ahmed Abdullah bin Yusuf did not have friends," the African man said. "He did not have family. Perhaps you were important to him."

"I was his student, that's all. I loved his art, and I respected him as a teacher and as a man. But that was a long time ago. I took classes from him for only a couple of years." She looked around the room. "He left all this to me? I just don't get it."

"But you *did* get it, *memsahib*. And now you will live forever in Uchungu House."

He gave her a dark look before leaving the room with Miriamu at his heels. Jess pressed her hands against her stomach as she gazed through the archways onto the balcony that faced the sea. Like a Möbius strip that had no beginning and no end, Solomon's words swirled around inside her head.

"And now you will live forever in the House of Bitterness."

Unable to sleep in spite of her exhaustion, Jess lay in the big bed and stared up at the ceiling through the filmy mosquito net. In London, she had imagined Dr. bin Yusuf's house as a quaint stone cottage by the sea. A haven for Splinter. A cocoon for her. Hannah would come, and Africa would wrap its benevolent healing arms around them all. Everything would be perfect.

Instead, she was burdened with a palatial stone mansion of great architectural significance, a household staff, and a gallery of valuable art. Would Splinter even be safe here? What if he tumbled off the cliff or fell down a well or got bitten by some strange tropical bug? Could she actually paint out here in the jungle? Could she afford to pay Solomon and Miriamu? How could she protect the paintings and sculptures?

Jess flopped onto her stomach and buried her face in the feather pillow. No, it wasn't any of that. She could handle Splint and the rest of the situation. Somehow or other, she would manage. She always had.

It was *him*. She couldn't stop thinking about him, couldn't get him out of her brain.

In Zanzibar town, the men had walked around the corner, the whole group of them. An African or two. Someone in a turban. A heavy white man with a bald head the color of a baked crab. And then those blue eyes. Rick McTaggart's blue eyes. No one else had eyes like that—deep-set, penetrating eyes that never wavered, eyes that always stared direct and straightforward, eyes that could pin a person to a wall or buckle her knees or make her weep.

But had she seen Rick's face? She couldn't remember. She had glimpsed a flash of tan skin, broad shoulders, brown hair. It could have been anyone, couldn't it?

Not with those eyes. The instant she saw them, everything had swept over her. Their meeting on a beach, their brief passionate romance, their wedding, the little house where . . .

She sat up and clapped a hand over her mouth. *Make it go away. Make the memories leave me alone.* Tears squeezed from the corners of her eyes. She blotted them with the sheet.

It's OK, Jessie. It's OK.

The words Rick had whispered in her ear that afternoon in Zanzibar held the same deep tones she remembered so well. *It's OK, Jessie.* He had called her by his special name. *Jessie.* So it was him. It was Rick McTaggart, and she couldn't escape.

Worse, even worse, he had picked her up and cradled her against his chest. She had felt the hard roundness of his biceps beneath her hand. She had rested her cheek on his shirt—warm khaki cotton, brown buttons, a pocket with a pen, a small spiral-bound notebook, a pair of sunglasses. And she had smelled him. Rick.

No one else smelled like Rick McTaggart—like salty sea air, sunshine, tanned male skin, and freedom. No one else walked like him, with that confident stride, shoulders thrown back, purpose in every step.

No one else called her Jessie.

She flopped back on the bed and pulled the sheet over her head. *Make him go away. Don't let me ever have to see him again.* The cry from her heart was meant to be a prayer, but she hadn't talked to God in so many years she wasn't sure she remembered how. And she wasn't sure he would want to listen. After all, ten years ago she had been so angry with him . . . raging and crying and begging . . . and finally turning her back on him.

Well, who wouldn't? No one wanted a God who would allow trouble like Rick McTaggart to invade. Jess had always believed God was sort of like Hannah. Benevolent, protective, loving. If she'd been around at the time, Hannah would never have let Rick McTaggart near Jess. Of course, Jess probably would have made her own choices anyway. Terrible choices. Horrible mistakes.

"God, if you're out there anywhere," she whispered into the silence of her room, "if you care about me at all, please fix this. Please help me get through this. Heal the brokenness inside me so I don't have to feel so awful anymore. I'm choking from it. I'm dying inside. Please just fix it!"

She doubted her prayer had the power to break through the thin web of mosquito netting, let alone find its way to God. Feeling empty and cold in spite of the hot night, she lay on the bed and listened to the surf until sleep took her.

◎ ◎ ◎

Just after sunrise, the roar of truck engines brought Jess bolt upright in bed. Had every car on the island of Zanzibar lost its muffler? She threw off the sheet, pushed out from under the mosquito-net canopy, and padded onto the balcony outside her room.

The horrendous sound came from the driveway just below. As Jess leaned over the stone railing, the ruckus stopped. Two khaki green trucks left over from some military campaign sat basking in an aura of diesel fumes. Two men jumped out of the first truck; three exited the second. Without preamble, they began hauling machinery, hoses, metal chests, and ropes from the truck beds and depositing them on the verandah of Uchungu House.

"I hope she's got eggs today." One of the men whisked off a battered white hat and bellowed at the house. "Hey, Miriamu! We're ready for breakfast."

Four of the visitors were Africans—shirtless wiry men who wore ankle-length skirts of native fabric wrapped around their waists and small white caps perched on their heads. The man who had hollered was white, bald, and he sported a paunch the size of a small beer keg. Barely visible beneath his girth was a tiny blue swimsuit. His thongs flipped on the crunchy gravel as he walked back and forth unloading equipment.

"Excuse me," Jess called down. "I don't think we've met."

"Great ghosts!" The bald-headed man's focus followed the direction of the voice. "You gave me the fright of my life, lass."

"Then we're even. I wasn't expecting visitors today. I'm Jessica Thornton, the new owner of Uchungu House."

"Owner?" The man scratched the skin on the top of his head. "I didn't realize anyone had been given the rights to this place. Ahmed . . . well, I didn't know he had an heir."

"I was his student. And you are?"

"John Wallace of Scotland, at your service." He gave her a deep bow. "Treasure hunter, marine salvager, expert on Indian Ocean sea life, and Scottish dancer extraordinaire. You may call me Hunky."

In spite of her irritation at the intrusion, Jess couldn't hold back a grin. "May I ask what you are doing here, Mr. Hunky?"

"It's simply Hunky, thank you. Now, don't tell me you've never heard of Wallace Diving, Ltd."

"I've been living in London."

"I fancied I was world famous."

"For diving?"

"For treasure hunting, of course. In my time I've found some fabulous loot. These past few weeks I've been exploring a sunken ship out in the bay. I discovered the ballast stones three months ago. I'm surprised you didn't know. The news was all over town. They had it in the newspapers."

Jess wondered if Zanzibar even had a newspaper. "I'm afraid I hadn't heard anything about it. I just arrived in town yesterday. Look, Mr. Wallace, I appreciate your situation, but I have a lot of work to do, and I want to keep things private around my house. I'm going to have to ask you to move your operation to another location."

"Another location? Lass, there's only one ship out there, and it sank in only one bay. That bay is yours. Have you had a look at it?"

She lifted her focus to the line of palm trees just beyond the verandah balcony. "Not yet, but—"

"You've a private beach, inaccessible to the public and worth a fortune should you choose to replace this crumbling old house with a luxury hotel. In the meantime, there's only one way for a diving team to get out to that ship, and that's from your beach."

"My *private* beach."

"It's private, yes, but I trust you won't shut it off to me and my crew. After all, we're doing a work of great importance."

"Treasure hunting doesn't seem all that important to me, Mr. Wallace. In fact, your presence here at Uchungu House feels an awful lot like an invasion of privacy."

Hunky Wallace glanced at his men before turning his focus on Jess again. "This is not merely a treasure hunt, you realize. It's a grand and important venture into the mysteries of the past. Wallace Diving, Ltd., is working with the Tanzanian government—"

"What?" one of his men cut in. "But, *Bwana* Wallace, you said we—"

"On the contrary, Karim. I have decided this wreck is of vital historical significance, and the government has the right to investigate."

"But just yesterday you told—"

Hunky put out a silencing hand. "Surely Ms. Thornton cannot object to the necessity of government exploration of this valuable relic of Zanzibar's past."

Jess crossed her arms and studied the persistent diver standing below her on the driveway. "Do I have a choice?"

"With the government? Not really. They do as they please, you know."

"How long is this going to take?"

"Another month or two at the most. Maybe three, but not more than four. Actually, it all depends on what we find. We've only just begun diving." He gave her a broad grin, then turned to one of his men and murmured a quick list of instructions. "We'll do our best not to disturb you, lass. You'll hardly know we're here."

The roar of one of the army trucks coming to life drowned out his last words. He gave a shrug as the vehicle pulled past him and headed back down the driveway. Jess shook her head. Treasure hunters. If Splinter got wind of this . . .

"You won't mind us having a bit of breakfast before we go out on the water, will you?" Hunky called up to her. "Miriamu usually manages to boil us a few eggs and stir up a little *posho."*

"I suppose I don't mind this morning, but—"

"Good. We've got to wait for our government man, anyway. Karim's gone to fetch him from town." He tipped his head in the direction of the verandah. "Come on, chaps. Let's go eat breakfast. It'll give Karim time to round up McTaggart."

A bolt shot down Jess's spine. "McTaggart?"

"He works for the Ministry of Something-or-Other in Dar es Salaam. Ministry of Antiquities, is it? Or the Ministry of Historical Development? Something like that. At any rate, he's been on my back for a month about this particular wreck. I'll let him poke about for a bit. That should satisfy him."

Jess gripped the stone balcony rail. "Are you . . . are you talking about Rick . . . uh . . . Rick McTaggart?"

"The very man." He gave her an expansive grin. "Come down and join us for breakfast, won't you, Ms. Thornton? I'll introduce you to my crew, tell you a bit about our work, and allay all your fears. Within the hour, McTaggart will arrive, and we shall all begin the most exciting adventure of our lives!"

RICK McTaggart studied the ocean from behind dark sunglasses as he drove his motorcycle down the bumpy road that led away from Zanzibar town. Ahead, one of Wallace Diving's two trucks led the way toward the site of a recently discovered shipwreck, a find Rick had been trying to document for several months.

As usual, Hunky Wallace had been bragging in the local pubs about the wreck he'd found—an undated bark, possibly loaded with gold, and completely untouched. When it came to revealing the exact location of the find, however, the veteran treasure hunter had been as tight-lipped as a clam. The Scotsman wasn't about to let any other scavengers at his prize. As for the government . . . well, Hunky always used the language of the sailor he was to describe how he felt about bureaucratic interference.

Yesterday in Zanzibar Rick had gone through yet another futile exercise. Earlier, he had scheduled a meeting with Wallace and crew. At his office downtown, Rick had shown them every official document he could find that set forth the rights of the Tanzanian government to investigate any excavation site on land or at sea. He had used his most persuasive arguments. He had even leveled a couple of

well-formulated threats. No good. Hunky wouldn't budge. In fact, the man denied he'd even found a wreck.

Rick had been ready to board the hydrofoil for the mainland this morning when Hunky's man, Karim, had appeared out of nowhere and instructed him to follow the truck to the wreck site. *Bwana* Wallace had decided to cooperate.

In spite of his concerns about this sudden about-face, Rick felt a tingle of excitement as he turned the motorcycle onto a narrow trail at the remote northern end of the island. An undocumented shipwreck. The possibility of hidden treasure. The hope of a magnificent discovery. A familiar tightening in the pit of his stomach set his pulse racing.

It was almost enough to quell the uncomfortable memory of the events of the previous day. Almost. Nothing could quite suppress the memory of when he'd walked around a corner with Wallace's crew and had spotted the beautiful, long-legged brunette in the alley ahead. Tall, slender, almost ethereal in her blue blouse and denim skirt, the woman had seemed to float toward him through the shadows. He had experienced an instant of paralyzing reaction so intense he had felt light-headed. His mouth dried up, his heart rate went berserk, and a sweat broke out on his forehead. He hadn't felt so off balance in years.

And then the woman had moved into a patch of sunlight. Her hair turned auburn, her eyes violet, her face familiar. Shock zapped through him. Recognition dawned in her eyes, and her cheeks drained of color. She clutched her stomach and crumpled onto the sidewalk. Sick, trembling, as white as the sand on the beach, she curled into a ball.

He could hardly remember what had happened next. Somehow he had found himself bending over Jessica. His Jessie. He had cradled her in his arms and carried her to a chair, murmuring soothing words.

And then she had hit him. Her camera bag smacked into the side of his head. She shouted at him. Somebody pulled him back. Escorted him away.

When he had finally rid himself of Hunky's crew and returned to the café where he'd left her, she was gone. Had the woman really been Jessie? He had been so sure. Positive. Now he could hardly believe it.

Rick drove his motorcycle up to the verandah of a huge old house, a relic of the years of Portuguese and Arab occupation of Zanzibar. He cut the engine and took off his helmet, determined to bury the incident and focus on the project ahead. Karim appeared beside him.

"Let us go inside Uchungu House, *Bwana* McTaggart. *Bwana* Wallace is eating his breakfast."

"How long has Hunky been working the wreck?" Rick asked as they climbed the steps into the cool shade of the verandah. "A month?"

"Not so long. Perhaps two weeks."

When he walked into the living room and spotted the painting on the wall, a faint memory pricked his spine. "Uchungu House. Isn't this where that artist used to live? The African van Gogh?"

"Yes, *Bwana* McTaggart. This was the home of Ahmed Abdullah bin Yusuf."

"I thought I read where he died recently. Cancer or something."

"I do not know, *Bwana*. There are many rumors."

They crossed a room with a stone *daka,* entered another room with a curving staircase, and then stepped out onto the porch surrounding the courtyard. Hunky Wallace and his men filled the chairs around a long table that had been piled with fresh bread, mangoes, boiled eggs, and white cornmeal *posho* mounded high in a bowl.

"McTaggart!" Hunky pushed back his chair and beckoned with a wave of his beefy hand. "Join us, won't you? We've a long day ahead of us, and a man needs a good breakfast when he's working the waters of the Indian Ocean. Make room there, my good lad. That's it."

A boy of ten or twelve moved down a chair to leave room beside the treasure hunter. Rick accepted the place of honor, cocked his elbows on the table, and eyed his host. "So, what's all this about, Wallace? Yesterday you claimed you didn't even have a wreck—said you didn't have any idea what I was talking about. You called me every name in the book. You announced that the government of Tanzania and I could go straight to—"

"Not in front of the boy, I beg you." Hunky clapped a hand on Rick's shoulder. "We've a special guest here this morning, Mr. McTaggart. Meet young Spencer. He insists we're to call him Splint."

The boy turned a pair of wide violet eyes on him. "Are you a treasure hunter, too?"

"I'm a marine archaeologist, Splint. There's a big difference."

Hunky snorted. "Ach, it's a fancy name for the very same thing. McTaggart searches the seawaters for shipwrecks, same as I do. And when he can't find any of his own, he comes pestering me to have a look at mine. Then he gets out all his fancy books and charts and pipes and chains—and he slows me down to a snail's pace. What I could do in a month, he stretches out to a year."

"What you could do in a month," Rick countered, "is blast a ship's fragile timbers to smithereens with your airlift, shatter conglomerate with a hammer, and haul off truckloads of valuable but undocumented historical data to throw in your warehouse and sell to the first antiques dealer who shows his face at your door."

"Now, listen here, McTaggart—"

"You listen to me, Wallace—"

"Can I go out to the wreck with you?" The boy's voice cut through the argument. "I'm a good swimmer, and I could help you—"

"Absolutely not."

The words spoken from the stairway in the hallway at the far end of the courtyard drew the attention of every man at the table. Rick swung around, and there stood Jessie. Jessie with her hair cut short and shining red brown in the sunshine. Jessie with her violet eyes rimmed in long, black lashes. Jessie with a yellow T-shirt over a gathered skirt of gauzy fabric in every shade of the rainbow. Beautiful Jessica. His wife.

"Did I give you permission to come down here, Spencer?" she asked the boy, her voice tight. "Get upstairs this minute."

"But I'm eating breakfast."

"Upstairs." One long arm shot out, a finger pointed at the rear staircase. "Now."

"OK, Mom."

The word skittered down Rick's spine like cold marbles. *Mom.* Jessica Thornton was a mother? He watched the boy push away from the table and plod sullenly toward the steps. How old was the kid? Eight? Ten? He had no idea. Had Jessie remarried? And what was she doing in Zanzibar . . . at Uchungu House . . . with Hunky Wallace?

"Jessie," he began.

"I have one thing to say, Mr. Wallace," she interrupted, her eyes trained on the Scotsman. "I want you and every single one of your men out of my house now. This is my home and my land. I want you all to get in your trucks and leave me alone."

"Now then, lass, you've a grand knot in your knickers, haven't you?" Hunky stood and rubbed his hands over his bare belly. "What have we done to distress you? We're merely eating our breakfast before we set out to sea. And you might like to know that we've been joined by an esteemed representative of the Tanzanian government. May I present Mr. Richard McTaggart? Rick, this is Ms. Jessica Thornton, the new owner of Uchungu House."

"We've met," she said, never taking her eyes from Wallace. "Look, I don't care about your shipwreck. I just want you off my property."

"You may not care about the wreck, but the government does. Isn't that true, Mr. McTaggart?"

"That's true." It was all Rick could make himself say. His mouth felt as dry as an old sea sponge. He could hardly believe he was standing in the same room with Jessie again. After all these years . . .

"The government has papers," Hunky told her. "Important documentation of their regulations. Don't they, Mr. McTaggart? They've a right to explore the wreck."

"I don't care who explores the wreck," she said. "Just don't come onto my property again."

"Listen to me now, lass." Hunky put a hand on Jessie's elbow and turned her toward the door. "Why don't you just come with me and see what I've got to show you? You'll understand in a minute how vital this shipwreck is. And you'll see why Wallace Diving, Ltd., and the Tanzanian government have no choice but to . . ."

Rick watched as Hunky led Jessie out of the courtyard toward the front verandah. He picked up a napkin and mopped his forehead. Jessica. Here in Zanzibar.

So he hadn't imagined it. She was living here in the old artist's house. She had a son. And she despised Rick McTaggart. Above all else, that last fact could not be denied. She hated him. Hated him so much she couldn't even bring herself to look at him.

He couldn't blame her. He'd walked out on their marriage years ago. How many years? He couldn't even remember. He'd been a kid, and things had been so . . . so confusing. So mixed up. At the time he hadn't known much of anything except that he loved Jessica Thornton. Loved her and was hurting her. Loved her and couldn't satisfy her. Loved her and would eventually destroy her.

"You're the guy my mom barfed on."

The voice at his elbow brought Rick back to reality. A pair of eyes the same luminous blue violet as Jessie's scrutinized him. "Hey, Splint," Rick said. "Gonna have another go at breakfast?"

"I guess so. My mom's weird, isn't she? You'll just have to get used to her. She goes along fine for a while, and then all of a sudden she heads off on an emotional tangent."

"An emotional tangent?" The boy's choice of words brought a smile to Rick's mouth.

"You know. She starts crying for no reason. Or she blows her top over some little thing. I chalk it up to her artistic temperament."

"Your mother's an artist?"

"Ever heard of the Kima the Monkey series? You know, *Kima the Monkey and the Appalling Anteater, Kima the Monkey and the Brilliant Baboon, Kima the Monkey and the Crafty Crocodile.* James Perrott writes them, and my mom illustrates. They've won scads of awards. They're working on the *Irritable Impala,* and that's why we moved to Africa. Mom thinks she'll paint better here."

"So . . . uh . . . where's your dad?"

"Who knows? He's been out of the picture a long time."

"Oh, I see."

"Hey, let's check out the beach. I can't wait to go swimming."

"You're a good swimmer?" Rick walked beside the boy through the cool interior of the house. He felt off-kilter. Like he had stepped onto a boat on a stormy ocean. Nothing looked quite right. Nothing seemed exactly the way it had before.

Who was this Spencer Thornton? Could the boy possibly be his own son? No, of course not. Jessie hadn't been expecting a baby when they separated. She would have told him about something as important as that. Wouldn't she?

He had to talk to her. Now. Had to straighten everything out. After all these years . . . How many years?

"I was on the swim team at my school in London," Splint was saying. "I won a lot of races. I even earned a certificate in lifesaving. I may be skinny, but I'm strong for my age."

"How old are you?"

"Ten. You?"

"I'm thirty-one."

"Getting up there, aren't you? I guess after a while a man has to rely on his intellect. The body starts to cave in, and the brain's all you've got to work with. So, how did you get to be a marine archaeologist anyway?"

They had reached the edge of the cliff that bordered the sea. A sturdy fence ran along the perimeter where the lawn of thick grass suddenly dropped a hundred feet down a coral precipice to the sandy beach below. Rough steps had been carved into the cliff, and a corroded iron railing was embedded in concrete to form a handrail.

At the thought of the boy starting down those narrow, uneven steps, a jolt of protective fear ran through Rick's chest. He put out a hand. "Hold up a second, Splint. You'd better wait right here until your mom gets back from her tour. She may not want you taking those steps on your own."

The boy shot him a look of utter disbelief. "I'm not hanging around up here in the yard. The swimming's down there." He grabbed the handrail and started down the steps two at a time. "You sound just like my mom. Gosh, you guys are two of a kind."

Jessica dug her bare toes into the sand. A playful breeze tugged at her skirt, flipping it this way and that around her calves. On any other day, she might have felt utter ecstasy. The beach below

Uchungu House was magnificent. A crescent of shimmering white sand, it was rimmed on one side by tall palm trees and on the other by the lapping turquoise waves of the Indian Ocean. High cliffs bordered the semicircle of beach, and where the sand ended, sheer rock precipices ran out into the water to form the arcs of an almost perfect circle. At the far end of the bay, the cliffs stopped abruptly, leaving an opening to the wide blue sea.

"There's a reef between those cliffs," Hunky Wallace said, his thick finger drawing a line across the ocean's horizon. "A reef of coral so sharp and jagged not a shark can pass over it. You've your own grand swimming pool here, lass. As safe and protected as any bathtub."

"Fine. I'm glad to hear it."

"That reef keeps out not only the sharks. A hundred years ago, more or less, it caused the destruction of a grand sailing bark whose bones lie rotting on the floor of your lovely bathtub. Now, if the bark couldn't cross the reef, you can be sure no little treasure hunter's rig can cross it either. In fact, I was forced to lower my diving boat over the cliff—and let me assure you, that was no easy matter. It took winches, pulleys, a large crane, and twice my normal crew. That killer reef is the sole reason the bark has lain undiscovered these many years."

"How did you find it?"

"A good treasure hunter lives and dies on rumors. Tales. Whispers around a saloon table. Like every other seaman in the area, I'd heard stories of gold coins washed ashore on the beach below Uchungu House—not to mention a hundred other Zanzibar beaches. The old artist, God rest his soul, wouldn't allow anyone to have a look in his bay. After his death, I was the first man out there, and within a couple of weeks I'd found the ballast. Now I've located the wreck itself, and a fine specimen it is."

"I'm happy for you. I just don't want you bothering—"

"We'll be no bother to you, lass. But you must understand that my crew and I cannot approach the wreck except by way of your drive, your front garden, your cliff-side stairway, and your lovely beach. Without your permission and cooperation, our task is impossible."

"Look, I'm sorry, but—"

"You mustn't discount the importance of the Tanzanian government's interest in this project. I assure you I've stood up to the bureaucracy many a time, and I'm not afraid of a good fight. But I can tell you one thing: Richard McTaggart is not a man to let go of things easily. If he wants something—*truly* wants it—he'll have it."

Jess thought of her whirlwind romance with Rick. His unbridled passion. His determination to make her his wife. And his easy saunter out of her life. Not a man to let go? Rick McTaggart was the quintessential quitter.

"You sound very sure of yourself, Mr. Wallace," she said. "Maybe you haven't known McTaggart very long."

"That man has dogged me for years about one wreck or another. I've never successfully outwitted Rick McTaggart. And now that he knows there's a virgin find in your bay, he'll be after it until he's got it all staked out, tagged, and recorded. I mean to have in on that business, lassie, and I'm not a man to turn loose of things either. You'd do well to pack away your privacy for a few weeks and let us have at the wreck."

Jess crossed her arms and stared into the treasure hunter's eyes. "You don't know McTaggart as well as you think. And you don't know me at all. I guarantee I'll get him off my back, and when he's gone, you'll have no choice but to leave me in peace too."

Anger, fear, and bitterness curled into a hard ball inside her stomach as she turned from Wallace and started toward the steps. Tears stung the corners of her eyes. She didn't know why she'd bothered to pray the night before. It hadn't done a bit of good. It never did. Look at this mess! Rick was back in her life. This stupid wreck was causing trouble. Things couldn't be worse.

At that moment Splinter bounded down from the bottom step on the cliff wall and jumped barefoot onto the white sand. Spotting his mother, he threw up his arms and danced around in crazy circles.

"Our beach!" he shouted. "Mom, this whole place is ours! It's great! It's the best!"

He raced across the sand, slammed into her with a bear hug that almost knocked her down, and turned her around and around. Unable to resist his joy, she wrapped both arms around her son and allowed him to dance them toward the water.

"I love this place!" he said. "I love Zanzibar. You're the best mom in the world! I'm going in, OK? OK?"

"Sure," she said with a laugh. "Go on. Mr. Wallace says it's safe. Just stay where I can see you."

"Come on, Hunky!" Splinter shouted over her shoulder. "Come on in. I'll show you how long I can stay under. I won first place at the swim meet last year!"

Before she could catch her son and tell him she didn't want him anywhere near the treasure hunter, Splint grabbed the man's hand and began tugging him toward the ocean. Chuckling, Hunky Wallace tore off his white hat, tossed it onto the beach, and splashed into the tide behind Splinter.

"Looks like he's found a friend."

She would have known Rick's voice anywhere. Jess swung around to find him standing on the sand two paces away. Her joy evaporated.

"I have just one thing to say to you," she said, unable to make herself meet his gaze. "Get off my land. Stay away from my son. And take your treasure-hunter friend with you."

"That's three things."

She looked at him for the first time since the afternoon before. Her breath caught in her throat. He was the same. The same man she had loved with such reckless desperation. The same deep-set blue eyes. The same brown hair. Same straight nose, same square jaw, same mouth that was reluctant to smile but always on the verge of humor.

And yet, he looked different, too. Ten years in the sun and wind had etched fine creases at the corners of his eyes and painted his skin a deep golden brown. Was he taller? Or had his shoulders just broadened and his waist narrowed? The flaxen down on his jaw had been replaced by the shadow of dark whiskers. Hair sprouted from the V neck of his white safari shirt. "That's *one* thing," she said before his physical presence overwhelmed her. "Get out."

He didn't respond. Didn't move. Didn't even blink. His eyes locked on hers, even and unwavering. She could feel her pulse slow, and she knew her blood was sinking to her knees. She couldn't suck in enough air to fill her lungs.

"What are you staring at?" she managed. "Didn't you hear me?"

"I hadn't forgotten how beautiful you are."

"I told you to leave."

"I thought I'd forgotten. I was sure I'd buried your memory. I was wrong."

"I mean it. I didn't come all the way back to Africa for this."

"I'd given up hope of finding you again." He took a step toward her. "Jessie."

"I am not about to let you—"

"Jessie, I need to—"

"Don't come another inch!"

"—talk to you. I want to—"

"Stay back!"

"Jessie." He touched her arm.

She let out a muffled cry and jerked back. "Don't! Don't call me that."

"Jessie."

"No!" She fought the tears that hung in the corners of her eyes. "Get out of here. Get out of my life, Rick. I don't want you. I can't—"

"Jessie, I have to talk to you. I have to tell you how I feel about what happened between us."

"Nothing happened. OK? Nothing." She drank in a trembling breath. "Look, this whole thing is a nightmare. You're a ghost out of the past, and I don't want anything to do with you."

"I'm no ghost. I've been looking for you for years, Jessie."

"You're a liar. A sick, drunken, lazy, hopeless liar."

"I was."

"You sure were. You're the biggest mistake I ever made. OK, I've looked you in the face. I've met my demon. Now what will it take to get rid of you again?"

He shoved his hands into his pockets and studied the sand for a moment. "It'll take about half an hour."

"What?" She shook her head. "You just walk up those steps and get in your car and head back to whatever hole you crawled out of. That ought to take about five minutes."

"I need half an hour. That's all." He met her gaze. "Give me thirty minutes to talk. You listen. Then I'll go."

"Thirty minutes of your lies? What's the point?" Anger welled up inside her. She relished it. The heat of her rage gave her power. "I don't have another second for you, Rick McTaggart. I'm going up to my house, and I'm calling the police. If you're not gone by the time they get here, they'll arrest you for trespassing and throw you into the Zanzibar jail."

She whirled away from him and ran toward the steps. She was halfway up when she realized she didn't have a telephone.

@@@

Splinter waded through the foamy tide. The sand felt spongy beneath his feet. In one hand he trailed a long string of black seaweed he intended to examine under his microscope. In the other, he held a small empty shell he had decided to put on the shelf in his new bedroom. He planned to collect one of every type of shell he could find, use his brand-new shell encyclopedia to identify them, and label them for future reference. Maybe he'd even find an undiscovered species and become famous.

Ahead on the beach, Splint's two new friends were deep in conversation. Hunky Wallace, still dripping seawater, was attempting to sign a sheaf of papers that Rick McTaggart supported on his leather case. They were talking. Arguing, really. It seemed to be the mode of speech in Zanzibar. If his mother wasn't shouting at Hunky or Rick, they were shouting at each other or at her.

"What's going on?" he asked the men as he approached.

"Mr. McTaggart here is applying a noose of bureaucratic red tape about my neck, with which he will slowly strangle me until he has drained every ounce of blood from my body."

"Can I watch?"

Rick laughed. "From a distance. It won't be a pretty sight."

"Are you guys going to hunt treasure together?"

"Hunky hunts treasure, Splint. I document underwater archaeological sites. Those are two very different things, but we're going to attempt to work on this shipwreck together. If I can keep the old buzzard from blasting holes in the wreckage and turning the seafloor into something that looks like a field full of exploded land mines, I'll be happy."

"And if I can get my hands on enough gold and silver to make the venture worth my while, I'll be a happy man too."

"Don't count on it, Splint," Rick said. "The only time Hunky's really happy is when he's raking in pieces of eight and gold doubloons—and he knows the government of Tanzania has the legal right to most of what we pull out of that wreck."

"Aye, well, the only time this bloke's truly happy . . ." The Scotsman paused. "When *are* you happy, McTaggart? You don't drink, you don't frolic with the women, and you're as pious as a priest. In fact, I doubt you've ever had a moment's fun in your life."

"You're wrong there, Hunky."

"Am I?" He gave Splinter a nudge. "This chap goes about looking as if he's lost his one true love, if you know what I mean. Works all the time, day and night. Never plays. Never sings. Never dances. You'd think he was paying penance with his life for something terrible he'd done."

"Unlike some people, I take my work seriously."

"And you'll work yourself into an early grave, too."

"I have a peace you know nothing about."

"Aye, you're at peace. I'll grant you that. But you have no joy. None at all."

The Scotsman scrawled his name on the final page of the contract Rick was holding for him. He tucked the pen back into the pocket of his new partner's shirt and turned toward the sea.

"I'll be out there with my men the rest of the day," the Scotsman said. "And whatever I find will be mine. Our contract begins tomorrow."

"I'll be here at dawn. And, Hunky, try not to move anything around down there today, OK?"

"Oh, you'll put it back together the right way 'round. That's your job, isn't it?"

The treasure hunter hailed his men on the small white boat bobbing a short distance from shore. Without a final glance, he crossed the sand and waded into the waves. Splinter watched as the heavyset man grabbed hold of the boat and swung himself onto the deck. As the boat's small engine coughed to life, the Scotsman busied himself putting on his flippers and arranging his air hoses.

"Has he really found gold and silver coins?" Splint asked the tall man at his side.

"A few."

"I'm going to be a treasure hunter like Hunky when I grow up."

"Your mom might not be too happy about that."

"My mom hasn't been too happy about anything since we got to Zanzibar. I think something's bothering her."

McTaggart studied Splint until the youngster started to feel like a specimen under a microscope. "Any idea what's wrong?" the man asked finally.

Splint shrugged. "My mom is tough. She went from coloring pictures at a card factory to designing the cards themselves to illustrating famous books. She's gotten us through winters where we didn't have much heat in the flat and months where she cooked beans at every meal. Nobody messes around with my mom."

"She sounds like a strong lady."

"She is. I don't worry about her too much. If something's bothering her, she'll get rid of it. She always does." Splint glanced down at the limp seaweed in his hand. "I'm going up to the house to put this under my microscope."

"Maybe I'll show you the microscope at my laboratory sometime. It's pretty amazing."

"All right!" Splint couldn't remember when he'd felt so happy. A bona fide treasure hunter was diving around a shipwreck in his own bay. A bona fide scientist had offered to let him see a real lab. Treasure might wash up on the shore at any moment. How could life get any better than this?

"Hey, Spencer," Rick said, catching him as he headed for the cliff-side stairs. "Tell your mom I'll be coming up to the house to talk to her in a few minutes."

"Taking your life in your own hands, huh? OK, I'll tell her, but I get the feeling she's not too crazy about you."

"I'm afraid you're right about that." Rick gave him a smile that filled a spot in Splinter's heart with a strange warmth. "Tell her I just need half an hour. Thirty minutes. After that, I promise I'll leave Jessie alone."

BY THE time Jess got up to her bedroom, Miriamu had already made the bed and unpacked two suitcases. Hannah had joined the young African woman in attempting to sort and arrange the vast numbers of pastels, colored pencils, markers, ink pens, paints, and other art supplies the new owner of Uchungu House had brought from London. As Jess entered, she could hear the two women laughing over some shared joke, their Swahili chatter filling the cavernous room.

"Ehh, the *memsahib!"* Miriamu leapt to attention at the sight of her employer. *"Jambo, Memsahib* Thornton."

"Good morning," Jess said. "Miriamu, you and Mama Hannah can leave all that. I'll do it later. I have a certain way I like to set up my tools."

"Of course, *toto."* Hannah gave a warm smile, her dark skin crinkling into a hundred tiny lines at the corners of her eyes. "This room will be a good place for painting. If you listen, you can hear the ocean. The light is strong, yet I think the room will be cool even in the middle of the day. You will paint many pictures at Uchungu House."

"Maybe so. But if I had enough money, I'd repack those suitcases and head back to London this morning."

"You have been disturbed by the visitors?"

"Do you realize who's here? And he's down on the beach right now! He's with Splinter, Mama Hannah. I don't know how to get rid of him."

"I think you must trust the Lord completely, *toto*. Remember? Don't ever trust yourself alone. Whatever you do, 'put God first, and he will direct you and crown your efforts with success.'"

The familiar words of comfort felt like sandpaper against Jess's heart. "At this point, I doubt that will do much good. I'm going to have to figure this out for myself."

"Even King Solomon, the wisest man in the world, did not try to understand everything himself. He wrote, 'Don't be impressed with your own wisdom. Instead, fear the Lord and turn your back on evil. Then you will gain renewed health and vitality.'"

"Turn your back on evil? Evil incarnate is walking around down there on that beach with my son, and I'm not going to find any healing or refreshment until he leaves us alone. Do either of you know where our own Solomon is this morning? I want to talk to him about the boundaries of the land around Uchungu House. I need to know my property lines." She had a sudden thought. "Maybe he can even help me run off these intruders."

"Solomon has gone in the car to the market in Zanzibar town to purchase fruit and vegetables for the kitchen," Miriamu said. "He will return before lunchtime."

"Great. Mama Hannah, will you please walk down to the beach and check on Splinter? Stay with him. I don't want him spending time with those divers . . . or anyone else."

"I shall teach your son how to dig for clams. Perhaps later Miriamu will show us how to cook a good soup."

The younger woman's dark eyes shone. "Yes, I can make soup."

Jess let out a breath. Her pencils and paints were calling her, but she knew she had to settle other matters first. "Look, Miriamu, I appreciate all you've done for me already. The breakfast this morning . . . making my bed . . . unpacking—"

"I work very hard at Uchungu House."

"I'm sure you do. But I don't have enough money to pay your wages. I'm sorry. If there were anything I could do—"

"You can give the paintings of Ahmed Abdullah bin Yusuf to *Bwana* Giles Knox. He wishes very much to sell them at his gallery in Nairobi."

"Giles Knox? Who's that?"

"*Bwana* Knox is a rich man. He comes to Uchungu House sometimes, but *Bwana* bin Yusuf will not sell the paintings. Maybe one or two. No more. This *Bwana* Knox will give you money for the paintings, and you can pay the wages of your helpers."

Jess thought for a moment. "I don't know about that, Miriamu. If Dr. bin Yusuf didn't want to sell his paintings—"

"This is no longer his house, *memsahib.* This is your house. You will sell the paintings of *Bwana* bin Yusuf, and then you will put your own paintings on the walls."

Jess had to smile. "That would be like taking down a van Gogh to hang a sketch of the Berenstain Bears. I'm afraid there's not much comparison between his art and mine. But you do have a point about the house." She looked around the room. "This *is* all mine now, isn't it? I suppose I can do anything I want."

"I believe you will bring good things to Uchungu House, *memsahib.* I believe you can make this a place of happiness." She struggled with an emotion Jess couldn't read, some hidden sorrow or pain, and then she forced it away and lifted her chin. "I shall go to the kitchen and prepare to make a good clam soup."

As the two African women left the room, Jess picked up a packet of colored pencils. Why couldn't she have as much faith as Hannah? Her old *ayah* always believed things in life worked together for the good of those who loved the Lord. Maybe Jess didn't love him enough.

Once she had loved Jesus with her whole heart. She had hung on the words of the Bible stories Hannah used to tell; she had rejoiced in the hymns all four Thornton children sang together; she had treasured the quiet moments she spent alone in prayer. Where had everything in her life gone wrong?

Rick McTaggart, that's where. He had walked into her heart and trampled everything—even her faith in Christ.

Seeking relief from memories of the past and fears for the future, Jess sat down at the table and took a sheet of clean white paper from her portfolio case. Almost as if she had surrendered control of her own will, her hand picked up a pencil and began to sketch. On the page appeared the half-circle of white beach . . . the bowing palm trees . . . the foamy waves . . . and her son. Spencer came bounding across the sand, arms and legs flying, head thrown back in ecstasy.

When had she lost her own joy? When had bitterness wrapped its roots so tightly around her heart? Would she ever again know childlike happiness, freedom, peace? Would she ever regain such hope? Would she ever hold the light of faith in her soul?

"Hallooo! Hallooo, the house!" The shrill voice echoed through the rooms, startling Jess into drawing a harsh blue line across the sand.

"Hodi, hodi!" The visitor called out the Swahili greeting used instead of a knock for houses without doors. "Is anybody at home?"

Jess barely had time to put her pencils back in their slots before Miriamu hurried into the room. "You have a visitor," she said. "Memsahib Cameron has come to see you."

Jess followed the housekeeper down the stairs toward the sitting room. "Who is *Memsahib* Cameron?"

"Your neighbor. She lives in the house just down the road and over the next hill."

Jess shook her head. "I wonder who else will show up. For some reason, I expected this place to be quiet. It's like Victoria Station on a Monday morning."

Miriamu led the way into the front room where Dr. bin Yusuf's huge painting filled the wall. A small woman with soft white skin and mounds of cottony hair sat in one of the chairs. She had on a pale blue sleeveless dress that matched her eyes. Red-painted toenails peeked from the front of well-worn green flip-flops.

"Ah, you must be Jessica Thornton!" the woman exclaimed, rising and holding out a cloth-wrapped bundle. "I'm your neighbor, Antoinette Cameron, but you must call me Nettie. I've brought you a lovely loaf of currant bread for your tea. I made it myself just this morning, so it's still hot."

"Thank you. That's very kind." Jess took the warm offering. "I've hardly seen my own kitchen yet. I'm still trying to unpack and put things in order around here. We just arrived in Zanzibar yesterday."

"We? Are you married?"

"I have a ten-year-old son, Spencer."

"Oh, how marvelous! A little boy. Everyone's buzzing with the news of your arrival. Another artist living at Uchungu House. Such a surprise!"

Jess felt the chilled edges of her heart begin to thaw. "Won't you sit down again, Nettie?"

"I shall prepare tea, *memsahib,*" Miriamu said. "I shall return with the warm bread."

"Thank you, Miriamu."

The African woman left the room, and Jess realized how easy it was becoming to accept her assistance. It would be wonderful to keep both Miriamu and Solomon at Uchungu House—not only to provide them with a livelihood but also to make things simpler for Splint and herself. Though she hadn't figured out how she could work through all the complicated details of life on Zanzibar, Jess felt determined to make everything right. And that meant Rick McTaggart—

"I live just down the road from you," Nettie Cameron was saying as Jess seated herself across from the little British woman. "It's an easy walk, not more than ten minutes. You must come and pay me a visit straight away. I do love company. Bring your son, as well. I shall teach him how to play Scrabble. I'm quite formidable at it."

"You may meet your match with Spencer. He loves words—the harder and more obscure the better."

"Ooh, lovely. We shall duel to the bitter death!" She laughed, a high tinkling sound. "When the Captain was alive, we'd stay up half the night playing Scrabble. I don't believe there was a harsh word between us all the years of our marriage—except on Scrabble nights!"

"The Captain?"

"Captain William Cameron, King's African Rifles. We were married for thirty-three years. A finer man could not be found in all the realm. I've been widowed a year now, much to my great sorrow."

"I'm sure it's been difficult for you." Jess tried to find words of sympathy, but her thoughts had returned to worry about her son. If Rick said anything to Splint about her . . . or if Splint somehow figured out that she and Rick . . .

"I've lived in Zanzibar all my life," Nettie continued. "I grew up in the house down the road. When my parents passed on, the Captain and I moved in, and there we lived happily until his death."

"Do you have children, Mrs. Cameron?"

"The Captain and I? Oh, no. We weren't able, I'm sorry to say. My husband had received certain injuries in the line of his duty to the Crown. It was always a great disappointment to us, yet we managed a satisfying life in Zanzibar all the same."

Jess forced her thoughts away from her own unhappiness and concentrated on her guest. "You must have seen a lot of changes in the island over the years. Did you know Dr. bin Yusuf well?"

"I don't believe anybody really knew the man. He kept to himself. As far as I could tell, he had no friends."

Miriamu entered with a tray and began pouring out the steaming amber tea. As she stirred lumps of sugar into her cup, Jess tried to reconcile Nettie's portrayal of the artist with her memories of the man who had been such an inspiration in her life. In the classroom, Dr. bin Yusuf had been lively, engaging, even funny. All his students had adored him. Had only sharing his art brought him to life—given him joy and peace? Had this House of Bitterness somehow closed his spirit?

"I understand the professor had no family either," Jess said.

"Oh, he had a family. Very much so. His darling sister lives in Zanzibar town. Fatima Hafidh—a very good woman." Nettie took a sip of tea. "No one can understand why he didn't leave her the house . . . instead of you."

Jess glanced away. Somehow she felt guilty for having been willed a house she wasn't even sure she wanted. "I . . . I don't know either. I've been trying to figure that out myself. I was Dr. bin Yusuf's student—but that was years ago."

"You must have been very special to him. The house itself is a historic landmark, you know. The land . . . oh, my goodness, it's worth a small fortune. And think of the art!"

Jess had opened her mouth to respond when she heard a car's wheels crunch on the gravel of the driveway. All thoughts of a quiet morning setting up her studio and exploring the grounds vanished.

The remote and isolated Uchungu House was turning out to be a beehive of activity. Footsteps sounded on the verandah.

"Ms. Thornton?" Mr. Patel peered into the living room. "Ah, you are at home. I would have phoned but . . ." His voice trailed off.

"But I have no phone. Come on in." Jess stood. "Mr. Patel, this is my neighbor Nettie Cameron. Mr. Patel was the executor of Dr. bin Yusuf's estate."

"Mrs. Cameron . . . the widow of Captain Cameron?" Mr. Patel executed a slight bow. "The honor is all mine."

After shaking hands, he seated himself on a third chair, laid his attaché case across his knees, and flipped open the clasps. Jess eyed Nettie, who showed no sign of making ready to leave. Apparently whatever Mr. Patel had to say would be public information.

"There has been a development of which you must be made aware, Ms. Thornton," he began. He extracted a pair of spectacles, set them on the end of his nose, hooked their wire temples around his ears, and peered down at the document in his hands. "I'm afraid there has been a change regarding the cause of death of Dr. bin Yusuf."

"A change?"

"It seems the professor was murdered."

Both women gasped. Jess leapt to her feet and grabbed the document. "You told me he died of cancer! Murdered? Who killed him? How did it happen?"

"Please calm yourself, Ms. Thornton." The lawyer held up both hands in a pacifying gesture. "At first everybody believed Dr. bin Yusuf had merely succumbed to the cancer that afflicted him. When the body was examined by the coroner, however, it became apparent that the professor had died after falling down a flight of stairs. Even this turn of events was not unexpected, considering the nature of his illness. He was a very sick man, and yet he was determined to work in his studio each day. While attempting to walk from his bedroom to the library, the professor fell down the steps. Or so the report read."

"Who gave the report?"

"The man who discovered the body. I believe his given name is Solomon Mazrui."

"Solomon! The chauffeur? The gardener?"

"I believe that would be the man."

"When did he say this?"

Mr. Patel took the document away from Jess and flipped to the second page. "That particular statement was taken down by the police after they determined that the body bore injuries commensurate with a fall. When Solomon Mazrui was questioned, he confirmed that he had found his employer at the bottom of the stairwell."

"So what's all this about murder?"

"Subsequent to the coroner's report, an autopsy was performed. The results arrived this morning. Apparently, Dr. bin Yusuf's skull was crushed by a heavy blunt object of unknown origin. According to the pathologist, such an injury could not have been sustained during a fall. It is believed that someone struck Dr. bin Yusuf in the head, and following that tragic event, he fell down the stairs and died."

Jess sank onto her chair. "Who did it?"

"A most appropriate question. Not an hour before I left town, the Zanzibar police located Solomon Mazrui and took him to their headquarters. He is being held there for questioning, as I'm certain you can understand."

"Surely they don't think Solomon did it."

"He reported the discovery of the body, which was lying on a settee here in this living room when the police arrived. Mr. Mazrui failed to tell the police about his employer's accident on the staircase until he was questioned directly. Instead, he allowed the police to make an initial report that he had discovered the artist dead on the settee."

"But why would Solomon kill Dr. bin Yusuf?" Nettie Cameron asked. "The man had worked here for years. He helped restore this house."

"It is not at all certain that Mr. Mazrui is responsible for the crime. In fact, I am certain the police will question everyone who had contact with Dr. bin Yusuf. Even you, Ms. Thornton."

"But I was in London!"

"Of course. Yet you stood to gain a great deal by his death."

"That's crazy. I didn't have any idea I was in Dr. bin Yusuf's will.

Until you contacted me about the house, I didn't even know he had died."

"And of this I will give testimony. I am sure you have nothing to fear." Mr. Patel pushed his spectacles up the bridge of his nose. "All the same, this turn of events may affect you in some way. The police will search the house, of course. And they will wish to interview you and everyone who was employed by Dr. bin Yusuf. Everything you can do to cooperate will be appreciated."

"Of course." Jess rubbed her temples. "Whatever they want."

"What about the house, Mr. Patel?" Nettie asked. "Does the estate go back into probate?"

"The house belongs to Ms. Thornton. Dr. bin Yusuf's will was very specific in that matter."

Jess stared down at her knees. She couldn't believe this. Murdered. How could her beloved professor have been murdered? Who would have done such a thing? And why?

"Splinter!" The image of her son at the mercy of a killer broke through the numbness in her brain. "Splinter's on the beach! I have to—"

"Spencer and Hannah are digging clams." The male voice came from the door. "I just saw him. He's fine."

Jess lifted her head to find Rick McTaggart standing inside the living room. One shoulder propped against the door frame, he was staring at her with those blue eyes.

"Jessie, are you all right?"

She squelched a moan and waved faintly in his direction. "Would everyone please leave me alone? Mr. Patel, thank you. I'll . . . I'll do what I can to help with the investigation. Nettie . . ."

"Say no more, duckie." The little woman stood and shook out the folds of her blue dress. "I'll be going. You've had a terrible shock. Terrible. You must go and lie down."

"I've got to see about my son." Jess tried to think of polite farewells and couldn't. Splinter was out there. A murderer was roaming loose. "Excuse me."

She pushed past Rick and fled across the verandah. Kicking off her sandals, she ran through the bare grass to the fence that lined the precipice. If anyone hurt Splint . . . if anything ever happened . . .

As she reached the cliff-side steps, a hand gripped her arm. "Jessie, wait."

"Let go." She turned on Rick. "I've got to find Spencer!"

"Your son is fine. He's down there with Hannah digging clams and having the time of his life."

She took two more steps and spotted Splint and Hannah huddled together at the edge of the beach. They were kneeling side by side, heads touching, as they poked their fingers into the damp sand in search of tiny clams. A tin pail sat lopsided, half buried in the sand.

Jess stopped and sucked in a shaky breath. She could see her son's brown-gold hair ruffling in the breeze. A transparent sheet of water left the sea and ran toward the beach, covering his knees and wetting Hannah's skirt. Splinter laughed and gave the old woman a little splash. Hannah took a fingerful of sand and wiped it on the boy's nose.

In a moment, the sound of singing drifted upward. *"Mungu ni pendo; apenda watu. Mungu ni pendo; anipenda."* God is love; he loves all people. God is love; he loves me.

"Let him keep his childhood, Jessie." Rick's voice was gentle. "At least as long as you can. He deserves that."

She slumped against the cliff wall, unwilling to admit he was right. "Would you just go away?"

"I want to talk to you."

"No."

"Yes. God allowed me to find you again. I need to tell you—"

"God? What makes you think he had anything to do with this fiasco?"

"Our meeting again is no fiasco. It's a gift."

She lifted her focus to his face. Sincerity was written in his eyes. She had read that expression before. Believed in it. Believed in *him.* Never again would she trust Rick McTaggart and his lies. Her heart was too strong. She had built the walls around it too thick. And over those walls grew the ivy of her hatred for him. Nothing could breach that. But she also knew from experience how persistent he could be.

"If I give you a chance to talk, will you leave me alone?"

"If you still want me to."

"I will." She sat on the stone step, her back to him. "Fine. Talk."

For a long time he didn't say anything. She wondered if her harsh words had driven him away. How many years had she imagined a moment just like this? How many times had she envisioned Rick coming after her, hunting her down, begging her to make peace with him? Sometimes she saw herself turning to him, tears streaming down her cheeks as she fell into his arms and accepted his repentance. But most of the time, she pictured herself laughing in his face . . . or slapping him . . . or rewarding him with nothing but silence.

Yes, that would be the best revenge of all—that he should have nothing from her. No pardons, no tears, not even a word of understanding. Nothing but total silence.

When he didn't speak, she began to wonder if that was all she would have from him, too. Silence. She glanced over her shoulder. He was sitting on the step behind her, his gaze trained on the waves. Arms resting loosely on his knees, he had woven his fingers together.

Rick's hands. They looked the same—strong fingers, brown skin, white nails. She had loved his hands once. Loved the way he had laced his fingers through hers, squeezing their palms together and swinging their arms as they walked. Loved the way he had slipped his fingers through the strands of her hair. Loved the way—

"I bet I've rehearsed this a thousand times," he began. "Now I can't even think where to start."

She shut her eyes, squelching memories. "Well, then." She made her voice harsh, careless. "I guess I'll just—"

He cut her off. "You could look at my life the past few years in two ways. The things I've done. And the things I've been."

"Whichever way you pick, make it short."

He fell silent again, and she knew she'd wounded him. She couldn't help it. Did he remember the time gone by as "a few" years? How about ten years? Ten long years in which she'd struggled to survive, worked to keep food on the table, labored to bring up her son as a happy, well-adjusted human being.

"What I've done with myself can be told without much trouble," he said finally. "After I left you, I went on the run. I'm not sure how long it lasted—maybe a year. I hitchhiked north into the desert. I traveled west through the rain forests of Zaire. I spent some time down south in Malawi. Mostly I logged a lot of time on the beaches—teaching skin diving to tourists, mostly. Eventually, I worked my way back to Kenya and started looking for you. I couldn't find you."

"Surprise, surprise."

"I don't know what I expected, but I'm sure I wasn't thinking too clearly. I was drinking a lot in those days, trying to escape any way I could."

"Escape what?"

"Everything. Past, present, future. I was angry with my parents for the years I spent in boarding school. Angry with myself for making a commitment to you I couldn't keep. Angry with God about the way my life was going. I couldn't figure out who I was or where I was supposed to go with myself. I didn't want to feel my own emotions—the rage, the fear, the guilt. I had to escape. So I ran . . . and I drank."

Jess realized her fingers gripping the iron stair rail were turning bone white, bloodless, and numb as she struggled to hold on. She felt as though she might tumble off the cliff at any moment. She didn't want to hear any more. And she wanted to hear everything.

"Remember my brother, Daniel?" Rick asked.

Jess nodded. How could she forget Daniel? He had been so kind, so gentle, so bewildered by the actions of his older brother. After the initial chaos following Rick's disappearance, she had lost track of Daniel and the rest of the McTaggarts.

"Daniel's a missionary in Dar es Salaam now," Rick said. "I don't know if you were aware of that."

Jess shook her head.

"Anyway, a long time before he became a missionary, he decided to track down his big brother, the black sheep of the McTaggart family. I think he finally found me lying on a beach somewhere in Kenya. I was at the end of my rope. Mentally strung out. Physically wrecked. Daniel took me to his place in Nairobi and helped me get my head on straight. I owe him my life."

He was silent again for a moment. Then he let out a deep breath. "After that," he said, "I did some course work at the University of Nairobi, and then I moved to Florida and picked up a couple of degrees in marine archaeology. I began to hear rumors that Tanzania was changing after Nyerere's little experiment with Chinese communism. Tourism was being encouraged, and that meant Olduvai Gorge and other archaeological sites would get some attention. I applied for a position with the Tanzanian government, and I got it. For three years I've headed up the marine archaeology team. Actually, the team consists of my coworker, Andrew Mbuti, and me. We chase treasure hunters like Hunky Wallace around and try to keep them from looting the ocean floor. I've put together a pretty comprehensive display in the Zanzibar museum, but there's a lot more—"

"OK, you've made a good life for yourself," Jess cut in. She could see Splint and Hannah washing the sand from their pailful of clams. They might be coming up the steps any moment, and Jessica didn't want Splint anywhere near Rick. And she didn't want to hear the rest of his story. It sounded true and honest—and she was afraid she might start to believe anything he told her.

"I have a good life, too," she said. "I have a new home, enough money to get by on, work I love—"

"And a son. Whose son is Spencer, Jessie?"

"Mine. He's my son." She swung around on the step to face him. "I've let you talk, Rick. I've given you what you asked. Now do something for me. Leave my house and my life, and don't ever come back."

He squeezed his hands together, and she could see his biceps jump. His blue eyes locked on hers, and for a moment she was afraid he could read everything in her heart. He let out a sigh.

"I can't leave, Jessie," he said. "I admit that in all the years I've known you, I've given you nothing and taken everything. But there's something else I need. Something only you can give."

He covered her cold hand with his own. His fingers were warm and strong as he stroked them over her white knuckles. "Jessie," he said, "I need your forgiveness."

FORGIVENESS.

Like a neon sign on a building in Piccadilly Circus, the word flashed fragments of a hundred Scriptures through Jess's brain—verses Hannah had quoted when her four *toto*s had been fussing, squabbling, arguing with each other as children do.

Forgive.

"Forgive us our sins, just as we have forgiven. . . ."

"If you forgive those who sin against you, your heavenly Father will forgive you. But if you refuse to forgive . . ."

"When you are praying, first forgive anyone you are holding a grudge against. . . ."

"Jesus said, 'Father, forgive these people, because they don't know what they are doing. . . .'"

"Instead, be kind to each other, tenderhearted, forgiving one another, just as God through Christ has forgiven you. . . ."

Jess could almost see dark-eyed Hannah gathering the Thornton children around herself like little chicks. Two would sit on her lap, another would crouch at her feet, the fourth would drape thin arms around her neck.

Hannah's rich voice would whisper, "Once upon a time, the

apostle Peter asked Jesus, 'Lord, how often should I forgive someone who sins against me? Seven times?'"

In response, all the children would chant the words they had heard so often from her lips: "'No!' Jesus replied, 'seventy times seven!'"

Seventy times seven? Jess couldn't imagine forgiving Rick even once. What he had done to her was nothing like dipping a pigtail in red paint, hiding a favorite doll, or pinching an arm in the backseat of the car. What he had done was devastating, life-altering, unchangeable. He had betrayed her. How could she forgive that?

"You expect me to ignore everything you did to me?" she asked. "You expect me to forget what I've been through at your hands?"

"I didn't ask you to forget." His voice was deep. "I asked you to forgive."

"Do you think I can just wipe everything out? Do you think I can say it doesn't matter anymore—that it's OK what you did to me?"

"No. It's not OK what I did. What I did to you was wrong, Jessie. I'm not asking you to deny that. I'm asking you to forgive me."

She swallowed against the gritty lump that was forming in her throat. Why did he have to sound so sincere? Why couldn't he be cocky or matter-of-fact about it all? Of course, Rick had always been a master at playing her emotions. He knew just how to get to her.

"Maybe when I figure out the proper definition, I'll forgive you," she snapped. "In the meantime—"

"Pardon," he cut in. "That's what it's about. You don't forget the sin, and you don't deny that it was wrong. Forgiveness means you stop feeling resentment toward the person who hurt you. You stop being bitter. You stop letting the past affect how you live in the present. When you forgive *me,* it will change *you.*"

"I'm happy just the way I am, thank you."

"Are you?"

"Yes, I am." She wondered why the words rang so false. "Listen, Rick, I can see my son coming up to the house now. I've heard your speech, and I want you to leave."

"I haven't told you the second part. I told you what I've done. I haven't told you what I've been through to get where I am today."

Jess chewed on her lip. Splint had spotted her and was waving as he carried the heavy pail toward the steps. She didn't want to hear any more from Rick. She had Splint to think about . . . Uchungu House . . . a treasure hunter . . . an incarcerated chauffeur . . . and a murder. . . .

"Mom, you should see all the colors we got!" Splint was taking the steps two at a time. The pail banged against his skinny calf. "We found blue ones and purple ones and brown ones. Some of them have stripes that look like rays of sunshine, and other ones are solid. Mama Hannah said we had to put back the tiniest ones so they could grow bigger."

Warmth calmed Jess's thudding heart. She stood and turned to Rick. "We've got a soup to make and a whole house to explore." Forcing down the lump in her throat, she willed her mouth into a smile. "It's good you're doing well for yourself, Rick, and I do understand why you wanted to talk. Now, if you don't mind—"

"I do mind. I'm not done." He raked a hand through his thick brown hair. A shock fell onto his forehead. "You may not want to be healed, Jessie, but I do. I've been working on this process for years. I've slogged my way through most of it—the stuff with my parents, all the moves we made when I was a kid, boarding school, my fears and frustrations, all that. I've made my peace with Christ. I've tackled everything head-on . . . everything except you."

"They have little gooey white feet that come sliding out from between the two shells," Splinter called up to his mother. "Mama Hannah says that's how they dig down into the sand."

"That's great, honey," Jess said. "Look, Rick—"

"I've been searching for you a long time, Jessie."

"Come on, Rick. Don't lie to me."

"It's the truth. I tried to talk to your dad. His secretary said he was too busy to see me. Your sister Tillie is living somewhere in West Africa. Mali, I think. Fiona's hiding out with her elephant research project and won't take visitors. About two months ago I finally found Grant near Mount Kilimanjaro. He told me you were living in London."

"Grant told you that?"

"Ask him. We had a good visit, but he wouldn't give me your

address. So I put in for a vacation at the end of September. I was going to fly to London. My coworker's sister has a flat there. I planned to stay with her family while I looked for you."

"Rick, please—"

"You know I'd have found you eventually, Jessie." He gently took her shoulders and turned her to face him. "With God's grace, I've rebuilt my life from the ground up. But there's still one big hole, and I can't figure any way to patch it. That hole is our marriage."

"We had no marriage."

"Eleven years ago, you married me. Unless there's something I don't know, you're still my wife."

Unable to speak, Jess grabbed the iron rail. A chill washed through her veins. She could hear her son's feet padding on the steps behind her, but she couldn't make herself turn around.

She *was* Rick's wife.

In all the years, she had done nothing about it. There had been no point. She'd had a son to raise. Work to do. A life to live. She hadn't been interested in dating anyone, and she had had no desire to fall into the marriage trap again.

Rick was long out of her world. A divorce cost money she didn't have. Divorce meant facing the pain of her past. Worst of all, divorce might mean she would have to locate Rick. Might have to tell him about Spencer. So she had let it go.

"Sometimes you find a clamshell where the animal's already out," Splint said, coming up behind her. "If the two sides of the shell are still stuck together, they look just like a butterfly's wings."

He threw one wet arm around her waist and gave her a noisy kiss on the cheek. Swinging the pail between Jess and Rick, he lifted it high to show them both his catch.

"How about this?" he said. "Does this look like lunch, or what?"

Jess stared down into the pail of tiny, colorful butterfly clams. "Wow," she managed.

"See, what you do is, you look on the sand right after a wave flows over it. If you search carefully, you'll see two tiny dots—little airholes with bubbles coming out of them. Stick your finger straight down between the two holes, and guess what?"

"You'll find a clam," Rick finished. "Way to go, Splinter! I know a lot about sea life, but I didn't know that."

"Mama Hannah taught me. She's awesome."

"Hey, ever tasted octopus?"

"No way! Can you eat an octopus? Which part?"

"The legs. They're a bargain, you know. Catch one octopus, and you get eight legs."

Splinter laughed as he pushed past his mother and grabbed Rick's sleeve. "Come on. Let's go put these clams in the kitchen, and then you can show me how to catch an octopus."

"You've got to have special equipment for that." Rick followed the boy up the last few steps. "Tell you what. One of these days, I'll show you all the equipment I dive with. I use most of it for excavating, but I need protection, too. You never know what you might run into around a shipwreck."

"Like what? Sharks?"

"Not too many of those inside a reef. I've had some trouble with moray eels, though. Sea urchins can be nasty, too, but about all you can do is avoid them. You want to watch out for scorpion fish. And have you ever heard of the Portuguese man-of-war?"

Jess felt her shoulders sag as she watched her son and his father walk toward the house. Rick had taken the heavy pail of clams in one hand. With the other, he clasped Splinter's shoulder. Only a blind man could fail to see how much alike they were. They even walked the same way—a long, loose, loping stride. Shoulders straight and heads held high, they continued to converse. Surely Rick knew. Surely it wouldn't be long before Splint knew, too.

Dear God!

"It is a beautiful day which the Lord has made," Hannah said, finally reaching the level where Jess stood. "Let us rejoice and be glad in it."

@@@

Jess decided she would rejoice and be glad in her first day at Uchungu House—no matter what. She had all but emptied her savings account to buy the airplane tickets to Zanzibar, and she wasn't about to back out now. Maybe she could be called unforgiving, hard-hearted, and cold, but no one could call her a coward. True, she'd never had to juggle a shipwreck, a murderer, and an unwanted husband all at the same time. But none of those things had to defeat her.

"I'll set up parameters for Hunky Wallace," she told Hannah that afternoon after a lunch of hot clam chowder and fresh pineapple slices. In spite of Splinter's pleas, Jess had not invited Rick McTaggart to dine with them. Now she and Hannah were working their way through the house, unlocking and exploring the rooms, rearranging furniture, straightening pictures, and setting up the few decorative items Jess had managed to fit into her suitcase.

"I'll agree to let Hunky cross my property so he can explore the shipwreck, if he wants," she said, "but in the process, he'll abide by my rules. No more sleep-shattering morning arrivals. And no more breakfasts at Uchungu House. If he comes quietly, does his diving, and then leaves, I won't protest. But I don't want him talking to Splint or to anyone else."

"Ehh," Hannah responded. As a Kikuyu from the highlands of Kenya, she used the favorite expression regularly. Jess knew it could mean anything from "What a great idea" to "I can't believe my own ears."

Picking through a ring of keys Miriamu had given her, Jess tried each of them in the lock of a door on the second floor. "Don't you agree I should keep Hunky Wallace away from the house, Mama Hannah?" she asked. "I mean, he's a treasure hunter—basically the antithesis of everything I believe in. He's a scavenger. I don't think he'd be a good influence on Splint."

"Any enterprise is built by wise planning," Hannah said softly. "I believe you will build this home wisely, *toto,* whether the treasure hunter takes his breakfast here or not."

"Well, I don't like him eating up our food when I can't even figure out how I'm going to pay Miriamu and Solomon."

"'If your enemies are hungry, give them food to eat. If they are thirsty, give them water to drink. You will heap burning coals on their heads, and the Lord will reward you.'"

Jess laughed. "I can't imagine Hunky ever feeling ashamed of himself for any reason. Oh, maybe he wouldn't be so bad to have around. Splint would enjoy looking over the things his crew brings up from the wreck. He's interested in that kind of thing. Did you see him organizing his clamshells?"

"Your son has great wisdom."

"And he feels morally responsible to share it with everybody he meets." Jess inserted a long iron skeleton key into the lock and turned it. "Finally!"

She twisted the brass knob and leaned her shoulder into the heavy wooden door. At first it didn't budge. Then the door slowly began to swing from its stone frame. Inside the long narrow room, sunlight poured through dusty windowpanes onto a collection of artifacts, some of them shrouded with canvas, others bare.

"Look at all this stuff, Mama Hannah," Jess exclaimed. "It's beautiful. Here's a brass tray from India."

"It is very green—many years without polishing."

"Are those rugs? See those rolled-up things propped over there?" Jess stepped across a small chest and walked between a pair of heavily carved chairs to the back of the room. "They are! Persian rugs! If moths haven't eaten holes in them, we can carpet almost every room in the house. This is amazing, Mama Hannah. Dr. bin Yusuf must have collected from China, India, Persia, Turkey—the whole Orient. I've never seen such a collection."

"Baskets, carvings, chests, tables, vases. Ehh, I am afraid your friend was storing up his treasures here on earth, where they can erode away or be stolen."

"Maybe I could be called a thief, but I'm going to take all these things out into the house so we can enjoy them."

"You are wise. The rich man believed he would store all his goods. He would lay them up for many years. But God says 'a person is a fool to store up earthly wealth but not have a rich relationship with God.'"

"I think you're being a little hard on Dr. bin Yusuf," Jess said. She picked up a large copper pot and an armload of dusty baskets and started toward the door. She intended to set them out on the verandah for cleaning. "Maybe he had some very selfless plans for these things. Or maybe just collecting them made him happy."

Even as she said the words, she remembered Solomon telling her that Uchungu House had never been a place of happiness. She found that hard to understand. Her art teacher had clearly had so much to enjoy, so much to bring him pleasure. He'd had money, this wonderful home, servants, rooms filled with treasures, and his enormous talent. What more could anyone want?

"Sikilizeni," Splinter was singing on the verandah as he sorted through his piles of clamshells. *"Furaha yangu. Mungu ni pendo; anipenda."*

I am happy. God is love; he loves me.

As Jess set down the copper pot and arranged the baskets in a row, she thought about the words to Hannah's song. Maybe her old *ayah* was right about Dr. bin Yusuf—as she was right about so many things. Perhaps the artist had tried to find happiness by storing up treasure on earth, instead of enjoying the richness of God's love.

Even so, Jess knew it was hard to feel much satisfaction with God when your life was filled with the kinds of trials she herself had gone through. Certainly something had been a big problem in Dr. bin Yusuf's life. After all, someone had murdered him.

"Where'd you get the baskets?" Splint asked.

"I unlocked a storeroom upstairs. It's filled with great stuff. I want to bring it all outside and clean it up. Then we'll decorate our house."

"Can I help? I'll bring things down for you! I'll clean! Can I use the spray wax? I'll be really careful, I swear. Hey, how about we turn on a garden hose? We could blast off the dirt!"

"Let's leave any blasting around here to Hunky Wallace and his crew. Go tell Miriamu what we're doing, Splint. See what kinds of cleaners she's got in the kitchen. Then you can help me bring everything down."

Splinter danced his way into the house singing Hannah's Swahili song. The African woman passed him as she walked out onto the verandah toting the large brass tray on her back. To it she had tied a strap, which went over her forehead just like the straps she had used to carry heavy loads of firewood. Jess was always startled when reminded that Hannah was not truly her own mother but a simple village woman who had taken on the role of caretaker for four little white children. How Hannah had blessed their lives. What happiness her love had given them.

"This is a very, very green tray," she said as Jess helped relieve her of the burden. "What a shame that the wealth has rotted away. As the Scriptures tell us, it will stand as evidence against its owner and will eat his flesh like fire."

"Mama Hannah, good grief!" Jess said with a laugh. "You're turning poor Dr. bin Yusuf into a demon just because he didn't keep his brass tray polished."

"Ehh," Hannah said.

"He was a good man. At least I think he was. I can't imagine why anyone would want to kill him."

Hannah straightened. "Someone killed him?"

Jess nodded and told her about Mr. Patel's visit. "The police have taken Solomon in for questioning."

"Why?"

"Apparently he didn't give an accurate police report after he found Dr. bin Yusuf's body."

"Ehh." She pondered a moment. "But why would Solomon beat his employer on the head? Was he caught stealing something valuable from this house? Or was he angry with Dr. bin Yusuf?"

"I don't think robbery was the motive. Mr. Patel didn't mention anything missing from the house. I don't know why Solomon would kill anyone. I'm sure the police have questioned him. After he had worked closely with Dr. bin Yusuf so many years, I can't imagine what could come between them that would cause such a huge problem."

"Lust, pride, envy, greed, gluttony, anger, sloth. All can cause sin."

"I guess that about covers it."

"But perhaps another person killed your teacher."

"Who? Both Solomon and Nettie told me he didn't have any friends. It must have been someone with whom he had a relationship. Someone he knew well enough to let into the house. Or a person already working in the house."

"Miriamu? I don't think so. She is a woman of great peace."

"Peaceful people can be driven to murder."

"When unforgiveness holds them . . . yes, this is true."

Unforgiveness. Jess flushed at the word. Was she capable of something as terrible as murder? Why not? How many years had she despised Rick McTaggart? How many ways had she imagined torturing her own tormentor? Of course, she felt sure she would never actually carry out such an act. Yet someone had taken revenge on Dr. bin Yusuf.

"The killer would be a person who knew him," Hannah said. "Who knew your friend? Solomon. Miriamu. Mr. Patel."

"Mr. Patel is a lawyer. He knew Dr. bin Yusuf only on a business level. He wouldn't have done it."

"Did he stand to gain wealth by the death?"

"Just attorney's fees. That wouldn't be a very strong motive." Jess thought for a moment, trying to make a mental list of anyone who might have had contact with the artist. "Well, our neighbor down the road, Nettie Cameron, told me Dr. bin Yusuf has a sister in Zanzibar town. Maybe his sister was holding something against him. Nettie told me everyone expected him to leave her the house."

"Perhaps you should pay this woman a visit."

"What if she knocks *me* on the head?"

"We should take Solomon with us for protection."

"Are you kidding? He's the primary suspect, Mama Hannah. Besides, he's at the police station in town."

"No, he returned in the Renault one hour ago. Miriamu told me."

"The police let him go?" Jess glanced around, instantly wary. She had assured herself the artist had been killed by someone who had a motive tied directly to him—and who would not be interested in coming after her. But she still felt uncomfortable. Had the death of Dr. bin Yusuf resolved the killer's problem and assuaged his rage? Or would he . . . or she . . . feel compelled to strike again?

"Miriamu told me the police could find no reason to arrest Solomon at this time," Hannah said. "He has returned to Uchungu House while the police continue their investigation."

"Do you think we're safe here, Mama Hannah? If anything happened to Splinter . . . or to you . . . Maybe we should move to a hotel in town. With so many people around, we'd be safer."

"'The Lord is my light and my salvation—so why should I be afraid? The Lord protects me from danger—so why should I tremble?'"

"Sounds good, but even David ran for his life when Saul was chasing after him. Remember the psalm? 'O Lord, how long will you forget me? Forever? How long will you look the other way?'"

"Ehh, you have not forgotten the Word of the Lord!" Hannah beamed. "I believed that perhaps the root of bitterness had eaten too deeply into your heart."

Jess leaned against an arched verandah support and stared up at the palm trees swaying in the afternoon breeze. Again, she found herself fighting a lump in her throat. It was an odd feeling. How many years had it been since she had allowed herself to cry? How many years since she had swallowed the ache and forced herself to feel nothing?

"This morning when we were sitting on the cliff-side steps, Rick asked me to forgive him," she said. Her voice was barely audible over the murmur of the palm leaves. "I don't want to."

"Ehh."

"Would *you,* Mama Hannah? I mean, I'll admit I played a part in the fiasco of our marriage. I was young and unrealistic. I expected Rick to conform to my image of the perfect husband. I pushed him too hard, and I was impatient with the struggles he was going through. I'd fallen in love with him for his wildness, for that rebel streak that made him do crazy things. But once we married, I wanted him to settle down and act like a responsible husband."

"You wished to change him. You forgot that only God can change a man."

"I made a mistake, and I acknowledge that. But I wasn't the one who drank beer until three in the morning. I wasn't the one who rode around on a motorcycle and spent nearly every waking hour scuba diving. And I wasn't the one who took off and left a pregnant wife."

She crossed her arms and glared out at a bougainvillea bush loaded with purple blossoms. Just the mention of what she had been through made anger eat at her insides. She could feel it gnawing. She could feel the pain as though it had all just happened.

"I don't see how I can forgive Rick for what he did," she said. "I just can't."

"God can do what men cannot, *toto.*"

"God's got his work cut out for him if I'm supposed to forgive Rick McTaggart. Just the sight of the man makes me sick. I hate him, Mama Hannah. I really do."

The old woman ran her dark fingers over the green tray. "You know what I have always believed concerning people. I have always believed that hate and love are very close to each other."

"I know, and I've always thought that was a bunch of bunk."

"What's a bunch of bunk?" Splinter stepped out onto the verandah carrying a bucket filled with warm soapy water and an empty bucket laden with a sea sponge, three rags, and a bottle of lemon oil.

Jess moved away from the pillar and went to inspect his finds. "Oh, Mama Hannah doesn't think love and hate are opposites. She says they're two sides of the same coin."

"Hmm." He cocked his hands on his hips and stared at the floor for a moment. "I'm with Mama Hannah."

"You would be."

"Sure, because she's right. It makes perfect sense. Remember how once in a while I used to come running in from Nick's house and tell you we'd had a terrible fight, and I hated him? I did, too! But see . . . I could only hate him that strongly because I liked him so much." He knelt down on the verandah floor. "Look, Mom, here's the deal. Pretend like this soapy water stands for my feelings for Nick. This bucket is love, and this one is hate. Are you with me so far?"

Jess nodded, always both amused and perplexed by her son's analogies.

"OK," he went on. "Now, see how much I love Nick? The bucket's full of my feelings. But if we get mad at each other, the hate bucket gets full." He poured the soapy water into the empty bucket. "The feelings don't go away, just like the water doesn't go away. The feelings just get transferred back and forth. The only way I could hate Nick this much—all the way to the top—is if I loved him this much."

"I still think when you're full of hate, you're empty of love. And that means they're opposites."

"Wrong. See, this is the *same* water, Mom. It can go right back from the hate bucket into the love bucket and make it just as full as it was before."

"Maybe."

"OK, now think about James Wiggins."

"Do I have to?"

Splint laughed at her reaction to the memory of the irritating little boy who had lived in a flat near theirs in London. "This is how deep my feelings go for James Wiggins," he explained, emptying all but a cup of the soapy water into the copper bowl his mother had brought down from the storage room. He showed her the barely wet bottom of the pail. "See what a small amount of feelings are in the bucket that stands for love? It's all I can muster. When James is hanging around and trying to be nice, I can sort of semilike him."

"You can remotely, slightly like him."

Splint chuckled as he poured the trickle of water into the second bucket. "Once in a rare while there might be the slender, barely negligible chance that I'd like him. But even when I don't like him, all I can make myself feel is a sort of inert apathy. See?"

"Inert apathy?" Jess repeated as she looked into the second bucket.

"I can't hate James Wiggins the way I can hate Nick, Mom. My feelings aren't full enough. So, it's just like Mama Hannah said. If you really, truly hate somebody, then that means you once really, truly loved them. And you could love them that much again."

"Oh, is that so?"

"Yeah, that's so! Who is it you hate, Mom?"

Jess glanced at Hannah. The old woman was rubbing a rag over the green tray and humming under her breath.

"I hate dust and dirt and cobwebs and rust," Jess said quickly. "Now, let's head back up those stairs and see what else we can bring down from the storeroom. The sooner we make Uchungu House into a home, the better I'll feel about living here."

"If there's a hammock up there, can I bring it? Could we hang it up on the verandah?" Splint was already halfway through the door.

"If there is one and the bugs haven't eaten it, we'll hang it this afternoon."

She could hear her son's *yippee*s as she started into the house.

"I have thought of one thing, *toto,*" Hannah said, her focus trained on the brass tray.

Jess stopped in the arched doorway. "What's that, Mama Hannah?"

"I have remembered that someone else knew Dr. bin Yusuf. Someone who wanted something very precious from him." She turned to Jess. "Hunky Wallace."

"I DON'T know why you won't let me go out on the boat with Hunky Wallace," Splinter said from the backseat as his mother drove the Renault down the bumpy road to Zanzibar town the next morning. "You won't let me do anything. I guess I might as well give up all hope of ever becoming an independent man. I should just tie myself to your apron strings and let you drag me around behind you for the rest of my life."

"I don't wear an apron," she said.

She and Hannah, who sat next to her, had been discussing what supplies they needed for the house. Sure, they were having a great time, Splinter thought. They had spent the whole afternoon and evening the day before lugging things down from the store-room and cleaning them off. Late into the night, Splint had heard his mother walking from room to room and setting up different objects. Decorating.

"I don't see why I can't go with Mama Hannah to the market!" Splinter spoke up. "I could help her carry all that stuff you're telling her to buy."

"You're coming with me, Splint." Her voice had a note of finality that made it useless to argue. But that didn't keep him from trying.

"To the house of the dead guy's sister? Wow, that sounds like a blast. At least with Mama Hannah I'd see some interesting people. In the market I might even find some shells for my collection. You never know, Mom. That collection I'm building could be worth a lot of money some day. A museum might pay a fortune for it."

Splint could see that his mom was paying zero attention to him. She and Hannah were trying to read street signs and navigate the car down narrow alleys toward Changa Bazaar. Suddenly Splint spotted an open-timbered building that Solomon had pointed out on their earlier trip.

"There's the House of Spices!" he shouted. "Turn here! Turn here!"

His mom swerved onto the right street just ahead of a taxi. What would she do without him? He let out a sigh.

"I'll pick you up right here in an hour," she told Hannah. "If I'm late, just wait. It means I got hung up."

"Or lost," Splint muttered under his breath.

As the car pulled away from Hannah, he waved at her through the back window. He had to admit, she was pretty neat for an old lady with holes in her earlobes and a dent in her forehead. She'd taught him to sing in Swahili and hunt for clams. This afternoon they were going to make rockets out of mango seeds. She had promised.

Hannah knew about a lot of things. Best of all, she didn't worry, she didn't gripe, she wasn't bossy. Not like his mom.

"You know, Hunky Wallace's boat stays inside the reef the whole time he's diving," Splint said, draping his arms over the front seat. "They never go anywhere dangerous. Plus, he has a whole crew of men who would watch out for me."

When she didn't respond, he decided maybe she was weakening. "They're hunting for treasure, Mom," he went on. "In our bay! I bet Nick's mom would let him go. And Nick's not even as good a swimmer as I am. I wouldn't fall in. I'd just wait on deck to see what they brought up."

"No, Splint." That little muscle in the side of her jaw was jumping up and down.

"Rick would be there. He likes me. He'd make sure—"

"I said *no,* Splint! You're not to go anywhere near Hunky Wallace or Rick McTaggart, and that's final."

"You're the strictest, meanest—"

"And you're the most persistent, tenacious—"

"Why don't you like Hunky? He's cool. He said I could go out on the boat with him. He said he wouldn't mind a bit."

"When did he say that? When did you talk to him?"

Uh-oh. Now he'd blown it. She was going to come unglued if he confessed.

"Spencer Thornton, when did you talk to that man about going out on his boat?"

He let out a breath. It never did any good to lie to his mom. He'd tried plenty of times. It was like she had some kind of lie-detecting radar on the top of her head.

"I went down to the beach this morning when his trucks came in," he admitted in a low voice.

"What? I told you to stay away—"

"I just wanted to say hi. Rick was there. Did you know he's going to work with Hunky every day from now on? They have a contract. Rick's not a treasure hunter. He's a scientist. He knows the names of all my shells. Plus, he said he'd show me how to catch an octopus. If you'd just give him half a chance, you'd like him a lot."

Splint ventured a glance at his mom. Her face was red. Not a good sign. She was pulling the car to a stop at the edge of the street beside a large white building. Things looked about as bad as they ever got.

"Spencer, honey." When she turned around, her eyes weren't spitting fire as he'd expected. Instead, they were red-rimmed, and her lips were trembling. It was like she was about to cry. He'd never seen his mom cry.

"Listen to me, sweetheart," she whispered. "I know you want to have fun, and I promise you will. But not with Hunky Wallace and Rick McTaggart. They're grown men. They're strangers. Please trust me, OK?"

What could a guy say to eyes brimming over with tears? It wasn't fair. Still, even though his mom was sniffling, Splint made up his mind that he wasn't about to agree to stay away from the one and only real true treasure hunt of his entire life.

"Don't worry, Mom." He patted her hand. "I'm going to be fine."

She nodded. "I'm counting on you to obey me, Splint."

Fortunately he didn't have to reply. They got out of the car and walked up to the door. Splint hammered on the thick wood. Just when he had decided nobody was home, the door opened.

A truly bizarre-looking man stared down at him. At first Splint thought he was African, because he had tight curly hair and dark skin. But then he noticed that the fellow's hair was deep brown, not black, and his skin was the color of caramel toffees. Even weirder, he had green eyes.

"I'm looking for the sister of Ahmed Abdullah bin Yusuf," Splint's mom told him.

"Yes, she is here. Please come in."

When the man held the door open, Splint felt the urge to take his mom's hand and run in the other direction. This guy could be a criminal for all anybody knew. He was broad-shouldered and tall. He had a bare chest, muscles rippling everywhere, nothing but a blue-checkered cloth wrapped around his waist, hanging down to his ankles—and he kept looking Splint's mom up and down, up and down.

Instead of doing all the things she had taught her son to do in dangerous situations—stop, drop, and roll . . . yell for help . . . scream and run—she flushed a bright pink and walked after the man straight into the courtyard of his house. *This* was the woman who had cautioned her son a billion gazillion times to be careful around strangers?

Irked, Splint followed her. The house wasn't that different from Uchungu House, he decided, except that maybe five families lived in it. Little kids were crawling all over the place, and laundry hung in eight rows across the open courtyard. The place smelled like a barbecue grill. Fragrant but smoky. Splint decided he didn't like it.

The green-eyed man led them across the courtyard and through the doorway of a dark little room. A woman dressed all in black from her head to her toes crouched on the floor in the cool shadows. Splint saw that she was knitting a blue blanket. Her whole head and face were covered by a black veil, and as hard as Splint looked, he couldn't even see her eyes.

"This is Fatima Hafidh, the sister of Ahmed Abdullah bin Yusuf." The muscle man held out a hand in the direction of the black figure on the floor. "She is my mother. I am her son, Omar Hafidh. She does not speak English."

Splint looked around the bare room and decided he wouldn't want to trade places with this lady. To live under a black hood all your life . . . to not know English . . .

"Mrs. Hafidh, my name is Jessica Thornton." Splint's mom took a chair and motioned for him to do the same. "Many years ago in Dar es Salaam I knew your brother. I'm the new owner of Uchungu House."

The muscle man, Omar, stiffened up like he'd been hit. He spoke to his mother for several minutes—a lot longer than it would take to translate what had been said.

"Why have you come here?" Omar asked.

Splint watched his mom put on a smile. "I wanted to meet your mother. I wanted her to know how much I respected her brother. I was Dr. bin Yusuf's student many years ago, and I admire his work very much."

"You were his lover?" Omar demanded.

Splint wanted to smack the guy. From the look in his mom's eyes, she felt the same. "Lover? Me? No! Of course not. No, I was just his student." She took a deep breath and went on. "I really didn't know him very well at all. Not personally, anyway. I've been trying to understand why he left Uchungu House to me. And . . . and I thought maybe you or your mother had been to the house to see him before he died. Maybe you spoke to him about it?"

"We do not ever go to Uchungu House. We are not welcome there."

Omar turned and talked to his mother for a long time again. Splint swung his legs back and forth and tried to think of a way to convince his mom to let him go out on the boat with Hunky Wallace. After all, it wasn't every day a boy had a sunken treasure ship in his own front yard. Besides, what was so bad about Hunky? He was friendly. He knew how to treat a kid with respect.

So did Rick McTaggart. Splint liked Rick even better than he liked Hunky. It might be fun to be a scientist. A marine biologist. The sound of the words turned over nicely in his brain.

"My mother wishes to know what it is you desire from us," Omar said to his visitor.

"Well . . . I . . . I thought maybe there was something in the house you might want. A keepsake of your uncle. You know, there's a lot of art still in the house."

"The legacy of a cruel man."

"Cruel? I can't imagine that. Dr. bin Yusuf was always kind to his students. He treated us like . . . like his children."

The woman in black uttered a string of loud Swahili words that told Splint she understood English perfectly well. And she didn't like the idea that her brother had been kind to other people—and not to her. It occurred to Splint that she probably had expected Uchungu House to be hers one day. Wasn't that the way it usually worked when someone died?

"My mother says we do not wish to have anything from the house of her brother," Omar said. "She wishes you to go away now."

Splint and his mom stood. "I'm sorry to have troubled you," she said softly. "I had hoped you could help me to understand."

"To understand why Ahmed left Uchungu House to a stranger? Or to understand how he died?"

"Both."

Omar led the way out of the room. "We do not know the answer to either question. My mother has chosen to put her brother's memory away. She does not wish to think of him. She will not want to see you again."

"She won't."

"Inshallah."

Splint followed his mom to the car. Inside, she turned the key in the ignition and pulled out into the street. Her knuckles were white on the steering wheel, and her lips formed a tight ashen line.

"What a creepy guy," Splint said. "What was that last thing he told you?"

"Inshallah. It means 'God willing' in Arabic."

He shivered. "Did you see those weird green eyes of his? That guy gave me the heebie-jeebies."

She shook her head. "If looks could kill . . ."

@@@

Who had murdered Dr. bin Yusuf? As hard as she tried to put it out of her mind, Jess found herself turning the question over and over.

Hunky Wallace might have done it to get access to the shipwreck.

Omar Hafidh might have done it to get Uchungu House for his mother. Or he might have done it in anger when he found out she wasn't getting the house.

Solomon Mazrui might have done it, though Jess had no idea why.

Or someone else might have done it.

Did it even matter?

Jess knew she could drive herself crazy trying to figure out who had killed her mentor. So she forced her mind to other things and decided to attack the house with a passion. Though she still wasn't sure how she would pay Miriamu, she assigned the young woman a long list of chores. While she and Miriamu worked at scrubbing, polishing, painting, and arranging, Hannah kept Splint entertained.

Solomon, enigmatic as ever, agreed to cut down the tall weeds around the house's foundation and to pull down and burn the vines that were creeping up the walls. He said nothing about his experiences with the police. Instead he seemed grateful to have been given something to keep himself occupied. Now and then Jess spotted him hauling huge empty clay pots out of the storage shed near the house or mowing the patch of coarse grass in the front yard or raking the gravel in the drive.

As though he were a cadet and she a drill sergeant, he reported his progress to her several times a day. But the detailed work orders he was fulfilling didn't come from her. Solomon followed some inner set of plans that demanded accomplishment—as though he had been setting goals for years and had never been allowed to meet them.

He placed clay pots all around the huge verandah, upstairs and down. He lined the walkways with them and set them along the fence by the cliff. Slowly he began to fill each pot with rich soil and ornate tropical plants—bird-of-paradise, split-leaf philodendron, poinsettia, hibiscus. Miriamu told Jess he was taking the plants from secret places on the island where they grew naturally. She said Solomon could make anything grow. Dr. bin Yusuf had kept him so busy restoring Uchungu House, he hadn't had time to work with his plants. Solomon had not been happy about that.

Unhappy enough to murder his employer? Over plants? In the week following Jess's visit to Dr. bin Yusuf's sister, the police came out to the house three times. They searched, asked questions to which nobody had answers, took a few items for investigation, and went away again. Determined not to stew over the situation, Jess decided to transform the house from a barren set of rooms into a warm and welcoming haven for her family.

She and Miriamu unlocked every door and inventoried the contents of each room. It turned out that Dr. bin Yusuf had not only filled storage rooms with native handicrafts, he had saved every tidbit of art he had ever produced. In the room Solomon had called the library, Jess found rough pencil sketches, lumps of half-molded clay, and stacks of canvases. Some of the canvases revealed completed paintings. Others were unfinished drafts—blocked-out skeletons of works that had never come to fruition.

And the sculptures. She'd had no idea her mentor worked not only in clay and marble but also in wood, metal, even paper. Once again, some of the pieces were beautiful and deserving of a place in the finest gallery. Others looked crude and twisted, as though Dr. bin Yusuf's dreams had turned into nightmares.

Near the small gas-powered refrigerator in the kitchen, Jess tacked up lists of her own dreams for each section of the house. New cushions for the chairs. Tablecloths. Curtains. A sofa. A rack for sweaters and hats. An outdoor shower to rinse off sand and seawater. More shelves in every room. Electricity. And a telephone. Definitely a phone. Jess knew her dreams would have to wait until more money came in, but she liked passing by her set of lists each morning. They spoke of hope.

Of course, she couldn't deny the realities of her fears—for Splinter, for Hannah, even for herself. There were times when confusion almost consumed her. Her most troubled thoughts centered in one area, like a sea urchin whose black spikes radiated doubt, dread, and despair. The center of her turmoil was Rick McTaggart.

As hard as she tried, Jess could not make sense of the disruption the man had caused in her life. Why did she wake each morning before sunrise and listen—with her heart pounding against her ribs—for the sound of two trucks and a motorcycle roaring up the driveway of Uchungu House? Why couldn't she stop herself from sliding out of bed and tiptoeing to the edge of the verandah to hide in the purple-pink shadows? Why did she wait, holding her breath, for the moment when Rick took off his helmet and raked a hand through his mop of brown hair? He always lifted his head and searched the windows of her bedroom. Always. She made sure he never saw her.

Every morning she lingered on the verandah until he had shrugged out of his jacket and hung it on the handlebar of his cycle. She waited until he had peeled off his T-shirt, slung a towel over one shoulder, and ambled to the cliff-side stairway. When he was gone, she loathed herself for having watched him.

She told herself she did it to remember how much she despised him and to rub salt in her wounds so they would stay fresh and raw. She wanted to keep her anger as it had always been—hot, alive, and easily touched off. She wanted to remind herself how much she hated the man who had cut at the core of her soul.

Instead, his voice haunted her.

"What I did to you was wrong, Jessie. I'm not asking you to deny that. I'm asking you to forgive me. . . . Forgiveness means you stop feeling resentment toward the person who hurt you. You stop being bitter. You stop letting the past affect how you live in the present. When you forgive me, it will change you."

Did she want to change? Of course not. Things were just fine. She had Splint. Her home. Her art.

"You may not want to be healed, Jessie, but I do."

Healed? Could broken lives be put back together, shattered hearts mended, lost years restored? The whole concept was ridiculous, Jess told herself again and again. Forgiving Rick would not make one iota of difference in her life.

"With God's grace, I've rebuilt my life from the ground up. But there's still one big hole, and I can't figure any way to patch it. That hole is our marriage."

Jess tried her best to shut off the memory of Rick's words. If there had been any healing in her life, she had done it herself. She had patched her own holes. Sealed off her own heart. Most important, she had blocked off the jagged scar left by her marriage. She wasn't about to let McTaggart tear into it again.

"Unless there's something I don't know, you're still my wife."

"There's a lot you don't know," she said out loud as she lit a citronella candle on the courtyard table one evening in preparation for supper. In the last couple of days, she had found it necessary to vocalize her mental arguments. It was the only way she could shut off the constant assault of Rick's words swirling around and around inside her head.

"Marriage means relationship," she said to the empty courtyard. "You and I didn't have one ten years ago, and we certainly don't have one now. You know little about my past and nothing about my dreams for the future. Most important, you don't know the woman I've become. I'm strong, determined, independent. The sooner you finish your work on the shipwreck and get out of my life again, the better."

She cocked her hands on her hips and stared at the three neat place settings on the table. Hannah, Splint, and Jess. They made a good team. A family. Starting tomorrow, Jess would get to work on her impala sketches. In two weeks, Splint would start school in Zanzibar town. In another month or two, the police would finish their investigation, Hunky Wallace would move on to a different shipwreck—or maybe go to jail if he turned out to be the killer—and Rick would leave. Things would feel normal. And that would be good.

"Einstein believed in time travel, you know." Jess heard Splint talking to Hannah as they walked from the yard onto the verandah. His voice drifted through the long narrow rooms almost as clearly as if he had been in the courtyard. He and Hannah had been on the beach all afternoon. Hannah would be tired. Splint would be sandy and sunbaked. Both would be happy.

"Just about every one of Einstein's theories has been proven," Splint continued. "He was a genius."

"As wise as King Solomon? This I cannot believe."

"Did King Solomon write about relativity and energy and time? I don't think so, Mama Hannah."

"Time? Oh yes, he did. 'There is a time for everything, a season for every activity under heaven. A time to be born and a time to die. A time to plant and a time to harvest. A time to kill and a time to heal.'"

"Whoa, dude," Splint interjected. "Did King Solomon really think about time way back in the olden days?"

"He thought about time and about many more things."

Jess straightened a chair and smiled. Hannah held the boy in the palm of her hand. If he wasn't telling her every thought that poured out of his overactive brain, she was busy teaching him a hundred wonders from her bag of tricks. The tender love blossoming between Hannah and Splint was the one part of coming to Africa that Jess could feel perfectly right about.

"Still, what King Solomon said has nothing to do with time *travel,"* Splint said. "See, Einstein was interested in the past and the future and how we could go back and forth between them."

"To go into the future before it has happened?" Hannah asked. "How can this be?"

"You're the one who's always telling me God knows everything past, present, and future. If he can see the future, then it must have been determined already, right? So that means we could go visit it, right? Huh?"

"Ehh."

"What's that supposed to mean?"

"It means she's thinking about it."

Jess jerked at the sound of the deep male voice. *Rick.*

"Just because God can see the future," he said to Splint, "that doesn't mean he's already set the whole thing up. If he had, we'd be like little robots. We wouldn't get to make our own decisions about how we're going to act and what we're going to do with ourselves."

Rick was coming toward Jess through the house. She could hear his voice getting louder and louder. She didn't want him in her house. He didn't have permission. He couldn't.

"God gave us the right to choose," he said. "Even though he's the king of the whole universe, God decided to put your future into your own hands. You're the boss of your life, Splint—unless you decide to give it to him." He stepped out of the shadows into the late-afternoon light. "Hey, Jessie."

"Guess what, Mom!" Splint skipped into the courtyard barefoot. He was followed by Hannah and Andrew Mbuti, Rick's African associate. "Hunky's crew found the mother lode today! Take a look at this buckle!"

Jess grabbed the back of a chair for support. She couldn't look at Rick. She didn't want to see him. Not this close. She studied the corroded black mass in her son's palm. It didn't look like a buckle. It didn't look like anything. But Splinter was dancing around in circles, and Rick was walking ever closer.

"I invited Rick and Andrew to have supper with us, Mom," Splint sang out. "I asked them if they'd tell me all about the day from sunrise to sunset. Every second of every minute. I knew you'd want to hear about it, too. Mom, just think of the book you and James could do about something this important. Treasure hunting is a ton more interesting than Kima the Monkey. Kids will love it. Rick said he'd talk to me tomorrow down at the beach, but I was sure you wouldn't mind if he and Andrew came up for dinner. You don't mind, do you?"

"Spencer Thornton—"

"If I could time travel, I'd go back to the day that ship sank," Splint went on. "Wouldn't it be awesome to watch the storm? Rick, do you think the captain was trying to get over the reef? Or do you think he just smashed into it on accident?"

"That's something I'll be trying to determine in the next few weeks."

Jess straightened and took a deep breath. "All right, Splinter. Now go wash your hands, and rinse the salt water out of your swimming trunks."

"OK!" The boy raced past her toward the staircase at the back of the courtyard. "What are we having for supper?"

"Fish. Hang up your trunks in the bathroom." She watched him disappear into his room. "Look in that chest by your bed for clean shorts."

"We don't have to stay, Jessie." Rick's voice was low, almost a whisper.

She couldn't turn around. He was standing too close. Right beside her shoulder.

"There's a kiosk near the main road," he said. "Andrew and I usually stop there in the evening. They have great samosas."

"It's OK." She let go of the chair and walked away from him toward Hannah. If she protested too much, Andrew would wonder why. Worse, Splint would wonder. "You can stay. I'm sure Miriamu fixed enough fish. We usually have leftovers. Mama Hannah, I'll go tell Miriamu we're having company. Would you mind coming to the kitchen with me for a minute?"

"Ehh."

It was all Jess could do to make herself walk the few steps into the long narrow kitchen. As soon as she was safely through the door, she swung around and took Hannah by the shoulders.

"How much time did they spend talking?" she whispered. "Do you think Rick knows? Does Splint suspect anything? Mama Hannah, I can't do it. I can't sit there and eat in front of him."

"Why not?" The bright brown eyes searched Jess's face.

"Why not! Because . . . because of the past. Because of what happened between us. I can't stand him, and I don't want Splint to suspect that Rick might be . . . that he was . . . Splint's my son, and I won't lose him, Mama Hannah. I won't have our relationship ruined because of some . . . some drunk who—"

"That man is a drunkard?"

"He was. You remember that, Mama Hannah. I told you everything. He was hopeless."

"In God's eyes no man is without hope."

"Oh, Mama Hannah, don't start that. Rick's drinking ruined my life, and you know it."

"He is drinking in these days?"

She gave a huff of frustration. "I don't know about now. I only know how he *was,* and that's enough for me."

"Perhaps he has changed, as you have."

"I don't care if he's changed. I don't care about him at all."

"Ehh."

Jess whirled away and grabbed two plates from the shelf. Hannah could be incredibly irritating when she wanted to be. Couldn't she see how devastating all this could be to Splinter? What if Rick wanted to be a part of her son's life? Splint obviously found Rick fascinating. What if he preferred the company of his father over the mother who had raised him from birth? How could she and Kima the Monkey compete with a treasure hunter?

"I am *not* going to do this!" she hissed, fighting the knot in her throat. "I refuse to put my son in jeopardy. I'm going to walk right out there and tell him to hit the road."

Hannah's warm hand covered hers. "It is you who bears the greatest pain in this matter, my *toto,*" she murmured. "The boy is the child of your flesh. His heart is tied to yours with ribbons of great love that nothing . . . and no one . . . can cut. The man is strong and wise. But he has no power over you. When he asked your forgiveness, he gave away his power. He gave it to you."

Jess brushed at the tear sliding down her cheek. "I don't want anything from him."

"Ehh. But he wants something from you."

"Forgiveness. I can't. It hurts too much. I feel too threatened by him. It's not just about me, Mama Hannah. It's about Splint."

"You fear if you cut down the vines of bitterness that have grown around your family, then your son will run away from you. In this matter you are wrong."

"But Splint might want to be with Rick. He might want a father."

"Does he not already wish for a father?"

"Of course he does. But I can't let him know his father is Rick. You remember what kind of person Rick is, Mama Hannah. He's irresponsible and wild. He's unreliable. He would be a terrible role model for my son."

"Do you know this?"

"I was married to him, wasn't I?"

"Ehh. Ten years ago." Hannah took the two plates from Jess, picked up a couple of napkins, and set some silverware on the stack. "In Swahili we say, *Ndovu wawili wakisongana ziumiazo ni nyika.* When two elephants fight, it is the grass that suffers. If you do not wish your son to suffer, *toto,* perhaps you had better strive for peace."

JESS managed to eat three bites of fish and a sliver of pineapple in the hour she sat beside her husband. She had decided to take Hannah's advice and observe Rick. If she couldn't get rid of Rick or keep him away from her son—and both were proving impossible—at least she should know what she was up against.

Unfortunately, during dinner he charmed the socks off everybody. She should have expected this. Rick had always been funny, an avid listener, a top-notch storyteller. He kept Splint enthralled with tales of his adventures on one shipwreck after another. He talked about airlifts and compressors and flotation drums. He explained magnetometers, grid systems, depth gauges, Aqua-Lungs. Splint's eyes grew bigger and shinier with each wonder Rick revealed.

Not only did Rick prove himself interesting, he left no doubt about the warm relationship he had with his coworker. Andrew Mbuti joined in every story with anecdotes of his own. "Remember the time we were caught in that storm off Pemba Island?" Andrew asked, and then he told everyone how Rick had rescued him from the rough sea. "I will never forget the day we used those empty barrels to try to bring up the anchor from the *Santa Louisa* shipwreck," he said and proceeded to relate how Rick and he had

brilliantly solved a sticky problem. As the dinner went on, it became clear that the two men relied on each other, expected the best of each other, trusted each other completely—and had done so for many years.

Even worse than the fact that her enemy was showing himself both interesting and trustworthy, Rick made every effort to be thoughtful toward Jess. She found it horrifying. He filled her glass with water when she ran out. He picked up her napkin when it accidentally slid off her lap. He asked all about her art. He complimented the house. He even offered to talk to the electric company about hooking up the power.

"I can do that," Jess said. "I'm going into town tomorrow to register Splint at school and buy his uniforms."

"Jonathan Wariru is the man to see at the power company," Andrew said. "He'll sort out the billing problems for you."

"Uniforms!" Splint said. "Aw, Mom."

"I used to wear uniforms at the boarding school where I went from third grade on up," Rick said. "Khaki trousers, khaki shirt. Boring, but useful as camouflage for sneaking around in the brush looking for the infamous three-legged, dog-eating leopard."

"You went to a school where they had a three-legged leopard?"

"That was the legend. My boarding school's still there—on the edge of the Rift Valley in Kenya. And the story about the leopard is probably still there, too. I never saw the animal, but I sure spent time looking."

"I didn't know you grew up in Africa." Splint chewed on a chunk of mango. "My mom grew up in Kenya, too. Did you ever meet her?"

"Splint, would you please finish up that mango?" Jess said quickly. "All of us are through with dinner, and you're still eating. I want you to get on up to bed, kiddo."

"Already? Why? Do I have to go into town with you tomorrow? I don't want to see that school. I don't even want to think about school."

"I'm going to town by myself, but you and Mama Hannah have been invited to Nettie Cameron's house to play Scrabble in the morning."

"Scrabble!" He pushed back from the table. "I'm gonna whip her. She thinks just because I'm ten, she can beat me. She doesn't know I can spell *ionium* and *qoph* and *subcutaneous.* I looked up *hydrofoil.* I've memorized the names of all my shells. Nettie doesn't stand a chance."

Jess stood and began to clear the table. "But you've been out on the beach all day long today, and she hasn't. If you don't get some rest, she might have the edge on you tomorrow."

"Yeah, she might pull *aoudad* out of her hat," Rick said. He leaned over to Splint. "It's a wild sheep from North Africa."

"Really?"

"Or *eosin.* It's a sodium or potassium salt we scientists use as a biological stain for cytoplasmic structures."

"If she knows scientific words, I'm dead meat." Splint studied Rick for a moment. "Hey, would you play Scrabble with me sometime?"

"I don't know about that. *Qoph* might do me in."

The boy laughed. "I'll see you tomorrow afternoon when you come ashore, Rick."

"Not tomorrow, pal. I'll only be here a couple of hours in the morning. I've got to fill out reports in town. You can ask Andrew what they bring up from the wreck."

"I sure wish I could go out there on the boat." Splint eyed his mom. "I know I'd be safe. I'm an ace swimmer."

Jess fastened her glare on him. "Upstairs, Spencer. Now."

Splint rolled his eyes and headed for the back staircase. Jess let out a breath. If she could get through the next few minutes . . . get Rick out the door . . . get him out of her sight . . .

Splint was halfway up the stairs when he stopped. "Hey, Rick. *Did* you know my mom back when she lived in Kenya?"

For the first time that night, Jess stared straight at the man. He looked at her, searching her eyes. Her heart lurched against her chest, and her breath caught in the back of her throat. Everything about him did the same things to her as ten years before.

"I met your mom a long time ago," he said, his eyes never leaving hers. "We were kids."

"Cool. So it's just like old times between the two of you." Splint started up the steps again. "I knew there had to be a reason you called her Jessie that day she barfed on you in Zanzibar town."

Jess let out a groan, grabbed the stack of dirty plates, and rushed them into the kitchen. Miriamu brushed past her on the way out to the table. Setting the plates in the sink, Jess bit her lip to stop the tears that were determined to fall. Her son would figure it out. He was too smart. Then he would want the father he'd never had. And how could she keep them apart? How—when Rick was kind and gentle and funny and everything a father should be?

"Jessie?" His voice in the doorway of the kitchen froze her tears. "Jessie, are you all right?"

"Of course I'm all right." She wiped the heel of her palm across her cheek and turned to face him. "I don't want him to know about the past, Rick. I don't want you to tell him."

"I won't."

In the low light of the kerosene lantern, she could see the broad silhouette of his shoulders. Hints of gold glinted in his hair. His skin glowed a deep bronze in contrast to the pale sea green of his T-shirt. He took a step toward her.

"Jessie, is Spencer . . . ?" He stopped and looked away.

She could see him struggling, and she knew the question he wanted to ask: Was Spencer his son? How could she not tell him? Didn't he deserve to know . . . ?

No! He had run off and left her. Left his own baby growing inside a young wife. Abandoned them both. No, he didn't deserve that child.

"You'd better go," she said.

"Yeah."

He rammed a hand down into his pocket. She stared at him, appalled at the urge she felt to tell him about his son. Mortified by the unbidden desire to touch him, to feel his arms slide around her. Terrified by her need to cry and rage and mourn . . . and heal. To heal him and to be healed by him.

Why had God allowed this to happen? Things had been so much better before. Now she had to look into Rick's eyes and read the mirror of her own emotions. He ached as deeply as she did. He carried the same torment.

"Jessie, I—"

"Rick—"

"Go ahead."

"No, you."

"I just . . . uh . . . thank you for the supper."

"You're welcome."

"Did you have something to say?"

"No."

He nodded. "I won't say anything to Splint. About us."

"Thank you."

He turned to go, then stopped. "Jessie, did you ever marry again after me?"

She jerked upright. "No." He was looking straight at her, trying to read her eyes. She squared her shoulders. "He's my son, Rick. Only mine."

"I guess you know that's a physical impossibility."

"You may know about genetics, but you know nothing about parenthood. Spencer has one parent. Me."

She could see him struggling to leash the turmoil bubbling up inside him. He crossed his arms over his chest, the muscles tight and bulging under the soft knit of his shirt. His jaw worked as he forced down the words he so obviously wanted to say. And then he let out a breath.

"God blessed him with you," he managed. "You're a good mother."

Before she could respond, he swung around and stalked out of the kitchen. Jess grabbed a dish towel and buried her face in it, stifling the scream that threatened. Out in the courtyard, Rick and Andrew thanked Miriamu for the dinner, said good-bye to Hannah, and left.

Jess heard the front door shut. She heard the motorcycle start up. And she heard the crunch of wheels on the driveway.

Forgive me. She heard the plea, but she didn't know whose voice spoke the words. Was it Rick's? Or her own?

◎◎◎

Rick wanted a drink. Wanted one badly. He pulled the motorcycle over to the side of the road near the little cliff-side kiosk where he and Andrew so often ate dinner after their work on the shipwreck.

"What's the matter, man?" Andrew asked behind him. "Why are you stopping? Let's go on into town. I'm full from that meal."

"Just a second. I've got to think."

Rick unsnapped his helmet and lifted it off. The night breeze blowing in from the ocean felt good. He shook his head to let the air dry his damp hair.

"This is bad news," he said.

"OK, man. You'd better tell me what's up." Andrew climbed down from the bike and took off his own helmet. "You want to go inside the kiosk?"

Rick let out a tired laugh. "Sure."

"Let's go then."

He swung one leg over the cycle and started for the small wooden hut. From inside poured the sounds of African rock music—a mixture of lively drums, horns, and singing. Through the open door, Rick could see the collection of tables, most of them sitting lopsided on the rough mud floor. A breath of wind carried the musky, enticing scent of rich African beer.

Rick stopped. "Can't do it, Andrew."

"Can't do what? Come on, let's have a Coke like we always do. Maybe get some samosas. We'll talk about this redheaded lady who has you all twisted up."

"I don't want Coke. I need something stronger."

"You got it bad, eh?"

"Seven years since I had my last beer. If I walk in there, buddy, I'm going to blow my streak."

Andrew's dark eyebrows lifted, and he shook his head. "Worse than I thought. So, what's the big deal? Go back to Uchungu House and ask the lady for a date. Tell her you think she's pretty. Give her a little kiss. You're a good-looking guy. What's the problem?"

"The problem?"

He studied the dimly lit interior of the kiosk. It would be so easy to walk in there. So easy to order up a beer. And another. So easy to make himself forget.

"Yeah, the problem," Andrew said. "You like her, that's obvious to anybody with two eyes. You stared at her all night like you were dying of thirst and she was a tall glass of ice water. She kept turning pink and white and red until I thought she was going to melt right into your arms. One kiss and she'll be yours just like that." Andrew snapped his fingers. "So what's the problem, man?"

"She's my wife. That's the problem, man."

Rick strode to the edge of the cliff and listened to the ocean waves crashing against the shore far below. High tide. He picked up a pebble.

"Excuse me, but did you say Jessica Thornton is your wife?"

"That's what I said, Andrew. My wife. I married her eleven years ago. Kenya. The bad old days. I ran off and left her more than ten years ago. And guess how old her son is."

"Surely not ten years."

"Surely so."

Andrew gave a low whistle. "That would tend to make a guy want a drink."

"Yes, it does." Rick flicked the pebble over the cliff. "But I killed my marriage with alcohol. I nearly killed myself."

"So I've heard." Andrew mused a moment. "You think Jessie is still your wife?"

"I think so."

"The boy? Could he really be your son?"

"He could. Or maybe not. She won't tell me. She doesn't want me around. I don't blame her."

"Maybe she won't tell you anything because she had the boy with another man. Maybe she didn't care that you left her. Maybe you don't owe the woman a thing."

"Maybe."

"But you think that boy is your son, don't you?"

"Yes."

"Me too. He looks like you." Andrew shoved his hands down into his pockets. "You want the boy? Or the woman? Or both? Or neither?"

"Both."

Andrew let out a low whistle. "OK, man. Now I see the problem."

Rick picked up another pebble and rolled it between his thumb and forefinger, back and forth, back and forth. He could feel the sharp edges of the coral chip digging into his skin. God had given him seven years of nourishment. Seven years of healing. Seven years to rid his body of the poison of alcohol. Seven years to beat his addiction. Seven years of transformation into a new man.

Why did he feel just like the old Rick McTaggart?

"You say she doesn't want you around," Andrew said. "I say you're wrong."

"The lady hates me, pal. I can see it in her eyes."

"That's not what I saw in her eyes."

"You weren't in the kitchen. She doesn't want me to have anything to do with the boy. She's not going to tell him we were married. She doesn't want the thought that I might be his father even to cross his mind."

"Because maybe you're not."

Rick nodded. On the one hand, he could handle the idea that he wasn't Splinter's father. It eased his guilt. So what if he'd walked out on Jessie? She must have run straight into another man's arms. Just thinking about that made him angry. He had left the marriage, but at least he hadn't gone to another woman. If Jessie had been unfaithful to her vows, she deserved the consequences.

Unfaithful to her vows? The thought slapped him in the face, and he felt his face burn with shame. What could you call walking out on a brand-new marriage? And how could he be sure Splinter wasn't his son? For all he knew, Jessie had been pregnant the night he'd left her. In that scenario, he had run off on a young, naive girl carrying his own child.

Rick hurled the pebble over the cliff and out into the surf. "I'm going back there. I'm going to make her tell me the truth."

"You can't do that. The woman will seal her lips as tight as a clamshell. You won't get a thing out of her." Andrew laid a hand on his friend's shoulder. "Come on, man. Forget her."

"Forget her?" Rick swallowed against the gritty lump in his throat. "I still love her, Andrew."

"You don't even know her. Ten years is a long time. Maybe you loved that girl when she was eighteen or nineteen. But she's a grown-up, angry woman now. For all you know, she's mean and tough and ugly inside. No man even wants to knock on the door of a woman like that. You forget what I've been telling you all these years? Lot of women out there, McTaggart. Why don't you go get yourself one?"

Rick shook his head. "Right now, all I really want to do is have a drink."

"So?"

"So, that's what *I* want to do. You know me better than anyone else, Andrew. You know I gave up my own will when I surrendered my life to Christ. The Lord's had seven years to work on me."

"I've seen you change a lot, brother."

"He's still got a long way to go."

"Hey, nobody's perfect. Look at me."

Rick found a smile for his friend. "I'm not going to take even one step backward. No matter how much I want to right now."

"OK, so what are you going to do? Go to the lady's house and make her tell you the whole story . . . or go inside the kiosk and have a Coke . . . or go home and go to bed?"

"I'm going to let you go into the kiosk and get us both a Coke." He nodded. "Right now, I'm going to pray."

"While you're at it, put in a good word for me about that woman, Miriamu, who cooked our dinner. A man would kill for a woman like that."

Andrew gave Rick a thumbs-up sign and headed for the kiosk. The two men had been through enough together to respect each other's privacy. Rick found a smooth boulder and hunkered down on it. He had told Andrew all about his past—the drinking, the surrender to Christ, the uphill walk away from addiction, the struggle to allow the Lord to mold him into a new creation. But he hadn't told his friend about Jessie.

All these years, she had been his secret. His hidden guilt. Though he had begged God for forgiveness for what he'd done to Jessie, he wasn't sure he'd ever forgiven himself. The only way he had been able to see an end to what haunted him was to ask forgiveness from Jessie herself.

"Father, I've asked her to forgive me," he murmured into the wind that rushed up the cliff from the ocean. "She can't. I don't know what else to do. I don't know how to fix this one."

He sat for a long time, watching the clouds paint patterns across the moon. At times like this, he felt frustrated and angry. Why wouldn't God just tell him what to do? Why couldn't the Lord send down an occasional blinding light like he had for Paul on the road to Damascus? That would be awfully handy. Or how about an angel—like the one who told Joseph to skedaddle into Egypt? Rick could do with an angel right now.

"Come on, Father. You know what's supposed to happen with this thing. Couldn't you just clue me in?"

He let out a breath. A little boy chased a puppy past the boulder. Unaware of the man watching him from the shadows, the child laughed and danced around the scampering pet for a moment before racing off into the night. An ache tore through Rick's heart at the sight of the child.

If Spencer Thornton was his own son . . . he wanted him! Look how many years he had missed. Look what he had turned his back on.

"Oh, God!" He buried his face in his hands. He could see Splint's bright eyes, hear his voice, his laughter, his thousand amazing questions. And what had he offered to his own son? A few paltry words of advice.

Just because God can see the future, he had said to Splint, *that doesn't mean he's already set the whole thing up. If he had, we'd be like little robots. We wouldn't get to make our own decisions about how we're going to act and what we're going to do with ourselves.*

"OK, Father," Rick prayed, realizing his own words were speaking to him. "I know you're not going to dictate this thing for me. I know you've given me free will. . . ."

God gave us the right to choose, his words echoed back to him. *You're the boss of your life—unless you decide to give it to him.*

"I give it to you, Father," he said. "I give it all to you. Jessie. Spencer. My urge to drink. My fears. The past. The future. This moment. I lay everything in your lap. Father, mold me. Take me where you want me to be."

He squeezed his eyes shut, letting go. Giving up. Surrendering. Accepting Christ's forgiveness. Forgiving himself.

"I got it, man! I got the answer." Andrew plopped down beside him on the boulder and shoved a glass of lukewarm soda between his hands. "You're going to be sweating blood in a minute with all that praying. Look, here's the answer."

"What are you talking about?"

"This." Andrew waggled the small Bible Rick had carried in his pack for years. "You're always shoving this thing in my face, man. Now it's your turn. I'm going to tell you what you're supposed to do." Rick reached for the book, but Andrew snatched it away. "I *said,* I'm going to tell you, brother," he repeated. "And you're going to listen."

"You don't even know where to start looking, you pagan."

"Oh yeah? It just so happens you've been giving me so many sermons through the years, I got myself my own Bible. I may not be a Christian, but I've been doing some reading in this book you talk about all the time. So don't call me a pagan. Before you know it, I'm going to be preaching to you."

Rick chuckled. "Preach on, Brother Andrew."

The African took a sip of his soda. "OK, we are now going to learn what this book says about being a husband, which is what you happen to be."

He flipped on a flashlight and brushed through the crinkly pages until he came to the concordance. After considerable fumbling and muttering Andrew cleared his throat. "'And you husbands must love your wives with the same love Christ showed the church. He gave up his life for her.' Tah dah! 'Husbands ought to love their wives as they love their own bodies. For a man is actually loving himself when he loves his wife.' Tah dah! 'So again I say, each man must love his wife as he loves himself, and the wife must respect her husband.' Tah dah!"

"Wait a minute. Is that in there? That *tah dah* business?"

Andrew rolled his eyes. "You think you're going to get out of this by making jokes, man? If you really believe what you've been telling me you believe, you're going to have to love that woman at Uchungu House, no matter how nasty she is. Love her. Respect her. Honor her. Even if she hates your guts from now to the day you die."

Rick studied his friend's face. "You think that's what it means?"

"How are you going to argue with it? Look at this one, man." He adjusted the flashlight on the page of Matthew's Gospel. "'They record that from the beginning "God made them male and female." And he said, "this explains why a man leaves his father and mother and is joined to his wife, and the two are united into one." Since they are no longer two but one, let no one separate them, for God has joined them together.'"

Andrew shut the Bible and set it firmly on Rick's thigh. "You're a man," the African said. "You got a wife. You believe this book. You better do what it says."

Rick picked up the book and stroked his fingers across the smooth leather. "'Let no one separate them, for God has joined them together.' I'm not going to be the man to break the sanctity of my marriage any longer, Andrew. I'm going to love Jessie. I'm going to love her . . . and I'm going to win back my wife."

"And I'm going to watch you do it. If you can pull this one off, man, I may just be tempted to start following this little book myself. You never know . . . I might even give my own life to your friend Jesus Christ."

JESS peered over Solomon's shoulder as he studied the intricacies of the Renault's engine. His dark hands stroked over the wires and hoses as she had seen them move over the leaves and flowers of a plant. He touched the battery, wiped off a blob of grease, tugged on a rubber belt.

"I do not know what is wrong," he said, straightening. "Perhaps I shall have to take it out."

"Take what out?"

"The motor."

"But it probably weighs several hundred pounds, Solomon. You can't take it out. Besides, I have to get into town. I have an appointment with the headmaster of Splint's new school. Can't you just pour some water in the radiator or something?"

The man stared at her. His dark eyes were hard, cold. "This car does not want to go to town today."

"Well, that's just great." She slapped her palm on the hood. "Fantastic. I don't have a car. I don't even have a telephone to let Mr. Ogambo know why I'm not coming."

Jess crossed her arms. It wasn't just missing the appointment with the school headmaster that was a problem. She needed to mail

some preliminary sketches to her editor. Without a phone, she'd had no contact with her publisher or with the Kima the Monkey books' author, James Perrott, since she arrived on Zanzibar Island. She had no electricity, so she couldn't send a fax or an E-mail message, even if she had a computer. For all she knew, they might have replaced her with a more accessible illustrator. She could have been dismissed from the Kima project, which would leave her an unemployed starving artist. Again.

"Do you think you can fix the car soon?" she asked Solomon.

"I will work on the motor this morning."

Jess let out a sigh. That told her nothing. "Look, I'm going to walk down to the village near the main road. Mdogo, I think it's called. Maybe I can get a taxi or a bus. Will you tell Miriamu?"

Solomon looked at her feet. "Those shoes will not wish to walk to the village."

"These shoes will walk wherever I tell them to. Splinter and Mama Hannah are over at Nettie Cameron's house. They'll be back around noon. If I'm not home by then, tell them where I've gone, OK?"

"You will not be home by then."

"And if you get the car started, come to town and look for me. I'll be at the school first, then the electric company, then the post office, and then I'm going to buy Splint's uniforms. All right?"

The man gave an unintelligible grunt and returned his attention to the Renault. Jess started down the driveway. The village wasn't all that far. She could make it, sandals or not. Finding a taxi might be another matter.

She brushed a hand around the back of her neck. The morning was going to be hot. So far, her visions of early-morning swims with Splinter and whole days of sketching and painting had barely materialized. She was doing well to spend any time at all with her son, whose fascination with the beach knew no bounds. Uchungu House demanded so much time—organizing, cleaning, and maintaining—that she'd managed to eke out only short stretches at her desk uninterrupted.

Jess studied the thick growth of vines and shrubbery growing along the sides of the narrow road. As the artist for the Kima series, she had no doubt Zanzibar was the perfect place to live. She could paint each type of flower, each variety of grass, each species of leaf onto the pages of her books. The series had won awards for the lush details of its art, and she knew the island was fertile with images that would enrich her work.

But could she ever get beyond the mounting problems that threatened her serenity? Her heart burdened with doubt, Jess plodded down the long dirt road. After twenty minutes, she finally walked into the little town that had grown up near the main thoroughfare. Tin-roofed shops lined Mdogo's single unpaved street. Hand-painted signs in bright colors advertised the nature of each business—shoes, groceries, clothing.

At this hour of the morning, the town bustled with activity. Children in patched and faded blue uniforms danced around in the yard of a small school. Women sauntered past the shops, large square tin cans of water balanced on their heads—the water drawn from a public faucet in an alley. Men strolled together discussing business and making plans. Few people offered even a glance at the white-skinned woman who had entered their town.

Jess stepped into a small grocery and approached the counter. A basket of fresh eggs sat beside a pyramid of mangoes on the clear glass case. Cans of lard; bottles of shampoo; and packets of rice, tea, and sugar lined the whitewashed walls. Flip-flop sandals slapping softly on the cool concrete floor, a young African man walked in from the back to meet his customer.

"Good morning, madam," he said in perfect English. "May I help you?"

"I hope so. Is there a bus going into Zanzibar town this morning?"

"The morning bus has already departed from Mdogo, madam. The next bus will leave at three."

"This afternoon? But I—" She stopped herself. "What about a taxi?"

The young man smiled, strong white teeth shining in his dark face. "Oh, madam, you will not find a taxi in Mdogo. But perhaps you will ride with my brother, Akim. He is carrying five hens and a goat into the market on his bicycle this morning. You may ride on the back, if you wish. I am certain my brother will not charge you more than twenty shillings."

Jess stared at the shopkeeper. On the back of a heavily laden bicycle, she wouldn't make it into town by noon. "Thank you, but I don't think—"

"Perhaps he may charge only fifteen shillings—if you will hold the goat."

"Hold the goat . . ."

"In your lap." The man smiled. "It is a small goat."

"I see. . . ." Jess blinked at the image of herself riding into Zanzibar on the back of a weaving bicycle—with a goat in her lap. She'd better come up with another plan. "Do you have a telephone I could use?"

"Not here. You must walk down the road to the petrol station. There you will find a telephone. It is not more than two miles."

Feeling sick, Jess nodded. "Two miles."

"I will tell my brother, Akim, to look for you there. Perhaps you will wish to ride on his bicycle after you have made your telephone call?"

"Perhaps." She tried to summon a smile. "Thank you, sir."

"Not at all, madam. Do come again."

Jess walked out into the blinding sunlight. She had no choice but to start for the gas station. At the very least she needed to cancel her appointment with the school headmaster. She could call the electric company, too, though she doubted they would do a thing toward restoring Uchungu House's lights unless she went in and spoke with them personally. And what about her sketches? Jess gripped the envelope she had so carefully prepared. Could she entrust that precious parcel to a stranger on a bicycle?

As she trudged down the shoulder of the main road, the occasional car blew past. Jess momentarily considered hitchhiking, but she abandoned the idea immediately. She was a mother, after all. She had responsibilities, and she knew thumbing a ride could be dangerous. Maybe she would find transportation at the gas station. She really needed to get into town. She had to buy Spencer's school uniforms. It wouldn't be long before—

"Jessie?" A black motorcycle slowed to a stop beside her.

She knew before she even looked that it was Rick. *Oh, Lord.* For the first time in years, she breathed a spontaneous prayer. *Lord, help me. I can't do this by myself anymore.*

"You're walking?" he asked. "Where's your car?"

"Solomon's working on the engine." She tried to sound casual, like tramping down a road on blistered feet under a burning sun was no big deal. "I needed to make a phone call."

"I thought you were going into Zanzibar town to run some errands this morning."

"I was, but . . . I guess I'll go another day."

He fell silent for a moment. The rumble of the motorcycle vibrated through Jess's sandals into her bare feet. She knew she should start walking again, move away from him, show him how little she cared that he had stopped to check on her.

When he looked at her again, his eyes were searching. "Can I give you a ride, Jessie? I'm on my way to my office."

She gave a disinterested shrug. "Oh, no thanks. I may go in with another man I heard about in the village back there. He's supposed to meet me at the petrol station."

"OK." He looked her up and down; then he turned away. She knew he wanted to say something, but she didn't want to hear it.

"Well, bye." She started walking. Maybe he would leave quietly. Maybe she wouldn't have to—

"Memsahib!" A bicycle bell jangled behind her. *"Memsahib,* my name is Akim! My brother told me you may wish to ride to Zanzibar town with me!"

The man swung his wobbly bicycle onto the shoulder just ahead of Jess. Five chickens tied by their scrawny yellow feet were hanging from his handlebars, wings flapping and feathers flying. A goat had been strapped to the rear rack, its spindly legs dangling on either side. Bleating, it regarded her with large brown eyes.

"You see, *memsahib,"* the man said, stopping the bike in a skid that sent up a small cloud of dust. "You can sit here on the rack."

"Well . . . there's, uh . . . there's a goat on the rack."

"You may hold my goat on your lap. You will keep her safe."

Jess glanced at Rick. His lips were working hard as he fought to suppress a smile. "I don't think so," she said to the man. "But thank you very much."

"Only twelve shillings. A good price for such a long journey."

"Thank you, but I think I'll just walk to the station over there and make my phone calls."

"Ten shillings. It is a small goat. You will hardly notice it."

Jess gave the goat a skeptical look. "That's kind of you, sir, but—"

"Eight shillings. A very good price, madam."

She glanced at Rick. He raised his eyebrows. "It *is* a nice little goat, Jessie."

Biting her lip, she faced the cyclist again. "I appreciate your offer, sir, but . . ." Finally she made up her mind. "But I think this motorcycle would be faster. I have an appointment in town, you see. I need to be there in half an hour."

"I see." The man nodded. "But this man will charge you much more than eight shillings. Perhaps next time you will ride with me."

Giving her a resigned smile, he pedaled off, his goat blinking at Jess as its owner wobbled toward town. Rick pulled his cycle onto the shoulder and let it idle. Turning toward her, he offered his helmet.

"It's a little damp," he said. "I was diving this morning."

Unable to make herself speak, Jess studied the helmet. How many miles of African roads had she and Rick flown along together in the old days? It had been their greatest pleasure—wind whipping at their clothes as miles of open grassland rolled by. Her first taste of freedom had come on the back of Rick's motorcycle. She had envisioned them riding forever, always together, always in love. But years ago, he had taken that motorcycle and ridden off without her.

"Put on the helmet, Jessie," Rick said in a low voice. "Come with me."

"Motorcycles are not really my thing anymore. I guess I've grown up some."

"We both have. I use it to get around, that's all. Best way to get where you want to go in Africa." He stuck a thumb in the direction of the black machine. "Transportation. Coming?"

"Better you than the goat, I guess." She settled the helmet on her head and fastened the chin strap. Against her better judgment—

or what was left of it—she climbed onto the bike behind Rick. When he pulled out onto the road, she had no choice but to grab two handfuls of his T-shirt. It was damp from his swim, and she could feel the heat of his skin through the thin cotton knit.

Praying that she could hang on, Jess vowed she would not drape herself over the man's back as she had when she was a girl. In those days, nothing had felt better than wrapping her arms around his chest and laying her cheek on his hard shoulder. No way would she do that now. Not even if it meant flying off the motorcycle and landing in a ditch.

The countryside flashed by, a blur of palm trees, small houses, blue sky. Rick navigated the potholes in the bumpy road, and he managed to steer his way between two humpbacked old cows without nudging either one. Jess hung onto his T-shirt until the fabric stretched into two big wads in her fists. Never—not in all her imaginings—could she have pictured herself riding a motorcycle again with Rick McTaggart.

At least she was on her way to town. She would make it to her appointment with the principal. She could take care of her errands. And maybe she was even conquering some of her revulsion for Rick. *Revulsion* was not the right word any longer, Jess had to admit. She was still angry with him, and she was more than a little fearful of him and of what he might do in regard to Splinter. But he didn't sicken her. He didn't enrage her. She was actually beginning to tolerate the undeniable fact that he was back in her life.

"You want me to take you to the school?" he asked. He turned around and leaned back into her. "It's right down that street."

"Yes." She barely managed the word. His face was inches from hers, so close that she could see salt from the dried seawater dusting his brown skin. Tendrils of still-damp hair curled around his ears. His blue eyes seemed to drink her in.

And then he turned to watch the road again. In moments, he was driving up to the front of a tidy white-and-blue school building, its lawn rimmed in bougainvillea and hibiscus. When Rick stopped the motorcycle, Jess practically jumped off. She whisked the helmet from her head and thrust it at him.

"Thanks," she said. "I owe you one."

"Make it up to me, then." He searched her eyes. "Have lunch with me today, Jessie."

"Oh, Rick. Really, I . . . I have a lot to do in town."

"You gotta eat sometime."

"Yes, but—"

"I *know* I'm better company than the goat." When she smiled in spite of herself, he leaned forward. "I'll meet you at the Kilau Coffee House on Baghani Street at noon. They make a mean shrimp-and-egg curry. And the mango milk shakes . . . unbelievable."

Jess could feel herself weakening. He was back, the old charmer. Smiling at her with his brown hair all windblown and his T-shirt molding to his chest, Rick looked like a million bucks. Worse, he hadn't done one thing to antagonize her. He was nice. Perfectly, wonderfully nice.

But it was all a front. She was sure of it. Underneath that gentleness, he must still be an irresponsible rogue. People just didn't change that completely. Did they?

"I have to buy uniforms for Splinter," she said, gesturing vaguely toward the town's center. "I'll just get a bite somewhere."

"Kilau's has cappuccino."

"Really?"

"And créme caramel."

"You're a rat, you know that? You really are."

He grinned. "That's what you've been telling me."

"It's true."

"Only way you'll know for sure is to hang around and find out. I might surprise you, Jessie."

"You've surprised me enough for a lifetime just by being in Zanzibar."

"I told you that was no accident."

She studied his blue eyes, trying to read the truth in them. Sometimes these days he looked so different to her. It was as if the rage inside him was gone. Something about him was calmer . . . more at peace.

"Baghani Street," he repeated. "Noon."

"Maybe," she called as he pulled away. "And maybe not."

As she turned toward the school building, she had the terrible feeling that just at noon Baghani Street would draw her like a magnet.

◎◎◎

The best elementary school on Zanzibar Island made no special provisions for its intellectually gifted students. Mr. Ogambo assured Jess that her son's precocious intelligence would be more than stimulated by the mixture of races, cultures, and languages at the school. There would be field trips to forts dating back three hundred years, to the city square where slaves once had been sold, and to the museum where students would examine memorabilia of Dr. Livingstone and Mr. Stanley. Spencer would be able to study the purest Swahili spoken anywhere. He would visit clove, copra, and fabric factories. And he would learn the history of the greatest market and meeting place in Africa.

By the time Jess walked out of the school building, Mr. Ogambo had convinced her that in exchange for modest school fees—though they seemed steep to her—Spencer would be receiving the finest education imaginable. Not only would he learn the essential academics, he would gain firsthand a sense of appreciation for the people and cultures of his world.

Jess fairly floated out into the street. As long as the Kima the Monkey series continued to sell well in the children's market, she believed she could afford the school fees. She hurried into the city center as she imagined the doors that would open for Spencer. With such a rich international background, he could go anywhere in the world. Do almost any job. Live successfully in any culture.

The relaxed, almost somnolent culture of Zanzibar Island nearly proved Jess's undoing in the next hour. She managed to get into the office of the electric company's manager, but he was reluctant to return service to Uchungu House. All the wires would have to be inspected, he said, and many would need replacing. It could take months.

At the post office, Jess had to wait in a long line at the single open window. No one was in a hurry, and Jess forced herself to calm down and adjust her timing to the tropics. Around her, good-natured laughter filled the cavernous office building. People chatted, read books, ate sack lunches. By the time Jess got up to the window it was nearly noon. She handed over her precious sketches and watched in trepidation as the clerk stamped the packet and set it on a counter behind him.

"That envelope must go to England today," she pointed out.

"Yes, madam. It will go."

"By air. Not sea."

"Yes, madam. We have good postal service in Zanzibar. Very few parcels become lost."

"That's not just any parcel, you know. It's very important to me. I don't want it lost."

"Please do not worry." He gave her a warm smile. "Perhaps you will feel better after eating your lunch."

"Perhaps." As she left the post office, Jess spotted the sign for Baghani Street. Her stomach knotted into a tight ball. Should she have lunch with Rick? What would he think she meant by it? Would it open a door better left shut?

Yes.

She turned around and started down the street in the opposite direction. It would be stupid to eat with Rick. Crazy to have anything more to do with the man.

On the other hand, what difference could a simple meal really make? She had eaten with him the night before, hadn't she? And no doubt she would see him at Uchungu House again. If he had something he wanted to say to her, she knew she was going to have to listen to it eventually.

She stopped walking. In fact, she might as well hear him out in the middle of Zanzibar town, safely away from Splinter's ears. Maybe they would just go at each other's throats. Spill the whole past onto the table at Kilau's Coffee House and be done with it.

Jess turned around and headed back down Kenyatta Road toward Baghani Street. When she rounded the corner, she spotted Rick at once. Leaning against the wall of the café, he was staring at the sidewalk. His face held a look of immeasurable sadness. She stopped again, suddenly in doubt. In the past, Rick had never been open with his feelings, never readable. A cocky grin had been his trademark, the perfect mask to cover his anger and rebellion.

Now, Jess felt she could see into his heart . . . but maybe she didn't want to. She gripped her purse. She should leave. This was a mistake. There was nothing he had to say that she wanted to hear. Or was there?

"Rick," she said softly.

He lifted his head. His blue eyes snapped to life, and a smile spread across his face. "Jessie. You came."

She shrugged. "You gotta eat sometime."

෧ ෧ ෧

Rick led Jessie through the dim interior of the Kilau Coffee House and out into the sunlit courtyard. He couldn't believe she had come. All morning, he had told himself she wouldn't be there. Why should she? He had done nothing but hurt her. Even now, he was clearly a threat to her peace of mind. He had stood on the street, waiting, turning over in his thoughts the hundred wrong things he had done to her in their brief marriage, trying to prepare himself for her rejection.

And then she was there.

Thank you, Lord, he prayed as he seated Jessie at a small metal table beneath the gray branches of a frangipani tree. *Please teach my mouth the right words to say to her. Speak to her heart through me.*

"I've got to try one of those mango milk shakes," she said. "That sounds outrageous."

He sat across from her, memorizing the play of sunshine in her auburn hair. She had on a simple yellow knit polo shirt and a plain blue denim skirt, but he thought he'd never seen a woman so beautiful. Her fingers were slender and long as she held the menu—artist's hands. Her skin glowed. Her eyes danced with life.

Rick felt like the teenager he'd been when they first met. Heart hammering, breath short, hands clumsy, he ordered a chicken sandwich. He doubted he could eat a bite. He was alone with Jessie. Beautiful, smart, intriguing Jessie. If he stood up, he'd probably fall flat on his face. He couldn't even think of anything to say.

"I'll have the curry plate," she told the waiter.

Rick fumbled his napkin into his lap. "So . . . uh, how did your morning go? The school . . . think Splinter will like it?"

Her eyes clouded, and he knew he'd made a mistake. *Don't talk about her son, you idiot! She's scared to death you'll horn in on their relationship.*

"I think it's a pretty good school," she said. "Mr. Ogambo is very proud of his teachers and curriculum. He says the students test well, too."

"Good. That's great." He turned his water glass around and around on the metal table. *Change the subject, McTaggart. Even the weather is a better topic than her son.* He hadn't been this nervous in years. He felt tongue-tied. Like a kid on a first date. "The . . . uh . . . the electric company? How did that go?"

"It's going to take months. I might as well get used to kerosene lamps." She shrugged. "I mailed some sketches to my publisher in London."

"It's great what you've done, Jessie. Your artwork."

"Yeah. Well, that's my living."

"It's more than that. It's a gift."

"It's a job." She fiddled with her napkin for a moment. "It's a good job. I've been very lucky."

"You've been blessed. Blessed with talent and the determination to develop it."

She leaned back and regarded him for a long time. The waiter placed their lunch plates on the table and refilled their water glasses. Jessie's focus never left Rick's face. Finally, she sat forward.

"You're weird, you know that?" she said. "Very weird."

"This is true. Sad but true."

"No, I mean it, Rick. You're not acting like you're supposed to."

"How am I supposed to act?"

"For one thing, you didn't order a beer with your sandwich."

"I don't drink beer anymore."

"No way. I don't believe it."

He chewed on a bite of his sandwich for a moment. It tasted like library paste. This was the opening he needed. *Give me courage, Father. Help me speak honestly.*

"I told you a lot had happened." He swallowed and gulped down some water. "There've been changes in my life."

"You don't drink beer *at all?*"

"I don't drink alcohol at all. I've been sober seven years."

"And you've held onto this job, too. You once told me you never wanted a job with a salary and an office. You were always going to be free. Free as a bird."

"The eagle has landed. Hard to believe, but I'm a responsible workingman, Jessie."

"Yes, it is hard to believe. I didn't think it was possible."

"Nothing's impossible with God." He let out a breath. There, he'd said it.

She set down her fork, folded her arms, and cocked her head to one side. "You know, you sound an awful lot like your missionary parents, Rick. God this and God that. I thought you hated that whole litany. You said it was shallow. Fake."

"'When I was a child, I spoke and thought and reasoned as a child—'"

"'But when I grew up . . . ,'" Jessie finished. "So, are you telling me you decided to follow in your parents' footsteps? You took on their faith after all?"

"No." He looked into her eyes. "That's not what I'm telling you. That's not how it is."

"Whew, you had me worried for a minute there."

"I'm following in *Christ's* footsteps, Jessie," he said. "Not my parents'. I don't have their faith. I have my own. It just happens that they were right."

"I wouldn't have expected that. Not from you."

"That day on the cliff-side steps, I told you there was more to my life than the years of wandering and drinking, the rescue by my brother, the university degree, and the job. Those are all things that happened to me. They're not who I am."

"OK, then. Who are you?"

He took a deep breath. "Easier asked than answered. Back in the bad old days—after I hit rock bottom—I decided I had to stop drinking. I'd killed our marriage, and I'd just about killed myself. By trying to run my own life, I had destroyed everything—and everyone—I'd ever loved."

Rick tried to read the look in Jessie's eyes, but she averted them. When she said nothing, he went on. "I started going to meetings for recovering alcoholics. One of the first things I had to do was admit I was powerless and seek help from a higher power. I thought *higher power* was a strange term for God—until I noticed how others in the group interpreted it. In their minds, this higher power could be almost anything from Buddha to a guardian angel to a person's inner self. So I went on a search for this power—for the highest power."

"And you found God."

"He found me." Rick bowed his head, praying he could break through the wall of bitterness and resentment around her heart—a wall built on the foundation of his mistakes. "God found me, Jessie."

She started to reply and stopped. Then she shrugged her shoulders. "Go on."

"One day in the middle of my search—at a point where I was clearheaded enough to realize what a total loser I'd become—I picked up a Bible at my brother's house. I started thumbing through it. I read verses I'd read a hundred times before, heard in a thousand of my father's sermons, memorized in Vacation Bible School. Boring, right? And then I read this one: 'So now there is no condemnation for those who belong to Christ Jesus. For the power of the life-giving Spirit has freed you through Christ Jesus from the power of sin that leads to death.'"

"You discovered your higher power."

"I discovered Christ's power. The Holy Spirit's power. That power set me free, Jessie. 'If your sinful nature controls your mind, there is death. But if the Holy Spirit controls your mind, there is life and peace. For the sinful nature is always hostile to God.'"

"You sound like your dad."

"My parents laid a foundation of faith in my life. I rejected it. Then I discovered my own path to the truth. It just happened that the truth I found was the same truth they'd been trying to show me all along. What I believe in is not a copy of my parents' religion, Jessie. My faith in Jesus Christ is my own."

She let out a deep breath. "Whew! Boy, you are different. I didn't know how different until now."

"'Those who become Christians become new persons. They are

not the same anymore, for the old life is gone. A new life has begun!' I didn't make that up. It's in Corinthians—and I believe it."

Jessie stirred her fork around and around in her curry. Rick watched, waiting, concerned that he might have pushed her farther away than ever. He'd never been much good at sharing his faith with people. As Andrew Mbuti had reminded him, Rick was forever tactlessly shoving his Bible in his friend's face. But they'd known each other for years, and Andrew still had no personal faith in Christ. With others he met, Rick found it awkward to talk about religion. Still, he wanted to tell people what had happened to him. He wanted to tell Jessie most of all.

"A brand-new person?" she said, lifting her head. "That kind of lets a person off the hook for the past, doesn't it."

"No. That comes when the people who were wronged are able to forgive. And just because I'm a new creation doesn't mean I'm perfect. Paul could have been writing my life story when he said, 'When I want to do good, I don't. And when I try not to do wrong, I do it anyway. . . . Who will free me from this life that is dominated by sin? Thank God! The answer is in Jesus Christ our Lord.'"

"Set free." Jessie stared blankly at her plate, as though the words had beckoned her into another world. Rick studied his wife and wished he could read her thoughts. Did she understand what had happened to him? Did she see the difference in his heart?

"Jessie?" he asked in a low voice. "I need to repeat what I said to you on the cliff. Can you forgive me?"

"Oh, Rick, I—" She looked up and sucked in a breath. "Rick, it's Omar Hafidh. He's coming this way."

"Who?" He turned to see a tall muscular man working his way between the tables in the courtyard. "Who's Omar Hafidh?"

She grabbed his hand and held on tightly. "I'm not sure, but I think . . . I mean, well—" her gaze met his—"he may be a murderer."

JESS looked up into the olive green eyes of Omar Hafidh and decided that at this moment she didn't care whether Rick was a con artist or a bona fide Christian, she was thankful to have his hand to squeeze. The towering African had traded his long cotton loincloth for a white shirt and dark trousers. A pair of mirrored sunglasses perched in the tight curls on his head. He stopped at the table, studied Rick for a moment, and then turned to Jess.

"Ms. Thornton," he said without a smile. "I have found you."

"You were looking for me?" She asked, trying to calm the terror that was making her voice quaver. "Was there something you wanted?"

"Someone would like to meet you." He stepped aside to reveal a pale, thin-boned man with a pair of small eyes that looked like hard brown pebbles. His hair had been slicked straight back from his high forehead and plastered into place with greasy pomade. The unsettling scent of roses drifted around him as he edged up to the table.

"Delighted to meet you, I'm sure," the man said in a clipped English accent as he held out a thin, long-fingered hand.

"This is Giles Knox," Omar informed Jess. "He has come from Nairobi to speak with you."

Jess took the man's cold fingers and gave them a quick shake. "I'm Jessica Thornton."

"Delighted, I'm sure," he said. "I have spoken with Mr. Hafidh about Uchungu House. I understand you're the new owner."

Jess nodded. Rick's hand felt warm and secure. She squeezed tighter in spite of herself. "Dr. bin Yusuf left me his house, yes. Why do you ask?"

"May we join you?" Before she could answer, the man slid into a chair and hefted a black leather briefcase onto the table. "My dear Ms. Thornton, I am the owner of Knox Galleries—Nairobi, London, Paris, New York. My galleries display only the very finest in native African art, and as I'm certain you can imagine, Dr. bin Yusuf's work is highly prized by collectors. Mine is the only gallery he permitted to display his paintings and sculptures. Of course I sold everything he left with me on consignment. The man was brilliant. A genius. I understand you're an artist as well, Ms. Thornton?"

"I do children's picture books."

"An illustrator. How very nice for you. How charming."

Jess glanced at Rick. He was clearly assessing the situation, his blue eyes shrewd and alert. Surprisingly, she felt thankful for the man, even grateful for his recurring presence in her life. As he unknotted her stiff fingers and wove them through his, a sense of peace slipped around her shoulders like a warm cape.

"Sir, as you can see, Ms. Thornton and I are having lunch," Rick said. "What exactly do you want from her?"

"Well." The man ran a finger around the inside of his collar. "Well, you do come directly to the point, don't you? Ms. Thornton, in my long and pleasant association with Dr. bin Yusuf, I came to realize he stored a great many paintings and sculptures at Uchungu House. In fact, I believe the entire house is filled with his work. Filled! I have only had the pleasure of seeing it once, but I believe you have *Storm at Sea*—the bird hovering over the ocean? The wind in the lone palm tree?"

"It's in the sitting room."

"The sitting room! Oh, dear heaven." He pulled a white handkerchief from his pocket and mopped his forehead. "Ms. Thornton, as an artist yourself, you surely understand the desirable qualities of such paintings. To leave them unprotected . . . to have them hang unseen . . . unappreciated! It's a tragedy!"

Jess was beginning to catch the trend of the conversation. "I've been concerned about the safety of the paintings, too. But clearly Dr. bin Yusuf wanted his artwork stored at his own house, or he would have placed it in your galleries a long time ago."

"What my uncle wanted no longer matters," Omar said. He had not taken a chair. Standing like a bodyguard beside the slick gallery owner, he crossed his arms over his massive chest and stared at Jess through hooded green eyes. "Ahmed Abdullah bin Yusuf is dead."

"I'm aware of that, but I'm attempting to respect Dr. bin Yusuf's wishes."

"Why?"

"Because I admired him. I want to honor his memory. He did leave me his house, after all. The least I can do is try to preserve some of its unique heritage."

"The least you can do to honor such a great artist," Giles Knox said, "is to place his paintings in a secure and protected environment. Surely you must be aware that a house by the sea—complete with humidity, insects, and crumbling plaster—is hardly an ideal setting for works that deserve preservation."

"Are you interested in preserving the paintings?" she asked. "Or do you want to sell them?"

"Well, of course I—" He coughed and cleared his throat. "Of course I wish to preserve Dr. bin Yusuf's art for posterity. This is my ultimate priority. These works simply must be removed from the house."

"And?"

"Additionally, it would be my honor and privilege to assist you in placing such fine work in the hands of collectors who would be able to care for it in the manner it deserves."

"You want to sell the paintings," Jess said.

"And the sculptures." Giles Knox gave her a little smile. "For their safety."

"For the money."

"That, too."

"And what is Mr. Hafidh's interest in all this?"

Omar stared at her. "My mother owns some of her brother's artworks. She does not wish to keep them. Knox will take the canvases for a price, but he tells me that if he can offer the whole collection to a buyer, my mother's paintings will be worth more."

"That is correct," the gallery owner affirmed. "You see, Ms. Thornton, I have among my clientele a certain . . . collector. This gentleman lives in the United States. Los Angeles, California, to be exact. The man is a rather wealthy entrepreneur who has elected to invest in an impressive collection of African art. He is particularly fond of Dr. bin Yusuf's work, and in past years he has purchased nearly everything I was able to obtain."

"And now that the artist is dead," Jess said, "the art is worth a lot more, and the collector wants it all as an investment."

"You are correct."

"I don't see how one man thinks he can pay the kind of price those paintings and sculptures should fetch. We're talking about a lot of money, Mr. Knox."

"That is also correct." He smoothed a hand over his hair. "The gentleman is . . . shall we say . . . more than a little wealthy."

"Who is he?"

"Confidential information. Let me simply say that this man has made his mark in the Hollywood entertainment industry. An award-winning comedic actor. A producer of films and television. Even a best-selling author of three books of humor. Oh, yes, Ms. Thornton, my client can afford the art. And as an African-American himself, he respects the work for its heritage and cultural value. You may rest assured that your benefactor's masterpieces will receive the finest care, the ultimate in security, and the most ardent admiration."

"Sounds like a marriage made in heaven," Rick said. "What does Ms. Thornton get out of this deal?"

Giles Knox glanced at Rick. Then he leaned toward Jess and lowered his voice. "My dear madam, would you not prefer to discuss financial matters in private?"

Her head a whirlpool of questions, doubts, and concerns, Jess stared down at her half-eaten curry. If she sent Rick away, she would be at the mercy of these two predators. It was obvious their motive was money. What would they do to get their hands on it? Could they have killed Dr. bin Yusuf just to get at his paintings? Clearly Omar Hafidh had no love for his uncle. He wanted the money for himself and his mother. Would he hurt Jess if she refused to agree to his demands?

She felt she needed Rick's presence for protection. She also knew he could act as a witness on her behalf if anything in the negotiations went awry. But did she really want Rick to be a part of the discussion? He was her enemy, wasn't he? He had abandoned her. Betrayed her. Why did he suddenly feel like her only friend?

"Speak bluntly," she told Knox finally. "Just tell me exactly what it is you have to say. Mr. McTaggart is—" She stopped and stared at Rick. *Mr. McTaggart is what? My friend? My confidant? My husband?*

"Mr. McTaggart is my . . . he's my . . ."

"I'm her protector," Rick said. "Ten years ago I made that promise, and it's still good. She'll make her business decisions on her own, but I'm here to stand beside her and see that you treat her right. Give her the facts."

"Very well." Knox opened his briefcase. "Here is the procedure, Ms. Thornton. First, I need to take a complete inventory of all salable artwork stored at Uchungu House. Second, I need to speak with my client in the United States and negotiate a price. So I need your agreement to offer the art and then, when we arrive at a figure all can agree on, to accept the terms of sale."

He pulled a sheaf of typed pages out of his case. "Now, Ms. Thornton," he went on, "if you agree to permit me to function as agent in this matter, will you please sign this form? It is a simple legal document. A contract, if you will. It merely gives me exclusive rights to work with you during the negotiation for the sale of the art."

Jess studied the papers he handed her. Signing them would mean turning over Dr. bin Yusuf's lifework to a stranger. A stranger she didn't fully trust.

"I'll take this contract with me, Mr. Knox," she said finally. "I need some time to read it over, perhaps talk to a lawyer, think about the offer. I'll get back with you in a few days."

"My dear Ms. Thornton, I assure you, there is no one more qualified to assess the art than I. Dr. bin Yusuf entrusted his works to me for more than thirty years. I will arrange absolutely the best price. You will be more than happy." Again, he leaned across the table. "If you place this matter in my hands, you will become a wealthy woman, Ms. Thornton. Very wealthy."

His brown eyes shone like wet pebbles in a stream. Jess stared into them, vaguely aware of the sickly sweet smell of roses that seemed to be wafting from his hair. She didn't like this man. She didn't trust him. She didn't want to work with him. He might even be a killer.

"What's your commission?" she asked.

"Minuscule. A drop in the sea. Thirty-five percent."

"You're kidding."

"Without me, Ms. Thornton, you have a moldy house filled with a lot of rotting canvases and mildewed sculpture. With me, you have a wealthy buyer, a contract, and piles of lovely green money. Thirty-five percent is more than fair, I assure you."

"And if I say no to the whole deal?"

"You will regret it." He dropped the lid of his briefcase and snapped the clasps. "Here is my card. I shall be staying at the Africa House Hotel on Kaunda Road for the next three days. Good day, Ms. Thornton. Mr. McTaggart."

He stood, offered his dead-fish handshake, and walked across the courtyard. Omar Hafidh studied Jess for a moment.

"I will visit you at Uchungu House soon," he said. "We will discuss this matter."

Before she could respond, he followed the gallery owner out into the street.

Jess let out a breath. "Oh, Rick. I don't know what to do. I don't need to keep the paintings and sculptures, but at the same time, I don't want to dishonor Dr. bin Yusuf. And that Giles Knox. He gives me the creeps. Why should I sell the paintings through him? He seems slippery. The way he handed me that contract—like I would sign the thing without even reading it. And Omar Hafidh. Did you get a look at that guy's eyes?"

She frowned. Rick was smiling, his mouth soft and his blue eyes filled with a warm glow.

"What's so funny?" she asked.

"Nothing's funny. I'm just glad you're talking to me like I'm Rick McTaggart instead of Attila the Hun. I also like the way you sent Knox packing. He'll think twice before he tries to pull anything over on you again."

"Yeah, I really intimidated Omar, too. He's so scared that he's coming out to the house to visit me. He wants to *discuss this matter."* She imitated the man's thickly accented English. *"What my uncle wanted no longer matters. Ahmed Abdullah bin Yusuf is dead."*

"You said you thought Omar was a murderer. What was that all about, Jessie?"

She looked away. If she told Rick her fears . . . if she continued to include him in the discussion . . . if she treated him like a decent human being instead of a traitor . . . if she began to forgive him . . .

"It's nothing, really," she said, drawing into herself. "Just a feeling. I met Omar a few days ago when I went to talk to his mother about something concerning the house. The guy gives me the heebie-jeebies, that's all."

"You don't think Omar had anything to do with Dr. bin Yusuf's death, do you? I thought the old guy fell down a staircase."

Jess took a bite of her curry. It was cold. "Let's just drop it, Rick. I need to find a taxi and get back to the house. Splinter and Mama Hannah went to Nettie Cameron's house this morning, and I want to make sure they got home OK. In fact, I'm beginning to think I'd better keep Splint closer to the house until all this settles down."

She started to get up, but Rick put a hand on her arm. "You're worried, Jessie. I can see it in your eyes. You don't have to tell me what's bothering you. But I want you to know I meant what I said earlier. Ten years ago I promised to protect you. Until now, I've failed at the job. I'm willing to watch over you, Jessie. Whatever you need, just ask."

Jess hugged her purse into her lap as unbidden tears stung her eyes. How many times had she longed to hear those words? How many years had she ached over Rick's broken promises? And now it was too late. Too late.

"It's OK, Rick," she managed. "I'll take care of it myself."

"Will you let me say a prayer about all this?"

"Pray? You mean right now? Here?" She stared at him, again

startled by such unexpected words from a man she had thought she knew so well. "I . . . I guess it would be all right. I don't care what you do."

"If you don't care what I do, then let me take you home. There's no point in paying for a taxi when I can have you there in a few minutes."

"No, Rick, really, I don't think so. I'm fine."

"I know you're fine." Before she could leave, he laid both of his hands over one of hers. Then he bowed his head. "Father, I give Jessie and her many concerns into your care, just like I have all these years. Comfort her. Bring her peace. Lead her through the valleys. Teach her your paths. And please protect Splinter. Amen."

Jess hadn't managed to shut her eyes. Instead, she had stared at the man's bent head, his thick brown hair, the slope of his deeply tanned nose. Then she had glanced around to see who was watching. Fortunately, nobody was. And then she had heard Rick's words. A prayer for comfort and peace. A request to lead, teach, protect. A blessing.

"Come on," he said, pulling Jess to her feet. "I'll have you home in twenty minutes. Fifteen, if we want to be daring."

He gave her a wink and started across the courtyard. As she followed him, Jess decided Rick McTaggart was the strangest man she had ever met. Strange, contradictory, and so considerate. She was beginning to think she might even like him just a little bit.

◎ ◎ ◎

Rick decided he hadn't been so happy in years. More than happy. Joyous. A deep-down, abiding, all-consuming joy filled him so full he thought he might burst. As he drove his motorcycle down the road toward Uchungu House, he had to work to keep from laughing out loud. Or even worse—singing. He couldn't carry a tune in a bucket. But at this moment, he reckoned he might sound like Enrico Caruso.

The reason? Jessie sat right behind him, her hands warm at his waist and her skirt fluttering around her knees. His Jessie. Ever since this morning when he'd picked her up on the road to Zanzibar, she had seemed just that again—his Jessie. She had smiled at him, asked his advice, eaten with him, even held his hand.

Lord, she held my hand!

It was impossible to contain the prayer of thanksgiving that lifted Rick's heart. Against all reason, Jessie Thornton was allowing him into her life again. Maybe she didn't trust him very far, but at least she wasn't pushing him away. In fact, she seemed to almost enjoy his company.

After lunch, they had walked down the street, picked up a couple of school uniforms for Splinter, and even stopped in at the telephone company. Jessie permitted Rick to speak to the manager on her behalf—and now it looked like she might have phone service by the end of the month. The smile she had given him at the news could have lit up Uchungu House for a year.

Lord, thank you, Rick prayed as he negotiated the dirt road that led to the driveway. *Thank you for softening Jessie's heart. Teach me how to win her back. And please, Father, please don't let anything come between us again. Don't let anything drive us apart.*

"There's Mama Hannah!" Jessie's long arm reached over his shoulder as she pointed at the small dark figure on the verandah of Uchungu House. "She's been so good to us. I wonder where Splint is."

"I bet he's down on the beach," Rick said. When he turned his head, he could see Jessie's face. So close. Her cheeks were blushed by the wind, and her violet eyes shone. "I've seen him roaming around on the sand every chance he gets. Splint loves to pick up shells."

"You should see his collection."

"I'd like to."

He pulled the bike up to the edge of the verandah and cut the engine. Jessie slipped off and began unfastening her helmet. "Hi, Mama Hannah!" she called breathlessly. "How was the Scrabble game?"

"Oh, *toto,* Splinter has gone away. I cannot find him!" The old woman's hands were clasped tightly together. "I have looked all through the house. Every room. Miriamu has looked also. Solomon has searched the gardens up and down."

"What? Splinter's not here?" Jessie ran up the steps onto the verandah. "What do you mean you can't find him? Did he come back with you from Nettie's house?"

"Yes, but after we ate lunch, he went up to his room to work on his shell collection. I took a small nap. When I did not hear him after some time, I looked for him in his bedroom. He was gone."

Rick plunged after Jessie into the cool interior of the big old house. Calling her son's name, she raced through the honeycomb of rooms. The thick white walls echoed her despair.

"Splinter! Splint, where are you?" She rushed out into the courtyard. "This isn't funny, Splint! If you're playing some kind of a game, I want you to come out right this minute."

"He is not here, *memsahib!*" Miriamu glided down the back staircase, her brown eyes wide with concern. "I have looked in every room. I think he went outside."

"Has anyone checked the beach?" Rick asked.

"Solomon looked there first. The boy is not on the beach."

"What about Hunky Wallace? Did he go out today?"

"The white boat of *Bwana* Hunky is far out in the water. Near the reef. He would not have seen Splinter."

Rick took Miriamu's arm. "I want you to go down the road in the direction of Mrs. Cameron's house. Maybe Splint left something there and went back for it. Take Solomon with you. Hannah, you wait here in the house in case Splint wanders in. Check all the rooms again—especially the ones he'd be most curious about. The studios and storage rooms. Jessie, come with me."

He grabbed her hand and strode back through the house. Fear had paralyzed the boy's mother. Jessie's face was as white as the walls of Uchungu House, and her fingers were stiff and icy. Concern prickled down Rick's skin, even though he knew enough about young boys to have confidence that Splint would turn up.

"I used to wander away from our house all the time," he assured Jessie as they hurried toward the cliff-side steps. "My mother would be frantic. Dad was always furious. Daniel and the others would cry. But I knew where I was. I was never afraid. And it always turned out OK. Boys roam, Jessie. We'll find him."

"But you don't understand." Her voice shook as she spoke.

"Splint could be in danger. Someone could be after him. They might want to hurt him."

"Hurt Splint? Why? He's just a kid. Come on, Jessie."

"No, Rick! I'm not being paranoid. There are things you don't know about here. Dangers. People resent the fact that I own this house. They want me to leave. Maybe they would . . . would hurt Splint to . . . to get rid of me."

"Who resents your owning Uchungu House?" He held her hand tightly as they ran down the steep coral steps. "You'd better tell me about this, Jessie."

"No, I can't. It's none of your concern. . . . Splint!" she shouted. "Spencer Thornton, where are you?"

"Jessie, who are you afraid of? Omar?"

"Omar. Hunky. Even Solomon." She stumbled on a loose chunk of coral. Rick caught her just before she fell. "Dear God, if anyone hurts my son . . . Why did I let him go to Nettie's? That was so stupid! Splint? Splinter, where are you, honey? Answer me, Splint!"

"Jess, Hunky Wallace couldn't care less about the boy. He's after the treasure."

"I know that. But I also know that while he was alive, Dr. bin Yusuf wouldn't let Hunky dive out in the bay. And somebody . . . somebody murdered the professor."

"What?" Rick stopped as his feet touched the sand. "Murdered him?"

Jessie raced past him. Skirt flying, she ran headlong across the beach as she shouted her son's name. Stunned at her revelation, Rick watched her search the gray coral caves that rimmed the white sand. She poked her head into rugged pockmarks carved by the crashing waves. She tore through tangles of shrubbery. She searched the fronds of every palm tree. Jess was weeping now, and her cries had taken on a note of desperation so poignant Rick felt tentacles of fear curl through his stomach.

Somebody had killed Ahmed Abdullah bin Yusuf? Who would have wanted to do that? Omar Hafidh—to inherit a house he believed would be his? Giles Knox—to get his hands on an art collection he had coveted for years? Solomon—over some kind of disagreement with his employer? Hunky—to gain access to a sunken treasure ship?

Rick narrowed his eyes as he studied the small white diving boat that bobbed in the bay. He could see the hazy silhouettes of the workingmen. Hunky wasn't a murderer, was he? Sure, the man was ambitious. Greedy. Even a little ruthless. But he wouldn't kill. Would he?

The familiar figures moved back and forth, and Rick knew their actions as well as he knew his own name. They would be checking air compressors, cleaning tools, hoisting baskets, breaking up conglomerate. He could just make out Hunky's rotund form as the treasure hunter climbed onto the diving platform. There was Tibias—tall and lanky. And there was . . .

"Splinter!" he shouted. "Jessie, I've found him!"

Her head emerged from a thicket of low-growing lantana and Cape honeysuckle. "Where? Where is he?"

"He's on the *Sea Star* with Hunky Wallace."

"With Hunky! Oh, good heavens, you've got to get to him, Rick! Hunky could throw him overboard. He'd drown!"

"He's fine. See him?" He helped her out of the tangled brush and slipped an arm around her shoulder. "He's right there at the end of the boat. Hunky's going in for a dive, and Splint's helping feed the air hoses into the water. Look, he's got on a life jacket, Jessie. Hunky's got him all rigged up so he can't get hurt."

"Really?" She was crying freely now, tears running down her cheeks and dripping off her chin. "Are you sure, Rick? I can barely see him."

"It's Splint all right. I'd know those skinny legs anywhere."

She cupped her hands around her mouth. "Splinter!" she shouted. "Spencer Thornton!"

"He can't hear you. Too windy." Rick pulled her closer, aware of her anguish but so thankful to be near this woman that he could hardly concentrate. He reached out and wiped her cheeks with the side of his finger. "I'll go after him, Jessie. I'll bring him back to you."

"How can you do that? You don't have a boat."

"I'll swim. It's not as far as it looks. Splint made it out there, didn't he?" He gave her a smile. "You know, I suspect he really is as good a swimmer as he claims, Jessie."

She sniffled loudly. "Yeah, he's good. And he's in big trouble, too. He'll be lucky if I ever let him set foot in the ocean again after this."

"Aw, don't be too hard on him. He's just a boy. I used to be just like him."

The look Jessie gave him sent a wash of chills down Rick's spine. Her violet eyes seemed to confirm everything he suspected: *You are just like him,* she was saying silently. *You're his father.*

"Jessie," he began. "Is Splint—"

"Give me a minute to change into my bathing suit, Rick." She cut him off as she turned away, pulling out of his embrace and heading for the cliff-side steps. "I'll tell Mama Hannah you found Splint."

"You're going out to the boat?"

"Of course. I'm Splint's mother."

Her auburn hair swung as she ran across the sand. *She's his mother,* Rick thought. *And I'm his father.*

JESS was mad. She knew her anger was born of fear, but she couldn't suppress it. Didn't want to. She was mad at her son for his disobedience. Mad at Hannah for neglecting Splint. Mad at Hunky for allowing the boy on board his diving boat.

"What are you mad at *me* for?" Rick asked as Jess splashed out into the low surf. "I'm the one who found him."

"If you hadn't told Splinter all those wonderful stories about your great treasure-hunting adventures, he wouldn't have been so tempted to break my rules."

She glanced at the man beside her. Never in a million years would she have believed she'd be wearing a bathing suit in the presence of Rick McTaggart. The one-piece suit was a deep solid teal with flecks of gold, and she hadn't worn it for years. She felt gangly and pale and out of shape. Rick didn't seem to mind. In fact, his blue eyes were positively roving—which made her all the madder.

"Splinter's been dying to get on that diving boat," she snapped, "and you did nothing but encourage him!"

"I didn't give him permission to swim out to the *Sea Star.* But, Jessie, there *is* a sunken ship under the water. And it's in Splint's own backyard. That's the greatest thing a kid could ever wish for."

"Oh, you sound just like him!"

At her second admission of the similarities between father and son, Jess made a shallow dive into the waist-deep water. Drowning her mortification in the cool depths of the tropical bay, she floated over a patch of dark brown seaweed. Farther out, the water turned a deep emerald. Almost crystal clear, it revealed a myriad of tiny fluorescent fish, chunks of coral, and rippled white sand.

She could hear Rick swimming beside her, matching her stroke for stroke. How many times had they swum together in their youth? They had drifted countless hours in the waters of the Indian Ocean, laughing, splashing each other, delighting in the joy of their passion. It was on a beach that she had first realized how much she loved Rick McTaggart. On a beach that he had asked her to marry him. On a beach that she had said yes.

"You know, you've got the best swimming hole on Zanzibar Island," Rick said. He had turned onto his back and was paddling along with his eyes closed. "There's not a stretch of water that's calmer, safer, or prettier from here to Bombay."

"I guess. I really haven't been out much."

"I've never seen you swimming here."

"That's because I haven't been swimming yet. I'm too busy."

"Too busy to have fun?"

"I have responsibilities, you know. I have to keep the house running, keep food on the table, keep an eye on my son."

"Busy, busy, busy on Zanzibar Island."

Jess scowled. She didn't like Rick teasing her so much. He had no idea what it meant to be the head of a household and carry the weight she had for so many years. No, she didn't have time for fun. Swimming, dancing, riding the motorcycle . . . all the things she used to love . . . took just too much time. They seemed silly to her now. Childish.

Maybe Rick thought she was a dud, but so what? She knew she was boring. Being responsible and mature was boring. Adulthood was boring. But what choice did she have?

"Hey, what's that down there?" Rick asked. He was swimming on his stomach again and pointing at something he'd seen in the water. "Right there by that piece of coral."

"I don't see anything."

"Hold on a minute. I'm going down."

Jess floated while he dived into the warm water. She didn't like to open her eyes in the briny water, so she couldn't make out what he had found. All the same, her heart began to beat a little faster as he emerged, hands cupped tightly and rivulets of seawater pouring down his hair.

"What is it?" she asked, swimming closer. "What did you find?"

"I'm not sure."

"Is it alive?"

"I don't know. Take a look."

He held out his hands, and she bent over to peer between them. A thin stream of water suddenly shot up straight into her face.

"Gotcha!" Rick laughed out loud. Before she could move away, he took aim and fired at her a second time. Water squirted into her mouth, her nose, her hair.

"Rick McTaggart!" She sloshed a wave over his head. "You sneak! You tricked me."

"Didn't think you'd fall for it!" He flicked a few drops of water into her face. "Uh-oh, there it goes again. I think it's after you."

"Rat!" She grabbed his shoulders and tried her best to dunk him. Spluttering, he sank in a fountain of bubbles. As she wondered what he might try next, she felt his hand wrap around her bare ankle and give a jerk.

She went under, struggled until he let her go, and came up laughing. Rick burst out of the water beside her. He blew a long stream straight up into the air and let it rain back down on his face. Then he turned and gave her a silly grin as water dripped off his eyelashes.

"You are a nut," she said.

"You're a squid."

"Well, you're a sea slug."

"You're a coelacanth."

"A what?"

By this time he was swimming again, outpacing her easily. She could see him just ahead, his strong brown arms pumping through the water. Jess followed, for the first time actually enjoying the warm waves, the steamy kiss of afternoon sunshine on her skin, the glow of having felt silly and girlish.

"What's a coelacanth?" she called. "Is that some kind of an eel? Are you calling me an eel, buster?"

Rick didn't answer, and Jess swam on. The buoyant water hardly tired her, and she was surprised when she looked up to find the dive boat just a few feet away. Splinter was standing under its white metal canopy, his face pinched and pale and his eyes round with the terrible anticipation of his impending doom. Jess had seen that look on her son's face a thousand times.

"Spencer Thornton," she called. "Is that you up there?"

"Yes, ma'am." His voice sounded so tiny it almost made her waver in her determination to be as harsh as she felt he deserved.

"I told you never to come out here, Spencer. You disobeyed me."

"I know, and I'm sorry, but Mama Hannah was asleep, and I just wanted to go down to the beach to look for some more shells. And then I saw Hunky's boat, and it didn't seem that far away, so I thought I'd just swim around a little. But then I realized I was getting farther and farther out, and then Hunky spotted me and waved, and so I just decided—"

"Spencer Thornton!" Jess grabbed the edge of the diving platform.

She was just about to haul herself up, when Rick emerged beside her. He leaned close and whispered in her ear. "A coelacanth is a prehistoric fish that everybody thought was extinct. The whole scientific community believed it was lost forever. But then some fishermen caught a coelacanth in their net, and now we know the species still exists. Everybody's rejoicing."

Jess studied his blue eyes. "What on earth are you talking about?"

"Coelacanths. You. Splinter. Once you were lost to me . . . and Splint was lost to you. But now you're both found. 'Always be joyful. Keep on praying. No matter what happens, always be thankful, for this is God's will for you who belong to Christ Jesus.' It's in 1 Thessalonians."

She stared at him for a moment. Maybe God really was as big a part of Rick's life as he claimed. He sure enjoyed quoting his Bible verses. *Always be joyful. Always be thankful. Easier said than done,* Jess thought as she hauled herself up onto the platform. But when she faced her son and saw the tears gathered at the rims of his eyelids, she couldn't keep from pulling the boy into her arms.

"Oh, Splinter, honey, I was so worried about you!"

"I'm sorry, Mom. I didn't think it all through carefully. It wasn't like I planned to come out here. It just sort of happened. And then when I got onto the *Sea Star,* I forgot about everything else." He glanced across the bay. "How's Mama Hannah? Is she mad at me, too?"

"She was concerned. Miriamu and Solomon went all the way back to Nettie's house looking for you."

"Well, that's OK. Gives 'em more time to smooch."

"Smooch?"

"Ah, Ms. Thornton!" Hunky climbed into the boat and deposited a large chunk of black conglomerate on the deck. "So you've decided to join us after all. And McTaggart, too? Well, isn't this a merry party?"

"We've been searching for Splinter," Jess said.

"And here he is. Safe and sound."

"When you realized what he was up to, Hunky, you should have taken him right back to shore."

"And forced him to miss the greatest moment of his life? Not ruddy likely. Look, I've put the wee chap into a life vest so he'll be safe and sound for his doting mother. But truth to tell, I've been grateful for his help this afternoon. The boy's a quick learner. He's good with the air hoses, and he's already done a fine job working on the conglomerate. Show her what you've found, lad."

The Scotsman's praise was all the impetus Splint needed. He raced to the prow of the boat and bent over a woven palm-leaf basket. In a moment he straightened, holding a fat, triangle-shaped chunk of metal.

"It's a padlock!" he exclaimed. "It was all covered by this black junk, see. But I broke through the conglomerate and got it out."

"Conglomerate?" In spite of her determination to be firm and uncompromising, Jess found herself walking toward her son to take a look at the padlock. She had rarely seen Splint so excited—and that was saying something, since the smallest details of life so often thrilled him. His eyes sparkled, and his grin stretched from one pink-tinged ear to the other. He was probably going to be sunburned and sore tonight, but she had no doubt he wouldn't care in the least.

"Conglomerate is this stuck-together gunk," he told his mother, holding up a chip. "Over the centuries, when iron and other materials chemically decompose, conglomerate forms. See how it's kind of pebbly? Hunky says you can't tell the difference between conglomerate and ballast rock just by looking. You have to hit it with a hammer. On ballast, the hammer bounces, but on conglomerate, a black residue puffs out."

"Yeah, and Hunky loves to hit things with hammers," Rick said, joining them in the prow of the boat. "Splint, I expect you to be extremely careful when you work with conglomerate. Remember, you're holding a piece of history there. If you pound it too hard, you'll break it. And that's destruction we can't afford."

"Aye, fill his head with your warnings and admonitions," Hunky put in. "Next thing you know, he'll be giving me lectures, too. Take a look at this, McTaggart, and see how patient and meticulous you want to be now!"

The bald Scotsman's blue eyes lit up as he lifted a hunk of coral-encrusted clumps into the air. "How does this sweet little biscuit suit you, Mr. Scientist? Do you know what this is? Aye, I can see by the look on your face you do. We found it this morning, and there's more down there besides. I think we're close to the mother lode."

"What is it?" Splint asked, hopping up and down for a better look. "Is it gold? Is it pieces of eight?"

"It's silver coins," Rick said, taking the distinctive chunk of coral from the treasure hunter. He held the coral in both hands so Splint could examine it. "We call this a biscuit. Coral grows around the coins and seals them together in the exact pattern they were in when they tumbled out of the ship."

"I want to break it apart! Let me do it! I'll get the hammer."

"No, Splint," Rick said, catching one skinny arm. "We don't break these. First I'll X-ray the biscuit to see how sturdy the coins are. Then I'll dip it in an acid bath that dissolves the coral. Sometimes the X-ray shows that only the coral covering is left, and the object inside has disintegrated. But even that can be useful to me. I can treat the coral like a mold and recreate what was inside it. That way I can study the artifact, even if there's nothing left."

"Wow! Can I help you? I'll be really careful, I promise."

"Right now you can put this biscuit into that tank of seawater. Exposure to the air can destroy these artifacts, Splint. Salt water keeps them safe until I have a chance to examine them."

"Rick, did you notice the date on this padlock?" Jess asked. She had been studying the hunk of rusted iron, her artist's eye combing it for interesting details. "It reads eighteen-something-or-other. Maybe that's an eight . . . or is it a three?"

"What!" He grabbed the lock and peered down at it. "Hunky, she found it! We've got a date! Oh, Jessie." He flung an arm around her shoulder, pulled her close, and gave her cheek a warm kiss. Then he was gone, striding across the deck toward the Scotsman. "This is fantastic! Hunky, where did you find the padlock? Which quadrant? Don't tell me you didn't write it down!"

"Calm yourself, Mr. Scientist. Even though we didn't have you or your chum Andrew Mbuti peering over our shoulders, we did mark the padlock on your pretty little chart. Take a look here."

The two men bent over a sheet of plastic-covered paper while Splinter turned the coral biscuit over and over. Jess fingered a strand of wet hair out of her eyes and sat down on the vinyl-upholstered bench seat in the prow. She felt damp, tired, and a little disoriented. This morning, she'd been focused on school and business. Now she was smack-dab in the middle of a treasure hunt. And she'd found a clue to the ship's date!

Strangely elated, she watched her son carefully sorting through the objects in the salt-water tank. The curve of his sun-browned back mirrored exactly the bare physique of his father a few feet away. Both were tall, well formed, handsome. More significant, they were twins in spirit and intellect. How long could she keep them apart? And did she really want to?

"Let me show you all this awesome stuff, Mom," Splinter said, wiping his wet fingers on his bathing trunks. He took her hand and pulled her to her feet. "See, these are the compressors. They feed fresh air through those hoses down to the divers. It's such a cool design, because this way the divers don't even need scuba gear! They can dive for hours without worrying about running out of air. And they're a lot freer because they don't have to carry a big tank on their backs. Now this is the motor, see? And here are the gas cans. We keep them really safe in this container off to one side. Hunky won't let me touch them."

"That's a relief."

"And here's some of the diving equipment. We have face masks, flippers, weight belts, snorkel tubes, and diving suits. If you don't have a weight belt, you can't go down. You won't sink! Did you know that, Mom? And guess what! Heavier people need *more* weights!"

"Is that right?" As usual, Jess felt a little overwhelmed at the rush of information pouring out of her son.

"Yeah, even though they're heavier, their bulk makes them buoyant. So they float! You should see the size of Hunky's weight belt."

"What are you saying about me, there, laddie?" The Scotsman tossed Jess a face mask. "Speaking poorly of my figure, are you? Well, sir, just for that, I'm going to have to ask you and your mama to follow me down into the water. Perhaps the both of you will learn some manners if you spend a little time in my company."

"No, Hunky," Jess said, setting the mask on the bench. "I'm not going to allow—"

"Please, Mom! Please, please, please! Just this once? I'll be so careful. You can come, too. You can watch me every second. Oh, Mom, let me go down and just see the wreck."

"Splinter, I've told you—"

"Just let me look at it really fast. Just so I can say I did. Please, Mom, you've got to let me!"

"I don't believe this." She glanced at Rick. Though his face was carefully composed, she could read the look in his eyes. *Let the boy go, Jessie. Give him this gift.*

"I swear I'll go to school every morning without complaining," Splint said. "I'll make my bed every day. I'll never argue with Mama Hannah. I'll brush my teeth six times a day. I'll—"

"That's enough, Splint." She let out a breath and looked at Rick. "What do you think?"

"I'll go down with him. I'll watch him like a hawk."

"I should have known where you'd stand." All the same, she was thankful for his offer. "All right, Splint. I'll let you see the ship. But I'm coming, too."

"Mom, you're awesome! You're the best! The greatest! I love you forever!" Splint threw his gangly arms around her neck and squeezed until she felt her face turning red. And then he went skipping off to try on face masks. "Treasure of Zanzibar, here we come!"

◎◎◎

Splinter slid off the diving platform at the end of the *Sea Star* and waved at his mom. She was doing her usual worried-mother routine. First, she'd made Rick go over and over the procedure of how to use the breathing gear. Then she'd fussed about making sure everyone's face mask fit tightly enough and all the flippers were the right size. Of course, Splint's were too big, but he didn't care. Now she was going round and round about the weight belts. Too heavy? Too light? Too bulky? Too flimsy?

Splint was surprised Rick didn't just dive in and leave her on the boat. Hunky Wallace already had. If he didn't think his mom would have a cow about it, Splint would have followed the treasure hunter straight down to the sunken ship. But what chance did a guy have to be bold when his mother was always hanging around nitpicking over this and that? All the same, he knew he should be thankful to get to explore the wreck at all. If his mom had followed her normal pattern, he'd be in his room right this minute, grounded for the rest of his life.

Zanzibar had changed Splint's mom. As he bobbed in the water, he could see the difference written all over her face. While Rick worked to fasten the weight belt around her waist, she was laughing out loud. No, she was giggling. Giggling! Splint didn't think he'd ever heard his mom giggle. She seemed to be smiling an awful lot the last day or so. She sort of bounced when she walked, too. And the way she flipped her hair behind her ear and tilted her head to the side when she looked at Rick . . . weird.

"You're sure there aren't any sharks down there?" she was asking him.

"Positive."

"What about eels?"

"Just a few sea slugs."

She laughed at that, as though it was the funniest thing in the world. Who could figure? Splint was grateful when Rick finally went into the water. Splint's mom slipped off the dive platform and took Rick's hand. There were more instructions, more giggles, and finally it was time to go down.

Gripping the breathing tube in his mouth, Splint allowed the weight belt to slowly pull him farther and farther under the water. Finally he understood what it would be like to be a fish. Such freedom! He could swim all over the place without having to come up for air. As they descended, Rick motioned Splint to grab his nose and blow hard in order to ease the pressure in his ears. Rick was amazing. He knew everything!

A vision of magic unfolded before Splint's eyes as he drifted down. He could see the anchor rope and air hoses running from the *Sea Star* to the ocean floor. Fish swam past him—angel fish dressed in black-and-white stripes, tiny fluorescent bluefish that swam in quick darting schools, and countless other unnamed species arrayed in shades of orange, blue, yellow, and red. Splint couldn't wait to look them up in his encyclopedia of sea life.

And then the wreck materialized before him. At first, it was a huge disappointment. There were a few spongy-looking timbers that had been mostly eaten up by worms. Some hunks of coral lay scattered at one end. Three large holes had been dug, but they were empty. And that was it. Sure didn't look like a sunken galleon to Splint. You couldn't swim in and out of portholes or climb undersea staircases or anything.

But then Rick drifted over and took Splint's hand. He pointed out the gridwork of chains that had been laid over the wreck. Then he showed Splint a large stiff plastic sheet onto which the grid had been drawn. Four stones held it pinned to the sand. Rick took a black crayon from under a chunk of coral and carefully marked and labeled the place where the biscuit of silver coins had been found.

After that, the time flew. Rick showed Splint and his mom where the coins had been found on the actual wreck. Then he taught them how to fan the sand away with their hands and search for more biscuits. After a while, one of the other divers brought over a big tube that looked like the end of a vacuum cleaner. Sure enough, the thing sucked up sand like nobody's business! Whoa! Anything of any size was uncovered in the blink of an eye.

While his mom did a little exploring, Splint got to work the wreck with Rick. They searched all around a pile of rounded stones, vacuuming everything with meticulous care. Splint loved the feel of his fingers working slowly over the rocks, turning them this way and that, gently searching for anything of significance. He watched Rick and copied the way the scientist picked things up and looked them over before setting them down in the exact place he'd found them.

Sure was different from Hunky. Twenty feet away, he and his men were attacking a hole they'd dug with the vacuum, going at it like demons. Sand drifted all around them like a mist, making the water murky and unpleasant. They were chopping at blobs of sea grass with big long knives, carving crevices into which they dipped and dipped, looking for treasure. Splint decided he liked Rick's scientific methods a whole lot better. When he grew up, he wanted to be just like Rick. A marine archaeologist.

He and Rick had just uncovered a big hunk of conglomerate when Splint's mom swam over holding something in her arms. You'd have thought Rick had been shot. He jerked toward her, took the thing, and cradled it carefully. Pointing at it, he gave Splint the thumbs-up sign about ten times, and then he spat out his breathing gear and planted a great big kiss on Splint's mom's cheek.

It was the second time he'd done that. Splint was beginning to think he ought to keep count.

In no time flat, everybody was floating up toward the boat. The minute Rick's head burst out of the water, he yanked off his mask.

"Wahoo! You did it, Jessie!" he shouted.

"What did I find? Isn't it some kind of a vase?"

"Aye, that it is, Ms. Thornton," Hunky shouted as he paddled toward the boat. "'Tis a porcelain urn, Chinese in origin. What dynasty, Mr. Scientist?"

"K'ang-Hsi."

"Worth a small fortune, if I'm correct. And it looks to be perfect!"

"But there's a small chip—"

"A small chip, she says. My dear lady, in this business, anything 80 percent intact is considered perfect. If we've only got half the piece we call it almost whole. And if it's at least recognizable, it's termed as almost intact. This is a treasure. A true treasure!"

"Yay, Mom!" Splint crowed. He had had no idea his mom was so cool. She had found a treasure, and she'd only been in the water once!

"The urn is worth more than Hunky knows," Rick said as they climbed aboard one by one. "K'ang-Hsi was emperor of China from 1661 to 1722. That gives us a definitive bottom line on dating the wreck. Plus, we know that Spain was a primary importer of this kind of porcelain. Since Spain had little to do with Zanzibar, we can deduce that this china was probably carried on board a Portuguese ship. We also know that in 1832, Seyyid Said bin Sultan moved his capital to Zanzibar from Muscat. So that establishes Arab dominance on the island. And we've got a padlock that's dated in the 1800s."

"What are you saying, McTaggart?" Hunky demanded.

"I'm saying that I calculate we've found ourselves a Portuguese bark that wrecked sometime in the early 1800s. If we search the records, we might find out exactly which one it is. And that'll tell us what we can expect to find on board."

"Well, I'll be a tongue-tied Scotsman. Do you mean to tell me that our reluctant Ms. America has not only dated our shipwreck but she's discovered it's nationality, too?"

Splint looked around at his mother. As usual, she was paying no attention to the scientific discussions that so fascinated her son. In fact, she had scrounged a pad of paper and a pencil, and she was sketching the K'ang-Hsi urn. Leave it to her to start drawing! And right after she'd made the best discovery of the whole adventure.

He squatted down beside the salt-water tank to watch Hunky hammering on the newest chunk of conglomerate. If only his mom would let him, Splint knew he could become a valuable part of this diving team. After all, he'd only been on board one afternoon, and he already could man the air hoses, break conglomerate, dive with the breathing gear, and work the vacuum. He could help a lot! Maybe he'd even find the biggest treasure of all.

Of course, his mom probably wouldn't let him on the boat again. Not after he'd disobeyed her like that. Splint looked over to where she was sketching. Rick McTaggart had sat down right beside her, and the two of them were going over her sketch. They kept pointing to this and that, their fingers touching. And then they would say stuff while they looked straight into each other's eyes. It was the weirdest thing.

Splint couldn't stop watching them, even when Hunky began to exclaim about something he'd found in the conglomerate. Splint just kept staring and staring at his mom and Rick McTaggart. And the more he stared, the more he realized how comfortable they were with each other. Like they knew things only the two of them shared. Like they understood each other without even talking. Like they fit together.

Right at that moment, Splint suddenly thought about how strange it was that his mom had auburn hair, but he himself had brown hair . . . the exact color of Rick's. His mom had a triangle-shaped face with high cheekbones, but Splint had a square face with a strong jawline . . . exactly like Rick's. And his mom had pale, creamy skin that burned to a crisp, but Splint had olive skin that tanned easily . . . just like Rick's.

Then he looked at his mom's toes. And then at Rick's. Splint had Rick's feet. Splint had Rick's hands. Splint had Rick's teeth and smile and ears and shoulders.

"Mom!" he shouted.

She glanced up, her eyes suddenly filled with concern. "What is it, honey? What's wrong?"

Splint stared at her. "Nothing."

"You sure?"

"Nothing."

He needed time to think this over. If his deductions were correct, he had just stumbled on the grandest, most glorious, most splendid treasure of all.

Rick McTaggart was his father.

11

JESS decided she had to restore normalcy to her life. Things had gotten out of perspective. Confusing. Disordered. Cloudy. She wanted to put the controls back into her own hands. She needed time to sort through her priorities. She needed distance from Rick McTaggart.

For nearly a week, Jess kept Splinter busy around the house. In the mornings he played with Hannah, and in the afternoons he and his mom went for walks, read books, and sketched together. Miriamu worked in the kitchen, as usual. Solomon, who had somehow managed to hang the car engine from the limb of a Red Hot Poker tree, tinkered with pistons and gaskets when he wasn't tending the yard. After the trauma of the encounter with Giles Knox and the adventure on the treasure ship, life began to feel almost calm.

Jess received a large royalty check for her work on the first eight Kima the Monkey books. She was relieved to be able to pay Miriamu, Solomon, and Hannah. Day by day, the illustrations for her ninth book began to come together. With the familiar figure of Kima the Monkey dancing around the pages, Jess finally captured the personality of this installment's star, the irritable and impatient impala.

Long, lyre-shaped black horns made the antelope a beautiful creature. Her seductive brown eyes had a delicate streak of white above, and gentle tan shading below. Two white patches on her face—one beneath the nostrils and above the mouth, the other under her lower lip—gave Impala the look of a lovely, pouty queen. Jess had no trouble transforming the natural beauty and grace of the antelope into an appealing but exasperating character.

Splinter loved to read aloud lines from James Perrott's rollicking text, and he enjoyed helping his mother plan the painting that would accompany the words. As long as Jess could remember, her son had dawdled at her side while she sketched and illustrated. In fact, Splint provided her with a strong dose of inspiration. She had never mentioned it to anyone, but the little monkey in her award-winning books shared many traits with a certain overactive, impish, and excitable boy.

"Let me decide where to put Impala on the next page," Splint begged one afternoon as he lounged, feet up on the table, in Jess's studio. "I'll remember what you told me about design and balance."

"OK," she said. "I'll close my eyes and listen while you read the words. Remember, on this page the monkey is doing most of the talking. Actually, he's scolding Impala, so we want to put Kima in the dominant position on the page."

"Here's what Kima says." Splint cleared his throat and held up the page of manuscript.

"'You fuss and gripe and irritate.
'You scold and push and never wait.
'And that is why, my dear Impala,
'No one's coming to your birthday gala.'

Kima finished and sat down.
He watched Impala start to frown.
But then that frown turned into tears—
A thing no one had seen in years!"

"Poor Impala," Jess said. "She's crying. Maybe Kima shouldn't have been quite so blunt with her."

"You're wrong, Mom. All the animals were talking about Impala behind her back, saying how grumpy and irritable she always acted. And none of them were planning to go to her birthday party. Kima did the right thing to just go right up to Impala and tell her the truth. People ought to tell the truth. You've always said that, Mom."

Jess studied her son. Splint had been trying so hard to please her and to obey the rules she had set for him. He hadn't complained once about his five-day suspension from all beach activities, even though she knew he was aching to get back to the sand and water. He had missed Rick and Hunky so much. . . . He talked of little else but the wreck, yet he hadn't laid eyes on the crew since the day of his escapade.

Although Jess had seen the men come and go each day, she had made it a point not to go down and talk with anyone. Rick's obvious interest in her, the fun they had shared in the water, and the instinctive trust she had placed in him all scared her half to death. He was beckoning her back to him. Calling her. Setting out lure after lure. Reeling her in so slowly she hadn't noticed she'd been hooked.

And Splinter? He'd already been landed. The boy could not have adored anyone more than he did Rick. The man was his idol.

"Don't you think I'm right, Mom?" he asked. "Don't you think we should always tell the truth? Even if it might hurt?"

Jess shifted uncomfortably. "Well, I think . . . I think Kima did the right thing to tell Impala why none of the other animals were planning to show up at her birthday party. James Perrott wants children to understand that in order to have friends, you have to be friendly."

"But don't you think there's another message in the story, Mom? It's not only what Impala's learning that's important. It's what Kima showed by his actions in going straight to Impala with the reality of the situation. I think James Perrott is trying to teach kids that even though the facts might hurt a little at first, it's usually better in the long run to tell the whole truth."

"I guess you're right. That's probably a theme in this book." She selected a charcoal pencil. "So where do you think we ought to put Impala? And do you think Kima should be in a tree or on the ground when he's confronting Impala?"

"Mom, do you always tell me the truth?"

"What a thing to ask, honey. I'm your mother. Do you think I would ever lie to you?"

"Well . . ." He rolled her wad of moldable eraser between his fingers. "I've been wondering about my dad."

An icy curl slid through her stomach. "Splint, I told you a long time ago about what happened between your father and me. Did you think I was lying to you?"

He shrugged one shoulder, his focus still fastened on the eraser. "I guess not."

"No, Splint, I did not lie. Listen, if it will make you feel better, I'll tell you the story again. Your father and I met when we were both very young. Too young, really. I was only eighteen, you know."

"So are you saying it was all a big mistake?"

Jess thought for a moment. She had discovered she had to listen very carefully to her son. Often his questions had several layers of significance. If she wasn't sensitive in her responses, he sometimes drew inaccurate conclusions.

"*You* weren't a mistake, Splint," she said finally. "You were a gift to me. My treasure. But your father and I were probably much too young when we got married. We couldn't figure out how to work through our problems—and you know every relationship has some problems, no matter how right it is. When your father decided to leave our marriage, I was pregnant with you. We lived in Dar es Salaam, and Mama Hannah helped us by taking care of you while I studied art with Dr. bin Yusuf. Then you and I moved to London where we lived until now. OK, sweetheart? That's the story."

It sounded so simple—too simple. For years, that story had been enough for the boy. Now? Now, her fingers were trembling as she sharpened her pencil. She couldn't make herself look at her son. Was she lying to him? Was it wrong not to tell him about Rick?

"I was just wondering," he began. "Wondering about something . . ."

Jess closed her eyes and took a deep breath. "What, Splint?"

"Well . . . what did my father look like?"

"Oh, he was sort of tall, I guess." She gave a casual shrug, but her insides were experiencing an earthquake that could knock the top off the Richter scale. "He had brownish hair. There was nothing very unusual or specific about him. Not anything you'd really notice. But he was nice looking, of course."

"Do I look like him?"

"Maybe a little. But you have my eyes."

"What color were my father's eyes?"

Her pencil made a wobbly squiggle across her sketch pad. "I guess they were sort of bluish."

"Bluish?"

"OK, they were blue."

"Could you draw a picture of him?"

"Splint, honey, I'm . . . I'm much better with animals, you know. I doubt I could draw anything that looked like your father. Remember the time I tried to do an illustration for that runners' magazine? You told me the man looked like he had frog's legs. And then I worked on that picture of Old Mother Hubbard, and you said—"

"Mom, have you looked for my father since you came back to Africa?"

She was silent, trying to calm her heart. "No, honey. I haven't looked for him."

"Why not? Don't you want to see him again? Don't you want to find out what he's doing these days? Don't you think he might want to meet me?"

"Splint . . . the past is . . . well, it all happened a long time ago. I have a new life now. Things are very different."

"Yeah, but what about my life? What if I wanted to meet my dad and get to know him? Didn't you ever think about that?"

"Of course I've thought about that, but, Splinter—"

"And what if you found out you really liked him after all? What if he's a great guy? What if he's like . . . like Rick McTaggart or something?"

"Spencer, listen to me, honey." She covered his hand with hers and forced herself to look into his violet eyes. "You know I love you very much. I always do what I believe is best for you. Right?"

"I guess."

"Now, I need you to trust that the decisions I've made about things that happened a long time ago are the best ones."

"Yeah, and I need something, too. I need you to tell me the truth."

"Spencer Thornton," she said, her voice stern, "I'll do what I think is right for you, and that's that."

"Even if it means lying to me?" He jumped up from his chair, big tears suddenly gathering in his eyes. "You mean you wouldn't tell me if you found my father? Why not? Just because you think knowing the truth might hurt me somehow? Well, that stinks! Kima the Monkey told the truth even though it made Impala cry. And I bet Impala gets adjusted to it. I bet Impala even changes herself so that everything works out great."

He grabbed the manuscript Jess had been working from and tossed aside the first half. Papers scattered across the floor like a stack of spilled hay as Splint pulled the last pages to the front and read rapidly. Before Jess could protest, he was flapping the manuscript in her face. "I was right! Impala even thanks Kima for helping her by telling her the truth! You're *supposed* to tell the truth! Kima did, and it helped Impala. She learned how to be nice. I could learn how to be a good son if I had a father. Every kid I know has a dad! It's not fair to come all this way to Africa and not find him. I want him, even if you don't!"

Jess stood, clutching her charcoal pencil. "Spencer," she said in a choked voice. "I am your mother, and I will make the right decisions for your life. Now I expect you to get control of yourself, young man. Nettie Cameron is coming here for tea any minute, and I'd prefer she didn't have to hear you having a tantrum."

"You think I won't find out the truth. You think you can hide it from me. But I'm smart! I'll figure it out. Then I'll have a dad, and he'll be better than you because he won't lie to me!"

"Spencer Thornton, I want you to go downstairs this minute and see if Nettie's here. And help Miriamu set the table."

"I'll go live with my father, and then you won't be able to boss me around anymore! He'll let me do what I want. He won't ground me from the beach for five days. He'll understand me a lot better than you ever did. I'll figure out who my dad is, and then you'll be sorry you never told me the truth!"

"Downstairs, Spencer!" she shouted back at her son. "Now!"

Splint hurled her eraser to the floor. It bounced in drunken angles as the boy bolted out the door. Jess could hear his footsteps pounding down the circular staircase near her room.

"Oh, Lord!" She sank into her chair and draped across her desk, cheek pressing the cool white sheet of her sketch pad and arms covering her head. "Lord, what have I done? What should I do?"

She needed help! But where could she turn? She had no close friends. With an issue as important as this, she couldn't trust even someone as kindly as Nettie Cameron. Rick would be the last person she should tell. And Hannah . . . Hannah would probably agree with Splint. A son should have a father.

"Oh, God!" she murmured again. "Help me. Help me."

God was supposed to be a friend. Hannah had sung a favorite chorus over and over to the four little Thornton children. Jess recalled it now, the words lilting through her mind as clearly as they had so long ago at her *ayah*'s feet.

What a friend we have in Jesus,
All our sins and griefs to bear!
What a privilege to carry
Everything to God in prayer!

Everything? Rick certainly gave a lot of weight to his newfound faith, Jess thought. The image of carrying everything to God—all her hopes for the future and her griefs from the past—was such a compelling picture it brought tears to her eyes. But hadn't she prayed just this way once before? Not long after she had moved into Uchungu House, she had prayed in this very room. What had she asked for? It had been something about Rick.

Make him go away. Don't let me ever have to see him again.

That certainly hadn't happened. God hadn't taken him away at all. In fact, she'd seen Rick McTaggart almost every day. Then Jess recalled the rest of her prayer. *God, if you're out there anywhere, if you care about me at all, please fix this. Please help me get through this. Heal the brokenness inside me so I don't have to feel so awful anymore. I'm choking from it. I'm dying inside. Please just fix it!*

"Heal me," she mouthed again. "Fix me."

All her efforts to keep the controls of her life in her own hands were crumbling. Her son wanted his father. If Rick knew the truth, he would want his son. Worst of all . . . Jess couldn't keep squelching the desire she felt to unite them . . . to bring father and son together . . . to have them both as a real and vital part of her own life.

"No!" she ground out, hammering the sketch pad with her fist.

Hadn't things been better when she'd been filled with anger? Filled with resentment? Filled with bitterness? Then she had known who she was, known who Rick was, known who Splinter was. Everyone had had a place, and she had been in control.

But it had been a lie. Rick wasn't the demon, the renegade, the ultimate betrayer. He was a man. A man who had made mistakes and regretted them. He had changed his life, and now he wanted her forgiveness. No, he hadn't changed his life—God had! Rick McTaggart was a committed Christian man . . . kind, loving, generous, responsible . . . a man who deserved to be a father.

And Splint? He wasn't a content, self-sufficient little boy who needed only a mother, good food, and a decent night's sleep. Splint was a complicated, intelligent man-child who understood concepts far beyond his years. He had the potential to contribute wonderful things to his world. Or to become as bitter and resentful as his mother had been. He needed the kind of love and strength that a man could provide. He needed the molding hands of a father.

The person Jess had been the most wrong about was herself. She wasn't the unconquerable fortress who needed no one. She was lonely. She was tired of grasping onto her anger and coddling her bitterness. Relief was possible. . . . She could let go. . . . She could give up the controls of her life. . . .

"Father," she whispered, "forgive me. Please come into my life the way you're in Rick's. I'm so tired of being the boss. Teach me how to forgive Rick. Help me know what to say to Splint. Even though my prayers have been angry and doubtful, you've heard them. You've been working in my life. Father . . . Jesus . . . I love you. Please heal me."

She lay across her desk for a long time, unable to move. Tears dampened the paper under her cheek and seeped into her hair. Her heart felt empty. Empty of hate and anger and frustration. And it felt full, too. For the first time in years, she felt full of something indescribable.

Maybe it was peace.

౯౯౯

"Mom, Nettie's here!" Splint shouted up the stairwell. "She's out on the verandah."

Jess lifted her head and brushed at her cheek.

"You better get down here, Mom. Miriamu's bringing out the tea. I'm going to get the Scrabble board and whip both of you!"

Jess gave a laugh that was half sob. Children were so resilient. "I'm coming, Splint," she called.

"Nettie brought you some flowers! Bird-of-paradise. You're going to need one of those urns out of Dr. bin Yusuf's storeroom."

"OK." Jess smiled as she ran a brush through her hair and straightened her collar. Splint was in his room now, but he could yell loudly enough to be heard all over the house.

"Want me to get an urn for you, Mom?"

"That'd be great, honey."

For some reason she couldn't explain, Jess felt almost serene as she descended the circular staircase. On the verandah, Nettie Cameron rose to greet her. She had pulled her white hair up into a chignon at the top of her head, leaving wispy tendrils curling around her neck. A blue cotton dress lit up her eyes.

"Nettie, you're looking beautiful this afternoon," Jess said, taking both of the woman's hands.

"Nonsense, my dear. I was just thinking about the Captain this morning, and it inspired me to put up my hair. He always loved it this way." She flushed as she sat down in one of the cushy verandah chairs. "He used to say it showed my neck to good advantage."

"He was right."

"You're a darling. Here, I've brought you some bird-of-paradise stems from my garden. They're perfect for Uchungu House." She held out a bundle of long green stalks, each topped by a spiky, birdlike flower in brilliant shades of orange and deep violet.

"Thank you, Nettie," Jess said. "How thoughtful of you. They'll look great in the sitting room."

"Or in the courtyard. Your friend, the late artist, used to keep batches of them out there. He said they were the only flower bold enough in size and color to do the house justice. They kept the perspective right, he always told me."

"Did he?" Jess could easily imagine Dr. bin Yusuf saying such things. Yet she wondered at Nettie discussing flowers with a man rumored to be so unfriendly and isolated.

"Oh, you know how Ahmed was—always going on about balance and design and proportion. I found it ever so tiresome. He made a painting of some bird-of-paradise blossoms once. Then sent it off to that nasty Giles Knox in Nairobi. He told me the canvas fetched a good price and that he would have something left over from his remodeling costs to stash away."

"Giles Knox the gallery owner? I met him in town the other day. Do you know him?"

"Repulsive man. I wouldn't put anything past that snake." She looked around in concern. "Now where has my young rival gone off to? We're the best of enemies, Spencer and I. Lay out the Scrabble board, and we're at each other's throats. Did he tell you he beat me soundly the last time he was at my house? Yes, he did. Gave me quite a drubbing."

Jess laughed. "Thank you for inviting him over, by the way. He loved it."

"Not half as much as I. He's a delight, that boy. Reminds me of the Captain. Very sure of himself. Very intelligent. But never quite willing to let anyone come too close. The Captain grew up without a father, too, you know. I'm quite sure it affected him adversely. A boy ought to have a father if at all possible. But some fathers . . . some fathers are simply too cruel. Too self-absorbed. They won't have anything to do with their children. It's a terrible pity."

Jess studied the elderly woman, reading clearly the pain reflected in her pale blue eyes. Did Nettie Cameron understand

Splint better than his own mother had? Maybe. She certainly seemed to empathize with the feelings Splint had expressed that afternoon in the studio.

"My son is a pretty well-rounded young man," Jess told her. "In fact, right now he's hunting for his Scrabble board. He's going to challenge both of us, I think. Would you like some tea, Nettie? Miriamu's fixing it in the kitchen. If you'll excuse me, I'll see what's taking her so long."

"Don't go, Jessica, my dear. I'm certain Miriamu will bring out the tea in good time. Lord knows the woman has a great deal to do, what with all those beaux vying for her time. It's a wonder she manages to keep your house clean at all."

"Beaux?"

"Don't tell me you haven't noticed?" Nettie dug around in her crocheted handbag until she found a bottle of hot pink nail polish. She propped her bare foot on the tea table and proceeded to paint her toenails. "Gracious, that Miriamu is quite the busy little bee. Surely you've taken note of how attractive she is. Dark flirtatious eyes. Full lips. Sumptuous figure. She may maintain her coy mannerisms with you, but she's quite the talk of this part of Zanzibar."

"Miriamu?" Jess couldn't fit the image Nettie was painting with her shy, gentle housekeeper. "Are you sure?"

Nettie pointed her nail-polish brush in the direction of the road. "You don't think Solomon Mazrui loiters about because he actually enjoys gardening, do you? And your poor Renault motor hanging from the Red Hot Poker tree! What a pathetic sight. Surely you don't believe Solomon has any knowledge about automobile repair, do you?"

Jess sank back into her chair and stared down the road at the dangling car engine. Even now, Solomon was puttering away on it, screwdrivers and monkey wrenches scattered all over the ground. He had gone into the nearest village umpteen times for parts—usually accompanying Miriamu on her way to market.

"I guess I really hadn't given it much thought," she said finally. "He seems to know what he's doing."

Nettie was laughing as Miriamu came out onto the verandah with a tray of tea things. Disconcerted, Jess thanked the woman and began to pour the steaming liquid into cups. Miriamu always worked with her eyes averted and her head down. She was humble and conscientious. A flirt? Not likely. But she was beautiful. No one could deny that.

"Miriamu, would you mind checking on Splint for me?" Jess asked her. "I think we stacked all the games on that table by his bed. Maybe Mama Hannah can find the Scrabble board for him."

"Hannah has gone down to the water, *memsahib,*" Miriamu said quietly. "At this time, she likes to pray."

"Oh, that's right. I forgot." She glanced at her guest. "Mama Hannah takes a nap, and then she has her prayer time. She's done that for years."

"Odd," Nettie said. "Is she a Muslim? I thought they were at their prayers five times a day."

"Mama Hannah's a Christian. Her faith is very important to her. Miriamu, if you'll just check on Splint, then you can take some time off until supper. I'll clean up the tea things."

"Yes, *memsahib.*"

As the African woman slipped back into the house, Jess recalled something Splinter had mentioned. He'd said Miriamu and Solomon would welcome time alone together. So they could smooch.

"Are Solomon and Miriamu . . . together?" Jess asked Nettie. "I mean, do they have a relationship?"

"Doesn't he wish they did! I've heard from my cook that Solomon likes to think of her as his possession. A sort of hidden treasure. He's very jealous. Very guarded. He won't let anyone near her. If she so much as looks at another man . . . well . . ."

Nettie took a sip of her tea and leaned across the arm of her chair toward Jess. She lowered her voice to a whisper. "I have heard some talk," she murmured, "that Solomon was jealous of Ahmed bin Yusuf's attentions to Miriamu. The artist, you know, could be quite the Don Juan. Apparently, Solomon got wind of something . . . a painting, I believe it was. Yes, I think Ahmed was using Miriamu as a model in one of his paintings, and Solomon didn't care for that at all."

"I can't imagine Miriamu posing for a painting."

"How little you know her." Nettie leaned even closer. "Some say Solomon's rage got the better of him."

"You mean they think he . . . that Dr. bin Yusuf was . . . that Solomon was jealous over Miriamu, so he . . ."

"It may be just talk." She wiggled her pink toes and let out a deep breath. "Oh, my. The tropics can be filled with such intrigue. Such dramatics! It's quite exhausting. Would you be so good as to pass me a scone, my dear?"

Jess picked up the plate of warm breads, but she could see that her hands were trembling. She had never really thought Solomon capable of killing anyone. He didn't seem the type. But now she knew he'd had a motive. A motive for murder.

"Mom, look what I found!" Splint said, stepping out onto the verandah. "It was in the storeroom."

Jess caught her breath as the boy lifted a small carved stone urn. Nettie Cameron turned to look, let out a squawk, and jumped up, knocking her teacup to the verandah floor. The china cup shattered into a hundred fragments.

"Where did you find that?" she cried.

"In the little storeroom at the bottom of the circular stairs. Look what's on it!"

"Yes, yes, I can see. Put it down, young man. Put it down at once."

Splint held out the urn. "Take it, Mom. It's got blood all over it."

12

"SPLINTER, please put down the urn," Jess said as calmly as she could. "Now go and wash your hands."

"But, Mom, it's dried blood. And look, there are little tiny black hairs all stuck in the—"

"Splinter!" Jess cut in. "Just go wash your hands. With soap and hot water!"

"OK, OK. Take it easy, Mom."

"I don't believe this," Jess muttered as her son scampered into the house. She knelt to pick up pieces of Nettie's shattered teacup. "He found it. He found the murder weapon."

"You can't be certain," Nettie said. "Maybe it's . . . maybe there's some other explanation."

"What other explanation could there possibly be? I'm taking that thing to the police this afternoon." She shuddered as she set the shards of china on the tea tray. "This is horrible. To think it was here in the house all the time. And Splint found it!"

"How are you planning to take it into town? Your motor is hanging from the Red Hot Poker tree. Oh, he has got you in a tidy little corner, hasn't he?"

"Who? You mean Solomon? You think he disabled the Renault on purpose?"

"It does isolate you, Jessica."

"But why would Solomon want to isolate me? If he killed Dr. bin Yusuf in a jealous rage over Miriamu, what would I have to do with it? I'm not a threat to him in any way . . . am I?"

Nettie shook her head. "One never knows how a man thinks. Listen, my dear, why don't you let me take that—that thing. I'll drive it to the police station myself."

"I'd hate for you to have to be involved in this in any way."

"Don't give it a second thought. You and your son have brought a joy into my life I haven't known since the Captain passed away. I'll do whatever I can to help you." She tilted the urn to examine it. "This is dreadful. It's simply macabre. Listen, before I take the urn to the police, we must wrap it carefully. We wouldn't want to destroy any evidence that might link it to the killer. Then you must think what to do about Solomon Mazrui."

"I don't want him near Splint, that's for sure. I can't believe this has all been going on under my nose, Nettie. I've been so preoccupied. What if I'm in danger? Or what if Solomon decides to hurt my son for some reason? If he realizes Splint is the one who found the urn—"

"Calm yourself, duckie." The older woman gave Jess a hug. "It will never do to have the boy see you trembling and looking so pale. I shall take that nasty bit of evidence to the police straight away. Perhaps they'll know what to tell you about Solomon. You can't very well go dismissing the man from employment at Uchungu House. That would enrage him all the more."

"You're right. He'd be furious if I forced him away from Miriamu." Jess stared half-paralyzed at the stone urn. It had a smooth glazed surface painted in Dr. bin Yusuf's favorite hues of bold yellow, blue, and green. But the tiny black hairs embedded in a blot of dried red blood could be mistaken for nothing but what they were. Evidence of murder. Even Splint had recognized the significance of his discovery.

"Nettie, if you wouldn't mind going home to get your car," Jess said, "you can pick this up on your way into town."

"Nonsense. I shall take it along with me."

"But it's heavy."

"I'm stronger than I look, my dear. The Captain used to tell me I was quite the workhorse. Oh, if only we had my dear husband with us now. He would know what to do."

"Expert advice would be very helpful at this point. I should probably call Mr. Patel. You remember my attorney?" Jess slid the tablecloth from under the tea tray and carefully wrapped the urn. "Maybe the surface is smooth enough for the police to collect fingerprints. If they can prove Solomon was the one who used it as a weapon, that would go a long way toward resolving everything."

"We can only hope so." Nettie lifted the bundle into her arms and gazed sympathetically at Jess. "Of course, the police will need to take your son's fingerprints. He handled the urn, you know. I think you'd better tell young Spencer what we suspect, my dear. Not only will it explain the presence of the police when they come, it may help him to be more alert."

"Alert to danger, you mean? Nettie, I'm beginning to wonder if I shouldn't just go back to London. I could probably sell Uchungu House. I might even give it to Dr. bin Yusuf's sister. I wanted a home for Splinter and me. I wanted a haven . . . but this . . . this is turning into a nightmare."

"Now, duckie, don't be too hasty. You must think things over carefully. I should hate to see you go. Perhaps it's much ado about nothing."

"Nothing? Nettie, you're holding a murder weapon there."

"Indeed I am, and I must get it to the police station at once. Do pardon me while I shuffle back home to fetch my car. Now, you tend to your son and your affairs here at the house. Put all this out of your mind."

Jess watched from the edge of the verandah as the elderly woman strolled down the driveway. She walked right past Solomon, who was fitting something onto the Renault's engine, stopped and spoke briefly with him, and continued on her way. Amazing. In her early years in Africa, Jess had known more than one woman like Nettie—resolute, tough, and anything but squeamish. It comforted her to know she had a capable neighbor who cared for her and Splinter.

"Where's the urn?" Splint asked, coming up behind her.

Jess nearly jumped out of her skin. "Don't sneak up on me like that! You scared me half to death."

"Hey, where's Nettie going? What about our Scrabble game? Did she take the urn with her? What's she planning to do with it? I'm the one who found it. I think we ought to keep it here at Uchungu House."

Jess took her son's shoulders. They felt small and fragile. He was so young. Like a scrawny baby chick, Splint was all skin and thin muscle stretched over a bony framework. And, like a mother hen, she wanted to protect him with every fiber of her being. Yet she knew sometimes protection meant he had to be told the truth about difficult subjects.

"Listen, Splint," she said softly. "I need to talk to you about some things that have happened. Nettie's going to get her car and drive the urn down to the police station in Zanzibar town. We think it might have been used in a crime."

"You mean like to kill somebody? Who?"

"A few weeks ago Mr. Patel, the lawyer, told me the police think Dr. bin Yusuf might have been murdered. Now I don't want you to get worried or scared—"

"Murdered! And you didn't tell me! How come? Mom, you said he fell down the steps." His face went dark. "You lied to me! You lied about it just like you've been lying about my father!"

"Spencer Thornton, I have *not* lied to you! Ever!" Jess's fingers tightened on her son's shoulders. "Now listen to me. I told you Dr. bin Yusuf had fallen down the stairs because that's exactly what Mr. Patel told me when I first talked to him about Uchungu House. That's what everybody believed had happened until a few weeks ago when they did an autopsy. I didn't want to tell you the new information because I thought you might worry about living here. I thought—"

"You think I'm just a little kid, don't you! It never occurred to you that I might find a bloodstained urn in the storeroom, did it? What about that? That would scare some people half to death. But

I'm not scared. I'm just mad. I'm mad because you didn't tell me the truth!"

Jess stared into her son's face, reading clearly the mixture of rage and defiance written across it. But she saw another emotion in his violet eyes—an emotion she recognized all too well. Splinter felt betrayed. Somehow, he sensed that his mother had not told him things he felt he should know. And the knowledge of her betrayal was making him bitter.

Betrayed and bitter. Just as Jess herself had felt for so many years. Like mother, like son.

"Splinter, honey, I want you to try to calm yourself." She ran her hands down his thin arms, hoping she was overreacting to the stress of the incident. "Sweetheart, you've been so angry lately. You've really been upset with me. Is it because I grounded you from the beach?"

"It's because you've been keeping things from me."

"You're ten years old, Splint. Moms don't tell their kids every little detail that happens. There are some things you just don't need to know about yet. When you're older—"

"Mama Hannah!" Splint tore away from his mother and dashed across the lawn toward the dark figure atop the cliff-side staircase. "Mama Hannah, guess what I found! Somebody killed Dr. bin Yusuf, and I found the bloody urn! Nettie's taking it to the police station. Oh, hi, Rick! Hi, Hunky! Did you hear the news? I found a murder weapon in the storeroom. It was an urn. Somebody hit Dr. bin Yusuf and killed him with it!"

Jess wrapped her arms around the verandah post as Hannah made her way across the lawn followed by Rick and the rest of the diving crew. Splint was scampering around, dancing back and forth among them like he'd just discovered the pot of gold at the end of the rainbow. No doubt the news would be all over Zanzibar by morning, once Hunky Wallace made his nightly rounds to the local saloons.

With all the energy she could muster, Jess stepped off the verandah and walked down the steps to meet the tired crew. They were carrying heavy bags filled with artifacts from their day's treasure hunt. The motley collection of faded bathing trunks they wore was dotted with white sand. Hunky sent his men to the trucks to deposit the haul, then he, Hannah, and Rick met Jess in the driveway.

"Splinter, I have found a new shell for you today," Hannah said softly, her warm brown eyes searching the boy's face. "I do not believe you have this one in your collection."

"Really? Let me see! Where'd you find it?"

"I was praying on the beach. When I opened my eyes, there it was beside my knees. Look." She unfolded her hand to reveal a small purple shell on her palm. "Do you have one like this?"

"No way! This is awesome. Hey, let's go look it up, Mama Hannah." He grabbed the shell. Then he paused. "Wait, you better look it up for us, Mama Hannah. I want to stay here and listen to this. Mom's going to tell them about how I found the urn."

The old woman gave a shrug. *"Haraka haraka, haina baraka."*

"What's that mean?"

"Hurry, hurry, and you will not have the blessing. If you wish to know the complete truth about this shell, you must take the time to look for it yourself."

"OK, I'll identify it later."

"Spencer," Jess said, "go look up the shell now. I'll call you when I'm ready to talk to you about everything."

"When you've made up another half-true story, you mean?" Splint hardened his jaw. "Rick, don't you think parents ought to tell their children the truth? You'd tell me the truth, wouldn't you? If I asked?"

Rick glanced at Jess. "I think children ought to obey their parents," he said. "Your mom loves you, kiddo. She's doing what she thinks is right, and you need to respect that."

Splint kicked at a pebble in the driveway. "OK, OK. I guess it's one of those grown-up conspiracies. Come on, Mama Hannah. I bet they haven't told you diddly-squat either."

As Hannah and the boy walked into the house, Jess let out a deep breath. "Nettie Cameron has taken the urn to the police station," she said. "I'm pretty sure it's the murder weapon."

"Ahmed bin Yusuf was murdered?" Hunky asked. He let out a low whistle. "McTaggart, you didn't tell me that."

"I figured you already knew," Rick said. "You're a suspect."

"Me? You must be joking. Why would I kill a harmless old man?"

"You wanted to explore the sunken ship in the bay," Jess explained. "Dr. bin Yusuf wouldn't let you. Now that he's dead, you're out here every day. Once he stood in the way of your goals, and now he doesn't. You got what you wanted."

"Great ghosts!" The Scotsman rubbed a beefy hand over his bald head. "What are you saying, lassie? Do the police have me on a list or some such? Do they truly think I did it?"

"Did you?"

"Of course not. I'll be the first to admit I'm greedy and ambitious. I fight for what I want, as McTaggart well knows, and woe to the man who blocks my path. But I'm no killer."

"You'd better hope your fingerprints aren't on that urn."

"How could they be? I've never seen the thing in my life! I wasn't even in Zanzibar when the artist died. I was searching through the maps-and-antiquities section in the Nairobi museum. You'll vouch for me on that, won't you, McTaggart?"

"Hunky, I don't keep tabs on your comings and goings."

"But I recall it clearly. When I got back to Zanzibar, I heard the news about the old man's death, and I rushed straight out here to have a bit of a look-see. Sure enough, the house was all shut up. Solomon said his employer had fallen down the stairs, and that was that. So I brought my boat in and set to work. But I didn't kill the man! Absolutely not!"

"I believe you're telling the truth, Hunky," Rick said. "You and I have had our troubles, but I've never known you to be cruel. You waited a lot of years to get at that ship, and I don't know of anything that could have happened a couple of months ago to push you over the edge. But you're going to need a documented alibi. Especially if your fingerprints show up on that urn."

"They won't!" He gave the waistband of his bathing suit a flip. "If I kept better records, I'd have my Kenya travel voucher for you in a second. As it is, I'll have to piece it all together. But mark my words, I'm innocent. I had nothing to do with it!"

He turned on his heel and stomped away, a flush spreading from his neck down his bare back. In moments, he had climbed into his truck with his crew and was pulling out of the driveway. Jess shook her head.

"This is so unbelievable," she said softly. "Splint found the urn, Rick. It was covered with dried blood."

"He doesn't seem too traumatized."

"He's in his Hardy Boys mode right now. This is all a grand adventure. But tonight in his bed, he'll start imagining the whole murder, and he won't get a wink of sleep."

"Jessie, if there's anything I can do . . ."

She studied Rick for a long time, unable and unwilling to break the bond between their eyes. If Splinter had a father to cling to, things would be so much easier. And sometime . . . sometime she would have to tell her son the whole truth. But not yet. She still wasn't ready to go that far.

All the same . . .

"Maybe there is something you can do for me, Rick," she said. "Nettie's pretty sure Solomon is guilty. I don't want my son hanging around that man. I just don't trust him. Would you be willing to take Splint out on the diving boat with you? School's starting soon, so it wouldn't be long. But if you were with him, I wouldn't worry so much. I know he can be kind of a pain but—"

"Jessie." He reached out to her but didn't touch. "There's nothing I'd like better than spending time with Splint."

"He thinks you hung the moon."

"I can't claim that one. But I figure the guy who did is on my side."

Jess smiled at the image of the benevolent Creator hovering protectively over this man . . . over the boy . . . their son.

"I'll watch out for Splinter, Jessie," Rick told her. "He'll be safe."

"What about Hunky? If he did it—"

"He didn't do it. Whoever killed Dr. bin Yusuf had a stronger motive than getting to a sunken ship. Under the waters around Zanzibar, there are a lot of boats that Hunky Wallace can't get his hands on. Some of them are rumored to be holding valuable treasure. It drives Hunky nuts. But it doesn't drive him to kill. Even if he had murdered Dr. bin Yusuf, Hunky wouldn't have anything against Splint. In fact, I think he's got a real heart for your son."

"Do you?"

"Sure. Splint's a little scamp, but he's a charmer, too. Hunky liked having his help on the boat the other day. He'll be fine." Rick looked into her eyes. "It's you I'm concerned about, Jessie."

"I'll be all right."

"At night . . . if you'd like me to stay—I could sleep downstairs."

"No. We'll be fine."

"I promised I'd protect you, Jessie. If you need me, say the word. I'll come."

For some reason her eyes filled with tears, and Jess had to look away. She did need Rick. She had needed him for so many years. But she was used to taking care of herself now. Sufficient. Competent.

Then she remembered her prayer that afternoon in her studio. It was time to let go of the controls of her life and stop being so self-sufficient. Time to allow Christ to be the Lord of her heart. Time to empty out the bitterness and be filled with his peace.

"Yes, you did promise to protect me, Rick," she said. "You know, I've been thinking you may have been right about something you said the first time we talked, on the cliff. I think God may have allowed you back into my life for a reason. Maybe he wants you to protect Splint and me. But I find it so hard to trust you. Hard to trust God. I'm afraid I'm not very good at it."

He touched the ends of her hair. "I hurt you a lot, Jessie. I broke the bonds of trust we had built. I don't deserve the faith you're putting in me to watch over Splint. But I'm thankful for it. I won't let you down this time. I promise."

"OK," she whispered. She took his hand and squeezed it. His eyes shone as bright and blue as the water behind him. "Thank you, Rick."

As she pulled away, he lifted his head to the balcony above. "Hey, Splint!" he called. "You up there, buddy?"

There was a moment of silence. "Yeah."

"Thought so. Didn't your mom teach you not to eavesdrop?"

"I can't hear a thing you're saying, no matter how hard I try. You're talking too quietly."

Rick gave Jess a wink. "Then I guess you don't know the big news."

"What? What big news?" Splint's head appeared over the balcony rail.

"I'm picking you up at seven sharp tomorrow morning. Bring your trunks, a T-shirt, a hat, and your notebooks. We're going treasure hunting."

To the whoops that echoed off the walls of the verandah balcony, Rick walked out to his motorcycle. "Tomorrow, Jessie," he said.

"Tomorrow, Rick."

◎◎◎

"Do you think everything's going to be all right?" Jess asked Hannah. They were sitting on the verandah just after lunch the next day, sipping mango juice and listening to the waves crash on the cliffs. "As hard as I try, I can't put all this out of my mind. I'm so worried about everything."

"Ehh," Hannah murmured. "The worry is written on your face like the words in a book. I understand that. Many things have happened to you in Zanzibar, and some of them are troubling. But in Jeremiah it is written, '"For I know the plans I have for you," says the Lord. "They are plans for good and not for disaster, to give you a future and a hope."' I believe God loves you and me, *toto*. When a father loves his children, he can use even the worst problems for good."

Jess smiled at the elderly woman. "You've always had so much faith, Mama Hannah."

"Not always. We all are little children in the Lord. We are growing, learning, becoming wise in him." Her dark eyes searched Jess's face. "But before we can even begin to grow in faith, we must first be born. Tell me, *toto,* do you feel this life inside you? Where are you in your walk?"

Pondering the question, Jess took a sip of her juice and let the cool orange liquid run down her throat. On the surface, her walk through life looked very good. She had spent the morning in her studio bedroom. The impala book was coming together beautifully at last, and she felt confident that her lavish illustrations equaled or surpassed her previous work.

Hunky had brought her a bundle of mail from the Zanzibar post office that morning. A letter from James Perrott was filled with snippets of verse from the author's new proposal, *Kima the Monkey and the Jealous Jackal*. James had wanted to know if Jess liked his idea. Did she think a jackal would make a good character? Jackals were carnivores, he reminded her. Would they run into the problem they'd had with Hungry Hyena, who had been more interested in eating poor Kima than in resolving his own problems? Did Jess think she could paint a jackal? Would the creature be vivid or boring? On and on. James Perrott had never been known for concise writing.

Jess loved the fact that her life was regaining a sense of normalcy. She was working steadily. Communication with the business world wasn't proving as difficult as she had feared. Splint was staying busy and mostly happy. Bills were being paid; food was on the table; school would be starting soon.

Other than the looming specter of an unsolved murder and the disconcerting presence of a long-lost husband, things were fairly average. She had to laugh at the image.

"Where am I in my walk?" she repeated Hannah's question. "Well, I'm in the middle of a murder investigation and a hunt for sunken treasure. But you know what? I'm all right, Mama Hannah. Yesterday I was up in my room alone, and I . . . I sort of just gave up. I realized I couldn't be the lord of my own life anymore. It wasn't working. I've been so hard and angry."

"Bitter."

"I've been choking on bitterness."

"Choking nearly to the death of your heart." Hannah studied the line of palm trees growing on the edge of the cliff. When she spoke again, her voice was filled with emotion. "I thank God he has opened your eyes at last. Many years ago, you gave your life to Christ, *toto*. At that time, I believed you were born into his kingdom. Do you remember it?"

"Yes," Jess whispered. "I was very young, but through your words I came to understand my own sin and my need for forgiveness. You taught me how to surrender my will and submit to Christ. After that, I believed I was growing, Mama Hannah. But then . . . then I met Rick."

"Ehh."

"I guess I stopped growing."

"Even the children of God can permit sin to creep back into their hearts. Like small vines from a bitter root, the unforgiveness wrapped around you. I saw this. Many times . . . many times, I have begged God to release you from these vines."

"He has, Mama Hannah."

"Has he? Have you forgiven your husband?"

Jess cringed at words she still could not accept. "I've forgiven Rick. But I can't think of him as my husband. I can't think of him as Splint's father. I can't let him back into my life."

"He is in your life already."

"Then I can't let him into my heart."

"What holds you away? Memories of the past?"

"Fear of the future. I don't know what life would be like with Rick. I can't imagine us ever . . . ever . . ."

She was lying. She knew it even as she spoke. Not only could she imagine it, she *had* imagined it. Now she faced the truth—even as she struggled with the concept—that she could easily picture herself in Rick's life—and in his arms. Though she tried to repress the images that had been sneaking into her mind for weeks, she had to admit that she could see herself and Rick together again, loving each other, building a home, creating a family. In spite of herself, she was as drawn to those images as she ever had been. But look what had come of her childish trust in the future!

"It scares me," she said finally. "I can give up my anger. I can let go of the bitterness. I think I've even forgiven Rick. But I'm too scared to place any hope in a life with him."

"Remember, *toto*. We are called to place our hope in Christ. Solomon, that wise king, wrote, 'Hope deferred makes the heart sick, but when dreams come true, there is life and joy.' I believe there is life and joy ahead for you. But I think you must put the hope in the right place. As the apostle Paul told that young boy, Timothy: 'Our hope is in the living God, who is the Savior of all people, and particularly of those who believe.'"

Again, Jess had to smile at Hannah's beloved words. To Hannah, the Bible was always so real. She called Solomon "that wise king."

Timothy was always "that young boy." Job was "the poor man Satan attacked." David was "the man God loved." These people walked through her life and spoke messages as real and vivid as those of any living person. Hannah breathed the Bible. Scriptures, prayer, and fellowship with other Christians were her nourishment. If only Jess could follow her example.

"I'll try," she said. "I'll try to put my hope in Christ. I guess he'll show me what to do about Rick."

"Of course he will show you." Hannah's brown eyes twinkled. "Perhaps he is doing so already. Look now, the boy comes with his father."

Jess glanced in the direction of Hannah's gaze. Rick was striding across the lawn, Splinter draped across his back like a lanky Ichabod Crane on his horse. The boy had his head thrown back toward the sunlight, and he was laughing at the man's efforts to tote the weighty burden toward the house. In all her life, Jess had never seen her son so filled with joy.

"Mom!" he shouted, spotting her and giving a wave. "Mom, you've got to come down to the boat! Guess what? We found the *real* mother lode! The captain's quarters! We came all the way back to get you. We need you."

"They need you," Hannah said, giving Jess a soft smile. "You need them. God knows this. And he will supply all your needs from his many riches in glory, because of what Christ Jesus has done for us."

Jess kissed the dark chocolate cheek. Hannah had been more than her caretaker all these years. She was her mentor. Her friend. Her mother.

"I love you, Mama Hannah," she said.

"Ehh," the old woman said. "Go now, *toto*. Your family calls you."

SOMETHING about Jessie was different. Rick noticed it immediately—in the way she carried herself, in the way she spoke to Splinter, in the way she looked at Rick. And she did look at him. Often.

Even though he had prayed Jessie would come out onto the diving boat again, he hadn't really believed he could talk her into it. Splinter had taken care of that, convincing his mom that the salvage project needed her artistic skills if history were to be recorded accurately. The kid's powers of persuasion were impressive. By the time Splint had finished, Rick himself was convinced that the sunken ship was the discovery of the century.

So here Jessie was in the boat, lounging on one of the padded benches with her sketch pad propped on her knees. A big straw hat with a yellow scarf tied around the band shaded her eyes. A filmy sea green tunic, its hem drifting around the deck in the soft breeze, covered her bathing suit. Her slender arms curved over the white paper as she rendered a faithful copy of the wine bottle that had just been brought up from the captain's quarters. And her long legs with their delicate toes . . . it was about all Rick could do to force himself to concentrate on his diagram of the shipwreck.

"What did you tell me you call this kind of glass?" Jessie asked, lifting her head and fixing him with those mesmerizing violet eyes. "It's so strange the way it's shedding."

"Onion skin. Glass that's been aging underwater for years peels off in layers like an onion."

"I'm finding it hard to sketch." She held her drawing at arm's length. "These pictures I'm doing for you aren't going to be displayed in public anywhere, are they?"

"I'll be using them for research purposes."

"Why don't you just take photographs?"

"That's the way I've always done it. I take pictures first on site underwater, and then I shoot the artifacts again up here. But it's never as good as a sketch." He left his maps and charts to join her on the bench. "Your pencil captures things my camera can't. Your artist's eye notices details a photograph would miss. See this ridge in the glass? Could be nothing—an insignificant bubble. Or it could be a mark made by the glassblower. Something like that can teach us a lot. On your sketch, you've shaded in the ridge. In a photograph, it would blend right into the bottle's surface. I'd miss it."

Jessie turned the wine bottle around. In spite of a thin crust of coral on the bottom and a couple of barnacles, the artifact had a hypnotic quality. Its peeling glass captured the afternoon sunlight and scattered marbles of green light across her bare legs.

"I would feel a lot better if I could label my sketch," she said. "For example, see how the bottle's lip juts out right here, but on the other side it's uneven? I can't really show that in the drawing."

"Write down all the details you observe. Anything we can add to the provenance will help."

"Provenance?"

"To an archaeologist, provenance is more important than a chest full of gold bars. Provenance is what we call any artifact that helps us authenticate a find and identify its origin. If I can use something to help me accurately date a site, it's invaluable."

"Like that vase I found?"

He smiled. "As far as I'm concerned, you hit the real mother lode that day. And you're the one who noticed the date on the padlock. Anytime you get a hankering to go back down to the wreck, I'll dive with you. See, I have a tendency to sift through tons of sand so carefully it takes forever. Hunky, on the other hand, uses his airlift to plunge into troves of valuable artifacts, and sometimes he blasts them to smithereens. But you're trained to look. You really study the world around you. I bet you'd find things the rest of us would miss."

"Maybe. All the same, I think I'll leave the undersea adventures to you guys. I like sketching up here where it's dry, and I don't have to wonder if I'm going to come face-to-face with an octopus."

"Or a coelacanth."

She laughed, and Rick's heart did a double flip. The woman was beautiful. Enchanting. Magnetizing. When she spoke, her voice ran through him like a warm waterfall. When she gazed at him from beneath those thick dark eyelashes, his skin tingled, and he felt his pulse rate step up to a quick military march. All she had to do was lean close enough to give him a sniff of the entrancing scent of tropical flowers that lingered on her skin, and his mouth went as dry as a washed-up seashell.

"Speaking of sea creatures," she said, "do you think Splinter's OK down there with Andrew?"

"Andrew Mbuti's like my own brother. I'd trust the man with my life. I do, in fact. He won't let anything happen to Splint."

"You were always close to your real brother, Daniel. Do you see him very often?"

"When I'm in Dar es Salaam, I do. I go to his church on Sundays. I'll see him tomorrow, in fact, and I'll tell him you asked about him."

"What does he think about all this?" she asked. "About us? That we ran into each other again, I mean. Doesn't he think it's strange?"

Rick searched Jessie's eyes, trying to read the significance of her questions. *Us,* she had said. Did she think of them as somehow together again? *Lord, that would be an answer to my prayers. Give me the words to say. Teach my mouth.*

"Daniel's a strong Christian," he said. "He thinks the lives of believers are in God's hands. He knew I was searching for you, Jessie. He prayed with me about it . . . that I'd find you . . . that you'd be able to forgive me."

"Mama Hannah's been praying about it, too."

"That's three of us, then. Ought to do the job. Remember what Jesus taught his followers? 'If two of you agree down here on earth concerning anything you ask, my Father in heaven will do it for you. For where two or three gather together because they are mine, I am there among them.'"

He sat in silence for a moment, waiting for Jessie's reaction. She had hurled her anger and bitterness at him so often he was steeled to accept it. And he knew the last thing she probably wanted to hear him say was that God had his hand in their relationship.

Jessie had made one thing abundantly clear: She wanted to hold onto the reins of her own life. They had been ripped away from her once, and she didn't trust anyone to hold them for her—not even God. Rick understood that, and it tore at his gut that he'd been the one to cause such pain in her life.

"I've been praying about it, too," she said.

He couldn't have been more surprised if she'd poured a bucket of ice water over his head. "You have? You mean, you've been praying about . . ." He gestured at himself and Jessie. "Praying about . . . about me finding you? That we . . . you and I . . ."

"Us," she said. "I've been praying about us. What to do. Where to turn. Mostly I've been trying to let go of the past."

He raked his fingers through his damp hair. Jessie *was* different. Something had happened to her. He'd never seen her so calm. So open. Even though he welcomed the change—even though he'd been praying for it from the moment he'd seen Jessie again—it was disconcerting.

Does this mean what I think it does, Lord? Can it be . . . ? Fearful of reading too much into her behavior, he shook off the thought. *I'll wait, Father. I'll wait and see what you're doing.*

"Hunky brought me a bunch of mail this morning," she said, placing the glass wine bottle back into the salt-water tank. She lifted out the corroded brass handle that once had been attached to a wooden trunk and set it near her sketch pad. "James Perrott wrote to me. He's the author I work with."

"Oh, yeah?" Fear sliced through Rick like a knife. James Perrott. Was she in love with the man? Could he be Splinter's father?

"James is working on our next book. It's going to be about a jealous jackal. James is great—so funny. I just love him." She sketched for a moment, a gentle smile playing around her lips.

Rick watched the play of emotions cross her face with increasing irritation. Maybe he'd been wrong. Maybe it wasn't God who had softened Jessie's heart but James Perrott and his letter. Maybe *he* was why she seemed so at ease. Rick fought a sudden urge to make disparaging remarks about a man who penned children's poems for a living. The green-eyed monster of jealousy reared its ugly head and assured Rick that the best fate for James Perrott would be a swift punch in his versifying visage.

"Anyway," Jessie was saying, "I also got a letter from my sister Tillie. She's living in Mali, you know? She married a writer."

Great, Rick thought. One Thornton sister had taken a writer for a husband. Maybe Jessie wanted to do the same. Could she be leading up to asking Rick for a formal divorce? They'd never gotten around to it, but he knew it would be a simple matter. After all, he had abandoned her ten years ago. What court would deny her petition?

"Tillie wrote me this long chatty letter," Jessie went on, sketching the outline of the chest handle. "She's so happy with Graeme. He sounds like a wonderful man."

"And he's a *writer?"*

"That's how they met. He was researching a book about a Scotsman who explored the Niger River two hundred years ago. Apparently, Tillie was kidnapped briefly by some local tribesmen, and Graeme rescued her." She paused for a moment. "I'm not sure I have the story exactly right. It's pretty exciting—escaping from hippos and crocodiles, exploring old gold mines, stealing rare manuscripts, all kinds of crazy things. You'll have to read it for yourself."

"OK."

"But the point is, Tillie told me that when she first met Graeme, he was really angry about some things that had happened to him in his past. Through the course of their relationship, Graeme decided to surrender his anger. Tillie said he asked God to take control of his life, and all that bitterness vanished. You know what she told me?"

"What?"

"She and Graeme have been praying for me. So that's two more. Isn't that weird? They've been praying that I could find a way to let go of my own bitterness. That I could come to some sort of resolution about what happened between you and me ten years ago."

"Are you planning to write back to Tillie soon?

"Maybe this evening after supper."

"What will you tell her?"

She let out a breath. "I don't know, Rick. I think I'll tell her . . . yes. Yes, God is answering prayers."

Trapped in his turmoil—jealousy, fear, confusion—Rick couldn't formulate an appropriate response. *What do you mean?* he wanted to ask. *Who is James Perrott, and how is God answering prayers, and what's happening here? What's going on, Jessie?*

"You know, I think I'll dive down to the wreck after all," she said, standing and setting aside her sketch pad. "I want to check on Splint. Would you rig up an air hose for me, Rick?"

I'd kiss the ground you walk on, Jessie! Just tell me why those eyes are drinking up my heart. Tell me how you feel. Tell me what's going to happen between us.

"And if you wouldn't mind," she said, slipping out of her tunic, "I'd like to visit Daniel's church in Dar es Salaam tomorrow. Do you think you could send a cab to meet the hydrofoil in the morning and take Splint and me into town? Mama Hannah will probably come with us, too."

"I'll pick you up myself. Dan's got a car."

"Great. Thanks."

"Sure."

His brain felt like it had been stung by a Portuguese man-of-war. Numb. Dumb. Paralyzed. He watched Jessie sort through the air hoses herself, select one that fit her mouth, pull on a face mask and weight belt, and climb out onto the diving platform at the back of the boat.

"I'll let you know if I find the treasure you've been looking for, Rick," she said.

With a single backward step, she sank from view and vanished under the teal water of the Indian Ocean.

Rick stared at the concentric circles spreading out on the calm water. "I've already found the treasure I've been looking for, Jessie," he murmured. And the words of King Solomon came to him. . . . *'You have ravished my heart, my treasure, my bride. I am overcome by one glance of your eyes, by a single bead of your necklace. How sweet is your love, my treasure, my bride! How much better it is than wine! Your perfume is more fragrant than the richest of spices.'*

Jess drifted in the half-light on the ocean floor, enjoying the total freedom of hanging suspended in salt water. Although at this depth the pressure made her ears hurt a little, she felt fairly comfortable with the breathing device. In the distance, Splinter worked alongside Andrew Mbuti. One by one they carried newly uncovered artifacts from their resting places to the hoisting basket. Rapt, the boy had hardly even noticed his mother's presence. He was as at ease in the water as a fish.

Since the discovery of the captain's quarters, the texture of the excavation had changed. All of Hunky's crew were gathered around the pit they had dug with the huge vacuum hose Rick called an airlift. The work progressed with great care as the men searched for any signs of hidden treasure.

Based on his knowledge of this sort of ship, Rick had predicted that the crew would be bringing up china, wine bottles, guns and knives, buttons, and clay pipes. If they were lucky, they'd find some jewelry. And if the wreck hadn't been plundered in the past, there was probably a chest down there somewhere. It ought to contain silver bars, uncut gemstones, maybe even gold.

Jess felt oddly pleased that Rick had asked for her help. Sketching the artifacts was proving to be interesting, even fun. And it gave her a reason to come out to the boat now and then. She told herself she wanted to be there to keep an eye on Splint. But she also enjoyed Rick's presence. She liked talking with him. Liked hearing his ideas. He was smart, funny, and good at what he did. What intrigued her most, though, was his obvious interest in her.

How long had it been since she'd enjoyed a man's attentions? Sure, her well-meaning friends in London had tried to fix her up with dates. She always made certain she was too busy to go. And when she met a man through some unexpected encounter, she felt dismayed when she recognized anything more than a casual interest in her company.

But Rick was different, Jess realized as she swam over to the plastic map of the shipwreck. She enjoyed the way his blue gaze flicked from her eyes to her lips and back again. When he touched her—a nudge on the elbow, a gentle guiding hand, a tentative finger on her hair or cheek—she reveled in the sensations that soared through her. The woman inside her felt awake again . . . a wife stirred by the powerful beckoning of desire for her husband. Was it wrong? How could it be?

Uncomfortable, even though she knew that she and Rick were married, Jess ran her fingertips over the evolving diagram of the wreck. Passion had once played such an important part in their relationship. Too important, perhaps. It had clouded her reason. She had built her marriage to Rick on romantic dreams and an unbridled drive for intimacy with him. Now, the fear of making a similar mistake riddled her with doubt. She couldn't deny how physically attracted to him she was. But she wasn't about to build anything on *that.*

Jess's newly affirmed resolve nearly evaporated when a current of water stirred her, and she turned to find Rick gliding down to join her at the map. Even underwater, his tanned skin and dark hair gave him an aura of masculine confidence. When he draped an arm around her shoulders, a shiver ran through her. He stretched his other hand toward the map, and she found herself noticing the shape of the muscle and the dark hair that covered his forearm.

Rick pointed out the location of the captain's quarters. He showed Jess where that area lay in relation to the spilled ballast that initially had led searchers to the wreck. Then he indicated other areas of interest on the grid—the possible location of the galley, the mizzenmast, and the wheelhouse.

Jess studied the diagram, imagining the terrible storm that must have driven the ship over the reef and into the bay so many decades before. She could almost see the sailors' wide eyes, smell the windblown rain, and hear the shouts of panic and cries of fear as the jagged coral reef ripped the bottom out of the ship. Timber had splintered; glass had broken; metal joints had wrenched apart.

Ballast stones had spilled across the sea floor like peas falling from an opened pod. The ship had begun to sink. The mast had snapped and tumbled into the sea.

But why had the long wooden spar come to rest at an angle perpendicular to the trail of wreckage? Odd. Jess left Rick's side and swam over the chain grid he and Hunky's men had laid across the actual wreck site. The sand where the prow should have been was smooth, barely disturbed by telltale lumps of conglomerate or coral growing on fallen timbers. She knew the potholes dug there by the airlift had turned up almost nothing.

Very odd. Splinter had told his mom there wasn't usually very much "good stuff" at that end. Only an anchor—and nobody had found it yet. Rick theorized that the ship's crew must have dropped the anchor on the other side of the reef in hopes it would prevent their crashing into the coral crags. But the water over there was deep, and no one on Hunky's salvage team had taken time to search for an anchor that had failed in its duty. Anchors had little value to a treasure hunter.

Jess drifted back to look at the map one last time. Then she signaled Rick she was going up. Enough was enough. Too much time in that salty water, and she was starting to shrivel up like a prune. Besides, she had a lot of sketching to do if she ever hoped to catch up with the growing piles of artifacts from the wreck.

When she broke through the surface and spat her mouthpiece from her lips, she realized Rick had followed. Brushing wet hair from her face, she tugged off her mask. A deep breath of fresh air filled her lungs.

"I like the way Andrew works with Splinter, including him in everything," she said. "He's having a ball down there."

"Splint's in his element." Rick's gaze roved over her face and down her neck. Then he met her eyes. "I guess I'll go back and help them get the hoisting basket ready to pull up. It looks like it's full of goodies."

"See you, then." She gave him a smile and started for the boat. Remembering her question, she paused. "Hey, Rick, how come the mizzenmast is lying at such a strange angle?"

He paddled toward her again. "A storm at sea can do weird

things to a boat. No telling which way the mast fell when it snapped. The underwater currents could have carried it off in a different direction."

"I noticed you've laid your grid out so perfectly in a straight line. But how can you be sure the front half of the boat's not lying somewhere else? Bits and pieces here and there?"

"Well, it's pretty clear from the ballast spill. . . ." He studied her. "The captain's quarters are right where they should be."

"But the rest of the dig isn't turning up a thing."

"The prow is usually pretty slim pickings."

She shrugged. "It just occurred to me that parts of the boat could be other places in the bay. You know what I mean? I saw those artist's renderings of the *Titanic* in *National Geographic.* When the ocean liner broke in half, part of it spiraled down like a spinning top. Couldn't that have happened to your ship in a big storm? Especially since it had hit a reef?"

He stared at her. "Jessie, do you want to take a stab at looking for the prow?"

"Me? I wouldn't know where to begin. I don't even know what I'd be trying to find."

"Angular shapes. Coral growing in unnatural patterns—straight lines, parallel lines, right angles, perfect circles. Obvious things like anchors or masts lying around."

"Needles in a haystack, in other words. No thanks. I'll leave the treasure hunting to you and Hunky." She paused. "But if I were you, I'd use that mizzenmast as a guide. Maybe the prow just broke off and swung around. I mean . . . it's a thought."

Again, she started for the diving boat. But Rick's hand closed around her arm. When she stopped swimming, she drifted against him. At the intimate contact, she caught her breath and drew back.

"What, Rick?"

"Come back down with me, Jessie," he said. "Show me where the prow is."

"But I don't know where it is."

"Come with me anyway. I'll help you look. We'll be a team."

Her instinct to snap back a sarcastic comment about the past was snuffed by the look in Rick's blue eyes. He wanted to be with her. He wanted her near. She could hear him beckoning even in the silence between them.

He held out a hand. Slowly she slipped her fingers through his. "Rick," she whispered. "I'm afraid."

As his eyes searched hers, she knew he understood what she meant. She wasn't afraid of the water. She could coexist with octopi and sea urchins. It was *him.* Rick McTaggart. She was scared to death of the way he made her feel.

"I told you I'd protect you, Jessie," he said. "That means I'm going to guard you from all pain. Even from hurt I might cause myself."

"I don't see how. How can we be a team . . . in anything?"

"We already are. Paul said, 'We are all one body, we have the same Spirit, and we have all been called to the same glorious future.'"

"Rick, how do you know all these verses? It's like you have a Scripture for everything."

"There *is* a Scripture for everything. God didn't create us and abandon us here without any guidance. You and I—and Hannah, Daniel, Tillie, Graeme—and everyone who has surrendered to Christ's call are on the same team." He ran a finger down the side of her face. "Jessie, please don't be afraid of me. I won't hurt you again. Try to trust me one step at a time."

Vibrantly aware of his touch, aching to know the warmth of his arms around her, Jess nodded. "All right. Let's go look for your ship."

֍ ֍ ֍

A huge coral head lay twenty yards from the place where Hunky Wallace's crew was salvaging. Jess had noticed it on her earlier dive. She had wondered briefly if it might be a home for some interesting fish, and then she'd dismissed it.

Now she and Rick left the others behind and swam toward the coral. Outfitted with scuba tanks to free them from staying near the diving boat, they kicked in unison to propel them forward. Jess didn't like the feel of the heavy metal tank on her back. She didn't quite trust the contraption, which took more getting used to than the simple breathing gear for the surface-air supply system Hunky used.

Before they left the diving boat, Rick had given Jess a brief refresher lesson. Years before, of course, they had dived along the Kenya coastline—but Jess had shelved her memories of scuba diving, motorcycling, parasailing, and anything else that might remind her of Rick McTaggart. For ten years, she had avoided even the taint of adventure.

Together in the Indian Ocean again, he had retaught her the importance of the buoyancy control, the device that could make her sink or rise at the press of a button. Then he had reminded her about the regulator, the exposure suit, the octopus tubes, and the underwater pressure gauge. The whole process had nearly dampened the limited enthusiasm she felt for the project. After all, what did she know about hunting for shipwrecks?

But once Jess and Rick sank beneath the surface and began making their way toward the coral head, her artist's fascination took over. The monolith was draped in waving fronds of seaweed. Large gorgonian fans decorated craggy nodes. A school of tiny, luminescent, turquoise fish darted away from Jess's hand as she swam toward them. Black-spined sea urchins nestled in pockets and clustered like miniature porcupines in the hollows. She could almost hear James Perrott exclaiming, *"Kima the Monkey and the Unfriendly Urchin!* Jessica, what a lovely concept for our twenty-first book!"

Scanning the bottom, she noted that the sand surrounding the coral head was vast and almost smooth. White ripples barely disturbed its surface. An occasional starfish with brilliant orange or red markings lay unmoving on the ocean floor. A sea cucumber rested near a broken conch shell. A large yellow-and-blue fish swam beneath her. Three striped angelfish glided past.

And then Jess swam right over the anchor. She sucked in a deep breath of air and nearly choked. Bubbles exploded from her tube. A sheet of her own hair drifted across her face mask, scaring her half to death. She managed to grab the end of Rick's fin, stop him, and point excitedly downward at her discovery.

In less than a minute, he had dived the dozen feet to the anchor. Jess stayed above, madly blowing through her nose to try to even the pressure in her ears. Oh, she had never been meant for deep-sea diving! But she ached to get to the anchor and examine it.

Breathing hard, she stroked downward to Rick's side. He was combing the enormous coral-encrusted hunk of iron, his gloved hands touching every surface. It appeared the crew of the ship had tossed the anchor near the coral head in hopes of securing a hold. But the ship must have been too far gone.

As Rick studied the anchor, Jess swam on alone around the coral head. She could hear her heartbeat hammering in her ears, and she knew she was breathing too fast. Rick had cautioned her to take it slowly. Chill, excitement, and fear could quickly use up the air tank of a novice diver, he had reminded her. She sucked a deep breath through the mouthpiece and willed herself to calm down.

Impossible!

She now recognized wreckage from the ship lying clearly outlined all along the seafloor. A mast here, another mast there. A large, round metal tank lay on its side. Timber ribs from the ship's prow jutted up from the sand. This was it! Half the ship had sunk right here!

Pinching her nose, Jess blew air into her ears again and swam deeper. *This* must have been what Splinter had imagined when he'd pictured a shipwreck. A large section of the ship was still intact, and Jess paddled toward the gray hulk. This was incredible!

Glancing behind her, she saw that Rick was still exploring the anchor. She debated going back for him, then decided to have a little adventure on her own—a private Jacques Cousteau moment. Running her hands along the sand, she picked up a crusty metal rod with a block of corroded iron attached to one end. Then she paused and dug out what looked like the center of an old wheel—a round central hoop with four two-foot-long spokes radiating outward.

Respecting Rick's commitment to archaeology, she set a couple of coral chunks in the places from which she had taken her finds. No doubt he would want to mark down everything on a new grid. For the first time, Jess understood his excitement. She felt a sense of the unmatched joy of discovery. And to know she held in her hands a piece of history—untouched for decades—thrilled her.

Swimming toward the intact section of the prow, she wondered what she might find next. Another anchor? A china plate? Perhaps even a sunken treasure chest? She ran her hand over the wooden timbers. Spongy, covered with wormholes, they were draped with dank green algae. They felt slimy to the touch, and she sensed they could be broken easily. If Hunky got into them with his airlift, they would disintegrate.

Jess took a breath . . . and nothing came. *Nothing.* Stricken with instant panic, she glanced down at the gauge on her air tank. Empty. She searched the murky waters. *Rick! Rick!*

Head down, he was engrossed in chipping the coral crust from the anchor. *Rick!* Her eyes filling with tears of terror, she kicked toward him. Her foot struck the timber prow. A long, snakelike shape darted out. Mouth open, rows of teeth bared, it lunged straight at her.

THIS was the anchor that had been fixed in the prow, no doubt about it. The plow anchor. Rick swam around the mass of corroded iron. Here was its ring, head, stock, shank, and crown. Both arms were intact, and both flukes—though coated with coral—still held. This was quite a find. The museum on the island would welcome the anchor, if there was any way they could figure out how to raise it. No telling how much the thing weighed.

Jessie was amazing, Rick thought as he used his knife to nick a barnacle from the anchor. She had led him almost straight to the anchor. In spite of her outward disinterest in the salvage project, she had an uncanny feel for the ocean and its mysteries. Wondering what she might have stumbled across while he'd been examining the plow anchor, he lifted his head.

Through the hazy gray water he could see a distant movement. Frantic movement. A discarded air hose. Arms and legs flailing. *Jessie!*

Adrenaline surging through him, Rick shot toward her as fast as his flippers would propel him. Instantly he could see she was in serious trouble. An eel hung suspended half out of its hole, darting at her with its long teeth bared. Jessie had lost the mouthpiece to her scuba tank, and she was futilely waving some kind of rod at the creature.

As he approached, Rick realized she was losing ground fast. Already her face had turned an ugly shade of blue gray, and her movements were lethargic. She was too deep. Too frightened. She was drowning.

Lord, help me! Please don't take her, God! Not now!

Surging forward, he threw one arm around Jessie and brandished his knife at the eel. Without a speargun, there was no way he could kill the thing. It was angry and aggressive in defending its territory. But Rick knew that almost any wild animal could be evaded. Holding Jessie around the waist, he paddled backward. The eel followed for a moment, taking nips at his fins, then it hung back.

The instant he felt they were at a safe distance, Rick grabbed one of the octopus hoses that was attached to his air tank. The secondary air source had been designed for a situation like this, but Rick had never used one except in training. As he kicked toward the surface, he placed the breathing gear in Jessie's mouth and turned on the air supply. She was limp, dangling in his arms. The light reflecting through the water gave her skin a gray pallor. As they rose, the water cleared to indigo, blue, and finally emerald green.

"Jessie!" Rick cried as he burst above the surface. "Jessie, can you breathe? Come on, sweetheart, breathe for me!"

He swam her to the diving boat. With a strength born of terror, he hauled them both on deck in seconds. Fighting fear, he jerked off his face mask and hers and began to compress her chest with his hands.

"Jessie, breathe. Breathe!" He covered her mouth with his and exhaled. Her rib cage rose as her waterlogged lungs filled with air. He pushed again. Breathed into her again. Prayed.

God, oh God, help me!

"Come on, Jessie! I love you." He compressed her chest. "I love you, Jessie."

She coughed. Water burbled out of her mouth. "Rick," she croaked, and curled into a fetal position. Coughing, groaning, she rolled against him.

"Breathe, honey," he whispered. "Breathe the air."

"I'm sick," she murmured. "I'm going to be sick."

He held her head as she retched into a bailing scoop he managed to grab in the nick of time. Smoothing back her hair, he could only thank God she had survived. Her skin felt cold, and her arms were covered in goose bumps. Cradling her, he wiped her face with a towel. Then he wrapped another towel around her and lifted her into his lap.

"You OK, Jessie?" he murmured, studying her ashen face. "Can you breathe?"

She let out a moan. "Rick . . ."

"I'm right here, Jessie. I've got you."

Her violet eyes flickered open. For more than a minute she stared at him, sucking in air, her gaze searching and memorizing his features. Then she let out a deep breath. "I was dead," she whispered.

"No."

"Almost."

"I should have stayed with you, Jessie. I promised I'd protect you, but I—"

"Shhhh." She shut her eyes. "I wandered away. Wanted to see the wreck. My fault."

He stroked his fingers over her wet hair, relieved at the gradual return of the pink blush in her cheeks. *Lord, I almost lost her again—this time forever.* Fear still ricocheted through his chest, making his heart hammer and his pulse throb in his ears. In his arms she felt light, fragile, a delicate treasure that had nearly slipped through his fingers.

"I love you, Jessie."

Her eyes slid open again. Wide, seeking. Damp black lashes nearly touching the arch of her eyebrows. Mouth parted. Lips flushed and full.

"Did you hear me?" he asked.

"Yes."

That was enough. He didn't expect a response. He just needed her to know. Maybe after she felt better, she would push him away again. Even so, he wanted her to understand how he felt. He loved her. He always had. Always would. Nothing could change that.

Head resting on his shoulder, she shut her eyes and seemed to sleep. He lost track of the time, content to let her trust in his strength, watching the sun sink into the pink-and-orange sea. And then heads began bobbing up around the boat. Hunky. Andrew. Splinter.

"Rick!" The boy waved a long skinny arm. "Wow, you should see what we've got in the hoisting basket. It's mondo awesome!"

"McTaggart, where've you been?" Hunky hollered. "We needed your help, man. We've found a chest!"

"It's embedded in coral." Splint heaved himself onto the diving platform. "We can't get it out, but—hey, what's going on with Mom? Are you OK, Mom?"

"She had a close encounter with an eel."

"An eel!"

"I hate eels," Jessie said, lifting her head and giving her son a warm smile. "Did you have fun, big guy?"

"Mom, it's totally unbelievable down there. You should've seen Hunky and Andrew and me working on that pit. We found dishes and teacups and a clay pipe and a little statue. We even found a gold chain! Did you know gunk doesn't grow on gold? Remember how silver clumps all together in those biscuits? But not gold. Gold stays shiny. We think there might be gold in the chest, but we can't get it out of the coral. It's metal. Hunky blasted it with the airlift, but it wouldn't budge. Are you sure you're all right? You look kind of green."

"I'm fine, sweetheart."

"Whoa, what's in this bailing scoop? Mom, did you barf on Rick again? Yuck-a-roli, how could you do that?"

"She missed me this time, scamp." Rick ruffled Splint's rapidly drying hair. "Hey, you'd better help Andrew haul that basket up. Looks like it weighs a ton."

"McTaggart, you're needed as well," Hunky hollered over his shoulder. "Enough lollygaggin' with your fair lady. Come and give us a hand."

Rick slid Jessie from his lap to the padded bench. "Are you going to be OK?" he murmured.

"I'm fine. I think I'll leave the Poseidon adventure to you professionals, though. I've had enough eels to last a lifetime."

"You found the entire front half of the ship, Jessie," he said. "You're as professional as any of us."

"I bet I'm the first diver who ever ran completely out of air."

"You're not. And I bet you'll be back in that water by tomorrow." He gave her a wink. "You've been bitten by the treasure bug."

"I've been bitten by an eel. I wouldn't be surprised if there are fang marks on my flippers."

He laughed. She was smiling as he turned to join the efforts of the crew in hauling up the hoisting basket.

"Hey, Rick," she called.

He swung around.

"Thanks. For everything."

"Anytime."

@@@

Standing at the rail of the hydrofoil, her hair blowing away from her face, Jess recognized the tall figure waiting at the edge of the Dar es Salaam wharf. In his Sunday suit and tie, Rick cut a handsome silhouette. He lifted a hand, and Jessie's heart turned over.

I love you, he had told her. *I love you, Jessie. Did you hear me?*

Yes, she had heard his deep voice reverberating all night long. He loved her. How long had it been since anyone had spoken those words to her? Other than Splint, with his boyish hugs and chocolate-cookie smooches, it had been ten years. *I love you, Jessie.*

The words felt so good, so warm, so right—and yet they frightened her beyond belief. A thousand questions had swarmed through her mind all night. Did he really mean it when he said he loved her? Or had it just come out of the impulse of the moment after he had rescued her? If he meant it, what would he do about it? What should she do about it? Did she love him?

"I believe a storm will come," Hannah said beside her. "Look there, in the east."

Jess looked back over her shoulder toward the island of Zanzibar. As Hannah had noted, a huge bank of gray clouds was building on the horizon. They would probably bring rain. A good thing, if Solomon's observations could be trusted. He had told Jess the plants were suffering. "They wish to drink water," he had said. "They are thirsty."

Strange man. Again she wondered if Solomon could have

murdered Dr. bin Yusuf. Possibly. In the days since Splint's discovery of the bloody urn, Jess had watched Solomon carefully as he went about his business. He was clearly enamored of Miriamu. Jess didn't know how she had missed it.

"I believe the rain is going to bring big waves," Hannah said. "This I do not wish to see."

"Mama Hannah? I've never known you to be afraid of anything. If it's a little choppy this afternoon, are you going to worry about riding back on the hydrofoil?"

"I think of that disobedient man Jonah."

"Jonah? Who spent three days in the whale?"

"Three days and three nights. 'I sank beneath the waves, and death was very near. The waters closed in around me, and seaweed wrapped itself around my head. I sank down to the very roots of the mountains. I was locked out of life and imprisoned in the land of the dead. But you, O Lord my God, have snatched me from the yawning jaws of death!'"

"Mama Hannah!" Jess couldn't hold back a laugh. "That's so morbid."

"I remembered it when you told me yesterday about what happened to you at the bottom of the sea."

Jess took the older woman's hand and held it tightly. The dark coffee-colored skin felt loose and soft, like an old well-worn handkerchief. How many times had Hannah's hands soothed the fears of her four *totos?* It had never occurred to Jess that one day her own hands could reach out, comfort, and reassure the one she loved so deeply.

"If it's too rough, we'll wait here in Dar es Salaam," she told Hannah. "We won't cross on a stormy sea, OK?"

The dark brown eyes glowed as they studied the approaching wharf. "I wait with great happiness for the day I will greet my Lord in heaven," Hannah said softly. "I am not afraid of death. But if I can choose at all, I will not wish to face it at the bottom of the ocean. Water is good for drinking. Good for bathing. Maybe good for swimming. But ehh . . . these old Kikuyu bones of mine wish to be laid to rest on the land."

Jess slipped her arm around the frail shoulders. It sobered her to think of ever losing Hannah. What would she do without the security of knowing this woman loved her and was always available to her? The thought dampened her spirits as she stepped off the hydrofoil onto the wharf.

"Rick, guess what!" Splint danced toward the tall man. "You know that chunk of conglomerate Hunky let me keep last night? I found something in it! Take a look at this!"

"Hey, it's a buckle." Rick clapped the boy on the shoulder. "It's in good shape, too."

"I was super careful chipping it out. You should have seen me. I did it with a little pick and a toothbrush, just like you showed me. And I found something else. How about this?"

"A spike. That's great."

"It was in the conglomerate, too."

"Morning, Jessie," Rick said, his blue eyes brilliant in his deeply tanned face. He held open the car door for her. "How are you feeling today?"

"I'm fine." She was so used to seeing him in his bathing trunks, she felt tongue-tied at this suave gentleman. "Mama Hannah thinks a storm is blowing up."

"She's right. Don't worry, Hannah, they won't operate the hydrofoil unless it's safe."

"Ehh."

On the ride to Daniel McTaggart's church, Splint chattered nonstop about the shipwreck. Rick listened and responded, but his focus was clearly on Jess. He complimented her dress. He asked if the breeze blowing through the open car window was bothering her. He commented on the high quality of the artifact sketches she had been giving him and how pleased he was with her work.

Jess let herself enjoy the masculine attention. In fact, she felt almost giddy, like a schoolgirl whose pigtail has just been dunked in ink by the cutest boy in class. She not only enjoyed Rick, but more and more she was growing to trust him. She trusted his words to be true. She trusted his promises to be fulfilled. She trusted his actions to be honest and fair. Was she a fool?

"Here's the church," he announced with obvious pride. "You can't imagine how hard it is to speak out for Christ in a Muslim environment like Dar es Salaam. But God has really blessed Daniel's efforts. And you should hear my little brother preach. Sometimes he out-hollers the muezzins on the minarets of the local mosque."

Jess chuckled as she led Splint and Hannah into the small, whitewashed building. Dan—a younger, shorter, and much more ebullient version of Rick—greeted her with warm enthusiasm. His wife and children scattered on the benches, mingling easily with the mixture of Africans, Indians, and Europeans who made up the congregation. Gradually the church filled to capacity, and the service began.

Jess had not been in a church for years, and she had almost forgotten the warmth and acceptance such a gathering could bring. Her bitterness had kept her away. Now, in the presence of other believers, her heart swelled with hope, peace, even joy. The hymns lifted her spirit and beckoned her into worship; the prayers brought her into close communion with Christ; the message stirred her.

Rick had been right. Daniel McTaggart could really preach. Unfortunately for Splint, the sermon was in Swahili. The ten-year-old concentrated for a while, and then he began to fidget. Jess did her best to translate the sermon—a retelling of Christ's parable of the prodigal son and its message of the heavenly Father's love for those who return to his arms.

Jess herself had been a wayward child, she realized as she pulled a piece of paper from her purse and began to sketch. Her drawings had always entertained Splint, and now with her renderings of the wheel spokes and the iron bar she had found at the new wreck site, she hoped the wiggly boy would settle down. Splinter had been in church only a handful of times in his life. The rituals so familiar to her were novel to him, and they would take some getting used to.

It bothered Jess to recognize in her son the consequences of her own self-centeredness. Whereas Hannah had molded and taught the four Thornton *totos* in the path of the Lord, Splint knew next to nothing about the Bible and the Good News it contained. As much as Jess loved her son, she had failed him in this most important facet of his upbringing. And all because of her own hardened heart.

As the service was ending, the first cracks of thunder echoed outside the little church. Rain began to pelt the corrugated tin roof and splatter on the sandy dirt of the courtyard. A bolt of lightning lit up the gray sky with a brilliant golden flash. Splint grabbed his mother's hand.

"Mom!"

"It's OK, honey," she whispered as they walked down the central aisle. "It's just a tropical thunderstorm."

"What if there's a hurricane? What if a tidal wave washes over us? Did you ever think about that? A tidal wave could travel all the way from India and sweep us all right out to sea."

"Splint, you're letting your imagination run away with you. To my knowledge, there has never been a tidal wave in the recorded history of East Africa."

"There's always a first time."

Jess was grateful when Rick slung an arm around the boy's shoulder. "Hey, buddy, after lunch how would you like to see my laboratory?"

"Really?" Eyes shining, Splint turned to Jess. "Did you hear that, Mom? Rick said he'd take me to his lab!"

"Jessie?" Rick asked. "Would that be all right with you?"

"It would take his mind off the storm. Sure." She gave a little shrug. "I'd like to see the lab myself."

Rick's smile broadened. "It's a deal."

"Mom made a couple of new sketches for you, Rick." Splinter held out the page. "Look, it's a wheel. And some kind of a bar-thingy with a block stuck on one end of it."

Rick took the sketch and studied it for almost a minute as the storm raged outside the little church. When he lifted his head, his eyes were narrowed in confusion. "Jess, I don't remember anything like these in the stuff we've hoisted up. When did you see them?"

"Yesterday. The new site."

"New site?" Splint cut in. "What new site? Mom, you didn't tell me there was a new site."

"I picked them up out of the sand," she told Rick. "But I left coral markers so you could plot them on your chart. I was very careful about that."

"Where are they now? These artifacts?"

"I must have dropped them when the eel attacked me. Rick . . . why are you looking at me like that?"

"Do you know what you've sketched here, Jessie?"

She studied her own drawings for a moment. "Well, I thought that first picture was probably a wheel. I mean, it has spokes and an axle. If you welded a metal rim around the edge, you could use it on a cart or a wagon."

He ran one finger over the sketch. "You've placed small double-barbed hooks at the end of each spoke."

"Yes. They were pretty corroded, but that's what I saw."

"This is no wheel, Jessie. This is what we call an iron necklace. Its purpose was control, confinement, and torture." He touched the other picture. "And this is a branding iron. It was created for one purpose—to burn an owner's mark into bare flesh."

Her heartbeat hammering in her ears, she looked into his eyes. "What are you telling me, Rick?"

"I'm telling you our wrecked ship didn't carry a cargo of gold. It didn't have tea or spices or uncut gemstones, either. The ship that sank in your bay had a human cargo, Jessie."

A chill poured through her. "Slaves."

◎ ◎ ◎

Splint decided tropical storms were for the birds. In fact, the whole day was turning into one gigantic drip. Sure, it had started out great—a pocket full of artifacts he had extracted from the conglomerate, a ride on the hydrofoil, the promise of a look at Rick's laboratory. Even the church service had been sort of interesting.

Rick's brother had preached the whole sermon in Swahili, but the singing had been fun. It was cool to see all the different kinds of people mixed together. And something had changed Splint's mom—he didn't know if it was Hannah or Rick or Zanzibar—but he knew she was calmer and happier. Maybe it was God. Anyway, Splint would go to church every day if he thought it would bring that pretty smile to his mom's face.

But then the storm struck. No matter how everyone tried to reassure Splint, he had no doubt a storm blowing in from the ocean could bring hurricanes and tidal waves and waterspouts and who knew what else? Hurricanes could smash buildings. Waterspouts could sink ships. Tidal waves could wipe out whole towns. He'd read about tidal waves plenty of times in his science-discovery books. As much as he liked diving, he didn't want to get clobbered by a monster wave.

And what about the lightning? There they all stood in a metal-roofed church building! Talk about asking for trouble! Rain was coming in through the open windows. Wind blew leaves off the trees and slapped them into the walls. Thunder made the whole floor shake.

As if the storm wasn't bad enough, Rick had just discovered that the wrecked ship probably had been carrying slaves. This had put Hannah into a funk, and she kept muttering things about human sin and the evils of Satan. Rick had decided he needed to inform Hunky of the development, a situation that meant the trip to the laboratory might have to be postponed. After all, Hunky Wallace would not be located easily on a Sunday morning.

The whole group raced out to the parking lot, Splint eyeing the sky every step of the way, searching for the bolt of lightning with his name on it. They were soaked to the skin by the time they all piled into the car. For some dumb reason, Splint's mom was laughing.

Correction, she was giggling.

In the front seat, Rick brushed her wet hair out of her eyes and wiped a raindrop from the end of her nose. Lo and behold, she leaned over and planted a kiss right smack-dab on his cheek! Then he chuckled and kissed *her* cheek. The next thing Splint knew, they were gazing into each other's faces like a couple of goo-goo-eyed puppies. It was as bad as one of those mushy movies his mom sometimes watched.

"Hey, can we get this show on the road?" he called from the backseat. He rolled his eyes at Hannah. "You realize what a target we are in a car, don't you? Lighting loves metal. It races right to it, and *zap!* You're fried! And a tidal wave? In this car, we'd be at the bottom of the ocean in two seconds flat."

"Ehh. We must be strong in the Lord," Hannah said. "Paul told us to give thanks in all things. Did you know my people were able to give thanks even when they were sold into slavery?"

"Give thanks?" Splint jumped as the car chugged to life. He felt like all his nerves were jangling. "Maybe the slaves gave thanks, but how can we be anything but freaked out when we're on the verge of being swept out to sea in a tropical hurricane?"

"Did I teach you the Swahili song of thanks?" Hannah closed her eyes and gave a hum. "Are you ready?"

"Let us go to heaven," Splinter finished in the traditional response.

"Asante sana, Yesu.
Asante sana, Yesu.
Asante sana, Yesu, moyoni.

"Asante sana, Yesu.
Asante sana, Yesu.
Asante sana, Yesu, moyoni."

Splint liked the tune, and the words were easy. Before long he could sing it as well as Hannah.

"What's it mean?" he asked as Rick pulled the car up to a small streetside restaurant.

"'Thank you very much, Jesus,'" Hannah translated. "'Thank you very much, Jesus, in my heart.'"

As he hurried into the restaurant, Splint hummed as loudly as he could in hopes of drowning out his fears. He was counting on things getting a lot better after he was inside looking at a menu full of good food. They weren't any better at all. The restaurant was an Indian curry joint!

It featured a big buffet with all kinds of unrecognizable stuff—mustard-colored stew with hunks of cauliflower, potatoes, and chicken floating around in it; mounds of fluffy yellow rice; chutneys that looked like something Splint had stirred up in his home science lab; and flat white bread hardly thicker than a sheet of paper. You'd have thought Rick and his mom had just stepped into paradise.

While the storm raged outside, the lovebirds ate and ate, talked and talked, laughed and laughed. It might have been OK if they'd been discussing the slave ship. But Rick had asked about the Kima the Monkey books.

He would say things like, "Did you do one on Kima and the Cranky Coelacanth?"

That totally hilarious comment sent Splint's mom into gales of giggles. Then she would say something equally hysterical like, "How about Kima and the Elusive Eel?"

Then they'd both guffaw. It was enough to make a kid want to hurl. After lunch, Rick drove them through the rain to his apartment where he could use his telephone to call Hunky. The apartment was pretty cool. It was small with bare white walls and a couple of chairs, a little square table, and a twin bed. Splint wouldn't have thought much of the place, but Rick had filled his shelves with all kinds of wonderful artifacts—every one of them labeled and tagged.

"I do not believe we will go home to Uchungu House today," Hannah said, assessing the storm through Rick's big window. "The ocean is very rough. The waves are big."

"Maybe we'll just stay here with Rick until it blows over," Splint said. "It would be OK to spend the night here, wouldn't it, Mom?"

"No, sweetheart. If we have to say, we'll take a hotel room."

"Aw, Mom! Rick wouldn't mind."

"Splint." Her voice held that note of warning.

"Look, Mom, this has been the worst day of my entire life, OK? I mean, I'm expecting a tidal wave any minute. And you and Rick take me to eat curry. And the treasure ship turns out to be a slaver. And now you're telling me—"

"Someone's knocking on the door, Splint," she said. "Now, answer it, please, and stop your griping."

"Or I'll give you something to gripe about," he finished under his breath. Moms didn't have a clue. They really didn't.

He pulled open the door. Two tall African men stood in the hallway, the shoulders of their uniforms splattered with raindrops. The one in front studied Splint for a moment.

"Spencer Thornton?" he asked.

Splint backed up. "Yeah."

"We will take you to the police station in Zanzibar. You must give your fingerprints to check for the possibility of murder."

"THIS is a ten-year-old boy," Rick said to the policemen who had stepped into his apartment. "He's capable of a lot of things. The murder of Ahmed Abdullah bin Yusuf isn't one of them. First of all, he and his mother weren't even in this country until several months after the artist's death. Second, he's not strong enough to have won out in a struggle with a grown man."

"Yes, *Bwana,* but Mrs. Cameron gave us a report that the boy discovered the container on which the blood of Dr. bin Yusuf was found. Was this not a true statement?"

"It is true, but—"

"I didn't do it!" Splint shouted. "I didn't kill anybody!"

Jess took her son's arm and pulled him against her. She could feel the trembles of fear radiating through every muscle in his body. Nestling him close, she ran her hand over his thick brown hair.

"Sir, my son is a child," she told the officer. "You're frightening him. I'm sure you can tell he couldn't possibly—"

"Madam, we are searching for the person who committed the murder of one of Tanzania's premier artists. Of course we do not have any reason to suspect your son. But if the boy touched the container that was used in the crime, his fingerprints will be evident.

We must record and study them in order to distinguish your son's prints from any others on the murder weapon. Surely you can understand why this is necessary."

"I didn't do it!" Splint hollered. "Mom, tell them I didn't kill anybody."

"They don't think you did it, Splint." She wrapped her arm around his chest, holding him tightly against her. "Sir, this is a Sunday afternoon. How did you even find us here?"

"Solomon Mazrui told us you had gone to Dar es Salaam to the church of Daniel McTaggart."

"Solomon!"

"He works for you, does he not?"

"He's my gardener."

"We went on the police boat to Dar es Salaam, and we questioned the minister, *Bwana* Daniel McTaggart. He directed us to this flat. Now we are eager to return to our headquarters in Zanzibar with this boy. Will you and your son come with us to the police boat, Ms. Thornton?"

"In this kind of weather?" Rick interjected. "You can't possibly take a little police boat safely across twenty-two miles of raging ocean. Why don't I drive Spencer to the Dar es Salaam police headquarters and get them to record his fingerprints? Then you can ferry the information over to Zanzibar whenever you want to."

The first policeman looked at the second, and they both shook their heads. "*Bwana* McTaggart, believe me, we do not wish to go across that water again today. It is a very bad storm. But we have been given orders to bring back the boy. The chief of detectives wishes to speak with his mother. And with him."

When Splint started to cry, Jess felt her ire rise. "I will not allow my son to travel in such dangerous conditions."

"Jessie, I'll go with Splint," Rick said. "There's no way these guys are going to agree to leave him here. I'll put him into my best life jacket, and we'll tough it out together. We'll be OK."

"I'm not letting my son go anywhere dangerous without me beside him," Jess said.

"But there's no need—"

"No, Rick. I'm going with you."

The light mood of the morning evaporated as Rick called his brother and relayed the news. Daniel affirmed that the police had been to his house just after noon to ask the whereabouts of Jessica Thornton and her son. Before hanging up, Rick asked his brother to pray for the safety of the passengers. Then everyone pulled on orange life vests. Even Hannah made up her mind to go along, announcing that she would not abandon Splinter in his hour of trouble.

"Jesus calmed the stormy seas," she reminded Jess as they trooped out to the police car. "Perhaps he will stop the wind and smooth out the waves."

He didn't.

The little police boat bobbed and dipped as it rose on the swell of one wave and plunged into the trough before the next. All around the boat, lightning flickered and flashed. Heavy gray clouds moved like a battalion of rumbling steamrollers across the sky. Sheets of rain pummeled the passengers. Thunder boomed across the water.

Jess didn't know when she had ever been so frightened. Though he put up a brave front, Splint's fear resounded into her like crashing waves as she sat cradling him in the bottom of the boat. Eyes shut tightly, Hannah sang hymn after hymn. Rick moved anxiously back and forth across the deck. When he wasn't giving the inexperienced policemen directions on how to pilot the boat through the storm, he was crouching beside Jess with his arms around her and their son.

The sound of Hannah's singing swept around the boat like a mournful dirge:

"I was sinking deep in sin,
Far from the peaceful shore,
Very deeply stained within,
Sinking to rise no more—"

"Mama Hannah, do you mind?" Jess called during the lull right after a loud clap of thunder. "That's not at all comforting."

"'Save me, O God,'" Hannah muttered, "for the floodwaters are up to my neck. Deeper and deeper I sink into the mire; I can't find a foothold to stand on. I am in deep water, and the floods overwhelm me.'"

"Mama Hannah." Jess laid a hand on the old woman's arm. "Come over here and sit close to Splint and me. We need your strength."

"Ehh, I am like the disciples of little faith," Hannah whispered, scooting into the protecting haven of Jess's embrace. "Oh, Lord! 'Pull me out of the mud; don't let me sink any deeper! Rescue me from those who hate me, and pull me from these deep waters. Don't let the floods overwhelm me, or the deep waters swallow me—'"

"Mama Hannah," Jess cut in. "Isn't there a verse that goes, 'Such knowledge is too wonderful for me, too great for me to know! I can never escape from your spirit! I can never get away from your presence! If I go up to heaven, you are there; . . . If I ride the wings of the morning—'"

"'If I ride the wings of the morning, if I dwell by the farthest oceans, even there your hand will guide me, and your strength will support me.'" Sopping, shivering, her voice still tremulous, Hannah began to recite verse after verse of God's comfort. "'Our fears for today, our worries about tomorrow, and even the powers of hell can't keep God's love away. Whether we are high above the sky or in the deepest ocean, nothing in all creation will ever be able to separate us from the love of God. . . .'"

On a good day, the twenty-two-mile crossing would have taken little more than an hour. This was far from a good day. Three hours after they had left the Dar es Salaam wharf, Rick finally spotted the coast of Zanzibar. Amid pouring rain and tossing waves, the policemen managed to bring the little boat into port. A few minutes later, the whole bedraggled crew stood in the Zanzibar police headquarters.

"Solomon put them up to this," Jess muttered to Rick as she watched the officers inking her son's fingers one by one and pressing them onto a sheet of white paper. "I'm going to fire him. He may have killed Dr. bin Yusuf, and he might turn on me. I don't want him around."

"I wouldn't blame Solomon for this," Rick said. "The police are just doing their job."

"On a Sunday afternoon?"

She turned to find a well-dressed African approaching from the rear of the building. He spoke to the two wet policemen. Then he examined Splint's fingerprints. Finally, he walked toward the sopping visitors.

"Madam, will you follow me, please?" he said in an educated British accent. "I wish to ask you a few questions regarding your acquisition of Uchungu House."

Jess spent the next hour confined in a small room with the chief detective of the Zanzibar police force. While she dripped onto the floor, he asked her one question after another, writing down her answers in his small notebook. Outside the narrow barred window, the rain finally stopped and the sun went down.

"Madam, during your residence in Zanzibar, have you encountered a gentleman by the name of Giles Knox?" the detective asked.

"The art-gallery owner? I've met him."

"And when did you first meet Mr. Knox?"

"Last week, I think it was. I was introduced to him by Omar Hafidh. He's the—"

"The nephew of Dr. bin Yusuf. Yes, I know him."

Jess went on. "Giles Knox had contacted Omar Hafidh, and together they looked me up. Knox wants to sell all of Dr. bin Yusuf's works that are still in storage at Uchungu House. He told me he has a buyer—some rich movie star in Hollywood."

"And Omar Hafidh? Did he expect to benefit from this sale?"

"Apparently his mother has a few paintings and some sculptures that her brother gave her years ago. Knox said the buyer would pay a higher price for the complete collection."

"Of course." The detective scribbled in his notebook for a moment. "Ms. Thornton, did you agree to sell the art collection using Mr. Knox as your agent?"

"I haven't made a decision about that. I really don't want to keep all the paintings, but I—"

"So you did not agree to his offer at the time you discussed this with Mr. Knox?"

"No."

"What was his response, Ms. Thornton?"

Jess thought for a moment. "He said . . . he said if I didn't take him up on the offer . . ."

"Yes, Ms. Thornton?"

"He said I'd regret it."

The detective's face betrayed nothing as he wrote down her words. Jess shivered. At the time she had spoken with Giles Knox she had found him manipulative and slightly repugnant, but not threatening. Now she wondered if his words had hinted at retaliation if she failed to comply with his wishes.

"Do you think Giles Knox might have killed Dr. bin Yusuf?" she asked the detective. "I mean . . . he really did want those paintings very badly."

"Did Mr. Knox give you any idea how much money would be involved in the sale of the artworks?"

"He didn't give me numbers, but he indicated that both he and I stood to earn a great deal of money."

"And Omar Hafidh also would benefit, of course."

Jess studied the man's dark eyes. "That's right."

"Thank you very much, Ms. Thornton. I apologize for the inconvenience we caused you and your son. Your husband also has expressed his displeasure."

"My husband? Oh, Rick. He told you he's my husband? Well, yes, he is . . . but . . . it's a little complicated. Anyway, I hope you don't need to talk to Splint. He was pretty frightened." Jess stood. Her skirt stuck to her legs like a piece of wet newsprint, and she made a feeble effort at detaching it. "You know, if you ask me, I think Solomon Mazrui might have killed Dr. bin Yusuf. At least Nettie Cameron says—"

"Solomon Mazrui's fingerprints were not found anywhere on the murder weapon, Ms. Thornton."

"But . . . but he—"

"Mr. Mazrui was, of course, our primary suspect. We have questioned him thoroughly. Twice. The first time was shortly after the murder, the second time was just after Mrs. Cameron brought the urn to the station. It is true, Solomon Mazrui found the body, and his original police report failed to disclose all the details of that event. But as you know, Mr. Mazrui has . . . shall we say . . . a distinctive style of communication. Sometimes it is difficult to determine exactly what he intends to convey."

"That's true. But you know, he's got my Renault engine hanging from the Red Hot Poker tree . . . and then there's Miriamu. And Nettie Cameron said—"

"Solomon Mazrui has not been eliminated as a suspect, Ms. Thornton, but I do not believe you should feel overly concerned about your family's safety in his presence. Again, thank you for your time. We shall call upon you again if the need arises."

I'm sure you will, Jess thought as she followed the man down the long hallway toward the front desk. Night had fallen, and Rick, Splint, and Hannah were eating spicy Indian samosas and drinking warm sodas in the lobby. When Splint looked up at her, his eyes revealed his continuing agitation over what had happened. She knelt at his side and wrapped her arms around his damp shoulders.

"It's OK, honey. They know you didn't do anything wrong."

He nodded and swallowed hard. "I want to go home, Mom."

Though Uchungu House had once been a place of threat, bitterness, even murder, tonight it was home. Jess lifted her eyes to heaven for a moment as she hugged her son. "Let's go home, sweetheart," she whispered.

The eerie wail woke Rick from a dead sleep. He sat up, fumbled for a lamp, and then remembered that Uchungu House had no electricity. What on earth was that noise?

"Aaa-aaa-aaa!"

His spine prickling, Rick swung his feet over the side of the couch in Jessie's downstairs living room and stood on the cool concrete floor. Moonlight poured through the long arched windows. Outside, the distant sound of waves crashing against the cliffs mingled with the rustle of palm leaves blowing against the glass windowpanes. Rick groped for his jeans, realized they were wet, and yanked them on anyway.

"Maa-aaa-aaa!"

It was a cry of desperation tinged with terror. Rick grabbed the first thing he could put his hands on—a carved ebony sculpture about the size of a baseball bat. Perfect. *Thank you, bin Yusuf.* For once, the man's artwork might prove useful. Pulse hammering, Rick followed the wail through the front of the house toward the courtyard. If anyone was hurting Jessie, he would—

"Maa-aaa-aaa!"

The sound was coming from Splint's bedroom.

"Maa-maa! Maa-maa!"

Rick took the back staircase two steps at a time. Emerging from the enclosed stairwell, he nearly ran full force into Jessie. At that moment, Hannah flung open the door of the next room.

"Splinter! I'm here," Rick shouted. "Stay back, Jessie."

He burst into the narrow room, and the door smacked against the wall. Brandishing his weapon, Rick looked around. No intruders. No thieves. No murderers. On the bed, inside a ball of wadded blankets, Splint groaned. Rick dropped the ebony sculpture and bounded to Splint's side, gathering up the damp tangle and cradling the boy against his chest.

"Hey, now. What's wrong, Splinter?"

"I want my mom!" he said, his voice trembling. "Mom!"

"I'm here, sweetheart." Jessie stepped into the room and sat next to Rick on the bed. She pulled the hood of blanket from around her son's head and kissed his cheek. "Shh, now. It's OK. I'm here."

Two long skinny arms snaked out from the blanket and wrapped around her neck. Rick looked up in time to see Hannah disappear from the doorway, a moonlit smile softening the lines on her face. As Splint lay half in Jessie's arms and half in his, Rick let out a deep breath.

"Whew," he murmured.

"I had a bad dream, Mom," Splint choked out. "These two bad guys were chasing me, and it was like one of those video games, you know, where the villains are throwing bombs and stuff at you? They were throwing pots and vases at me, like that one I found in the storage closet."

"Oh, sweetheart, it was just a dream." Her hand smoothed over his sweaty hair. "I know it must have been scary."

"Yeah, and I ran and ran, but they kept on throwing pots at me. Then the pots would explode. *Boom!* I was going down all these narrow hallways, and then I ran outside and jumped into a little boat. But then a storm came, and these huge waves were crashing onto me just like . . . just like . . ."

"Like this afternoon."

"Yeah."

For a moment Rick thought the realization of the dream's source had calmed Splint. Then the boy burst into a fresh round of sobs. His body shook, and he pressed his head against his mother's neck.

Never in his life had Rick felt so completely helpless. He had faced sharks. He knew what to do with an angry eel. He could handle a sea snake or a puffer or a stonefish. But a frightened little boy? His whole heart poured out for the child, and he felt the strongest urge to nestle Splint close and kiss his downy cheek—but what right did he have? For all Rick knew, something like that might scare him even further.

"The worst part of the dream, Mom . . ." Splint said in a strangled voice. "You were chasing me."

"Me?" Jessie looked up at Rick, her eyes alarmed. "I was chasing you, Splint?"

"Uh-huh. You weren't throwing pots, but you were after me. You weren't like my real mom. You were different. You were scary. You kept calling me, but I kept running away from you because . . . because I didn't trust you."

"Oh, Splinter!" Jessie hugged her son more tightly, burying her own face in his blankets. "Splinter, you know I would never hurt you. You can always trust me, honey. I've always taken care of you, haven't I?"

"Yeah."

"I'm always here for you. I always tell you the truth. Don't I?"

"I guess. Except when you think I'm too young to know it."

"Splint, we've talked about this before." Jessie tucked her hair behind her ear. "Now, I want you to settle down and try to get back to sleep. Hannah's right next door. I'm just down the hall, and Rick is in the living room. Nothing's going to hurt you, OK?"

"OK." Sniffling, Splint detached his arms from his mother's neck. Then he lifted his head and gave Rick a quick peck on the cheek. "I wish you wouldn't have to go back to your apartment tomorrow. I wish you would stay here with us."

Flooded with warmth at the boy's need for him, Rick had to force out his words. "This is a good safe house, buddy," he managed. "If I didn't think it was, I wouldn't leave you and your mom alone here for a second. You're going to be OK."

"What if I have another nightmare? Will you sleep in my room, Rick?"

"You don't need me looking over you. God is always with you, Splint. How about if I say a prayer and ask him to keep an extra-close watch on you tonight?"

"I'd like that."

Rick prayed words his own father had spoken when he was a little boy frightened by scary dreams. As he prayed, he could feel the tension ebb out of Splint's body. When he tucked the boy back into his bed, those long arms slipped around his neck once again.

"Good night, Rick," Splint murmured. "I love you."

A lump formed in Rick's throat. "I love you, too, Splinter."

He made it out of the room before the tears that had welled in his eyes spilled down his cheeks. Jessie caught up with him before he could make it down the stairs. Her hand fell on his arm, and he stopped. He leaned on the balcony rail and stared down at the courtyard, unwilling to let her see his face.

"Rick," she whispered, "thank you."

"For what?"

"For being here with us. For going to Splint. For your prayer."

He nodded. It wasn't enough. He wanted more than the occasional afternoon visit with the boy. More than childlike hero worship. More than the rare "I love you." He ached to become a part of Splint's daily life—to share with him not only his knowledge but also his values. He wanted to have a hand in molding Splint, in creating a strong man capable of becoming everything God intended him to be.

But what right did he have to desire any of that? Jessie might be his wife, but they didn't live together. They'd had no relationship for ten years. He had forfeited his rights with her—and with her son.

Jessie had been correct that night she had lashed out at him in the kitchen of Uchungu House. Splint was *her* son, and only hers. Rick had no idea who the child's father really was, and what difference did it make anyway? Even if Splint was his own flesh and blood, Rick had no right to him. For the first time in his life, he fully understood Jessie's anger and bitterness toward him. And he knew he deserved it.

"Looks like Dr. bin Yusuf's artwork is doing a lot of double time as weaponry these days," Jessie said.

Rick tried to smile. "Yeah. I guess you grab what's available."

"Are you available?"

He lifted his head. "What?"

"You've been coming in awfully handy these days." She took a step closer to him and slipped her arms around his waist. "Maybe I'd better grab you while I've got the chance."

Rick stared down in paralyzed shock as she laid her head on his chest. His heart felt like it was going to hammer its way right through his ribs. Uncertain, unwilling to risk breaking the spell of the moment, he gingerly laid a hand on her back. She let out a deep breath.

"I am so tired of fighting everything," she said. "Just when things seem to be falling into place, they get out of whack again."

"Yeah," he said. Not exactly eloquent, but it was about all he could manage. Her hair smelled like rainwashed lilacs, and he struggled to keep from burying his face in it and drinking the scent like a famished man. She was thinner than he remembered, and her skin felt warm through the fabric of her robe. He let himself run his fingers up to the ends of her hair and touch it gently. She tightened her arms around his chest.

"All these years," she murmured.

"Mm-hm."

"I've been doing the best I could all these years."

"You're wonderful."

She laughed a low husky laugh. "I'm talking about Splint here."

"Oh, yeah." He sifted his fingers through her hair, reveling in its silkiness. "Splint."

"He's just such a handful, you know. One minute he's spouting off words like he's Daniel Webster himself. The next he's sobbing about nightmares. It was always OK, just the two of us. Somehow I was all he seemed to need. Mommy this and mommy that. But as he gets older, he's so complicated. He's either brave or scared to death. He's angry or he's dancing up and down. He's sullen or he's talking a blue streak. You know what I mean, Rick?"

He tried to pull himself back from the heady ecstasy of holding Jessie tightly against him, smelling her skin, touching her hair, feeling her arms pressing him close. He needed to listen. Needed to hear what she was saying. But he needed her, too! It had been so long since he'd held this woman in his arms, and now it felt so very right.

"Splint's growing up," he said. "I remember how that felt. Things get crazy when you're ten, eleven, twelve. Thirteen and fourteen—I don't even want to think about those years. Hormones zinging and zanging. Voice up and down like a Swiss yodeler. Hair sprouting on my chin—"

He sucked in a breath as Jessie reached up and touched his jaw. "I don't think you were this bristly ten years ago."

"Maybe not."

"Definitely not." Her fingers stroked toward his ear, grazing the dark stubble he had to shave off every morning. "I don't know what I'm going to do when Splint starts into his teenage years."

"Pray," Rick said. "Pray hard."

She fell silent for a moment. Then she looked up into his eyes. "That's another thing. All these years I thought I was doing such a great job as a mother, and I failed to give Splint the most important foundation he needs to succeed in life. I rarely took him to church. We almost never prayed together. He doesn't know . . . he doesn't know the Lord, Rick."

"It's never too late." Dismayed at the tears glistening in Jessie's eyes, he pulled her closer. "You can always—"

"No, *you,*" she said. "You showed me how important faith is. You convinced me it can change a person. You taught me how to let go, how to forgive. *You* teach Splinter, Rick."

"Me . . ."

"You heard what he said about his dream. He can't trust me. He doesn't think I tell him the truth." Openly crying now, she swallowed down tears that threatened to choke her. "He's right. I haven't told him the truth."

"Jessie . . ."

"No, I mean it. He has to know!" She pushed back from him. "Splint is your son, Rick. You're his father. You tell him about Christ. You help him into his teenage years. You be there for him when he's scared and angry and sullen. Show him and teach him. I can't do it all. Not anymore. Not since he found you. Splint needs you, Rick. . . . Will you be his father?"

Breathing hard, Rick gripped Jessie's shoulders. "I'm his father? Are you sure?"

"Yes. I was pregnant when you walked out on me. I found out a week later. Mama Hannah stayed with me."

"Hannah knows?"

"Everything."

"Does Splint know?"

"He suspects." She took a step backward and gave a laugh that was half sob. "The two of you look exactly alike, Rick. You walk the same. You talk the same. You like the same things. It's so obvious! I've been so scared you would both find out—and tonight . . . in Splint's room . . . I suddenly knew you both *had* to find out. You need each other so much."

"Jessie . . ."

"Be a good father to him, Rick," she said. Then she turned and ran down the hall to her bedroom.

Splint is my son! Rick thought. *My son! Oh, God, how I need him.* He heard the bedroom door shut. *I need her, too, Lord. I need my wife so much.*

"I DON'T believe I did it," Jess whispered to Hannah the next morning in the kitchen. The two women, along with Miriamu, were preparing to carry breakfast out onto the courtyard dining table. "It seemed so right at the time. But then I lay awake all night worrying and praying and wondering if I'd made the biggest mistake of my life."

"You used to tell me that marrying Rick was your biggest mistake," Hannah said. She scored a mango half and flipped it inside out to expose the orange fruit. "I did not agree with you then. And I do not agree now. You were right to tell him. When will you tell the boy?"

"I can't even think about that!" Jess handed Miriamu a basket of fresh rolls and croissants. *"Bwana* McTaggart spent the night here at Uchungu House, Miriamu. He slept on the sofa in the living room, so we'll need to put away the blanket and pillow later. He'll be joining us for breakfast this morning."

"Yes, *memsahib*. And tomorrow?"

"I don't know about tomorrow." Jess paused. "No, definitely not. He'll be going back to his apartment this afternoon."

"Memsahib," Miriamu said. Her dark eyes stared intently at Jess.

"Two policemen came yesterday morning to talk to Solomon. They think someone killed *Bwana* bin Yusuf."

"Yes, Miriamu. I know they talked to Solomon about it."

"Solomon believes there may be danger here at Uchungu House for you and the boy."

"He does?"

"Perhaps it would be good for *Bwana* McTaggart to stay here with you until the policemen catch the bad man."

Jess picked up a bowl of steaming scrambled eggs. It was odd to think of Solomon Mazrui expressing concern over her and Splint. For so long now, she'd been thinking of him as the prime suspect.

"No, Miriamu," she said. "I don't believe that's necessary."

"Then Solomon can sleep here at Uchungu House. We have no children, so my husband is not needed to protect a family each night."

"Your husband? Wait a minute—are you telling me you're married to Solomon?"

Miriamu's black eyebrows arched. "Of course, *memsahib*. We are married for two years."

"I didn't know that. Then no wonder he walks you home at night. And the village . . . you always go together."

The young woman's face broke into a radiant smile. "Solomon and I live in the village near the shop of Akim, who offered to take you to Zanzibar town on his bicycle."

"You know about that? About the goat?"

"In the village, nothing is a secret." Miriamu hitched the basket of bread onto the curve of her hip. "Maybe one day you will come to the house of Solomon Mazrui. I will serve you a cup of tea."

As she strolled into the courtyard to finish setting the breakfast table, Miriamu left the scent of frangipani blossoms in her wake. Jess turned to Hannah.

"They're married. Did you know?"

"Ehh. She told me one day. They wish very much to have children, but God has not given them any babies. It is a great sadness to them."

"Mama Hannah, why didn't you tell me all this?"

"You must learn to look and ask questions for yourself. You

study many things with your careful eyes. You see the colors and shapes and shadows of everything you paint. But in some things, *toto,* I believe you are completely blind."

Chagrined, Jess followed the old woman into the courtyard in time to catch Rick emerging from a dip under the outdoor shower. Shirtless and barefooted, he was clad only in the jeans he had put on before their boat ride the day before. He rubbed a towel over his wet hair and gave her a lopsided smile.

"Morning, Jessie," he said. He hooked the towel around his neck, leaving his hair standing on end in a mass of damp spikes. "Sleep all right?"

"OK, I guess. You?"

"Not a wink." He walked toward her, so close she could see the water droplets glistening on his neck. "About last night. I've decided not to say anything to Splint. I think that should be between the two of you."

Jess nodded. For all her self-admonishments about how stupid she had been the night before, it was all she could do to keep from slipping her arms around Rick again. He looked so warm and real. So perfect in his damp jeans and messy hair and goofy grin. Thank goodness Hannah and Miriamu had both gone back into the kitchen.

She swallowed. "OK. I'll tell Splint. I'll tell him today."

"Will it be all right with you if I take him out on the boat this morning?" He held the ends of the towel in his fists. "I'd like to be with him, if you wouldn't mind. Sort of just observe him. Get used to the whole thing, you know."

"Thank you for asking my permission, Rick. I guess you've figured out you really don't have to anymore. You do have certain rights as his father."

"No, Jessie. I surrendered those rights ten years ago. I'll only take what you choose to give me."

She laid her fingertips on his arm. "Rick, I—"

"Come with us, Jessie," he urged her, his blue eyes intense. "Come out on the boat with Splint and me. We'll dive around the new wreck site. You can sketch whatever we haul up in the basket. I'd like to . . . I'd like to be with you, too."

She shook her head, feeling off balance with him standing so close. "I really need to paint today. My illustrations are due in London soon, and I can feel the deadline looming. James Perrott wrote me a letter. He wants sketches for the new book."

"The jealous jackal?"

Jess nodded, her eyes filling with tears again over the fact that Rick knew. He knew about the jealous jackal. He knew about her life, her work, her son. And he cared. He had made her important to him once again.

"Oh, Rick, I'm so scared about all this!" she said and covered her face with her hands.

"Jessie, I've got you." He pulled her into his arms, held her close, cupped the back of her head with his hand. "I promised I'd protect you. I said I'd never hurt you again. Please try to trust me—"

"Mom, did you know some of the caves in the coral cliffs along the coast of Zanzibar . . . were once used . . . to hold . . . slaves . . . ? Hey, what's going on?"

Splint was halfway down the stairs before Jess managed to stiffen and pull out of Rick's arms. Flushing like a guilty teenager caught spooning on the front porch, she brushed at her skirt. Rick cleared his throat.

"That's good research, Splint," he said. "At Mangapwani, about fourteen miles north of town, there's a slave hole. It's been covered by a stone slab."

"Oh yeah? I'd like to see it sometime." Splint walked down the steps, his eyes darting back and forth between the two adults standing in the courtyard. "So, what's going on?"

"Breakfast time," Jess said. "Did you wash your hands?"

"I mean what's going on with you guys? Have you been crying, Mom?"

"I'm just a little tense, Splint." She pulled back her son's chair. "I didn't sleep much last night. How about you, sweetheart? No more nightmares?"

"Nah. To tell you the truth, I think I was just kind of hungry last night." He picked up his fork. "Remember we had to eat that Indian curry for lunch? And then for supper all we had was samosas. I bet it was just hunger pangs."

Jess glanced at Rick. He gave her a wink.

"Hunger'll do that to you," he said, sitting down beside Splint. "We'll take along some extra snacks when we go out on the water today."

"Hey, am I going with you again? All right! Can we explore the new wreck site? Are you going to let Hunky go at it with the airlift? A slave ship—that's amazing. You know, the first thing we ought to do is put down a grid. I'll help you with that. But what about those eels that nearly got Mom?"

"I'll take my speargun."

"Cool! So, what do you think we'll find at the new site? Draw me a diagram of everything you discovered so far."

Splint slid a paper napkin in front of his father and grabbed a croissant. Rick took a pen from the back pocket of his jeans. He took a bite out of a roll and set it on his plate as he leaned over the napkin and began to sketch.

"See, here's where the anchor lies," Rick said around a mouthful of bread. "It's crusted over in a lot of places, but it's in remarkable shape for the number of years it's been underwater. The ring's still in place, and both flukes look great."

"Flukes?" Splint asked, his own mouth so full of bread it came out sounding like *fooks.* "Are those the finlike projections on the ends of each of the anchor's arms?"

Jess watched the two of them for a moment, and she had to bite her lip to keep from laughing out loud. Brown heads touching, they were bent over the diagram shoulder to shoulder. Oblivious to the world around them, munching on bread they weren't even tasting, they discussed the anchor as though there were nothing more important in life than the condition of the anchor and its *fooks.*

"Bwana Hunky has come," Hannah said, passing by Jess with a plate of sliced mangoes. She paused beside the younger woman and studied the two at the table. "I think they do not see or hear anything but each other."

"Like father, like son," Jess murmured.

Hannah smiled. "This is a good thing you have done, *toto.* In Swahili we say, *Mwana umleavyo, ndivyo akuavyo.* As you nurse your child, so he grows up."

"I hope you're right, Mama Hannah," Jess said. "Tell Hunky and his crew to come on in and join us. We might as well get this day off to as crazy a start as possible."

After the divers left for the morning, Uchungu House settled into an uncharacteristic calm. The rainstorm had left everything damp and muggy. Jess thought about Dr. bin Yusuf's artwork as she cleared the breakfast table. Giles Knox had been right about one thing. The paintings and sculptures did belong in a safe, dry environment.

But should she do business with the gallery owner? Undecided, Jess spent the morning painting impala and monkey illustrations in her studio bedroom. From the balcony, she could see Solomon laboring over the engine that still hung from the Red Hot Poker tree. Miriamu was singing in the kitchen below. Later in the morning, Hannah strolled down to the beach to have her usual prayer time.

At noon, Jess ate lunch on the sand with Hannah. They could see the diving boat out in the bay, but it was almost impossible to distinguish one figure from another. After lunch the police showed up again. This time they talked to Solomon, Miriamu, Jess, even Hannah. They examined the small storage room behind the stairs where Splint had found the bloody urn. Then they counted steps, took measurements of distances from one room to the next, and drew diagrams of the house.

The policemen had just left when a crew from the electric company showed up. They examined wires and drew more diagrams. Jess tried to keep painting, but her thoughts were on Splint and Rick anyway, so it hardly mattered that her work had been disrupted all afternoon.

She was putting the final touches on Impala's big birthday gala—complete with visitors from the previous books: Anteater, Baboon, Cheetah, Dik-Dik, Elephant, and so on—when Giles Knox drove up in a long white limousine. Jess watched him from her balcony as he emerged, looked around, smoothed down his natty ecru safari suit, and tucked his mirrored sunglasses into his shirt pocket. As he walked past his chauffeur toward the verandah, he ran his hand over his hair. Beneath her, Jess caught the unmistakable scent of roses.

Not wanting Miriamu to have to make the trip upstairs to alert her, Jess went on down to the sitting room. If Giles Knox was a killer, he was certainly the most dainty one she had ever heard of. He looked as slender and fragile as a hothouse flower. On the other hand, despite the urn's weight, both Splint and Nettie had managed to carry it without too much trouble.

"Mr. Knox," she said, pulling open the carved front door. "I see you decided to pay me a personal visit."

"I should have preferred to ring you up first, of course, but it's quite impossible to telephone Uchungu House," he replied, holding out a thin-fingered hand. "I'm sure you're well aware of that."

"Yes. Won't you come in?"

He was already walking through the door, his gaze fixed on the large painting of the storm scene that hung over the sofa where Rick had spent the night. "This is simply magnificent, isn't it?" he gushed. "But what's this? Oh, dear! Oh, my goodness gracious . . . do you see this? Look, Ms. Thornton. *Mildew!"*

He presented the small green spot as though he were announcing an Academy Award. Jess leaned over the sofa and squinted. "I see it," she said. "It could be mildew. Or it might just be a speck of green paint."

"I should think I know mildew when I see it! This is worse than I had anticipated. A painting of this caliber . . . covered with mildew."

"It's not exactly *covered."*

"Ms. Thornton, may we speak frankly?"

"Sure." She gestured to the sofa. Knox declined to sit. "But you might as well know up front that I haven't made up my mind what to do about Dr. bin Yusuf's art."

"I gathered that. I awaited your decision in Zanzibar, of course. When you failed to respond, I was compelled to leave the island and return to the business of overseeing my galleries. In the meantime, my dear Ms. Thornton, I have had further contact with the collector I mentioned to you who lives in America."

"The Hollywood guy?"

"My client is a most distinguished patron of the arts, madam.

He is quite concerned about the status of Dr. bin Yusuf's art. And when I tell him about the . . . the—"

"The mildew. Yes, I'm aware I need to make a decision."

"Today I have come for one purpose and one purpose alone." He paused and cleared his throat. "I beseech your permission to begin cataloging every single work of art in Uchungu House."

"But that would take days."

"I am prepared for that eventuality. Once again, I have booked a hotel room in Zanzibar in the fondest hope that you will give my request serious consideration." He took a step toward her and leaned close, his cloud of rose water enveloping Jess. "Madam, once I have organized and cataloged all the valuables, I shall consult my client. Within a few days after that telephone call, I should be able to present you with a concrete offer."

"Are you telling me you want me to give you free rein of Uchungu House? For as long as it takes? There are pictures and sculptures everywhere, Mr. Knox. The storerooms are full."

"Full!" He took a monogrammed white handkerchief from his pocket and mopped his brow. "Oh, my. Please, Ms. Thornton, I cannot overstate the urgency of this matter."

"I understand your feelings of urgency. You've had this big offer dangling for . . . for a long time. . . ." Jess stopped speaking and studied the gallery owner. "By any chance, did you work with this famous Hollywood client before Dr. bin Yusuf's death? Did you know how badly your client wanted the art?"

"Of course I knew! I am the primary worldwide supplier of African art, madam. I am intimate with my clientele."

"Did you personally ask Dr. bin Yusuf if he wanted to sell his work? Did you ever come out here to Uchungu House and talk with him?"

"I visited briefly. The man refused to consider selling even one piece. His behavior toward me was . . . it was . . . unconscionable!" He wrapped his thin fingers around Jess's upper arm and pulled her from the west sitting room into the east. "Do you see this portrait? It's very small and quite badly framed. The canvas is almost inconsequential in size. In this very room, Dr. bin Yusuf and I were discussing the matter of my valued client, and I begged him to let me show the portrait. Just this one tiny painting! Do you know what he said to me?"

Jess shook her head. Though she hadn't paid much attention to the picture since her initial sweep-through cleaning of Uchungu House, she remembered the haunting expression of the little boy. Now she took a step forward and studied the portrait carefully. There was something about the light-skinned little boy . . . something about the child's green eyes. . . .

"Did you see those weird green eyes of his?" Splint spoke those words once, but when? "That guy gave me the heebie-jeebies. . . ."

Omar Hafidh.

"Ms. Thornton?" Giles Knox asked. "Do you have any idea what Dr. bin Yusuf said to me about this small, inconsequential painting? He said, 'You may not have it. And you may not have this one, either,' at which time he pointed to this little painting of the woman with only half her face revealed. 'You may not have any of my works,' he told me. 'They are my life, and you will not take my life.'"

Jess swallowed. "You will not take my life?"

"That's what he said! Can you imagine? This little painting, clever though it is, can hardly be considered extraordinary. The one in the sitting room, however—*Storm at Sea*—now *that* canvas! That canvas is a masterpiece!"

Jess walked over to the picture of the woman. Suddenly she recognized it, too. The woman was Miriamu.

"I tell you, I have never met such a stubborn, willful man in my life," Knox continued, oblivious to Jess's epiphany. "Artists can be temperamental, of course. Well, you should know that. You're an illustrator of some sort, I believe you told me. At any rate, I've dealt with some difficult artists. But Dr. bin Yusuf . . . that man . . . he was exasperating. So easily outraged. So very . . . bitter."

"Bitter?" Jess turned.

"Oh, indeed. He was a man eaten through with bitterness. Impossible to see why, of course, with all his talent. He had so much. But the longer I knew him, the more I watched him wither. Devoured by his personal demons."

"That doesn't sound anything like the artist I knew in Dar es Salaam."

"People change. Something happened to him in the last years of his life. I don't know what it was. Something quite dreadful, I think. He never got over it. Never forgave. It consumed him. The man became totally impossible to reason with. But his works were still brilliant—still magnificent! Dear Ms. Thornton, do consider my request to catalog the contents of Uchungu House. I assure you I have the utmost respect for this art. I shall handle it with the greatest care, and when I am finished, I have no doubt you will thank me generously for my work."

"Thirty-five percent, as I recall," she said. "That's pretty generous, all right."

Jess crossed her arms and regarded the gallery owner as he strolled around the room inspecting the paintings. Had Giles Knox murdered Dr. bin Yusuf the day they argued? Clearly both men had been angry. The artist had stated he felt his life was threatened. When he refused to give up his artwork, had Giles Knox picked up the nearest thing he could find and bashed Dr. bin Yusuf in the head?

Shuddering, Jess followed the man with her eyes. Maybe Knox was a killer. But he didn't scare her. In fact, she was getting just a little tired of this whole business. She wanted to know who had murdered her friend, and she suddenly decided it was time to find out for herself.

The Zanzibar police detectives said they were doing all they could. But she lived right here at Uchungu House. She could study, question, examine—even draw diagrams of her own. She could spend hours at a time in the company of every person who might have been involved in the murder. Solomon Mazrui. Miriamu. Hunky Wallace. And now she had Giles Knox within reach.

"All right," she said. "I'll give you three days. You can come first thing in the morning along with Hunky Wallace and his divers. I'll expect you to go at sunset when they leave. Don't talk to my son, and don't bother my employees. I'm painting under a deadline—yes, I'm aware that's not very artistic, but it's how I make a living, Mr. Knox—so I'll ask you not to disturb me unless it's an emergency. When you've finished, I want to see everything you've cataloged. Give me a complete list. Only then will I consider what your client has to offer. This is no guarantee I will accept it. Agreed?"

Giles Knox's face blossomed like an unfolding rose. His eyes lit up. His nostrils flared. His lips parted. "Oh, my dear Ms. Thornton!" He ran across the room and grabbed both her hands. "You're a dear! I knew you'd come round. Three days! Yes, that's superb! Magnificent! Thank you so much."

"You're welcome."

"Tomorrow morning, then! I'll bring pastries, shall I? Enough for the divers and everyone!" He gave each of her hands a kiss. Then he whisked out of the room.

Jess couldn't help but chuckle as she watched the man practically skip to his limousine. As the long white car crunched across the gravel driveway, she turned back to the painting of the green-eyed boy. Why had Dr. bin Yusuf painted a portrait of Omar Hafidh? Omar was his nephew, of course, but why had the artist kept this particular painting for himself—when he'd given several others to the boy's mother? Was family much more important to Dr. bin Yusuf than anyone had suspected? Maybe he and Omar had developed a special relationship through the years, and no one but the two of them knew about it.

But why had Dr. bin Yusuf so vehemently refused to part with the other little canvas? Jess turned to the portrait of Miriamu. Only half a face. Why had he painted her that way? And why Miriamu? Had she just been an available model? Or had Dr. bin Yusuf pursued her romantically, as Nettie Cameron claimed. If Miriamu had been Solomon's wife at the time, of course her husband would have been angry at the situation. Angry enough to kill?

Why hadn't Dr. bin Yusuf put these little paintings in his storerooms? Why did he keep so many far more valuable canvases in storage while giving these two paintings a place of honor in his home? Why wouldn't he even consider selling them?

"They are my life," he had told Giles Knox, *"and you will not take my life."*

But someone had.

◎ ◎ ◎

Giles Knox wasn't the last visitor of the day. Andrew Mbuti, Rick's coworker, roared up on his own motorcycle at sunset to meet the divers. He came loaded down with a stack of mail for Uchungu House. Jess greeted him, sorted through the letters, read the lengthy missive from James Perrott, and then wandered down toward the cliff-side staircase to watch the boat come in.

In spite of the bustle, she had been lonely all day, she realized. Lonely for her son. Lonely for Rick. How could she have changed so much in such a short time? Not many weeks ago, she would have sworn she despised Rick McTaggart. Now . . . now how did she feel? She liked him. She trusted him. She cared about him. Did she love him again? Could forgiveness ever take her that far?

"I have received a letter from your sister Tillie and her husband in Mali," Hannah said, joining Jess at the top of the steps.

"How is Tillie?" Jess asked.

"She has good news."

Jess took the letter and scanned the familiar handwriting. "Tillie's pregnant! She's going to have a baby. She's going to be a mother. Oh, Mama Hannah, I miss Tillie so much. I was always closer to her than I was to Fiona. I wish I could see her."

"She has written that she may come to stay in Nairobi for the baby's birth. In Nairobi they have good hospital care. Also, Tillie's husband, Graeme, is wishing to write a story about another explorer of Africa. This time in Kenya."

Jess glanced down at the letter. "He wants to write about Joseph Thomson, the guy who explored Maasai Land in the late 1800s! I bet Grant could help him with his research. You know my brother—he does those anthropological studies all the time. I think he's on Mount Kilimanjaro with the Maasai these days. I wonder how Grant would get along with Graeme."

Hannah smiled. "I believe they are two of a kind."

"That would be great, wouldn't it, Mama Hannah? Tillie and Graeme could move to Nairobi, and then Splint and I could fly up there for a visit. Tillie hasn't seen Splint in years. Maybe we could even track down Fiona. She's somewhere out in the Serengeti with her elephants. I'll bet Grant knows where to find her."

"Ehh." The old woman folded the letter and slipped it into her bodice. "Perhaps one day I should go to visit your brother."

"But we need you here. Splint needs you. We don't know who

killed Dr. bin Yusuf. And I told Rick all about Splint, which could turn into a big problem. I still have to tell Splint who his father is. That could throw him off kilter for days . . . even weeks. School is starting, and who knows how he'll react to that. My paintings are due in London. And Giles Knox—"

"Ehh. We are blessed to know that God is always with us," Hannah murmured.

Below on the beach, the divers were straggling out of the water and onto the sand. Splint had spotted his mother and was waving tiredly. Jess realized once again how thankful she was for Hannah's presence in her life. She had come to rely on her beloved *ayah*'s strength and wisdom. To Splint, the old woman was a best friend.

Jess slipped her arm around Hannah's shoulders. Together they watched the boy, his father, Hunky Wallace, and the rest of the heavily laden crew climb the staircase. Andrew Mbuti met the divers halfway up and helped carry the baskets and sacks of treasures from the wreck. As the men reached the top, everyone set down his haul and began talking.

Splint grabbed Hannah and pulled her over to his bag to show off his finds. Andrew cornered Rick. Hunky and his crew knelt on the lawn to compare the booty. Jess watched the scene for a moment, thinking how familiar it felt. Familiar and right. She had prayed for peace. For the first time, she felt it slip around her heart.

When someone tapped her on the shoulder, she jumped at the unexpected touch. "Yes?"

"Jessica Thornton."

Jess turned to discover one final visitor of the day. As she lifted her head, she looked into the bright green eyes of Omar Hafidh.

SPLINTER couldn't believe it when he glanced up from the hoisting basket to find his mother deep in conversation with Omar Hafidh—that green-eyed goon! The guy had come right up behind her when nobody was looking. Now he was talking to her, staring into her eyes, and . . . he was touching her!

"Mama Hannah, he's holding her hand!" Splint hissed. "That's totally putrid!"

"Perhaps the man wishes to ask her a question. It is the African way to hold the hand of a friend."

"She's not his friend."

"But you are my friend, and I have missed you today, *toto."* Hannah took Splint's hand. "Did you know I saved all the mango seeds from breakfast? Shall we play our game on the verandah while we still have some daylight?"

Splint gave the old woman a smile. There was almost nothing he liked better than their mango-seed game. Hannah had taught him how to play right after he got to Zanzibar.

First they took two of the four-inch-long seeds that were shaped like bars of soap—and when coated with stringy mango pulp were just as slippery. They set the seeds side by side at one

end of the long verandah. Hannah would count in Swahili, *"Moja, mbili, tatu!"*

Then she and Splint would stomp on their seeds with their bare feet. Each seed would shoot like a rocket down the concrete floor. The seed that traveled farthest was the winner. It was a gooey, sticky, slippery, messy game—and Splint loved it.

But right now he was much more interested in what his mother was saying to Omar Hafidh. She had tucked a strand of hair behind her ear, and she was nodding like she agreed with everything he told her. Splint glanced at Rick.

Now there was a sight. Rick's blue eyes were fairly shooting flames as he watched the couple on the edge of the cliff. The back of his neck had turned bright red, and Splint knew it wasn't a sunburn. He elbowed Hannah in the ribs.

"Rick's going to clobber Omar Hafidh," he whispered. "Rick doesn't want my mom to have a boyfriend. Not unless it's Rick himself."

Hannah studied the scene for a moment. *"Toto,* perhaps you should take *Bwana* McTaggart to play the mango-seed game on the verandah."

"No way. I'm going to find out what that freakazoid is up to with my mom. Watch me in action." Splint put down the heavy piece of conglomerate he'd been showing Hannah and walked across the lawn to his mother.

"Hey, Mom," he said. "What's up?"

She reached out a hand and smoothed down his damp hair. "Splint, you remember Omar Hafidh, don't you? He's Dr. bin Yusuf's nephew. We met him in Zanzibar."

"I know who he is." Splint stuck out his hand. "Hello, Mr. Hafidh."

"Good evening." Those green eyes scrutinized the boy until he felt like a squid under a microscope. Then Omar again focused on Splint's mom. "Tomorrow evening, then? We shall dine at one of the beach hotels. The Bahari. They have good dancing."

"Dancing?" Splint exclaimed.

His mom gave him one of her withering looks. Then she turned back to Green Eyes. "I'd enjoy that. You'll pick me up, then? Around seven?"

"Seven o'clock will be very good." He lifted the hand he'd been holding and gave the knuckles a kiss. "I shall look forward to seeing you then."

Splint thought he was going to barf! His mom was going out on a date with Omar Hafidh? Omar the green-eyed monster? Omar the Incredible Hulk with shoulders the size of Zanzibar Island? How could she do that?

"Mom!" he screeched as the man walked away toward his car. "Mom, what are you doing?"

"Splint, please get control of yourself. You're practically foaming at the mouth." She started off toward the house as though nothing momentous had happened. "Wash your hands for supper, please."

"Mom! Mom!" He scampered to her side as she strode past Rick. One look at him and Splint knew things were as bad as he'd feared. Rick didn't look happy at all. He had two white spots on his cheeks, and a vein on his forehead was twitching. "Mom, are you going out on a date with that guy?"

"Omar? Sure. I haven't been out to dinner in a long time."

"And dancing! Did you say you'd dance with him? Mom?"

"Will you please calm down, Splint? I've had people combing through the house all day, and I'm exhausted. The last thing I need is your histrionics."

"Mom, you can't go out with him." He caught up close enough to grab her arm. Giving a quick glance behind to make sure they were alone on the verandah, he stood on tiptoe and whispered his message. "Rick likes you! He told me so himself. Today on the boat! You can't go out with Omar Hafidh. You need to go out with Rick!"

Splint's mom put her hands on his shoulders and stared into his eyes until he had no choice but to be quiet. "Rick McTaggart has not asked me to go out, Splint. Omar Hafidh has."

"But, Mom, that guy's a total Frankenstein."

"He's a nice man."

"You just like his muscles."

"I do not like his muscles. Well . . . I don't hate them. But I'm not going out with his muscles, Splint. I've been wanting to talk to

Omar for some time. There are things we need to work out about Uchungu House and about Dr. bin Yusuf's art. Giles Knox is going to spend the next three days here, and I'm trying to get a feel for the relationship between him and Omar. There are some things I need to know, Splint, and I think I can get my answers tomorrow night."

"If you marry Omar Hafidh, I'll never forgive you. I don't want him to be my father. I want Rick to be my father!"

She let out a breath. "Splint, honey, I'm not going to marry Omar. We're just going out to dinner, that's all. Now, come over here and sit down on my lap. I need to tell you something very important."

Splint had always liked cuddling up with his mother. She was soft and warm, and she smelled good. He had been crawling into her lap since he was a little baby, and he hoped there would never come a time when he'd be too big. When she cradled him, his mother always looked deeply into his eyes. She always told him how much she loved him. It was the time they connected best.

Now he climbed onto her lap and folded his long legs into the big pillowy chair on the verandah. He knew his mom would get water and sand all over her skirt, but she wouldn't mind. He had just laid his head on her shoulder when Rick McTaggart walked up to the edge of the verandah where his motorcycle was waiting. He studied Splint and his mom for a moment. His face was rigid, like he was trying hard not to show how he felt when he looked at the two of them.

"I understand you'll be busy tomorrow night, Jessie," he said in a low voice.

"She's going out to dinner with Omar Hafidh," Splint told him, "and dancing, too. They're going dancing at one of the beach hotels."

"Is that right, Jessie?"

"Yes," she said softly.

Rick raked his fingers through his hair. Splint could see the vein leaping around in his forehead. Rick clenched his jaw like he had something to say and was trying to hold it back. Then he hooked his leg over the cycle, started the engine, and roared off in a blast that sent gravel spraying across the verandah.

"He's mad," Splint said. "He likes you, and you're going out on a date with that green-eyed gorilla instead of with him."

"Rick could ask me out on a date if he wanted to."

"Would you go?"

She hardly hesitated a moment. "Yes."

"You didn't used to like him."

"That's true."

"It's because of the past, isn't it, Mom? It's because of when you and Rick knew each other before. A long time ago."

She nodded. "Splinter, honey, I've told you about some of the things that happened when I was very young. But not everything. You were right when you said I had held some information back from you. At the time, I didn't think you needed to know. Now you do."

"Rick is my father," he said. "Isn't he?"

She stiffened. "Splint . . ."

"Am I right? Is Rick my father?"

"Yes, sweetheart. He is."

"I figured it out. You wouldn't tell me, but I guessed it anyway." Splint felt so strange all of a sudden. A mixed-up ball of feelings rolled around in his stomach—joy, anger, disbelief, resentment, loss, exhilaration. Even though he didn't want them, tears filled his eyes. "Mom, why didn't you tell me?"

"At first, it didn't seem to matter. You were little. We lived in London, so far away from Africa. I didn't think I would ever see Rick McTaggart again."

"And here he is. Right here in Zanzibar. Mom, God wanted you to find Rick again."

Her arms tightened around him. Hannah walked across the verandah into the house and gave them one of her smiles, as though she knew exactly what they were talking about. Splint brushed a tear off his cheek. He really hated it when he cried, but sometimes he just couldn't help it. And finding out who his father really was seemed like as good a time as any. Especially since his father was Rick McTaggart, his favorite friend in the whole world.

"God did want Rick and me to find each other," Splint heard his mom say. "I had been very angry with him for leaving. I couldn't forgive him, and I'd grown bitter. But now—through a lot of prayer and a lot of long conversations with Rick—I understand why he went away. He had many problems to work his way through. He needed to grow up before he could take his place in your life. He needed to find out who he really was. Most of all, he needed to give his heart to Jesus. Rick did all those things, Splint. Now he's truly ready to be your father. And I'm willing to let him."

"Does Rick know I'm his son?"

"I told him last night."

"What did he say?" He wiped off another tear. "Did he . . . did he sound glad? Does he like me, Mom? Does he want me?"

She kissed his wet cheek. "He loves you, Splint. He asked me if he could take you out on the dive boat today just to watch you. He wants to be with you more than anything in the world."

"I noticed he was awfully happy today. Every time we were up on deck, he was singing and laughing and telling stories. I thought it was because of you."

"Me?"

"I asked him why he was grinning, and he started singing one of his goofy songs about a 'purty little gal.' So I said, 'Who's the purtiest little gal you know, Rick?' And he said, 'Your mother, Jessie.' So I asked him if he liked you, and he said he sure did. Then he got real serious, and he told me you were the most beautiful woman he'd ever known. He said you have a good heart, and you're talented and sweet and on and on until I thought I was going to get sick. Then he told me I was blessed to have you for a mother. So I said, 'If you think she's so great, why don't you ask her out on a date?' And he said he thought he just might do that."

"Really?"

Splint sat up and looked into his mother's eyes. "But you're going out with Omar Hafidh!"

"Yes, I am. There's more to it than you know." She shook her head. "And no, I'm not going to tell you everything that happens in my life—everything I'm doing and thinking and feeling. There are some things ten-year-old boys just don't need to know. This is one of them."

He nuzzled back into her shoulder. "I'm glad you told me about

Rick," he said. "I think you made a good choice when you married him—even if he did run off and leave you and me alone for a while. I'm going to like having him for a dad. We'll be the best family ever."

Splint could hear his mother catch her breath. He knew she didn't have any plans to be Rick McTaggart's wife again. But then, Hannah always said God knew best. And Splint had no doubt God was planning to give him a mother . . . a father . . . a family. The sooner the better.

Rick sat on the edge of the coral cliff just beyond the kiosk and watched the sun slip into the Indian Ocean. He turned the ice-cold beer bottle around and around in his hands. The malt scent drew him like a sweet perfume. He lifted it to his nose and took a sniff. Rich dark beer. Escape.

He had bought the beer with the few shillings he found in the pocket of his still-damp jeans. Damp from the storm the day before. He had huddled over Jessie through the storm, watching her, protecting her. He had slept at her door all night . . . guarding her. In the night she had given him the greatest gift imaginable. He had a son!

Equally wonderful, Jessie herself had melted into his arms. She had slipped her hands around him. She had touched his cheek, laid her head on his chest, wept in his embrace. He had been so sure of everything. So sure he was walking through the door into a new life. An hour ago, the door had slammed in his face.

Rick wiped a bead of water from the lip of the brown beer bottle. *"She's going out to dinner with Omar Hafidh. And dancing, too. They're going dancing at one of the beach hotels."*

Wait a minute, Rick had wanted to shout at her. *You can't do that! You're Splint's mother! You're my wife!*

No. She wasn't his wife.

He had lost her ten years ago. Walked away.

Rick thought back to the last time he had sat on this rock near the kiosk. He had told Andrew Mbuti the whole story of his youthful marriage and the mess he had made of his life. Andrew had challenged Rick to win Jessie back. To love her with all the love a husband had to give a wife. To fulfill every commandment in the Bible. To make it happen.

"God!" Rick ground out. "I don't know how! I've tried. Tried so hard. But I can't. Can't force it."

His grip tightened on the beer. If he drank it . . . and another . . . and another . . . he could silence his grief. He could stop the pain. At least for a few hours he could escape his failures, his mistakes.

Couldn't he? Rick lifted the bottle and studied the last of the sunlight glowing through the amber glass. If he drank this beer, he knew he would only add one more mistake to the list.

"God," he said again. "I can't do it. I give it to you. I give Jessie to you. My son. My future. Everything."

He tilted the dark bottle and let the beer run out onto the sandy soil. It foamed like the ebb tide. Then it seeped into the earth and vanished. A sacrificial offering. Pouring out of sin.

Why didn't he feel any better?

"Rick!" Andrew's voice pulled him up sharp. "There you are, man! Why didn't you wait for me? Hunky said you blasted out of the driveway like a demon was after you."

Rick turned around. Andrew was sauntering toward him. And right behind him . . .

"Jessie."

"Hi, Rick." She looked down at the empty beer bottle in his hand. Then she glanced at the wet spot in the sand.

Rick shrugged. Maybe Jessie understood the choice he had made moments before, maybe she didn't. If he told her he had rejected the easy escape, he didn't know if she would believe him. Didn't know if she could ever believe him, ever trust him, after what he'd done to her.

He stood. Jessie looked great, dark hair blowing around her shoulders, eyes shining. He felt wrinkled and wet and miserable. Why had she come? What did she want?

"Your lovely lady said she needed to talk to you," Andrew told Rick. "So I brought her along. Excuse me, but I'm going to the kiosk for a samosa. Anybody else want one?"

Rick shook his head. Jessie declined, too. They watched Andrew walk away. Then Jessie sat down on the rock and tucked her knees up under her chin.

"Sit with me, Rick?" she asked.

He hunkered down again. She was too close. He could smell her. Her hair blew against his shoulder. Soft. Like a warm breath.

"Rick," she said. "I just wanted you to know I told Splinter about you. Us. Well . . . really, he told me. He had it figured out already."

She leaned against his shoulder. At the contact, every muscle in his arm stiffened. He could hardly breathe, let alone talk.

"Smart kid," he managed. "So, how did he take the news?"

"He cried."

"That bad, huh?"

She gave him a little whack on the arm. "He's thrilled. You should have seen him running around the house shouting the news to Mama Hannah and Miriamu and Solomon. I bet he'll never get to sleep tonight. It's more exciting than Christmas." She leaned against him again. "I wish you hadn't left. I know he'd really like to be with you right now."

"I needed to do some thinking."

"Big changes are never easy." She tapped her toes on the stone. "Rick, could I ask you to help me out with something?"

Uh-oh. What was this going to be—to look after things while she went on a date with Omar Hafidh? He knew jealousy had curled through his stomach like a poisonous snake. But how could he stop it? He wanted Jessie in his life so much. He'd prayed for her. Prayed to make it work. And now?

"What is it you need?" he asked.

"You."

His head jerked up. "What?"

"I need you. I agreed to talk with Omar Hafidh tomorrow night. He's Dr. bin Yusuf's nephew, you know. I have a suspicion he might have been involved in the murder, maybe as a henchman for Giles Knox. Anyway, I thought if I could question him, maybe I could get to the bottom of it all. But . . . I'm scared."

She brushed her hair back from her neck. It was all Rick could do to keep from touching her. His heart felt like a jackhammer in his chest. What was she telling him? What did she want?

"So I was wondering if you could follow us," she said. "Omar and me."

"Follow you?"

"You said you'd protect me, Rick. And tomorrow night I'm going to need you. If Omar killed Dr. bin Yusuf, and if I can get him to disclose something that would prove it, we've got our murderer. But if he figures out what I'm doing, I'm afraid he might turn on me. If I knew you were close . . . I'd feel so much better. Safer."

The jackhammer stopped. His breath stopped. Everything stopped.

"You want me to *protect* you from Omar?" he said.

"Yes. There's something about that man I don't trust. He's been wanting to talk to me. Trying to tell me something. He may have the idea he can intimidate me into leaving Uchungu House. If he got rid of me, he could have the house and all the art. He'd be rich. Wouldn't that give him a motive for murder?"

"You agreed to go on a *date* with a guy you think is a murderer?"

"What is it with this *date* business? You and Splint—you're just alike. I'm going out to dinner with Omar Hafidh to try to solve a crime."

"And to dance."

"Omar may think it's a date, but I'm just interested in getting to the bottom of all this mess. I want life to feel normal again. I want to be able to relax and . . . and start over. You know what I mean?"

"I think so."

"Good."

She leaned her head on Rick's shoulder, and he could feel her hair sift over his bare arm. Her words danced around inside his head. *"I need you. . . . I'm scared. . . . You said you'd protect me, Rick. . . . If I knew you were close, I'd feel so much better . . . safer. . . . I want to be able to relax and start over. . . ."*

Start over? With him? The jackhammer started up again.

"So what do you think, Rick?" she murmured. "Will you help me?"

He slipped his arm around her shoulders. She was looking up into his face, her eyes shining. He'd never seen anyone so beautiful in his life.

"I'll help you, Jessie," he said.

"I knew I could trust you." She smiled. "There's another thing, too. Rick, would you mind spending a few more nights on my living-room couch? It's not only Omar Hafidh who concerns me. Giles Knox is going to be prowling around the next three days. And Solomon Mazrui is still an enigma. It turns out he's married to Miriamu."

He watched her lips move over the words.

"I think you have a lot more strength than you know," he said.

"I'm growing in my faith. Learning to trust God's strength." She ran her fingertips up the length of his arm. "Rick, back at the beginning, you asked me to do something for you. You asked me to forgive you. I didn't think I could."

She looked up at him again. Her mouth was so close. He forced himself to focus on her eyes.

"I just wanted you to know," she whispered, "I forgive you. I've been angry. Bitter. I want to let it go. I'm so sorry, Rick. Can you forgive me?"

"Of course I forgive you." Unable to hold back any longer, he bent and brushed his mouth across her lips. "I love you, Jessie."

She leaned closer. Her hands slipped around his neck. Pulling her into his arms, he kissed her again. Her response was warm, beckoning, sweet. She moved against him, holding him tightly.

"Rick," she murmured. "Oh, Rick . . . it's been so long, I—"

"Well, well, well." Andrew's voice sounded somewhere in the background. "I believe I'm witnessing my first miracle. Looks like I'd better take my samosas and go home. That God of yours certainly does keep his promises. *Tutaonana,* man."

Rick barely heard the putter of the motorcycle as it pulled out onto the main road.

◎◎◎

Jess didn't know when she'd ever felt such a mixture of joy and anxiety. At five o'clock the following afternoon, the dive crew came in from the ocean. Arm in arm, Rick and Splint climbed the cliff-side staircase. Splint announced that he'd decided to call Rick "Dad." Rick had given his blessing on the new title, and there they were—father and son. Jess could hardly contain her happiness.

At six o'clock, Hunky Wallace and his crew left for Zanzibar town. Since learning that the sunken ship was a slaver and not a treasure galleon, the Scotsman had lost interest in the dive. He was planning to spend a few more days helping Rick bring up things for research purposes, and then he would head out in search of richer loot.

Hoping to keep Splint out of any unexpected problems that might crop up with her plan, Jess had arranged for him to spend the evening playing Scrabble at Nettie Cameron's house. Hannah would fetch him at bedtime and walk him back to Uchungu House. Splint grumbled as the old woman tugged a lightweight jacket over his shoulders.

"I don't want Nettie Cameron to be my sitter tonight," he said, taking Hannah's hand as they started down the road. "I like you better. She won't stomp mango seeds with me. She doesn't even know how to weave birds out of palm leaves. Why can't I just stay here tonight, Mama Hannah?"

Worn brown hands reached out and cupped the small white face. "Are you ready?" Brown eyes searched violet ones as her lips formed a knowing smile. "Let us go to heaven. *Mungu ni pendo; apenda watu. Mungu ni pendo; anipenda . . .*"

Splint sang along, but he glanced back at his mother as he walked away. Jess waved, lifting up a prayer of thanksgiving. Hannah had brought so much healing, so much peace into her family.

At six-forty-five, Rick drove off on his motorcycle, headed for the road toward the Bahari Hotel, where Omar and Jess had agreed to dine. With him he carried a big straw hat and a newspaper to hide behind. He told Jess he was doubtful he could remain inconspicuous.

"Just stay close to me," she whispered as she kissed him goodbye.

At seven o'clock, Omar Hafidh arrived at Uchungu House. He was wearing a white shirt, a dark tie and trousers, and a jacket. Tall, well built, and flashing those intriguing green eyes, he nearly filled the arched doorway. "You are ready to go," he said. Glancing behind her, his brows narrowed. "Where is the boy?"

"He's spending the evening with Antoinette Cameron. Do you know Nettie?"

"I know her." He followed her out to the car. "Antoinette Cameron is my mother."

"HOW can Antoinette Cameron be your mother?" Jess asked, trying to force herself to relax. She had knots as big as fists in her shoulders. "Nettie told me she never had any children."

Omar Hafidh said nothing as he steered past the dangling Renault engine on the Red Hot Poker tree. Alone with the man in his car, Jess felt a lot more frightened than she had anticipated. She wedged herself as close to the door as she could, as though that could give her some measure of security. Occasionally, she glanced at the road behind, but she could see nothing in the blackness of the Zanzibar night. Was Rick following as he'd promised? Would Omar really take her to the hotel he had proposed the night before? The Bahari Hotel. She'd never heard of it. Maybe there was no such place.

"When I visited you in Zanzibar town," Jess tried again, "you told me Fatima Hafidh was your mother. You know—the woman at your house . . . the woman in the black *bui-bui?"*

"Yes, Fatima Hafidh is my mother."

Now *that* made a lot of sense. Clearly Omar Hafidh was leading her through a verbal maze. Cat and mouse.

Was he driving the car into a maze as well? Jess leaned her cheek against the window. The occasional dim street lamp gave her hope

they were headed in the right direction. Still, she had been to this part of the island only once or twice. She was disoriented. Lost.

Had Omar managed to lose Rick, too? Could she even trust Rick to stick close to her? Maybe she had been foolish to rely on Rick. Look what had happened when she had placed her faith in him ten years before.

Where was Hannah now that Jess needed her strength? If Hannah were in the car, she would come up with a comforting verse. A scriptural promise. A psalm. All Jess could think of was *"Yea, though I walk through the valley of the shadow of death . . . shadow of death. . . ."*

"I have a good mother," Omar said into the darkness. "Fatima Hafidh. Also Antoinette Cameron is my mother."

"That's very interesting," Jess remarked. "You have two mothers. Do you have two fathers?"

"I have no father."

"Oooo—OK."

Two mothers and no father. Well, that made things clear—as clear as mud. Omar turned the car down a steep gravel road. Jess held her breath. A small, poorly lit sign emerged over the top of the palm trees. Bahari Hotel.

Thank you, Lord.

"The Bahari Hotel has African food and dancing," Omar said as he pulled the car to a stop in front of a large whitewashed building with a thatched roof. "Sometimes the tourists like our ways. Sometimes not."

"I'm sure the hotel is charming." Jess opened the car door and stepped out before Omar could make it around to her side. She scanned the parking lot, but she saw no sign of Rick's motorcycle.

Alone. Rick had left her alone. Why had she trusted him?

"We will eat fish," Omar said. "You like fish?"

"Yes."

"Good. I am a fisherman."

"Really? I notice you have a nice car. Do you have a boat?"

"This is not my car. I borrowed it." He took her elbow and led her toward the hotel lobby. "To have a car in Zanzibar is to have great wealth. I have a bicycle. Also a small boat."

The Bahari Hotel was definitely not one of the high-class tourist lodges that catered to wealthy European vacationers. In fact, it must have had no more than ten rooms. Huts, actually. Half-hidden in vines and brush, the little bungalows were scattered outward from the main building.

Jess tried to assess her situation as she walked through the cement-floored lobby. Africans were gathering in the open-air dining room. For a Tuesday night, the place was packed. Jess was the only white person in sight. That would be all right if not for Rick. There was no chance he could be inconspicuous in a place like this. Had Omar planned it that way?

It hardly mattered. Rick was nowhere to be found.

"Sit down," Omar said, pulling back her chair. "I will bring drinks."

"Fanta for me, thanks." Jess watched the man stride through the crowd toward the open bar. Hands on the glass-topped table, she half rose and scanned the bougainvillea bushes for any sign of a straw hat, a newspaper, a white face. Nothing.

Oh, Rick. She missed him so much. At the same time, fear curled through her. Had she fallen into the same trap that had snared her ten years before? Had she let herself love a man who was destined to abandon her when she needed him most?

How easily they had slipped back into the warmth of their love. The evening before had been bliss. Sitting on the rock under the stars . . . listening to the waves break on the cliffs below . . . holding each other tightly . . .

"Your Fanta," Omar said, plunking down a glass. "I have ordered our dinner. Grilled eel."

"Eel?"

"You will like it. Very tasty."

Swallowing hard, Jess shook out her napkin and laid it in her lap. By now the noisy crowd had filled almost every table. Waiters scrambled back and forth taking orders and pouring drinks. Omar sat down and crossed his arms over his chest. His green eyes studied Jess for a moment.

"This is an African place," he said, defiance giving his voice an edge. "You like it? Or do you only like the places of white people?"

"I like this. I grew up in Africa, you know. Kenya mostly. My father taught at the university in Nairobi."

Omar nodded. "Then you understand me."

"Actually, there are a lot of things about you that confuse me, Omar." She took a deep breath, determined to probe his past. "For example, how did you meet Giles Knox?"

"He was searching the island for the art of Ahmed Abdullah bin Yusuf. Nothing is secret in Zanzibar. He found me."

"So you and your mother . . . Fatima . . . have several of his paintings. But I noticed you don't own the portrait Dr. bin Yusuf painted of you when you were a little boy."

Omar sat up straight. "You have seen that picture? Where is it?"

"It's at Uchungu House. Dr. bin Yusuf kept it in the second living room, the more secluded room to the east."

"How did you know that was a picture of me? He painted it when I was very young."

"Your eyes."

The man looked away, and for the first time Jess saw pain written in his bearing. His big shoulders sagged, and he nodded sadly. "Yes," he said in a low voice. "I have green eyes. You think I am strange."

"I don't think you're strange. I think you're . . . a mystery." She turned her glass on the table, her fear of him giving way a little. "I like your eyes."

"Yes?"

"Yes. They're very nice. Interesting." She cleared her throat, uncomfortable at allowing the conversation to turn personal. "Omar, why do you say Nettie is your mother? She told me she was married to Captain Cameron."

"That man was not my father."

"You had no father."

He nodded again, unable to look at her. A waiter brought two steaming platters. The eel flesh had been filleted and grilled in garlic and butter. Actually, the dish smelled so good Jess thought she might almost be able to eat it.

"You speak in riddles, Omar," she said. "There's something else that puzzles me. Why did you ask me to have dinner with you?"

"To talk." He took a sip of his drink. "I wanted to understand why Ahmed Abdullah bin Yusuf liked you—why he chose to give Uchungu House to you. Now I begin to understand. You are not the same as other white women. You walked into my home, and you did not seem afraid of us. You spoke to my mother as though she deserved your respect. You looked into my eyes, and you did not shut me away."

"Why would I shut you away, Omar? Have you done something that should make me fear you?"

"People fear me because I am different." He stared at her. "You see this skin? This hair? These eyes?"

"It doesn't matter to me how you look. What matters is your heart."

"To many people it matters how I look. Because I am different, they hate me."

"Then they're foolish."

"That is why I like you, Jessica Thornton." He took a bite of his eel. "You also are different."

In spite of herself, Jess began to relax a little. If Omar Hafidh had killed Dr. bin Yusuf, he would need to reveal a better reason than the ones she'd come up with so far. He seemed disinterested in the art, in Uchungu House, and in Giles Knox. He appeared relatively content with his lot as a fisherman. In fact, if Jess hadn't convinced herself that he was a killer, she thought she might actually be able to like Omar Hafidh.

She stabbed a chunk of eel with her fork. Sucking in a deep breath, she put it in her mouth and chewed. Not bad.

Omar was watching her, a grin forming on his face. "You like?"

"I do," she said. "Not too long ago an eel nearly had *me* for dinner."

He laughed out loud, a deep warm sound. "Never fear something unless you are a threat to it. That is the rule of Africa."

"I'm learning," she said. "Omar, what do you find threatening? Africans who call you different? White people who reject you? The fear of poverty?"

"Not poverty. I do not care so much for money. I have my home. My boat. My work. Of course, I would not turn away from wealth. You already know I would like to give the money from Ahmed bin Yusuf's paintings to my mother."

"Which mother . . . Fatima? Or Nettie?"

"You ask a lot of questions, Jessica Thornton," Omar said. "Eat your dinner. I am going to tell you a story about Uchungu House. Because you live there, you will wish to know this tale."

"Is this why you asked me to dinner?"

"No. And yes. Listen, please. Many years ago, there lived a man whose name has been forgotten. He had a very wealthy trade, and he built himself a beautiful white house filled with rooms. In the coral caves below his house, he kept African slaves for export to Arabia, England, and America. The slaves called that place *uchungu.* Bitterness. To be sent to Uchungu House was the worst of fates. A sentence to living death. A sentence to hell."

"The shipwreck Hunky Wallace found in the bay," Jess said. "Did you know it was a slaver?"

"No. But it does not surprise me. Hundreds of slave ships came and went around Zanzibar Island. Near Uchungu House, slaves were taken out of the coral caves and ferried to the reef in small boats. At low tide, they were loaded onto huge ships. The tales say that one stormy night a slave ship was driven over the reef. Its holds were full. Hundreds died."

"Omar . . . that must be the ship we found. How terrible."

"Terrible, yes, but also wonderful. The slaves gave their lives for a good cause. With the destruction of that ship, the owner of Uchungu House was ruined. Already British blockades had cut into his business. The man left his house and was never heard from again. Years passed, and Uchungu House fell into disrepair. Then another family moved in. Squatters. An African family with many children and no wealth. One of those children did a terrible thing."

"What was it?"

"When he was still a young man, he fell in love with a girl who lived nearby. By him, she conceived a child. Though she loved him, she knew her parents would never approve of their union. The young man himself refused to marry her. You see, he had many selfish plans for his own life. In fact, he grew tired of the girl. He abandoned her. So she gave the baby away to a friend—the childless sister of her lover—and married another."

A sudden realization swept over Jessie. *The child must have been—* With a quick intake of breath, she leaned back in her chair, listening intently. If she was right . . .

"After many years, the young man became a famous artist. The girl, who was now a woman, lived not far away with her husband. The child grew up in a loving home. He was told nothing of his birth. Then one day the artist became ill."

As Omar spoke, Jess couldn't help but think of herself and Rick. Their union had been secretive and forbidden. Rick had abandoned her and her child, just like the man in the story . . . just like—

"You're talking about Dr. bin Yusuf," she said quietly.

Omar looked up at the moon. "Tell me something, Jessica Thornton. Did Ahmed bin Yusuf know you at the time you had the little boy, the child with no father?"

"I was his art student in Dar es Salaam right after my son was born. Dr. bin Yusuf knew about Spencer. In fact . . . I remember he was intrigued that I had chosen to keep my baby. He said he admired me."

Omar nodded. "Now I understand the true reason he gave you Uchungu House. In you, he could see what he himself had failed to do."

"But who was the woman—?"

"At the time of bin Yusuf's illness, the woman who had been his lover allowed her bitterness about their past to burn within her."

"Omar . . ." Jess felt breathless, on the verge of understanding something amazing and awful. "Omar, was that woman Nettie Cameron?"

He focused on her. "No more questions, Jessica Thornton. Let us dance."

Before she could respond, he pushed back his chair, took her hands, and pulled her onto the dance floor. The throbbing African beat swirled around them—a mixture of drums, guitar, piano, and trumpet. Lost in a twirling, swaying sea of bright dresses, Jess could hardly keep up with Omar. He danced her around the floor, spun her back and forth, and nearly left her breathless.

When the music changed into a slow languid rhythm, he took her hand and led her through the front door of the dining room onto the open sand. Fear instantly clutched Jess's throat again. Omar was leading her away from the crowd, far from the security of the lights and music. She stopped walking.

"Omar, let's go back to our table," she said, trying to sound casual. "You can tell me the rest of the story while we eat."

"I will tell you when we are alone."

"No. I . . . I want to finish my dinner."

"You fear me?" He shoved his hands into his pockets and looked down at his feet half buried in sand. "I know you are not at ease with me, Jessica Thornton. But this story I cannot tell in such a place."

"Why not, Omar?"

He fell silent for a moment. "When I speak the words, I do not want you to see my face."

"Then tell me now. Here."

"All right." He took a deep breath, and Jess could hear the shudder in his chest. "That woman went to the home of the child she had borne. By this time, he had grown up. He was a man. Against the wishes of the man's second mother, she told the whole story of his birth. She insisted that the boy must go to his father and demand his inheritance. Money. A car. Land. And Uchungu House."

"Did he go to his father? Did he make such a demand?"

"No."

"Why? Surely he was angry and bitter. Didn't he want the rights that belonged to him?" Jess squared her shoulders, more certain than ever that she was right about the child's identity. "I think he went to his father and made his demands. I think his father refused to acknowledge him. In his anger, I think the son struck the father—"

"You are wrong." Omar grabbed her shoulders. "I never went to Ahmed Abdullah bin Yusuf. I did not want him! Only once in my life had I seen that man. He had come to his sister's house—to the home of my mother Fatima—and he had asked to paint my picture. I went to Uchungu House. He painted me. A small picture. And he said to me, 'You have green eyes. Who is your mother? Who is your father?' I told him, 'Fatima Hafidh is my mother, and I do not have a father.' And he said, 'May God go with you.' After that, I never saw him again."

"Do you think he knew you were his son, Omar?"

"Maybe. But he did not claim me. Why should I have gone to the man when he was sick and ready to die? Why should I demand an inheritance I did not want? In my life I want only peace. Peace for my mother and myself." He shook his head. "I did not go to him. I hated him. But *she* went. She went to him in my place!"

"Who?"

"She went to Uchungu House. Her bitterness ate her like stinging ants. She could not forgive him."

"Who, Omar? Who went to Uchungu House and confronted Dr. bin Yusuf?"

"My mother."

"Fatima Hafidh?"

"Fatima Hafidh is a cripple. You saw her sitting on the floor. She cannot walk." He shook his head. "No, Fatima Hafidh is not the one. It was the other. That angry, bitter, unforgiving woman."

"Nettie Cameron." A wash of ice poured through Jess's veins. "Nettie went to Dr. bin Yusuf. She demanded compensation because he had abandoned her. She wanted revenge. She told him to give her the house. The paintings. The sculptures. And when he wouldn't . . ."

"I do not know what happened that evening. I know only one thing. Antoinette Cameron said she once had loved Ahmed bin Yusuf beyond all reason. And now she hated him with equal passion. She told me she had given everything for him—her heart, her body, her only child. She said she had been given nothing in return. It was time for him to pay. In great anger, Antoinette Cameron drove away from my home. The next morning, we heard that Dr. bin Yusuf had fallen down the stairs and died. Soon the secret came to be whispered . . . someone had hit him in the head. Someone killed him."

"Nettie." Jess stared into Omar's green eyes. "Nettie did it. She couldn't stand being rejected again."

"Perhaps."

"Yes! Omar, my son found the murder weapon. It was a stone urn. When he brought it out onto the verandah, Nettie said she would take the urn to the police herself. Now she has an alibi for the fact that her fingerprints will be on it. She tried to turn the blame on Solomon. But it was Nettie all along." Jess covered her hand with her mouth. "She killed Dr. bin Yusuf—and I've left her alone with Splinter!"

She grabbed Omar's arm. Her breath wouldn't come. Nettie would be looking for some way to make Jess leave. It was clear she had no legal claim to the house, but if she was deluded enough to kill Dr. bin Yusuf, would that truth have any effect? Probably not. And what better way to get rid of Jess than to use Splint? If he met with an accidental death, Jess would want nothing more than to escape the memories. To Nettie's way of thinking, Uchungu House would be free again. *Oh, God!*

"Take me home, Omar!" She began to cry. "You've got to take me to Uchungu House right now. She'll kill my son!"

"Calm yourself—"

"No! No! You've got to help me!"

"Jessie?"

She swung around to see Rick walking toward them.

"What's wrong?" he asked. "Is Omar hurting you?"

"Rick!" She ran to him and grabbed his sleeves in her fists. "Oh, thank God! You've got to do something. Nettie did it! She killed Dr. bin Yusuf, and Splint is alone with her!"

@@@

Nettie Cameron was a pretty cool old lady after all, Splint decided as he followed her flashlight beam down the narrow rutted trail. They had played Scrabble for a while, but she could tell he wasn't into the game. Then they got to talking about the sunken slave ship in the bay. At that point, Nettie had come up with her idea. A visit to a hole where slaves had once been kept before they were shipped off to Arabia or the Caribbean.

"Is the slave pit we're going to visit covered with a stone like the one Rick told me about?" he asked.

"Like the pit at Mangapwani? I believe this one is covered." She swung his hand as they walked. "But you can get the general idea of how it used to be anyway. Dreadful place, but fascinating all the same. Ah, here we go. Follow me down this little path."

They turned onto a narrow trail in the tall grass. Splint could feel the evening dew dampening his bare legs, but he didn't care. To have the chance to see a real slave pit was worth anything. Rick . . . his dad . . . would think it was wonderful. Maybe they could visit it together. Just the two of them.

"Look just there!" Nettie said, giving Splint a little nudge from behind. "Do you see that ragged lip of coral?"

He left her side and moved ahead. "There's no covering, Nettie! It's an open pit."

"Is it really? My goodness, I was certain this one was covered. Do be careful, my dear."

His heart racing, Splint knelt at the edge of the deep black hole. To think that slaves had been lowered into such a place and kept for days. How cruel people could be.

"Do you suppose iron rings are embedded into the walls down there?" he asked. "Rick told me they kept the slaves chained up all the time so they couldn't escape."

"Rings. Hmm . . . I don't know." Nettie crouched beside him. "Is that a ledge? Partway down. Yes, I can just pick it out with the light. Do you see it? I wonder if there's a ladder. Surely they kept one in the pit."

"It's really deep."

"Yes, it is. Fascinating, isn't it?" Her smile was barely visible in the moonlight. "I wonder if there are remnants of the slave trade in the cave at the bottom. Bits of fabric, perhaps. Or beads. I suppose if one could find a ladder, the search would be quite easy."

"My dad would just love this."

"And think how pleased he would be if you brought him back a real artifact. He could put it on one of those shelves in his apartment that you told me about. It would have a tag and a description saying you'd found it. Spencer Thornton."

Splint grinned. It was pretty neat the way Nettie looked at things. She understood him a lot better than he'd thought. "I'll bring my dad here tomorrow," he said. "He might even want to put this place on a map in the museum."

"Why not take him a little treasure tonight? Just to whet his appetite. If you climbed down onto that ledge, you could check to see if there's a ladder."

Splint swallowed. "It's pretty dark."

"Don't forget we have the flashlight, silly!"

"Oh yeah." He could feel his hands grow damp with sweat. His mom would kill him if he pulled a stunt like this. On the other hand, it would show Rick how glad Splint was to have him for a father. Rick would understand that even though they had spent a lot of years apart, his son was just like him. A scientist. An explorer. A bold adventurer.

"What do you think?" Nettie asked, excitement tinging her voice.

"It's deep."

"I'll hold your arm."

Splint took a deep breath. "OK. I'll do it."

"That's my boy!"

Nettie held out her hand, and he took it. While she held the flashlight, he gingerly lowered one leg down into the slave hole. His toes didn't quite touch the ledge. He scooted closer to the edge.

"You're going to have to hold on tight," he said.

He glanced down into the darkness below him. Then he looked up at Nettie's face.

She smiled. "Don't worry, Splinter," she said. "You can trust me."

@@@

"Nettie Cameron?" Rick looked at Omar. "Are you sure?"

"I believe there is cause for concern," the tall man said. "Where is the boy now?"

Jess glanced at her watch. "He should be back home in bed by now. Mama Hannah was supposed to pick him up at eight-thirty."

"I will take Jessica to Uchungu House in my car," Omar spoke up.

"My motorcycle will be faster. Omar, look, will you go to the police station in town? Will you tell them what we think happened?"

"I will do it."

Omar turned on his heel and headed off through the crowd.

Rick and Jess dashed to the motorcycle. Jess wrapped her arms around Rick's waist as he gunned the engine and spun out onto the road.

Trying to see through her tears, she clung to his back. *Dear God!* If Nettie hurt Splint . . . if anything happened to her son . . . *Please, Father, protect him. Watch over him. Don't let her hurt him. . . .*

But Nettie could do anything! Splint trusted her implicitly. He was completely vulnerable to her. She could push him down the stairs. Shove him off a cliff. Feed him something poisoned. Take him somewhere and lose him.

"Hang on, Jessie," Rick called over his shoulder. "We're almost there."

"I'm so scared for Splint!"

"Are you absolutely sure Omar didn't have anything to do with the murder? Are you positive Nettie was the killer?"

"She and Dr. bin Yusuf had an affair when they were young. Omar is their son. Dr. bin Yusuf abandoned her, and she never forgave him."

As Jess spoke the words, she recognized her own story in the tale. Bitterness demanded such a price. Unforgiveness became a demanding, vengeful master. Destruction could be the only result.

Oh, Splint! Please be all right!

The motorcycle shot down the road toward Uchungu House. The looming building was dark. Every window utterly black. Jess searched her heart for hope. Maybe Splint and Hannah were in the courtyard having a snack. Maybe they'd lit a little lamp . . . a candle. Maybe they were eating cookies and sipping milk. Maybe everything was all right.

As the motorcycle slowed to a stop, Jess jumped down and ran up the steps onto the verandah. The carved front door stood ajar.

"Spencer?" she called. She stopped in the living room. The picture over the sofa was gone. Panic clutched at her throat. "Mama Hannah! Splint!"

"Are they here?" Behind her, Rick was breathing hard. "How about the little room next door?"

He took her hand, and they sprinted across the room. The

pictures there were gone, too. No green-eyed little Omar. No Miriamu.

"Splinter!" Rick shouted. "Hannah? Where are you and Splint?"

Rick ran just paces ahead of Jess through the honeycomb of rooms. Dark. Empty. Nothing. They dashed out into the courtyard. The Scrabble game lay spread out on the dining table. The two chairs were vacant.

"I'll check Splint's bedroom," Rick said. "You search the storage rooms and the kitchen."

Sobbing, Jess ran from room to room in the house's lower level. All were empty. Silent. She could hear Rick calling his son as he searched the upper floor of the house. His voice took on a note of desperation.

"Splint! Splinter, this is your dad. Where are you, buddy?"

In moments Rick was racing down the front staircase. "Any sign of either of them?" Jess asked.

"Nothing. I'll check the beach."

"I'll go with you."

"No." He put his hands on her shoulders. "Trace our path back down the driveway toward the road. Search the lawn on both sides. If Omar's as good as his word, the police should be on their way by now. The minute you spot the police car, tell them what's going on. If you can't find me right away, go with them to Nettie's house. I'll catch up on my bike."

"Rick, what if she hurt Splint? What if he's lying wounded somewhere . . . bleeding. . . ?"

"We'll take care of him." He held her close for a moment. "I love you, Jessie. We'll find our son."

Tearing apart, they ran in opposite directions. Jess could hear Rick calling as he started down the long cliff-side staircase. She closed her eyes, shuddering. One push. One shove, and Splinter would tumble over the rail. Fall to the cliffs below.

Blinded with tears, Jess hurried down the driveway. "Splint! Splint, it's Mom. Where are you, sweetheart? Mama Hannah, please answer me!"

She searched around the pots Solomon had organized in long

neat rows. She combed through a stand of palm trees. She lifted back a tangle of vines. She looked up into the Red Hot Poker tree.

The Renault engine was gone. The Renault itself was gone.

"Rick!" she screamed. Grabbing her skirts, she hurtled back down the road. She stopped at the rail and hung her head over. "Rick! The engine is gone. The car—it's not there!"

In moments, he was racing back up the stairs. "The Renault?"

"It's gone. The whole thing. When Omar and I left this evening, the engine was still hanging from the branch. Now it's vanished."

"Solomon must have driven it away."

"How can you be sure? Maybe whoever stole the paintings stole it, too."

"Too heavy to steal. The engine's got to be back in the car. That means Solomon's been here tinkering most of the evening. Maybe he knows where Splint is. Maybe he's seen Hannah. Any idea where Solomon lives?"

"In the village down the road."

"Let's go."

"What about searching Nettie's house?"

"Omar and the police will be there any time. Maybe Splint and Mama Hannah are there. Let's find Solomon first."

In moments they were back on the motorcycle, flying down the road with moonlight sparking off the gravel that shot out from under the tires. *"In the village, nothing is a secret,"* Miriamu had told Jess. Maybe someone there would know. Maybe someone had seen Splint.

"Stop here!" she called when the motorcycle approached the small grocery store. "I know these people."

Rick stopped the bike, climbed off, and hammered on the door. A man's dark head peered around the corner of the corrugated tin building. He gave Jess a broad smile of recognition.

"Jambo, madam. You would like me to take you to Zanzibar town on my bicycle?" he asked. "I have no goats tonight."

"Akim!" Jess exclaimed. "Akim, do you know where I can find Solomon Mazrui's house?"

"Ndiyo, memsahib." He emerged from behind the building. "You would like me to show you?"

"Yes, please."

"Come, come. We shall walk. It is not far."

Rick slipped his arm around Jess as they followed Akim down the single narrow road. The African strolled along, waving at friends and pointing out the homes of his many family members. He was telling them all about his most recent trip to the Zanzibar market when Jess interrupted.

"Akim, this is a very urgent matter," she said. "Can we please walk faster?"

"In Africa, nothing is urgent, *memsahib*. All things are *shauri la Mungu.*"

"The affair of God." Rick held Jess tightly. "Trust God. Trust him. We have to."

"Aha! This is the house of Solomon Mazrui!" Akim pointed at a small, tin-sided bungalow. "Thank you very much."

"Thank *you,* Akim."

"It's OK, anytime. And if you wish to ride on my bicycle, just come to the shop. There you will find me."

Jess gave him a faint smile as Rick knocked on the green door. It opened a crack to reveal a pair of dark eyes.

"Ni nani?"

"Miriamu? It's me, Jess!"

"Memsahib!" Miriamu drew open the door. "Come inside."

"Miriamu, something's happened to Splint!" Jess rushed in and took the woman's hands. "This evening, I found out that Nettie Cameron killed Dr. bin Yusuf. When I went back to Uchungu House, Mama Hannah and Splint were both gone. And then I noticed that the Renault engine isn't hanging from the tree anymore. Did you see anything unusual? Does Solomon have any idea—"

"Hi, Mom!" Splint walked into the front room. "Hi, Dad. What's up?"

"SPLINT!" Jess threw her arms around her son. Sobbing, she held him as if she'd found the greatest treasure in the world. "Splint, oh, sweetheart, I've been so worried. What happened? Where's Mama Hannah? Why are you here at Miriamu's house?"

"Don't have a cow, Mom." He looked at Rick. "She can be so emotional sometimes."

"I'll try to get used to it," Rick said, wiping his own cheek with the side of a finger.

"I came over here to Solomon's house to play *bao* with him," Splint explained. "It's this really cool game where you have a board with two rows of cups. You put rocks in the cups, see, and then you—"

"Spencer Thornton, what happened tonight?" Jess said, gripping her son's shoulders. "What happened at the house? Where's Mama Hannah? Where's Nettie Cameron?"

"Nettie went down to the police station."

"The police came for her?"

"Just to talk, you know. See, here's how it all happened. Nettie knew how interested I've been in slavery ever since we found out about the shipwreck. So she told me about a place she knew of that

had a really deep pit where they used to keep slaves—like the one Rick said he'd visited at Mangapwani. Nettie said the slave hole she knew about had a stone covering it, but she was wrong. When we got there, the pit was wide open. And really deep, too! You should have seen it. If anyone ever fell into it, they'd be a goner."

"Oh, Splint!" Jess covered her mouth with her hands.

"Anyway, Nettie suggested I climb onto this little ledge partway down in the pit to see if I could find any steps or a ladder or anything. She had me by the arm, and she was letting me down into the slave hole, when all of a sudden Solomon drove up in the Renault! Can you believe that? He fixed it!"

"That's wonderful," Jess choked out.

By this time, Solomon himself had stepped into the front room. He looked at Jess, his dark eyes hard.

"The motor wished to begin working again," he said.

"I'm so glad," Jess whispered.

"Yes. It was a good day for me to follow the child and the woman."

"Thank you, Solomon."

He nodded. "The police had spoken to me and Hannah at Uchungu House. They were searching for *Memsahib* Cameron. They had decided to question her."

"Something about the fingerprints," Splint put in. "See, they could only find Nettie's and mine on the urn. So they wanted to talk to her about that. I guess she'll remind them that she was the one who took the urn into town that day."

"I expect she will," Jess said.

"Mama Hannah stayed with the police—that's where she is now—but Solomon went over to Nettie's house to check on things. One of her workers told him where we had gone. When Solomon got to the slave hole he jumped out of the car," Splint said. "He walked right over and grabbed my arm away from Nettie and pulled me back up. He said it wasn't a good idea for me to go down into the pit. Slave holes don't like visitors."

"I see."

"And then here came the police with Mama Hannah. They talked to Nettie for a while, and off she went with them. After that,

Solomon suggested I come over to his house for a game of *bao.*" Splint leaned close to his mother. "I think he guessed I was kind of nervous about that slave pit."

"That was very nice of him."

"Yeah, and Miriamu made me this awesomely good kind of African bread with sugar on it. *Mandazi.* We've had *mandazis* and tea, and Solomon and Miriamu said I could come and visit them anytime, because they don't have any kids and they really do like children. Can I come back for a visit, Mom? I promise I'd let you know where I was going."

"I'd be very happy to have you come and visit Solomon and Miriamu." Jess smiled at the African couple. "I don't know how I'll ever repay them for what they've done tonight. Rick, would you mind taking Splint outside for a minute while I talk to Solomon. Splint, go with . . . go with your father."

Beaming, Splint linked his arm through Rick's. "Good night, Miriamu," he said. "Good night, Solomon."

"Good night, *toto,*" Miriamu said.

When the door shut, Jess took both of Solomon's hands and held them tightly. "You saved my son's life," she said. "How can I thank you? What can I do for you?"

"You give us good work. That is enough."

"But Solomon—"

"For many years I worked for Ahmed Abdullah bin Yusuf. That man was empty. His heart had no love. Then he saw Miriamu. He painted her picture. You saw it? He painted only half her face, because she would not turn to him."

"I love Solomon," Miriamu said softly. "Only him."

The big man slipped his arm around his wife. "That man wished to be like the bird in his big painting. You know it? Ahmed Abdullah bin Yusuf wished to fly above the storm. But he could not. He was like the palm tree in his picture, always bending to the ground. Before he died, he became empty no more. His heart was filled. But not with love. Anger."

"Bitterness," Jess said. "He couldn't forgive himself for giving up something he recognized he desperately wanted. A child."

Solomon looked at Miriamu. "We have no children," he said. "But we do not grow bitter. *Shauri la Mungu.* It is the affair of Allah."

Miriamu's lips curved into a beautiful smile. "And now we have the happiness of the *toto.*"

"Yes," Jess said. "Enjoy Splinter. Teach him. Open his eyes to your food, your games, your whole way of life. Help him learn to love as you love."

"Ndiyo, memsahib," Solomon said. "Tonight I will go to the police station and get Hannah. Then I will return the Renault to Uchungu House, now that the car likes to go."

Jess nodded and leaned toward Miriamu. "The painting Solomon spoke about with the palm tree in the storm . . . and the painting of you . . . they are missing from the house."

"No, *memsahib.* The thin man who smells of roses came in the evening and moved all the paintings to another room."

"Giles Knox?"

"He said he would begin to measure them and take photographs in the morning."

"I guess we can find something else to hang in the living room," Jess said. She now knew she would agree to sell most of the collection. Omar Hafidh could be sure his mother would live in comfort. "Good night, Solomon. Miriamu."

"Good night, *memsahib. Mungu akubariki.*"

God bless you, Jess thought as she stepped out into the dusty street. She could see Splint and Rick conferring under a palm tree. Moonlight silvered their hair and outlined their twin profiles. Father and son. *Thank you, Lord!*

"So, Mom," Splint said as Jess approached. "What happened to Omar?"

"Omar went back to Zanzibar town."

"Then it's just us?"

"Just us."

"Forever?" Splint asked.

Rick met Jess's eyes. "How do you like that idea, Jessie?" he asked. "Us. Together. Forever?"

"I do," she whispered. "Forever."

"I love you." Rick pulled her into his arms, and she melted thankfully into her husband's warmth.

"I love you," she murmured against his lips. "I love you, Rick."

"Jessie, oh, Jessie."

"Oh, barfola!" Wedging himself between his parents, Splint wrapped an arm around each of them. "Come on, you two. Enough's enough."

"Never enough," Rick said, looking into his wife's eyes. "May I walk my family home to Uchungu House?"

"I've been thinking Uchungu House needs a new name," she said. "I want to call our home *Masamaha*. House of Forgiveness."